Echoes
in
Death

Titles by J. D. Robb

ANTHOLOGIES

Silent Night

(with Susan Plunkett, Dee Holmes, and Claire Cross)

Out of This World

(with Laurell K. Hamilton, Susan Krinard, and Maggie Shayne)

Remember When

(With Nora Roberts)

Bump in the Night

(with Mary Blayney, Ruth Ryan Langan, and Mary Kay McComas)

Dead of Night

(with Mary Blayney, Ruth Ryan Langan, and Mary Kay McComas)

Three in Death

Suite 606

(with Mary Blayney, Ruth Ryan Langan, and Mary Kay McComas)

In Death

The Lost

(with Patricia Gaffney, Ruth Ryan Langan, and Mary Kay McComas)

The Other Side

(with Mary Blayney, Patricia Gaffney, Ruth Ryan Langan, and Mary Kay McComas)

Time of Death

The Unquiet

(with Mary Blayney, Patricia Gaffney, Ruth Ryan Langan, and Mary Kay McComas)

Mirror, Mirror

(with Mary Blayney, Elaine Fox, Mary Kay McComas, and R.C. Ryan)

Down the Rabbit Hole

(with Mary Blayney, Elaine Fox, Mary Kay McComas, and R.C. Ryan)

ECHOES
IN
DEATH

J. D. Robb

ST. MARTIN'S PRESS

NEW YORK

ECHOES IN DEATH. Copyright © 2017 by Nora Roberts. All rights reserved. Printed in the United States of America. For information, address St. Martin's Press, 175 Fifth Avenue, New York, N.Y. 10010.

www.stmartins.com

Library of Congress Cataloging-in-Publication Data (TK)

ISBN 978-1-250-12311-4 (hardcover)
ISBN 978-1-250-12314-5 (e-book)

Our books may be purchased in bulk for promotional, educational, or business use. Please contact your local bookseller or the Macmillan Corporate and Premium Sales Department at 800-221-7945, extension 5442, or by e-mail at Macmillan SpecialMarkets@macmillan.com.

First Edition: February 2017

10 9 8 7 6 5 4 3 2 1

O love, they die in yon rich sky,
They faint on hill or field or river:
Our echoes roll from soul to soul,
And grow for ever and for ever.

—Alfred, Lord Tennyson

A sad tale's best for winter.

—William Shakespeare

ECHOES
IN
DEATH

1

WAS SHE DEAD?

She felt like a ghost, untethered and insubstantial.

Was she floating?

Everything around her seemed blurred, faded, and unimportant. Maybe she was blurred, faded, and unimportant while the world moved around her full of color she couldn't see, sound she couldn't hear.

If so, death was the same as life. What difference did it make, really? Unless . . . unless. Could death be a kind of freedom?

But freedom from what?

Something, something scraped like tiny fingernails on the edges of her mind—a need to run, to hide. But why? *Why?*

What was the point of it all? What would death need to hide from? The dead could sleep, couldn't they? Just sleep, sleep, sleep.

And yet, she felt as if she'd just woken, still groggy and vague.

She wandered. Puzzled, yes, but detached, and wondering if she'd reached heaven or hell. There was something oddly familiar about the faded colors and blurry shapes here. Colors suddenly so strong they hurt her eyes, shapes so sharp they might slice and gash.

Then they faded and blurred again, and there was comfort in that. Odd, quiet comfort.

But . . . she caught a scent, yes, yes, the rich and funereal scent of lilies. Blood. Lilies and blood, surely that meant death.

She should just lie down, lie down and sleep. Lie down and just go away. Surely someone would come tell her where to go next, what to do next. An angel. Or a devil.

Because the idea of either—the image that flashed in her mind that was somehow both—made her shudder, she didn't lie down. Could the dead fear?

She paused when she came to a door, stared at it. Out or in? In or out? Did it matter?

She saw a hand reach for the knob. Was it her hand? Something was wrong with it. Blood and lilies. Something was wrong with the knob. It moved, sneaking just out of reach, right, left, up, down.

A kind of game, she thought, smiling a little. She would play.

The hand reached for the knob, drew back. Reached again, swept right then left. Then closed around the sneaky knob. So she laughed in a sound that was thin and tinny and very, very far away.

In or out, out or in.

The door opened; she walked through.

Bright and dark was the world of the dead. Surrendering, she walked into it.

All Eve wanted in the world of things to want was to get out of the excuse for a dress and the ankle-breaking heels she was wearing. She'd done her duty after all, and considered she'd earned a big red checkmark on the plus side of the Marriage Rules column by decking herself out and painting herself up for an evening of playing wife of the business god.

Who'd invented the charity winter ball anyway? she wondered. Sane people wanted to stay home in warm, comfortable clothes when February reared its ugly frozen head. Even the not-so-sane were mostly huddled up somewhere at damn near two in the morning on a bitter night, which was why she'd had no excuse not to do her marital duty.

Maybe 2061 had started off with a bang—nearly literally—in the professional sense, and murder and mayhem had followed.

But murder had taken a breather, which had provided time and space for a really nice three days of hot beaches and hotter sex on Roarke's private island. And if that had to be followed up with a fancy ball with fancy clothes, well, it was checked off now.

But come Monday, she'd be back in the saddle, wearing boots and sensible clothes. Carrying badge and gun.

Not that she didn't have the badge and weapon with her—stuffed into the silly, sparkly purse. Lieutenant Eve Dallas always had her badge and weapon.

At last she slid into the car—already cozily warm—and considered the elegant East Side hotel, its obsessively winter ballroom decor and the crowd inside, all happily in the rear view.

Roarke leaned over, took her chin in his hand, brushing his thumb over the shallow dent as he kissed her. "Thank you."

Here she was, Eve thought, looking into the wild blue eyes of a man conjured by the gods on a particularly generous day, and she'd mostly griped internally for the bulk of the evening.

That, she decided, violated the spirit, if not the letter, of those Marriage Rules.

"It was okay."

He laughed, kissed her again before he slid away from the curb. "You hated nine out of every ten minutes in there."

Humor and echoes of Ireland wound through his voice, the perfect accompaniment to that gorgeous face framed by a mane of black hair.

The gods, she decided, had opted to mix together all the best elements of warrior, poet, angel—the fallen variety to add some spice—and then deemed he'd love an unsociable, badass murder cop.

Go figure.

"Maybe seven and a half out of every ten. It was nice seeing Charles and Louise and the Miras. I was okay, right?"

"Flawless."

"Flawless my ass." She snorted that away. "Maybe you didn't hear me tell that woman with the hair like a tower of whipped cream"—Eve demonstrated by swirling a finger over her own short, choppy brown hair—"that, no, I don't want to chair her committee for reintegrating rehabilitated offenders into society because I was too busy tossing offenders in prison."

"I heard you, and was grateful, when she went on to explain to you how the police were far too focused on punishment rather than reintegration, that you refrained from punching her."

"Thought about it. You can bet your fine ass that if one of her *ROs*—as she called them—walked up, conked her on her whipped-cream head and ran off with the glitters she was dripping in, she wouldn't be lecturing me about how the law needs heart and compassion and forgiveness."

"She's never stood over a body or had to tell someone the person they loved is gone. And so has no idea the heart and compassion those duties require."

"Yeah, well, I didn't punch her—or anybody." A little smug about it, she snuggled more comfortably in the seat. "Score for me. Now we can go home, get out of these duds."

"I enjoyed seeing you in your duds almost as much as I'll enjoy getting you out of them."

"And we can sleep late tomorrow, right? Laze around like a couple of slugs and—"

She broke off as her habitual cop-scan of the street arrowed in. "Jesus! Stop!"

He'd seen for himself an instant before the woman stepped out into the street and into the glare of his headlights.

Naked, bloody, eyes wide and empty as moons, the woman continued to walk.

Eve leaped from the car, started to yank off her coat, but Roarke beat her to it, wrapped his own around the woman.

"She's near to frozen," he said to Eve. "You'll be all right now," he began, and the woman lifted an icy hand to his face, pressed.

"Are you an angel?" she asked. Then those wide eyes rolled up white as she crumpled.

"Get her into the car. Is there a blanket in the back?"

"In the boot." He carried the woman to the car, laid her in the warmth as Eve grabbed a blanket. "I'm back here with her. Toss me that stupid purse thing. Closest hospital is St. Andrew's."

"I know it." He tossed Eve her bag, got behind the wheel, and floored it.

Eve pulled out her 'link, contacted the hospital. "This is Dallas, Lieutenant Eve." She rattled off her badge number. "I'm bringing in an unidentified female, early to mid-twenties, injuries undetermined, but she's unconscious, shocky, and likely heading into hypothermia. Five minutes out." She judged Roarke's speed. "Make that three."

She used the 'link to take a photo of the woman's face, of what she saw now were ligature marks around the neck.

"Someone tuned her up, choked her, and, odds are high, raped her. She's got some cuts, plenty of abrasions, but I don't think all this blood's hers."

"She can't have been wandering around in that state very long. Not only because it's barely into the single digits, but someone would have seen her."

"Blood in her hair," Eve murmured, probing. "She took a hit, back of the head." Wishing she'd grabbed her field kit, she did a visual exam of the hands, the nails. Then glanced up when Roarke swung into the turn for the ER.

She hadn't given them much notice, but two doctors or nurses—who could tell—stood outside with a gurney. Eve shoved the door open even as Roarke braked. "She's back here. She's been choked—rope, scarf—has a head wound, likely from a blunt object. She needs a rape kit."

As she spoke, Eve moved out of the way while they transferred the woman to the gurney. They rolled her inside at a run, with the one who barely looked old enough to order a legal brew snapping out orders.

"Keep up." He glanced back at Eve and Roarke. "I need any information you have."

They banged through the doors of an exam room where more medicals waited. "On three!"

On three they lifted the unconscious woman from gurney to table.

"Core temp's ninety-one point four," someone shouted over the rest.

"I'll get the car out of the way," Roarke murmured to Eve. "And be back with you."

IVs, warming blankets, poking, prodding.

God, she hated hospitals.

"Tell me what you know." The doctor, Eve assumed, glanced briefly at Eve while he worked.

He didn't appear to be much older than his current patient, with a mop of loosely curling brown hair around a pretty face roughened by a long-night's scruff and fatigue shadows under his clear blue eyes.

"She stepped out into the street—Carnegie Hill. Just like you see her. Walking like she'd had a few too many, shocky, speech slurred. She asked my husband if he was an angel, then passed out."

"Core temp's ninety-three point two and rising."

"I need you to bag her hands," Eve said. "After I get her prints. Not all that blood's hers."

"Just let me finish saving her life first."

Eve gave them room, kept her eyes on the woman's face.

Young, very attractive under the bruising. Mixed race—some Asian, some black. Slight build, no more than a hundred and ten on a little over five feet. Manicured fingers—very pale pink nails, same for the toes. Pierced ears but no earrings. No tats she'd seen. Nearly waist-length black hair, in knots and tangles.

She started running a facial recognition with the photo she'd taken in the car. Might not work, she knew, considering the battering that face had taken.

She looked up as Roarke walked toward her, with her field kit.

"I thought you'd want it."

"I do, thanks. If she doesn't come to by the time they've finished, I need her prints for ID. She's going to be from that general area. She's got the hands and skin of somebody with enough money to pay for good care, and no way she was walking for blocks. So she lives or works in the Carnegie Hill area, or was there when she was attacked."

She looked back at the exam room doors. "From the blood on her you'd say she put up a fight, but I don't see any defensive wounds. No blood or skin under her nails—at least not that shows on a visual."

"You're worried someone was with her, someone else was attacked."

"I've got to put it as a possibility. If this one got away, the other—"

She broke off when the doors opened and the doctor stepped out. "Her vitals are stabilizing, and her core temperature's up to ninety-six plus. The head wound's the most severe of her injuries—which include multiple facial contusions and lacerations, abdominal bruising, some cuts that look like shallow knife wounds. She has a concussion. She was raped, more than once, and violently. You'll have your kit there. The drunken walking and the slurred words are likely from the hypothermia and shock. We're running a tox, but that's most likely."

"I need her prints. Not all her blood," Eve reminded him before he could object. "Someone else might be out there in the same condition as she is. I ID her, maybe it leads us to saving another life tonight."

"Sorry, didn't think of it." He rubbed at his eyes. "Double shift."

"I hear that."

"Sorry again. You probably saved her life getting her here so fast. Sure as hell saved her from brain damage. Dr. Nobel. Del Nobel."

Eve accepted his hand. "Dallas. Lieutenant Dallas. Roarke."

"Yeah, that got through about two minutes ago." He shook Roarke's hand in turn. "Nice dress," he said to Eve.

"We were at a thing."

"Hope your cleaners can get the blood out of it. Let's get your ID. Somebody's probably worried about her."

They stepped back inside. "I want pictures of the injuries," Eve said. But ID came first.

She moved to the side of the table, took her pad out of her kit, gently pressed the woman's fingers to it.

"Okay. Strazza, Daphne, age twenty-four. Got an address about two blocks from where we found her. Married to . . ."

She glanced up, saw Del's face. "You know her."

"No, never met her. But I know her husband. Everybody in this hospital knows Anthony Strazza. Jesus. She's Strazza's wife?"

"Let's keep that under wraps until I can . . . She's waking up."

Eve saw the long, dark lashes flutter. Then the eyes—almond shaped and strikingly, softly green—opened. Stared blindly.

Del held up a hand to stop Eve, as he leaned over Daphne. "You're okay. You're in the hospital. Nobody's going to hurt you. You're safe now."

Those eyes darted around the room. As her breathing began to rush and hitch, Del took her hand. "You're okay," he repeated. "I'm a doctor. You're safe. I'm going to give you something for the pain."

"No, no, no."

"Okay, okay, we'll wait on that." His voice stayed calm, stayed easy. And though the monitors charted her vitals, Eve noted he laid his fingers on her wrist, taking her pulse the old-fashioned way. "I just want you to relax," he continued, "to breathe slow. Can you tell us what happened to you?"

"I was dead. I think I was dead."

Her gaze landed on Eve. "Were you there?"

Eve moved forward. "What do you remember?"

"I . . . went away. Or the world did."

"Before that. Can you remember before that?"

"We had dinner, a dinner party. Dinner for fifty at eight, with cocktails beginning at seven-thirty. I wore the Dior with the crusted pearl trim. We had lobster medallions, seared scallop salad and winter squash soup, prime rib and fingerlings roasted with rosemary, with white and green asparagus. Croquembouche and coffee. The wines were—"

"That's okay, what happened after dinner?"

"Our guests left at eleven-thirty. If I'd planned better, they'd have left at eleven. My husband has rounds in the morning. He's very busy.

He's a surgeon, so respected, so talented. We'd normally go to bed after the guests left, and the house droids cleared up. We'd go to bed, and—"

Her breathing shortened again. This time Eve gripped her hand before Del could interfere. "You're safe, but you need to tell me what happened when you went up to bed."

"Someone in the house." She whispered it, like a secret. "Not a guest. Not. Waiting. A devil, it's a devil! His face is a devil. My husband . . . He fell. He fell and the devil laughed. I don't know. I don't know. Please. I don't know."

She began to sob, tried to curl up into herself.

"That's it," Del snapped at Eve. "She needs to rest. Give her some time."

"I'm going to check under her nails. If she got a piece of who did this, I need it."

"Make it fast."

The visual with microgoggles showed nothing, but she got her tools, gently scraped. Nothing.

"Either she didn't fight back, or didn't get the chance." Eve studied the ligature marks on the wrists. "If she tells you anything else, I need to hear about it. I'll be back in a few hours, and I'll be assigning a uniform to sit on her room."

Eve stepped out with Roarke.

"Are you assigning a uniform to keep someone out, or to keep her in."

"I don't know yet." She pulled out her 'link as they walked. "Let's go check on Anthony Strazza."

Not exactly the end-of-the-night plans they had expected, Eve thought as she did a quick run on the Strazzas during the short drive.

The surgeon had more than twenty years on his wife—his second wife, Eve noted. Wife number one—divorced five years ago—currently lived in Australia and had not remarried.

Current wife, of three years had been a student and part-time event planner (or assistant planner) when they'd married. No updated employment listed.

As trophy wives went, Eve supposed Daphne fit the bill. Young, beautiful when her face hadn't been pummeled. Probably an excellent hostess with the event-planning bent.

Eve wondered, though she was Roarke's first and only spouse, if some considered her a trophy.

She glanced at him as he maneuvered into a street slot outside the double redbrick townhouse where the Strazzas lived.

"You didn't get a shiny prize."

"I'm fond of shiny prizes," he said. "Why didn't I get one?"

"Your own fault. As trophies go, I'd be in the dull-and-dented category."

"Not in the least. But then again, you're no trophy."

She got out, navigating from curb to sidewalk in the stupid fancy-girl shoes. "That's a compliment?"

"It's truth. If I'd wanted a trophy, I'd have one, wouldn't I?" He took her hand, rubbed his thumb over her wedding ring. "I much prefer my cop. You're thinking of Daphne Strazza, and the generational difference in age with her husband."

"How do you know? You haven't had time to do a run."

"Simple enough as Strazza's a surgeon of some repute—and the name rings a dim bell. He's bound to be twenty years or so older than she."

"Twenty-six. Second wife. First, close to his age, divorced after about a dozen years. Lives in Australia, on a sheep ranch, which is a pretty far ways from New York and dinner parties in town mansions on the Upper East."

She gave the house a study. Three stories of old elegance, New York style. Strazza had merged two townhomes into one, widening one entrance to highlight the main with carved double doors. Tall slim windows, privacy screened for the night, stood like blank eyes in their frames of dark wood. A pair of glass doors on the second floor led to a kind of Juliet balcony with a stylized S centered in the rail.

The same ironwork flanked the three steps leading from sidewalk to entrance.

And there, Eve noted, he had top-of-the-line security.

"Cam, palm plate, intercom, double swipe," she said as they approached. "He paid for the dignified look, but he's got a pair of high-end police locks on here. Audio, visual, and motion alarms."

"Back in the day, this is just the sort of house in just the sort of neighborhood I'd have targeted." The thought of those days as a master thief brought a nostalgic smile to his lips. "It's quiet, settled, and inside? That's where all the goodies are. Art, jewelry, cash as well."

"If we were back in the day, how long would it take you to compromise the security?"

His hair blowing in the wind, Roarke angled his head to study the locks. "With proper due diligence and preparation? Two or three, I'd say. Likely closer to two."

"Minutes."

"Of course."

He wasn't bragging, she mused. Just stating a fact.

Eve rang the bell. She expected an automated comp response, but got nothing at all.

She rang again. "I'd call that a security lapse. No warning, no response from the system, no attempt to scan."

As they waited, Roarke took out his PPC, ran some sort of scan of his own. "The system's down," he told Eve. "Deactivated, and the door, Lieutenant, is unlocked."

"Shit." She took her weapon and badge out of her bag, tossed the bag on the stoop, clipped the badge to her coat. And wasn't surprised, as she also clipped a recorder to her coat, when Roarke took a clutch piece out of an ankle holder.

"Hold it. Record on. Dallas, Lieutenant Eve, and expert civilian consultant Roarke entering unsecured residence of Anthony Strazza. Two attempts at contact elicited no response. There is reason to believe Strazza is injured or under duress. I have armed the civilian."

She shoved open the door, went in low. Roarke went in high.

She swept the foyer. Overhead a silver and white free-form chandelier dripped dim light, and illuminated drops and smears of blood on the white marble floors.

"We've got blood—and footprints through it. Bare feet—probably Daphne Strazza's."

She gestured him one way, went the other, each calling out "Clear!" when they'd swept a room.

She didn't need Roarke to tell her someone had walked off with some trinkets. She spotted a couple of empty wall niches—and the dinner-party debris no house droids had dealt with.

They rounded back, started up to the second floor, once again separated.

She caught the scent as she walked toward the room in line with the balcony, the one with double white doors open.

Blood and death . . . and flowers.

She found all three in the spacious suite with its wide bed flanked with high posts of burnished gold. Like the floor, drops and smears of blood marred the knotted white linens. A chair with gold finish lay with its back broken and trailing duct tape—bloodied and ragged. Trampled white lilies swam in a pool of blood or scattered bruised petals over the white and gold carpet.

A large vase of deeply cut crystal had spilled its flowers and water over the carpet and lay smeared with blood and gray matter.

More blood on the footboard, at the edge where board met post, and what looked like blurry handprints, red against the white of the carpet.

Among the blood and gore Anthony Strazza lay like a penitent at the altar, arms and legs outstretched. Still fully dressed, he wore a dark gray suit with a paler gray shirt. Cuff links winked at his wrists. His face, barely recognizable, showed red and purple from a beating in the slice of profile Eve could see.

Blood, gore matted his dark blond hair where it had seeped and run from the gaping wounds in the back of his skull.

"I've got a body!" Eve called out.

Roarke joined her, standing in the doorway with her.

"No one does this to steal—and then not take so much that's easily transported."

"Maybe it got out of hand," Eve said. "We still have to clear the third floor."

"Why don't you do that, as we both know whoever did this is long gone. I'll go out and get your field kit."

Long gone, Eve agreed, but procedure was procedure for a reason. She cleared the top floor, Strazza's office suite, a bathroom, a kind of media room in the contemporary and manly style, a shiny automatic kitchen, a full bar, a secondary workstation . . .

And an open safe built into a small cabinet.

She went down as Roarke came up.

"Nearly empty safe on three. At a quick glance it didn't look compromised. I lean toward the assailant beating the code out of Strazza, but you could check it out."

She looked down at her shoes—needle-thin heels attached to her feet by a bunch of glittery straps. Resigned, she took them off, sealed her bare feet, her hands, handed him the can of Seal-It. "Haven't cleared the closets or the master bath. Why don't you seal up and do that? I need to officially ID the vic, call it in."

"You'll be getting Peabody up early, I take it."

"It's never early when you're a cop. I need real clothes, damn it."

"I'll take care of that."

"How?" she demanded when he put the can back in her kit.

"By getting Summerset up early."

She thought of Roarke's majordomo, the pain in her ass. "But—"

Amused at her expected reaction, Roarke skimmed a finger over her bare shoulder before he went into the bedroom. "Your choice whether to do what you do more comfortably or in formal wear."

"Damn it. Clothes. And boots. And my regular coat. And—"

"He knows what to send along. Another safe in the closet—his closet—open and empty."

Eve tossed her coat behind her, walked over the soiled carpet, crouched in a sheer dress of red and silver. The skirt consisted of dozens of thin, floaty panels that swirled like ribbons when she walked and exposed a long length of leg. Straps, as narrow and sparkly as those on the discarded shoes crisscrossed over her bare back.

She pressed dead fingers to her Identapad.

"Victim identity verified as Anthony Strazza of this address." She took out a gauge. "TOD, zero-one-hundred-twenty-six. COD to be determined by ME, but by visual exam of primary most likely the skull fracture."

"That would do it," Roarke said from behind her. "No safe in the wife's closet. I'd suggest the one in his is large enough to hold her jewelry and any he might have had. And I'll take a look at the one upstairs."

"Check the security feed first, would you? He likely cleared it out or compromised it, but we could get lucky. And the doors and alarms."

"As an expert consultant, I'd have to say burglary wasn't the point here, or the primary one."

"No, just a really big bonus to top off rape and murder." She started to reach for her 'link. "Damn it. My 'link's in that shiny thing."

"No, it's in your field kit, and the shiny thing's now empty in the car."

"Oh, yeah, here it is. Thanks. Look, I'm going to tell Peabody to bring McNab as this place is loaded with electronics. You could head home, catch some sleep."

When he just raised his eyebrows, she shrugged. "Or not."

"Or not. I can tell you the . . . intruder bashed the components in the security room. As I was clearing I didn't look beyond that—or the droids—a trio of house droids, also smashed."

"He likes violence—animate or inanimate. Whatever you can get."

"I'll see what I can do."

Alone, Eve looked down at the body, thought about just what one human could do to another.

And called it in.

2

WITH THE CRIME SCENE AND THE BODY *IN SITU* ON RECORD, EVE ROLLED the victim.

"Multiple facial injuries. From fist and some sort of sap, I'd say. Nicks and shallow cuts on the throat. Similar to those inflicted on the second victim. No sign Strazza was gagged during the assault. Bound to the chair, restrained at the wrist. Zip-tie restraints still on wrists."

She angled for a close zoom on the thin plastic.

"Fought those. We've got deep lacerations and contusions at the wrists, what appear to be splinters from the chair both in the flesh and stuck—by blood and bits of adhesive—to the zip ties. Some tape still attached to the pants legs, the sleeves of the jacket. Vic's knuckles are bruised, so he might've gotten a couple shots in."

She eased back a little, studied the shattered chair.

"Broke the chair, broke out of the chair, went for the assailant. That's how it reads. Assailant grabs the big-ass vase, bashes him—temple

wound—frontal assault there. Puts him down. Then *bam, wham*, finishes him where he lays.

"What does she do?" Eve wondered as she took samples of blood
from several locations, labeled, sealed them. Still crouched, she studied the blood on the footboard.

"Second vic has a head wound. Gash at back of the head. Does
she try to help, get knocked back? Hits her head, passes out. Maybe.
Wakes up, in shock, concussed, disoriented. Brain just shuts down
so she walks out, goes downstairs, goes outside—naked."

Eve blew out a breath. At eight years of age, she'd been beaten and
raped, and had walked in that dreamy fugue state away from the
dead—covered in blood not all her own—out on the street.

"The mind shuts down," she murmured, "so it doesn't go crazy."

She stood up, breathed in, shut her eyes—shut out those memories.
She couldn't allow them to color the now. Tried instead to see how it
had been in the here, in the now.

Dinner party's over, time for bed. Did they walk up together, chatting about who'd said what? That sort of postgame commentary. They
walk into the bedroom, surrounded by that illusion of safety, by that
quiet fatigue of having a social event over and done.

Was he waiting for them in here? Someone they knew? One of the
party staff? Caterer, valet, server? Or someone who took advantage
of the comings and goings, slipped in, strolled upstairs.

Cased the house first—knew enough about the house first. Had to.

Incapacitate the biggest threat—Strazza. One way or the other. Grab
the woman, knife to the throat. Or knock him down and out. Take him
out—smarter—smack the woman around a little. Maybe force her to
bind the husband to the chair, zip the ties around the arms of the chair.
Restrain her, too. On the bed, tie her to the posts.

Frowning, Eve picked up the white dress from the floor, studied
the lacy underwear.

No, no, he didn't rip or cut this off her. Made her strip, made her strip down. Made the husband watch. Wants that power, wants the husband to be helpless, enraged.

She looked over as Roarke came back. "Does he get the codes for the safes first—get that out of the way? I won't hurt her/you. I just want what you've got. She didn't have the codes."

"You're sure of that?"

"The safes are both in his areas, not hers. She's the trophy—and, however he felt about her, he was in charge. Nothing around here *feels* like her. He's got the entire third-floor domain. She doesn't even have a sitting room deal, an office. His house, his money—that's impression, speculation. The perp knocked her around pretty good, but he knocked Strazza around more. I'm talking before the kill. He didn't have to. Give me the codes or I'll cut up her pretty face—or I'll mess you up."

Messed him up anyway, Eve thought, as she looked down at the body.

"Most people finding themselves in that situation give the codes. They sure as hell give them after a couple of punches in the face or with a knife to their throat or the throat of a loved one. It's things—insured things—in the safes."

Roarke nodded. "So you project the killer dealt with the practicalities first. Cleared out the safes, destroyed the droids and the security feed—we may get something back on that—then came back in, added some flourishes, raped the woman."

"Multiple times, the doc said. Maybe he rapes her straight off to show the husband he means business. Threatens to rape her again, kill her. He made her strip."

Eve gestured to the dress. "It's got some blood, likely from where he hit her or cut her. But it's not torn. He didn't tear or cut it off her. Husband's bound in the chair, and the killer stands behind him, knife to his throat. Take it off, all off, or I slit his throat. Then he ties her to the bed—no defensive wounds. You get raped, you're probably going to fight, even a little, scratch. And she did, from the wounds on her wrists and ankles, she fought the restraints, at least at first."

She studied the bed, imagined the war.

"After that, maybe he wanders around some, picking up a few more goodies—some things that catch his eye. Cocky bastard. Comes back, rapes her again, pounds on both of them again, rapes her again. Strazza manages to break the chair, lunges at him. Bruised knuckles—didn't break the skin, but he got at least one or two shots in. She's not restrained—she's passed fighting the rapes—maybe she tries to help or just run. She gets knocked back, hits her head hard on the footboard, there at the corner. She's out or plenty dazed. Killer grabs that vase slaps it against Strazza's head. He's down, and plenty dazed. The killer finishes him."

He hadn't noticed the blood on the footboard. There was so much blood spilled, smeared, spattered. He wondered if she knew the dark poetry of her skill in reading a murder scene.

"But not her?" he commented. "Why not finish them both?"

"That stands out. I would have—he *should* have, being a vicious fuck. Maybe it's his first kill. The kill's sloppy, and it's of the moment."

She stood in the stunning dress, blood soiling the hems, gestured to the body.

"I mean, Jesus, the guy *attacked* him."

"The gall of it," Roarke added.

"Exactly. He attacked. He deserved to die. But the woman? She's nothing now that he's done with her, so he leaves her. It's going on forty minutes between TOD and when we found her. She spent part of that unconscious, part of it walking around in shock. And the killer had plenty of time to pick up his toys and go home."

Eve stopped, hands on hips, studying the room. "That's a basic read of the crime scene, the two vics. The order of things may be different, but I don't think the murder was premeditated. Daphne Strazza wouldn't be alive if so."

"I'd agree there."

"Or he thought she was dead. She's lying there, out, bleeding from the head. He's a little panicked—so he gets his toys and runs home."

"Either way he'd be a sadistic bastard."

"Yeah, he would. And while this may be his first kill, it's not his first time with the rest. We'll look there."

When the doorbell sounded, Roarke turned away. "I'll see to that. It's either your change of clothes or your partner."

"If it's Peabody, send her straight up, and McNab can start on electronics."

Alone, she took another slow study of the room, the positioning of the furniture, the body, the suspected murder weapon, the pile of the female vic's discarded clothes. She started toward the male vic's closet, heard the unmistakable clomp of Peabody's winter boots on the stairs, then a quick, high-pitched squeal.

She had her hand on the weapon she'd set on her field kit when she heard the follow-up, and just rolled her eyes.

"The shoes! Holy sacred stilettos, the shoes!"

"Zip it, Peabody."

Rather than zipping it, Peabody made a *yum* sound, and stepped into the doorway holding one of Eve's shoes as if it were a priceless gem.

"They're so awesome mag it's beyond all magnitude." Peabody completed the pink theme—pink coat, striped cap heavy on the pink, pink fuzzy-topped boots—with her square face flushed pink with awe.

"Put the damn shoe down. Are those my clothes?"

"What? Oh, yeah, we got here just as the driver pulled up with—" Peabody squealed again as she finally tore her eyes from the sparkle of the shoe and looked at Eve. "The *dress!*"

"Shut up." Eve snatched the garment bag from Peabody's other hand.

"Oh, but it's *gorgeous!* It's . . . sexigance."

"It's a dress, and that's not even a word."

"Sexy elegance. It's all so . . . you got blood and matter on the hem, and some blood— A good cleaner can get all that out."

"That is my immediate priority. The dead guy over there? He's an afterthought."

"It's just that—" Peabody broke off, focusing on the body and finding her inner cop. "He won't have to worry about having that suit cleaned. He was a doctor, right? No physician healing himself this round. Any update on the wife's status?"

"No. We'll get to that. I've notified the sweepers and the morgue. I've got TOD, and the obvious on-scene COD. Seal up, start on the room. I'm using the bathroom to change."

Shutting herself in the elaborate white and gold bathroom, Eve stripped out of the dress. Relief was immediate.

In the bag she found everything she needed. She tried not to think of Summerset selecting and packing her underwear—that way lay madness—but pulled it on, dragged on soft wool trousers, blissfully black, a pale gray sweater, her weapon harness and main police issue, sturdy black boots, a black jacket with needle-thin gray stripes.

He'd included the cases for the jewelry she wore, so she took it off, piece by piece, puzzled out the coordinating cases. He'd also included her ankle holster—she had to give him props for that as she strapped it on.

That left her coat, the snowflake hat she'd grown fond of, a scarf with black, gray, and red stripes—she could live with the red—and a pair of surely insanely expensive fur-lined gloves she'd lose in no time.

Feeling like herself again, she rolled her shoulders, glanced at the ornately framed mirror over the long vanity. Said, "Shit!"

Real clothes (even if they were embarrassingly fashionable) aside, she still had on her fancy party face. And had no way to take it down to cop.

She grabbed the garment bag, stepped out. "Peabody!"

"Sir!" Snapping to it, Peabody stuck her head out of Anthony Strazza's closet.

"Do you have any gunk? You know the gunk that takes off the gunk?" To illustrate, Eve circled a finger in front of her face.

"Cleanser? Enhancement remover? No, not with me."

"Crap, crap, crap."

"You look good."

"Another of my top priorities."

"No, really. You still look like a hard-ass. In fact, the lip dye only boosts the hard-assery."

"Bullshit." But since previous experience had taught her soap and water simply smeared everything so the skin looked like one livid bruise, she opted to forget her face.

But when she walked over, started to shove the shoes into the bag, Peabody leaped toward her.

"No! You can't just shove them in there. Aren't there shoe bags? Let me do it. Let me! Dr. Strazza strikes as more than a little OCD."

"Because?"

"His closet. It's obsessively organized. He has about sixty white dress shirts—same shirt like sixty times. White shirts, black shirts, a smaller amount in gray. Black pants, black suits, gray suits. No color. Everything's in order," she continued as she bagged the shoes. "Everything's precisely hung. He's got some casual wear in drawers—a built-in—and workout gear same deal, though he loosened up there enough for a little navy blue. Even his casual clothes are precisely folded and coordinated. Same with underwear and socks. Oh, and every shirt—even the casual—have his monogram on the cuffs.

"He has two pair of white athletic shoes," Peabody went on, "two pair of black—all four the same brand and style, all pristine. All the rest are black dress shoes. About fifty pair. His closet comp not only lists each article of clothing, when he last wore it, and where, but when and where it was purchased. Nothing is more than a year old."

"So he was fussy."

"And then some."

"Check out the other closet."

Eve moved to a bedside table, opened the drawer. She took out a tablet, and at her swipe saw it was passcoded. She tagged and bagged it for McNab to take into the Electronic Detectives Division. She bagged a bottle of prescription sleep aids, another bottle for male sexual enhancement, a white silk blindfold, and a long white silk cord.

Considering all, she walked around the bed to the other night table. Another tablet—no passcode. On it she found a number of books on entertaining, hostessing, menus.

Peabody stepped out as Eve sniffed a small bottle with a gold lily as a topper. "Perfume. And her bedside tablet's filled with domestic stuff. No photos, no personal data, no music, no novels."

"Her closet's nearly the female version of his, organizationally. Not quite as precise, but close. Nearly everything's white, but there are some prints, some color—but it's either gold or silver over white. And the underwear runs from virginal to deep slut city. Same with her nightwear."

"Interesting. No sex toys. He's got his performance enhancer candy and that's it." She circled the room. "Could be a kind of theme, right? Bedroom's all white and gold. Like a church or temple. Anyway . . ."

They went back to it. By the time Eve finished the bathroom—a lot of bath oil and female products in the same scent as the perfume— the morgue team and the sweepers were at work.

She turned a tube of cleanser in her hand, sorely tempted, but put it back.

"Lilies and white. Lily-white. Maybe the guy wanted that from the wife. Or wanted her to project that. That image shattered when she was raped."

"You think the killer knew them, or one of them?"

"He knew enough to get into the bedroom undetected," Eve said as they started out. "He knew enough. Daphne Strazza said he was in the bedroom when they came up for the night after the party. She said he was the devil. She's still in shock, but that's how she described him."

"A mask?"

"That's my take. We need the name of whoever catered the party, any outside staff. Valets, bartenders, servers, extra housekeeping, decorators. Some of that's on her tablet, as is the guest list."

"Handy."

"Considering, to the best of my knowledge, all the regular household staff are droids, now kicked to hell and back, it is pretty handy."

"Next of kin?"

"He has parents—divorced. Mother's in France—a retired physicist, remarried. Father's a neurologist, department head in a private hospital in Switzerland. Her parents were killed in tsunami in Asia while the whole family was vacationing. She was nine. She was raised by Gayle and Barry DeSilva—family friends and the appointed guardians through the parents' wills. They, like Daphne Strazza's deceased parents, live in Minnesota. I haven't made any notifications, or done any deeper runs."

They stood outside Strazza's home office, looking in.

"I can start the runs," Peabody said.

"Do that, and check on the e-geeks. They've obviously been here, taken Strazza's desk comp and comm center. I want to look around." Eve checked her wrist unit. "I'll contact Strazza's parents shortly. We need to see about another interview with Daphne Strazza, and we'll see if she wants her guardians contacted."

"She has to have a pal," Peabody pointed out. "Probably on the guest list. Everybody's got a pal."

Though Eve nodded as she moved into the office, she knew differently. She hadn't had anyone remotely like a pal. Until Mavis Freestone. She'd lived two decades of her life without someone close enough to be considered a friend.

A short round in Strazza's office added weight to Peabody's OCD diagnosis. Everything in the room was meticulously organized. Every drawer and door secured. Roarke or McNab—or both—had bypassed the locks and codes so she sat in Strazza's custom-built leather chair, fishing through his desk.

McNab pranced in on plaid airboots, his blond hair streaming back in a tail, earlobes forested with glittery hoops. He wore a sweatshirt sporting a madly gyrating Elvis over sapphire-blue baggy pants with a half dozen emerald and ruby pockets.

"Hey, Dallas, early start. Wanted to let you know I had a team come in to haul in the murdered droids. We got some non-humanoid domestics. We'll look at them, but don't expect much there. Gathering up 'links and comps and tabs. Peabody said you got his and hers tabs from the bedroom."

"His passcoded, hers not."

"Follows what we're finding. He had that desk customed for his thumbprint on the drawers. Even the supply closet has a lock code.

Same with the half bath there." He jerked a thumb. "Who puts a security code on their office john?"

"Apparently Dead Strazza." She looked up again, winced. "Can you turn that thing off?"

He glanced around, his pretty face puzzled. "What thing?"

"That thing on your bony chest. It's distracting."

He looked down at Elvis, grinned. "Oh, sure. Forgot." And tapped a finger on Elvis's midsection. The long-dead king froze mid swivel.

"So, anyhows, we looked at the three safes, including the one inside a cabinet in a man-type den on the main level. All cleaned out—all opened with codes. Looking like one of the vics gave him the codes."

"Strazza—it's pretty clear his wife wouldn't have them."

"Right. Burglarizing, raping killer didn't bother with electronics—at least there are plenty of high-end and portable still on the premises. Roarke says there are empty spots around where maybe art's gone missing."

"We'll get insurance info, cross-check. Art, jewelry, any cash that may have been in any of the safes. Passports and IDs, credit and banking info. All that's lucrative if you know how to turn it, and I'm not finding passports, IDs."

"We'll check the comps for financial info. We can take a whack at the security system, but like the house droids, whoever bashed them knew how to bash. And took the main drive with him."

"You talk to the machines." Eve pushed out of the chair. "I'll be talking to people."

"We do what we do. Hey, you look good."

Eve narrowed her eyes. "What did you say?"

"Nothing personal." He all but froze in place. "Just an observation. Lieutenant."

"She does look good, doesn't she?" Roarke spoke cheerfully, slapping a hand on McNab's shoulder as he came in behind him. "Particularly considering she's been up about twenty-four hours straight now. Your morgue team's taken the body out and, as dawn has broken, your uniforms have barricaded off the early morning gawkers."

"Okay." She stared through McNab. "Have you run out of things to do, Detective?"

"Always something," he said and vanished.

Roarke moved in, laid his hands on Eve's hips. "You do look good."

"I don't have any of the gunk to take off the gunk." She tapped her cheek.

"You'll survive a few more hours of it." He kissed the cheek she'd tapped, then the other. "I'll take your other clothes with me as I need to go home and change myself at some point. Your car's out front."

"Appreciate it. I think he ruled her."

"You're talking about the Strazzas' relationship."

"Yeah. All her devices, open, all his passcoded. His spaces secured, right down to the office john. Hers, open again. Her closet mirrors his. I think he selected her clothes. I get you pick out most of mine," she said quickly. "But . . . they work. For me. And even when I find sexy girl underwear or whatever in my drawers, you don't go Slut City on me."

"Well now, my mind's taking a stroll down Main Street of Slut City, and considering."

"You think of me. The boots, say, may be styling in a way I wouldn't think of, but they're sturdy, comfortable, made for legwork, for chasing down bad guys. There's a difference between that and filling my closet so I have to wear what you want."

"I certainly hope so."

"I hate to shop. You, for some reason, consider it entertaining. She doesn't have a space in this house. Her own space."

"That I noticed."

"You made one for me. Here? He's got the third floor, plus this office, a sort of manly den going downstairs, according to McNab. Nothing reflects her, is made for her. Maybe she wanted it that way, maybe she liked being ruled. Some do. But . . ."

She turned away, circled the room.

"You think not."

"I don't think yet. What I know is that her personal tablet reads like she's staff. Lists and chores and menus. No photos, no notes to friends, sent or received. She lost her parents when she was nine, but there's nothing in the tablet, nothing I've seen in the house to remind her of them. Or of the people who raised her. They have a daughter about her age. Were they friends or foes?"

"What would any of that tell you about the assault and the murder?"

"Don't know until I know." She leaned back on the desk. "He had male enhancement pills in his nightstand—not surprising for a man twice his wife's age. And a silk blindfold and binding cord."

"A little sexual bondage between willing partners is hardly surprising, either."

"If it's mutual," she agreed. "He's got a full med kit in the bathroom, and that's not surprising for a doctor. It's not surprising he kept it in a medical bag. A fancy one with his initials engraved on it, and with a lock it took me nearly ten minutes to pick."

"I'm proud of you. But ten?" Roarke shook his head. "We need more practice, Lieutenant."

"A lot of stuff in there—bottles, pills, syringes. I'm going to have everything analyzed. Just to be thorough. I need the vic's lawyer, the insurance company. I have to hope EDD can pull that out of the comps straight off, save me time and trouble."

"I think you can count on that."

"Okay, then I'm going to leave the house to the sweepers for now, and head out, work down the guest list, see what kind of party we had going. Hit the party staff, swing by to see if I can get more out of Daphne Strazza, and . . . so on. Sorry about the quiet Sunday at home."

"I don't think either of us is to blame for nearly running into a naked, traumatized woman on the street."

"Yeah, but only one of us is a cop."

"And thank God for it." This time he kissed her enthusiastically. "Your vehicle's out front, and I have my own. I may wander into EDD myself later in the day."

"Because you find geek work as entertaining as shopping."

"I do. Meanwhile?" He tapped a finger on the dent of her chin. "Take care of my cop."

When he left, she sat down again to make the notifications.

She made notes, revised others, checked on Daphne Strazza—under mild sedation, sleeping, undisturbed. No visitors.

She took a pass at the guest list she'd copied onto her PPC, devised a system for the first half dozen guests.

And found Peabody downstairs doing a search of the manly den.

"I figured I'd hit the more personal spaces," Peabody began.

"Good figuring. Anything?"

"More meticulous organizing, so what's out of place sticks out. I think there are some things missing. You can see the vic had a bunch of awards and photos—or his photo with important types. But whatever was on that pedestal thing's gone, and there's a couple spaces on those shelves. See how it's all precise? Everything pretty much equidistant from each other. Except for that glass plaque and that framed wedding photo."

"I get you. Something was between them, and between that really ugly bowl and that other ugly bowl."

"Yeah. We can surmise whatever was there took the killer's fancy. He didn't bother with, say, this throw—handmade silk batik, and probably worth several thousand. And that lamp? It's a signed Terrezio. That's about ten grand."

"For that lamp?" Flabbergasted, Eve stared at the triangular gold base, the triangular shade with its white and gold glass panels. "Seriously?"

"Deadly. I know because Mavis and I went with Nadine to this fancy auction last week, and Nadine bought one. She got hers for eight-five, and I like it a lot better than this one, but—"

Flabbergasted yet again, Eve waved a hand. "Nadine bought a lamp for eight and a half large?"

"She's got that big new apartment to furnish."

"How am I friends with any of you? How is this possible?"

"Hers is really pretty—not gaudy like this one. Anyway, it was fun to look at all the stuff, and I picked up some things—I mean what they are, not actually picking them up. I was literally afraid to touch anything. What I'm saying is there's a lot of pick-and-go stuff around here I can spot that's worth bunches. Weird-ass burglary that leaves tens of thousands behind with a DB."

"Some specialize. You come for the jewelry or the electronics. How many people would look at that lamp and think it's worth ten grand? But you're right, it's a weird-ass burglary if that was the goal."

Eve frowned at the empty place on the shelf. "He went through grabbing what caught his fancy along with cleaning out safes. Maybe weird, maybe just a flourish. We're leaving the rest of this to the sweepers for now. We have the chief of surgery at St. Andrew's and her husband on the guest list last night. We'll hit them first, then the hospital, go from there."

Peabody picked up her coat from where she'd tossed it, began to wind her mile-long scarf around her neck. "Notifications done?"

"Vic's parents, yeah." Eve pulled on her snowflake cap as they headed out. "Shock from both of them. Some tears, a lot of questions. And what struck me as a kind of emotional distance."

She realized she'd forgotten just how freaking cold it was when the first gust of winter wind blasted her. She strode straight to her car, parked considerately at the curb. "I asked them both when they'd last seen or spoken with their son."

Eve got in, hit the heat, the seat warmers. "Coffee," she told Peabody. "Get us coffee."

"Don't have to ask twice." Peabody immediately programmed the in-dash AutoChef for two coffees: one black, one regular.

"The father told me he saw Strazza three years ago when the father came to New York for a medical conference."

"That's a long time between visits."

"Yeah, and with a little pressing it comes out they met for lunch. Strazza junior was very busy, blah-blah. The mother? Five years, she believes."

"But—how long ago did Strazza get married?"

"Three years. Neither parent was invited. Neither have met the wife. Again, with a little pressing, it sounds like the mother had specifically asked the vic if she could come to New York, spend some time, take the new bride to lunch, whatever. Too busy."

"That's pretty harsh."

"Maybe they were shit parents. Maybe one or both abused or neglected him. Maybe he was a shit son. Hard to say. But they're both flying in to New York, dropping whatever they've got going to come here and see what's left of him, to see his widow. So I lean toward shit son until I lean differently."

"It's sad. I know I only see my parents, my family, a couple times a year now, but we talk every week. Same with McNab and his."

"Say he was a shit son, and a shit husband. Odds are, if so, he was a shit in other areas."

Peabody embraced her coffee. "And the burglary deal is a cover. Somebody wanted him dead." As she considered that a strong possible, Peabody gave a nod. "But then why beat and rape the wife?"

"To torture Strazza, maybe to torture the wife. Maybe because the killer likes beating and raping women. We'll look for similar crimes."

Coffee, Eve thought, pleased traffic was light enough so she could enjoy it as she headed the few blocks to Dr. Lucy Lake and Dr. John O'Connor's condo.

She knocked the last of the coffee back as she swerved to the curb in front of an impressively refurbished building. She figured the nice jolt of caffeine would add a buzz to slapping back the doorman in his forest-green livery.

"Don't get excited." Peabody anticipated her. "I looked it up. It's Roarke owned."

Slightly deflated, Eve reached for the door handle even as the doorman whisked it open for her. "Lieutenant Dallas, how can I help you today?"

Eve reminded herself that a cooperative doorman saved time, even if it was a buzzkill. "We need to speak to Drs. Lake and O'Connor."

"You come on in out of the cold. I'll ring up and tell them you and Detective Peabody are here."

He led the way into a classy lobby decked out in Deco style. It smelled, very faintly, of pomegranates.

3

It took the cooperative doorman under two minutes to contact the doctors' apartment, relay the information and clear them up.

"Apartment 1800," he told them as he escorted them to an elevator. "They're expecting you."

Since he was being so damned helpful, Eve sized him up. "Lake and O'Connor. Impressions."

Probably weighing duties and ethics, he scratched the back of his neck. "Well, they've had 1800 for about ten years now. I've been here twelve myself. Doctors hours, so a lot of late nights, early mornings. Most always have a word, though. Got two grown kids, a couple of grandkids—visit pretty regular. Never had any trouble with any of them. In fact, a few years back when my boy took a header off his airboard and was in the hospital a couple days, they both went by to see him. That says something to me."

"Okay. Were you on when they got in last night?"

"I came on at six. We have Droid Denise on from midnight to six.

She's in the storeroom if you want me to activate her. Or I could tag up Pete at home. He had the evening shift."

"We'll hold on that. Thanks."

They rode up to eighteen in the smooth, blissfully silent elevator.

"It looks like Roarke," Peabody commented. "The building. Old-world class with modern efficiency. And it does say something when people take time to look in on their doorman's kid."

"Maybe. We'll see what they have to say for themselves."

The eighteenth floor was as silent as the elevator. There the air carried the faintest drift of something herby—maybe rosemary.

Apartment 1800 had the west corner. The double doors opened almost as Eve rang the bell.

The woman who greeted them was round—body, face, even the ball of pale blond hair on top of her head. She wore bright blue pants and a boldly printed top under a starched white apron. "Lieutenant, Detective, come right in. My husband's on the job. Sergeant Tom Clattery out of the one-one-three. Twenty-two years. And wait till I tell him who came to the door early this morning. Have a seat."

The housekeeper chattered away as she led them into a living space made cozy by a long, narrow electric fire built into the far wall. "Would you have some coffee? There's fresh as the doctors are just finishing up their breakfast. Never knew a badge to say no to coffee."

"We wouldn't want to break the record," Peabody said just as cheerfully. "Black for the lieutenant, coffee regular for me."

"Two shakes. Now sit down and be comfortable. The doctors will be right with you."

She walked off, a ball of cheer on sturdy black shoes.

"Kind of homey," Peabody commented. "A couple of doctors in a big apartment in a swank Upper East building, but it's homey.

Somebody needlepoints," she added, tapping one of the mountain range of pillows scattered over sofas and chairs. "And really well, too."

Eve could admit a sofa where your ass snuggled right in hit the homey mark. In addition, framed photos—kids various ages, vacation shots, holiday poses—fit into that. But she'd developed enough of an eye to recognize important art on the walls and the elegant gleam of a few antiques perfectly placed.

So homey, sure, she thought, with a foundation of comfortable wealth.

The doctors came in together. She was tall and lean, her hair clipped short and dark around a sharply defined face with deep-set eyes more gray than green. A flawless complexion just a shade richer than Peabody's beloved coffee regular. She wore her age—sixty-three according to her official data—as stylishly as the trim suit of steel blue.

He was taller, leaner yet, with thick black brows over keen blue eyes. He'd allowed his dark hair to streak silver at the temples. Sprinkles of that silver dashed through his narrow goatee. His smoke-gray suit complimented hers.

In fact, Eve thought their looks and body language spoke of unity.

Lake touched a hand to her husband's arm before she stepped forward.

"Lieutenant, Detective. Alice recognized your names. You're homicide. It's not about our children."

Before Eve could speak, could reassure, O'Connor spoke up. "We contacted them as soon as Greg called up. We know they're all fine. Who isn't?"

"Anthony Strazza."

Lake let out a stream of air as she sat. "We just saw him last night. A dinner party at his home. Which you know, of course." She drew in more air, let it out again. "We were there until about eleven. Johnny?"

"Yes, about eleven." Now he sat beside her. "We were the first to leave, actually. I have rounds this morning, and Lucy has an early meeting."

"Should I reschedule that?"

"This shouldn't take long," Eve told her.

"I—" She broke off when Alice wheeled in a coffee cart. "Alice, would you contact my office? Have Karl push my morning meeting an hour."

"I'll do just that, don't you worry. Now there's good black coffee for you, Lieutenant. And I'll have yours here, Detective. You'll have your second cup," she said to both doctors, pouring and serving. "I'll be right back in the kitchen if you need me for anything. Don't you worry," she repeated, and left them.

"If something happened after we left." Lake looked at her husband. "Someone would have contacted us. If something happened to Anthony during the dinner party."

"He was killed after the party."

"I don't understand how— Oh God, Daphne. His wife." With a hand pressed to her heart Lake came halfway out of her chair. "Was she killed, too?"

"She's in the hospital," Eve told Lake. "Your hospital."

"Her condition?" O'Connor demanded, even as he pulled his 'link from his pocket.

"Just hold off on contacting the hospital. I've just checked on her. She's in stable condition, mildly sedated."

"Her attending?"

"Dr. Delroy Nobel."

The tension in O'Connor's face eased, and his wife rubbed a hand on his thigh. "Then she's under excellent care," Lake said. "Can you tell us her injuries? There's nothing we can do for Anthony," she added.

"You'll have to get the medical details from Nobel, but I can tell you Mrs. Strazza was physically and sexually assaulted."

"Raped." Lake's eyes stayed level, but something in them hardened.

They'd get the details, Eve thought, so she laid it out. "Shortly after two this morning, Mrs. Strazza was found near her home, wandering outside, naked, in shock. She'd suffered numerous contusions and lacerations and was hypothermic. Dr. Nobel stabilized her. I interviewed her. Her memory is spotty, but she stated there was someone in the master bedroom when she and her husband entered after the last guest left. Dr. Strazza was restrained, Mrs. Strazza was repeatedly raped and assaulted."

"She saw who did this?" O'Connor covered his wife's hand with his.

"She was unable to describe or identify the assailant, and was too distraught to press on it at that time. During the assault, Dr. Strazza was killed. Mrs. Strazza suffered a blow to the head. I need to ask— to eliminate—can you verify the time you returned home and verify your whereabouts from eleven-thirty to two this morning?"

"We left about eleven, as we said." O'Connor rubbed his temple. "We'd have been home before eleven-thirty. I think it was about ten or fifteen after eleven, actually. We're practically neighbors. The security feed would verify it, and would verify we didn't leave the house once we got in."

"Is it all right if I check the feed?" Peabody asked. "Just to cross it off."

"Yes, yes. Alice can show you." Lake gestured. "A home invasion?" she continued as Peabody left. "Their home seems very secure."

"We're investigating. What was your relationship with Anthony Strazza?"

"We were colleagues. I'm his chief."

"And you socialized?"

"Yes. That's part of being chief. Anthony was a brilliant surgeon. Orthopedic surgeon. His talents will be sorely missed."

"Just his talents?"

"I had no issue with Anthony." She spoke carefully, politically. "I respected his skills. We weren't friends, but colleagues."

"He was a difficult man. Lucy," O'Connor said, when she shot him a sharp look. "It's no secret. Surgeons are often difficult." He gave his wife's hand a squeeze as he spoke. "He was well respected, admired for his skill. He was not particularly well liked."

"Anybody particularly dislike him?"

"Enough to kill him?" Lake shook her head. "I could see a dozen who might get into an altercation, might take a swing in the heat of the moment. But to invade his home, to kill him? To attack his wife? No."

She leaned back on the couch, shook her head again. "No. And people tend to like Daphne. It would be easy to disdain her. The young, beautiful trophy wife, marrying status and money. But she simply didn't fit that slot. There's a shy sweetness about her, and a kindness. She doesn't flaunt and strut and demand. Initially she volunteered at the hospital once a week in the pediatric unit. But after a few months, Anthony said it was too stressful for her."

"Was it?"

"I couldn't say. I do know she won over a lot of skeptics during that time. She has a quiet way, remembers everyone's name—their children's names. She hosts lovely parties, and faithfully attends all the often-tedious events required of a doctor's spouse. We don't know her very well—again, we're not friends—but I like her."

"As do I," O'Connor confirmed. "A sweet girl. And, I think, browbeaten."

"John."

"Lucy," he returned, in the same exasperated tone. "You asked if anyone disliked him particularly. I did. Very much disliked him. He was cold, arrogant, egotistical. Some would say a perfectionist, a fine trait in a surgeon. I'd say overbearingly demanding of perfection. There's a difference."

"Yeah, there is. I appreciate your candor. Did he have any altercations with colleagues, staff, patients?"

"Altercations, yes. Incidents, no," Lake said firmly. "We work in stress, in life and death, every day. Altercations happen. I've fielded complaints, formal and informal, regarding Anthony's behavior, his treatment of other doctors, interns, nurses, orderlies. I've done the same for any number of doctors on staff."

Eve changed tacts. "You say most like Mrs. Strazza. Could anyone you know have misconstrued her kindness, wanted more from her?"

"An affair?" Lake's eyebrows winged up. "Absolutely not. Believe me, that's the sort of thing that runs through the hospital grapevine like wine. I'd have heard."

"Let's go back to the party. Was there any trouble? Any arguments? Any sort of tension?"

"No. It was a lovely evening."

"Do you know who catered it?"

"Mmm." Lake frowned. "I imagine Jacko's. I asked Daphne last year who she used, as the company I'd used for years changed management—and wasn't working out well. It was Jacko's, and I recognized a couple of the servers, as we've used Jacko's a few times since."

Peabody came back. Eve caught the signal, wrapped it up. "We appreciate the time," she said as she got to her feet. "If you think of anything else, please contact me."

Lake rose. "Please let me know how—when—we can make arrangements for Anthony. Daphne may need help in that area. We weren't friends, but I was his chief."

"Understood, but his parents are coming in, so—"

"His parents." Lake's brows drew together. "I was under the impression they'd cut him off, wanted nothing to do with him."

"That wasn't the impression I got when I notified them. Where did you get yours?"

"I— Anthony said as much to me. That when he refused to kowtow to their every wish and whim, they stopped speaking to him."

Interesting, Eve thought. "What about his ex-wife?"

"I didn't know her very well. She was distant, and I'd say on the brittle side. She— He said she'd tried to clean out their accounts, and had had one too many affairs. She ran off to Europe, I think.

"I can't verify any of that," Lake said quickly. "I don't interfere with the personal lives of my people unless it overlaps the work. But Anthony was up-front about the divorce, took a month's leave to sort things out. I don't see how that could apply."

"Information's information. Thanks again."

Peabody waited until they were back in the car. "They got home at eleven-thirteen. Locks engaged. No activity until Alice arrived at seven sharp. She adores them, by the way. I prodded some. She's family—that's how they think of each other. She's been with them nearly thirty years. Her impressions of Strazza aren't as warm and fuzzy. Can't say she knows him, but he's been around for parties and such. Likes people to stay in their place—or his idea of their place, according to Alice. No chitchat with staff. You don't suspect them."

"I don't see O'Connor sneaking out of his house, sneaking back into theirs, laying into the wife—you can see he's soft on her. Like paternally. Can't see him killing Strazza and walking around taking goodies. But they gave me a picture. We're swinging by the hospital first. I guarantee the two doctors won't be far behind us."

"What's the picture?"

"Strazza was an asshole, disliked if respected. And very likely a big, fat liar. Claimed his parents cut him off, which I don't buy. And his ex-wife had one too many affairs. A guy like Strazza? It would only take one. We're going to want to talk to the ex, and the parents. Get some finer details on the picture."

"I hate when the vic's an asshole."

"Happens."

"Yeah, happens. And it widens the suspect pool."

"It can. Caterer was likely Jacko's. Check on that, and get us a list of who worked the party."

"Can do." Peabody pulled out her 'link as Eve drove to the hospital.

Two cups of coffee helped, but Eve wondered if she could just get a shot of straight caffeine. It was a hospital, after all. She hated shots, but she'd suffer through it for a good, strong jolt.

She badged her way to the ER desk, and after some dithering got the section and floor where Daphne Strazza had been relocated. Worked her way there, to that desk, badged again.

Yeah, she'd take the shot.

"I have to contact Dr. Nobel," the nurse told her.

"Fine by me, but we're going to her room now. Which way or I'll just swagger around with my badge and weapon until I find the uniform on her door."

"Down this corridor and to the right. She's in 523."

"Got it."

"I'm not sure I can pull off a swagger," Peabody commented as they started down.

"Not in those sissy boots."

"They're not sissy boots."

"They're pink and have fluff. That's the definition of sissy."

She spotted the uniform in a chair outside 523, playing on his PPC.

He heard her non-sissy boots on the tile, rose, sliding the PPC into his pocket as he came to attention.

"Lieutenant. No one but medical staff in or out. The nurse checked her about ten minutes ago. She's awake."

"Good. Stand by, Officer. We'll order in your relief."

Eve walked in.

Daphne lay in the bed, her upper body slightly elevated. Her color looked nearly normal, and medical treatment had eased a lot of the bruising and swelling on her face. She stared blankly out the window until Eve moved into her field of vision.

Daphne blinked. "I . . . know you."

"I'm Lieutenant Dallas. I brought you in."

"Yes. With the man. He has blue eyes. I remember his blue eyes."

"Hard to forget. This is my partner, Detective Peabody."

"Oh." Daphne shifted her gaze. "Hello."

"Mrs. Strazza." Eve pulled her attention back. "I regret to inform you, your husband was killed early this morning."

Daphne continued to stare. "Killed? But he's very important."

"His body was found in the bedroom where you were attacked."

Daphne lay still, but her breathing quickened. The monitor beeped faster. "But . . ." She turned her head, eyes still wide but dry, staring toward the window. "I wasn't dead. I thought . . . My husband is dead."

"I'm sorry for your loss, Mrs. Strazza," Peabody said.

"My husband's dead. Something terrible happened. Do you know what happened?"

"Do you?"

Daphne closed her eyes. Her hands lay still on the white sheets, as if she were asleep. "It's like looking through a curtain. In some places it's thin, and I can see. In others it's thick, and I can't. I feel as if I could float away, just float away." She opened her eyes again. "Am I floating?"

"It's the meds."

"It feels good to float. It feels free. I can't see my husband. Not through the curtain, not when I float. I can't see what happened to him. Maybe he's not dead. He's very important. He's very strong. He's a very skilled surgeon. He's—"

"I'm sorry," Eve interrupted. "I identified his body."

"His body," Daphne whispered.

"What do you see? What do you remember?"

"The devil. But it's not the devil. It's a man. How can the devil be a man? I think a man can be a devil."

"What does the devil look like?"

"His face is red, burning red and there are little horns here." She touched the top of her forehead. "He has a terrible smile. I think his eyes are red, but then I think they're yellow. The lights are flashing, red and yellow. Someone's screaming. Someone's laughing. Anthony? No, my husband's not laughing. He's not screaming. I can't breathe, I can't breathe."

"Yes, you can." Eve laid a hand on Daphne's shoulder as the woman jerked up gasping. "You can breathe. No one's hurting you now."

"But it hurts. It hurts." The tears came now, spilling out of those wide eyes. "You can't go away because he brings you back. I had sex with the devil, and it burns, it tears. I don't want to. I don't want to."

"He can't touch you now." Eve slapped down the bed guard, sat on the side of the bed. "He can't get to you now."

"He'll find me." Daphne gripped Eve's arm, used it as a lever to sit up then, still holding tight, looked wildly around the room. "He can find me. He can find me anywhere."

"No, he can't. He won't."

"He chose me. Devil's whore. It hurts when he makes me his whore. It burns. It glows red and it burns." She gripped Eve's hands hard, spoke in a whisper. "If you beg, if you fight, he'll make it hurt more."

"You're safe here."

Daphne collapsed back, shut her eyes as tears ran down her cheeks. "Nowhere is safe."

Del rushed in. "Hey. Back off," he snapped at Eve, then laid a gentle hand on Daphne's wet cheek. "It's okay now. It's all good. Remember me?"

She opened her eyes, stared at him. "You're the doctor. You're noble."

"That's my name. I want to take a look at you, okay? See how you're doing." He glanced back as a female nurse stepped in. "And this is Rhoda. She's going to help me with the exam."

"Do you have to touch me?"

"We'll be careful. I promise."

Rhoda stepped up, smiled. "Dr. Nobel's a sweetheart."

"Aw," he said.

"He's been looking out for you. He's going to keep looking out for you."

"If the devil comes—"

"The police won't let the devil in here. Neither will Dr. Nobel."

Del glanced over his shoulder at Eve. "Give us a minute."

In the corridor, Eve paced. "Get that fresh uniform in here."

"She's on her way. I thought, under the circumstances, a female officer."

"Yeah, yeah, good. She's not faking."

"No, she's not. Hallucinogenic?"

"We'll see what Nobel says. They ran a tox screen. Maybe he wore a mask, or makeup. Made himself look like a devil. See if you can find assaults, murders, rapes, break-ins where the perp disguised himself as a devil."

"I'll get on it. But the eyes—red or yellow?"

"Could've dyed them. Could've brought his own light show—red and yellow flashing lights—to add to the trauma and confusion. Or she's fucked up over it all and just sees it that way."

"Yeah. And the glowing red penis—you can get condoms in all sorts of glowing or sparkling or—"

"I know about condoms, Peabody. Maybe she saw his hands. If he wasn't gloved up she might be able to tell us race. We need to—"

She stopped when Nobel stepped out.

"I can't have you pressuring her that way. She's weak and fragile right now."

"I wasn't pressuring her. It's not my first round with a rape victim. I had to notify her. Anthony Strazza was killed."

"Killed?" Del took one short step back. "He's dead?"

"That's what happens when you're killed."

"Jesus." Rubbing the back of his neck, Del closed his eyes. "Jesus Christ."

"She remembers bits and pieces, and what she remembers goes back to that devil business. Tox?"

"Clean." After hissing out a breath, Del opened his eyes. "No illegals, no drugs whatsoever. No DNA from the assailant. He sealed up there, fucker." On a second hissing breath, Del pinched the bridge of his nose. "Not my first round, either, but she hit a chord. God, Strazza. Look, I need coffee. Break room's down here."

He turned, started walking.

"Have you been on all night?"

Del shrugged. "I hit the bunk for a couple hours. She knows me, or remembers me enough, trusts me as far as she can. So I need to be around until she's steadier."

He swiped them into a room not very different from the break room off her own bullpen. It smelled not very different. Bad coffee and fatigue.

"Want?"

Eve studied the dilapidated AutoChef. "Absolutely not."

On a half laugh, he glanced at Peabody, got a firm shake of the head. "Just me then. Here's the deal, and forgive all the medical jargon. She got the crap beat out of her, the crap raped out of her, got choked, cut, terrorized and bashed in the head. Her brain's pretty scrambled."

"I think I can pick through the complexities of your medical jargon."

"Good." He gulped coffee, said, "Praise Jesus," gulped again. "Add the hypothermia. Her memory of the events that happened in that house are bound to be confused, and some pieces missing. Some pieces may stay missing. It's not only the physical trauma—the blow to the head, the hypothermia—it's emotional shielding. And now that I know her husband was probably killed in front of her, I suspect that shield's thick and sturdy at this point. Her brain blocks out what she can't handle."

"I'm aware," Eve said evenly. "I don't need lectures on trauma. I've been a cop longer than you've been a doctor."

He studied her over the rim of the ugly gray mug. "I don't know. I made my debut playing doctor with Cassie Rowling. We were six."

"That's not vocation. That's being a perv."

"A six-year-old can't be a perv."

"The seeds are there."

He laughed again. "I like you. I didn't get to see the vid or read the book. I used to see vids and read books," he said, wistfully. "But I looked you up. You'd be Peabody?"

"Yeah, nice to meet you."

"I'd like you just from this conversation. I'd like you for getting a woman in distress to the hospital. But I really like both of you after looking you up. I know Daphne's in good hands with you guys. But she's in my hands first. Has to be. To add more complicated medical jargon. She's a fucking wreck. We're going to help her, and she'll get stronger and steadier. I'm just asking you not to push from your end."

"How much stronger and steadier will she be when she knows the bastard who did this to her, who killed her husband, is in a cage?"

"You make a good point. Let's try this. We'll both do what we do. I'll try to cut you some slack. You cut Daphne some slack."

"I can agree to that. We're keeping a cop on her door. She should know that. It may help her."

"Officer Marilynn Wash," Peabody said with a glance at her 'link. "Just checked in. She'll be on for eight, then her relief—already in line—is Karen Lorenzo, followed in another eight-hour shift by Zoey Russe."

"All girl cops. Good touch." Del glanced at his wrist unit, dumped more coffee into his mug. "I had to give Daphne something to soothe her out. She has a hard time with the exams. Give her a few hours, okay? She's not going to remember anything else right now. And I need to ease her into talking to a rape counselor. Add on a grief counselor now."

"I have one on tap who can serve as both."

"I don't want some—"

"Dr. Mira."

The defensive look on his face eased away. "Dr. Charlotte Mira?"

"That's right. Objections?"

"Not only none, but I'd be grateful for her."

"She'll contact you. Set it up. If any of those missing pieces shake loose, I want them asap."

"You'll have them. I'll feel a lot better myself when the bastard who did this is in a cage."

With a nod Eve left him contemplating another mug of terrible coffee.

"Get me a meet with Mira," she told Peabody as they walked. "And see who in the bullpen can handle some interviews. Odds of it being a party guest are pretty slim at this point, but they have to be covered. We'll take the caterer."

"On it. Hey, wait, wait. I got a sort of something on the like crimes." Hustling to keep up, Peabody studied her screen. "We got a pair of assaults, rapes, beatings. In-home deal, same as this. First one last summer, and the vics said he looked like Dracula. Second this November. Described assailant as a ghoul."

"Mask or makeup?"

"Unsure, both cases. And in both cases he restrained the male, beat him with fists and a sap, beat and choked the female, raped her. He put on sound effects. Howling wolves in the first, screams and rattling chains in the second. Added lights in the second. A strobe light."

Peabody glanced up quickly as they moved into the elevator. "Had a knife in the second attack, cut both vics a little, threatened to slit their throats if the male didn't give him the combo of the safe, and the female didn't shout he was the best. That she wanted more. He left all vics alive, releasing them—evidence indicates—he took the contents of the safe, a few other items, and raped her a final time."

"Who's on it?"

"Detectives Olsen and Tredway, Special Vics Unit."

"Reach out. We need everything they have."

4

MORNING TRAFFIC THICKENED WITH LOADED MAXIBUSES LUMBERING, cabs and cars inching along the black ribbons of roads, and pedestrians pouring onto sidewalks.

Air blimps blasted their relentless hype. Their current focus beat the retail drum for Valentine's Day.

Eve didn't get it, just didn't get it. Who the hell decided everyone was supposed to go mad with romance and gift buying on some random day in February. Hadn't everybody just gone mad with good cheer and gift buying in December?

When would it end?

When she said as much, snarling her way through the next vehicular tangle, Peabody sent her a sad, sad look.

"But it's for sweethearts."

"Oh, bollocks. It's just another scam designed so restaurants and shops can con people into spending money on expensive dinners, bunches of flowers, and the sparkly things some poor schnook buys on credit thinking he'll get lucky. You want to be sweethearts, stay home and bang your brains out."

"It's kind of nice doing that after a special night out."

"Eat in bed, bang more. I caught this case a few years back. Couple's doing the V-Day deal, big time, retro, dinner and dancing at the Rainbow Room."

"Romantic, classic."

"Yeah, and while the guy's dropping about two grand on overpriced pork medallions, the wife goes off to the john. While she's in there, her 'link signals—left it or forgot it on the seat of the booth—and he takes a look. Turns out it's a text from the guy she had a romantic room-service lunch and hotel sex with that same afternoon. So the husband takes a closer look, finds lots of sexy texts between his wife and hotel-sex guy where they have a couple of good chuckles about her clueless husband and his substandard banging."

"Ouch."

"So—" Eve spotted her chance, zipped to the curb in front of a massive delivery truck, which expressed its annoyance with a barking horn. "This caterer place should be about a block and a half west."

She got out and, after judging the traffic, Peabody managed to nip out of the passenger side and squeeze between bumpers to the curb.

"What did the husband do?"

"He asked for the bill, signed for it. When the wife got back, he gave her the 'link, said 'Happy Valentine's Day, bitch,' and stabbed her in the neck with his dinner knife."

"Holy shit. He *killed* her, right in the Rainbow Room?"

"They had a candlelit corner booth. Nobody noticed this woman bleeding out while her husband polished off the rest of the champagne. Let that be a lesson to you."

"To me?"

"Stay home and bang."

Peabody, muffled in her scarf, aimed a suspicious look. "You made all that up."

"Elina and Roberto Salvador, 2055 or '56—not quite sure. You can look it up."

The minute they stepped into Jacko's, the siren's scent of yeast and sugar assailed them. Peabody audibly moaned.

"I didn't know it was a bakery." Peabody closed her eyes, drawing in the scent. "I didn't know."

Not just a bakery, Eve noted. Through a side opening were tables and chairs, a bar, and a hostess podium stood in the dark. But here, in this section, the lights were on and sparkling on glass displays of muffins and pastries, coffee cakes and breads with drizzles of white icing.

Staff in white smocks bagged, boxed, and rang up purchases briskly. Customers waited while others carried out those fragrant bags and glossy boxes.

"Wipe the drool off your chin," Eve advised, walking to the far end of the counter where a pretty girl of about twenty constructed more boxes.

"Need to speak to whoever's in charge."

"I'm sorry, ma'am, if there's a problem, I . . ." She trailed off, big blue eyes going bigger as Eve palmed her badge, held it up. "Oh. Oh, gosh. Just a minute, okay? Just a minute."

She bolted, down the counter and through a swinging door.

"I know you personally can go days without actual food—which makes no sense as you have no body fat stored—but I need to eat." Peabody huffed out a breath. "I was going to settle for a yogurt bar and egg pocket from a cart or Vending, but jeez."

"Get something when we've finished the interview."

"They have cinnamon buns," Peabody said reverently. "Cinnamon sticky buns."

"Don't bitch about your own sticky bun after you scarf one down."

"They are not to be scarfed, the cinnamon sticky bun, but savored."

The pretty young thing hurried back. "Ma'am," she began in a stage whisper. "Jacko can't come out of the kitchen right now, so if you could go back?"

"Sure. We'll go back."

At the girl's direction, they moved down the counter. On the other side of the swinging doors, the baking smells nearly had Eve's reputedly zero body fat moaning out loud.

Besides a wall of busy ovens, she spotted some sort of mixer nearly as big as the woman running it, a line of stainless-steel cabinets, what she took to be a mammoth refrigerator, racks full of trays and supplies.

At one counter, a man in a skullcap used some sort of tool to add tiny petals and leaves to a towering cake. At another, a girl used a different tool to squeeze batter into a tray filled with pleated cups.

At the center of it all, at an island counter, a big, broad-shouldered man wearing a white trailing cap and smock rolled out dough while he sang about getting down to live it up. He had a voice like a foghorn.

"Uncle Jacko? Here's the police."

"Huh? Oh, okay, okay. You're a good girl, Brooksie. Go on back out." Still rolling, he gestured at Eve and Peabody with his chin. "Come on over. We got a run on the buns like always. Gotta see the badges."

He worked as he studied them, nodded. "Okeydoke, what can I do for you?"

"You catered a dinner party last night."

"Had four events last night—two dinner parties. Which one?"

"Anthony and Daphne Strazza."

"Ah, Mrs. Strazza. Sweet thing, knows her party planning. Yeah, we catered that. Party of fifty. Appetizer course, served in the living area, lobster medallions in a piquant sauce. Main dining room, warm salad—seared scallops, haricots verts, and bell peppers in a walnut vinaigrette with a main of roast prime rib—"

"Got it. Don't need the menu."

"It sounds amazing," Peabody put in, making him smile as he spread butter over the rolled-out dough.

"You gonna eat, you should eat good." From a bowl he sprinkled a mixture—Eve could smell the cinnamon and sugar—over the butter. "What's the problem?"

"The Strazzas were attacked by an intruder after the party."

His hand stopped, mid-sprinkle, and all the easy levity died out of his face. "Is she okay? Mrs. Strazza? I mean, are they okay?"

"Mrs. Strazza's in the hospital, and she's stable."

"What hospital? Gula!"

The woman at the mixer looked over with a scowl. "In a minute, Jacko."

"Gula, little Mrs. Strazza got hurt. She in the hospital."

"Oh no!" She hurried over, and stood beside him. Her head barely reached his breastbone. "What happened?"

"These are cops here, and they're saying she got attacked. They, I mean to say. Mr. Strazza, too?"

"Yes. He's dead." Eve said it flatly, watching reactions.

She saw shock in both as the woman gripped Jacko's thick arm. "Oh, well, God! When? They were both fine last night."

"You worked the party?" Eve asked Gula.

"We both did. Mrs. Strazza, she always asks for us to be there. Jacko heads the kitchen, I head the servers."

"After the party, she said. An intruder."

"That place is like a vault." Gula shook her head. "Nothing's ever safe, is it? Oh, that poor girl. How bad is she hurt?"

"She'll be all right," was all Eve would say. "Can you both tell us what time you left the Strazza residence, and where you went? We need to establish a timeline."

"We served the croquembouche just about ten, ten-fifteen, wasn't it?" Gula rubbed her temple. "With the fancy mints, coffee, and liqueur. Jacko and I left about ten-thirty and went on home."

"Together?"

"We've been married twenty-six years, so we go home together," Jacko told Eve. "We left Xena, our daughter, and Hugh, he's our nephew, in charge. She's out front, you can talk to her, but she said this morning she and Hugh left about eleven—more like eleven-fifteen—turned it over to the house droids. Still guests there when they left, she said."

"We're going to need a list of your employees who worked that party."

"Sure, sure." Shaking his head, Jacko began to roll the sheet of covered dough into a tight roll. "But I can tell you nobody who works for us would hurt anybody."

"That's the truth." Gula patted his arm. "But I'll get you a list."

"We work in a lot of high-end homes and event areas," Jacko continued and, taking a lethal-looking knife, cut the roll into slices.

The girl who'd been filling paper cups brought him a saucepan. "Perfect timing," she said.

"Thanks, sweetie. She didn't work the party," he added when she had walked away, then he poured something that smelled obscenely delicious into a pan. "I have to trust who works for me, so I have to know them. A lot who do are family. And nobody works an event for Jacko's until they're trained. I've been doing this for better than fifteen years. Never had an employee so much as take a napkin from a client. Nobody who works for me and Gula is going to hurt somebody."

"They might have impressions, might have seen something, someone. You might have," Eve added.

"I stick to the kitchen mostly." He covered the pan with a cloth.

"And you know everyone who worked the event? Every server, every cook, every valet."

"Every one. Know a lot on the guest list, too. Not all, but more than a few. Professionally. Dr. Hannity snuck back into the kitchen. We did his daughter's wedding a couple years back. He had a beer and some samples. And Mrs. Wyndel came back for a bit. We do all her catering. She wanted to talk to me about a party next month— baby shower for her niece. Like that," he said with a shrug. "Otherwise, I don't much mingle. Hate parties."

Eve laughed before she could stop herself. "Me, too. But I figured you'd love them."

"Like cooking and baking." He wiped a big hand on his apron. "Might as well make a living doing what you like."

"I hear that."

He walked over to another counter, picked up a rack of cooling cinnamon buns. "Have a sample."

"We'll buy some on the way out," Eve told him. "We're not allowed to . . . take samples."

He lowered his brows, jabbed a finger at two of the buns. "These two aren't for sale. I'm not sure they meet my standards. I'd like an opinion."

"Dallas, I'm dying here." Flanked by Jacko's beetled brows and Peabody's pleading eyes—and assaulted by the scents—Eve surrendered.

"Fine. Okay." She picked up a roll, took a bite. And wanted to weep.

"Terrible," she said over another bite. "I don't know how you stay in business serving something like this. I ought to confiscate the whole bunch."

"Batch," he said, grinning. "I'm going to box these up. You take them with you."

"Really, we can't—"

"You can, too." He said it fiercely, and Eve caught the faint glitter of tears as he grabbed a box. "You do your job, I do mine. I like that girl. I've got a girl of my own about the same age. Don't know what I'd do if somebody put her in the hospital."

Eve waited a moment. "But you didn't like him. Anthony Strazza."

"Didn't really know him. I worked with her." Then he shrugged. "Didn't like him much. He'd give you the cold eye. Some people figure if you feed them or do for them, you're less. He was like that. She's not. She was afraid of him."

"Why do you say that?"

"You wanted impressions, right? Back a year or so ago, we were working out the details, the menu for a party. Sitting in the dining room of their place with charts and lists and the samples of desserts I'd brought. Having some coffee. Having some fun with it, and she was laughing. He came in, and I saw it. Just for a second. I saw fear in her eyes. She covered it, jumped up, reminding him who I was, what we were doing. All bright and shiny. But her fingers were trembling when she reached for one of the charts we'd worked on."

Jacko's mouth tightened. "We never met like that again. Mostly worked things out via 'link or e-mail."

The woman who'd been ringing up sales came in through the swinging doors, studied Eve, Peabody. "Mom said to give the police this disc." She pulled it out of her pocket. "It's got the names, contact numbers, addresses of everybody who worked the Strazza event. And how long they've worked for us, if they're family."

She looked at her father. "Mom's taken over for me on the counter. I'm supposed to talk to the police."

Leaning down, Jacko gave her a smacking kiss on the top of her head. "Nothing to worry about, baby."

"Dr. Strazza was killed? And Mrs. Strazza's hurt?"

Xena had the same big blue eyes as her cousin, and a bundle of gold-streaked chestnut hair under a white cap. She took a bright red water bottle out of her apron pocket, guzzled. "I just can't believe it. But it couldn't have been any of us. I mean, none of us would ever . . . Plus, everybody left before me and Hugh. All of us, I mean."

"You're sure of that."

"I know everybody on that list. My brother's on that list. He worked as bartender, and he left before dessert. Nat and I served that, then I sent her home. All the kitchen staff but Elroy left during dessert. And he left with Nat. We had Bryar, Zach and Hugh on valet—Hugh served as runner. What I mean is, he worked wherever he was needed. Hugh told me Zach and Bryar left together, walking to the subway. Even in a good neighborhood, Dad doesn't like any of the girls to walk by themselves after an event. Lacy served as bartender with Noah, my brother, and she left with Rachel, Trevor, and Marty—kitchen staff. Rachel, Trevor, Marty, and I live together. They were still up when I got home."

"Okay. Did you notice anything, looking back, anything that seemed off?"

"Honestly, no. You've really got to be on your toes when you're doing a multicourse, sit-down dinner for fifty. We served the first course in the living area, and set up the dining room table while that was being served. Cleared the first course while the main was going on, made sure the right wine was offered, glasses were filled. Mrs. Strazza had a playlist, so there was that. Then it was back to the living room—but without the tables and chairs—for dessert."

"What do you mean 'without the tables and chairs'?"

"Well, not *her* tables and chairs. The rentals, for the fancy first course."

"What company?"

"Loan Star," father and daughter said together.

"We've done events with them for years," Jacko continued. "They're solid."

"When do they bring in the rentals, take them away?"

"They brought them about five," Xena told her. "I was there to supervise the setup. Nat and I did the table decor—with Mrs. Strazza. She likes to have a hand in. They picked them up at eight-thirty. We cleared, they came in. In and out in about ten or fifteen minutes."

"Did you know the crew?"

"Ah . . . mostly. I mean . . . I'm not sure. We were so busy." She looked at her father. "Oh, Dad."

"You don't worry." He came around the island, pulled her to him. "You don't worry about this."

"He's right," Eve said. "Do you remember how many in the rental crew?"

"Four—no, five. Five. I *do* know a couple of them. But I was busy, just didn't have time to think about it."

"If you remember anything more, contact me or Detective Peabody. We appreciate your time, the help. And everything else."

Rubbing his daughter's back, Jacko looked over her head. "Can Mrs. Strazza have visitors?"

"I wouldn't say right now."

"Can we check with her doctor, see if we can send her some soup?"

"Delroy Nobel at St. Andrew's. You do what you do, Jacko," Eve said. "We'll do what we do."

On the street, Peabody hunched inside her coat. "If I could afford to have something catered, I know who I'd use." She tapped the top of the box she carried. "Those were seriously amazing sticky buns. Are you taking these into Central?"

She considered it. "Cull one out."

"You're going to eat another one?"

"No. Cull one out. Roarke's earned one."

"Aw. See, for you, every day is Valentine's Day."

"Oh, yeah, I'm a romantic fool 24/7. Just cull one—hell, cull two, one for McNab. Seal them in evidence bags. And find out where Loan Star Rentals is."

"Next stop?"

"I tend to think Jacko's got a firm hand on his people. Not that one couldn't go nuts. But with the similar attacks, it's more likely this is a serial offender. I don't see Jacko and Gula fooled for long. So, the rental company's next. We'll talk to the rest of the catering staff, but let's pull them to us, after the rental company and the morgue."

"Right. Wait. It's Sunday."

"So what?"

"Rental company might be closed. I'll check."

"If it is, find the owner, the manager, whoever can get us the names of who worked this job."

"On that." But first, she got two evidence bags from the field kit in the trunk. Once the buns were all secure, Peabody started on her PPC.

"Open, by appointment only on Sundays. I'll dig up the manager."

"Do that. So, morgue first."

"Oh, joy. Got her." Peabody settled in for the drive. "Want me to contact her—the manager?"

"Start there. Get the names."

As Peabody went to work, Eve let her mind play with what she'd gathered.

Daphne liked. Strazza disliked. Daphne interacted—liked her hand in, had coffee with the caterer, briefly volunteered at hospital. Strazza was cold, arrogant. So an older, wealthier husband, a demanding and domineering one.

If Jacko was right about the flash of fear, would they add abusive to that list?

She used her in-dash to do some digging of her own while Peabody talked with the rental manager.

No reports of domestic abuse, no nine-one-ones from Daphne or from the house itself. No visits to the ER or hospital.

"Five guys," Peabody reported. "I've got names and contacts."

"Run them."

"Running them."

Still, he was a doctor, Eve thought. He'd know how to hurt her without letting it show, if he was the physically abusive type. And where, if so, would that play in this?

A cold, abusive, jealous husband. A young, beautiful wife. Maybe a fling there, or someone who wanted a fling. Someone she'd discarded or rejected outright. A kind of payback.

If it turned out to be a single attack, maybe.

She went back to the dash 'link.

"We have the case files from Olsen and Tredway. And a request for a sit-down asap. We'll work it in."

"I'll schedule it. Got one here with some bumps. Two assault charges, a couple drunk and disorderlies, an indecent exposure. Did three months on one assault, other one charges dropped. Community service and mandatory counseling on the D and Ds. Time served on the indecent exposure."

"No B and Es, muggings, theft, sexual assaults?"

"Nope. Got another one with vandalism, but it's small change. Got caught tagging a building when he was eighteen. Ten years ago. Nothing shaky since."

"Let's pull them all in, have a chat. I need to talk to Mira."

"I sent her the details with a request she contact Nobel for a possible consult." Peabody yawned hugely. "Man, sugar rush, now sugar crash."

"Okay." Eve scanned for a spot to park. "Contact the five guys from the rental place, set up interviews at Central. If any of them balk, we'll send uniforms to convince them. That doesn't do it, we go to them. And see what we've got from the other party guests."

As they entered the white tunnel, Eve kept walking. "Find a place to work this out. I'll take the body."

The tunnel echoed, smelled of harsh lemon, maybe something like vinegar. But under it lingered the smear of death. Nothing much touched that.

Bodies in, bodies out, she thought. Bodies opened, bodies closed. And somewhere in that process, the bodies talked to the ME.

No one she knew understood the language of the dead as fluently as Morris.

She pushed through the swinging doors into his work area. He had music on low, something with a lot of bass and a charging drum beat. Over his snappy midnight-blue pin-striped suit he wore a clear protective coat. No tie today, she noted, but a turtleneck the same hue as the thin gray stripes. He'd twisted his long, dark hair into some sort of a complicated knot where a single thin braid spilled from the center.

His exotic, clever eyes met Eve's. "An early morning for you."

"Actually we'll call it a long night. Roarke and I ran into his wife"— she gestured to the body on the slab—"almost literally, about two this morning on the way home from a fancy deal."

"I see. As she hasn't joined him here, she survived."

"In the hospital. Beaten, raped, naked when we spotted her wandering the streets. Memory's spotty, so far," Eve added.

Eve stepped closer. Morris had Strazza opened with his precise Y-cut. She didn't flinch at such things. Couldn't remember if she ever had.

"The way it looks," she continued. "Somebody accessed their

house during a dinner party, laid in wait in the bedroom. Party's over, they're attacked. Husband is restrained, she's restrained and raped, both are knocked around. A couple of safes in the house open and empty. A few other valuables appear to be missing."

"A straight burglary doesn't do this."

"Nope. Could be that part of it is more of a bonus. We'll see."

"I can tell you the victim fought. He struggled enough to abrade his wrists and ankles. There are, as you see, numerous cuts—none life-threatening—inflicted with a thin, sharp blade. I'd vote for a scalpel."

"Vic's a doctor, a surgeon. That may play."

"Most of the blows were to the face. Fists—gloved, likely smooth leather—and a sap of some sort. I'd say leather there as well. The body blows are well placed to inflict damage and pain. Kidneys, abdomen, kneecaps."

He handed Eve microgoggles, put on his own. "The zip ties bit into the flesh, and we have splinters of wood, and what I expect the lab will verify as adhesive from duct or strapping tape."

"Yeah, zipped him, taped over that. Wood from the chair he broke out of."

"This blow here." Morris moved up to the head. "A sweeping strike with a blunt instrument. I would time this as at least an hour after the other injuries, certainly not what incapacitated him before he was restrained."

"Likely the first blow, to put him out so he could restrain him. After the assault, the vic broke the chair he was tied to. Managed to bust it, and I'm seeing him gain his feet enough to try to charge the attacker."

"That fits, as the angle of this wound indicates they were facing each other, with the assailant slightly to the left side."

"Big, heavy crystal vase. Had to put him down, right?"

"Even considering adrenaline, a hit like this would have flattened him."

"Medical term."

"Of course. He'd go down, certainly lost consciousness."

"The assailant gave him two more whacks for good measure."

"Not right away."

Eve's eyes sharpened. "How much of a gap?"

"I'm going to tell you the initial head wound bled for at least fifteen minutes. Fifteen to twenty. The blood had time to begin to coagulate. The killing blow—and either of these to the back of the head, would have done it, was delivered after the heart continued to pump blood for a good fifteen minutes. And this one? The angle suggested the victim was moving, getting to his feet. The last, he was prone."

"Okay. Okay." Eve closed her eyes a moment, pulled off the goggles, paced. "Vic breaks loose enough to go after the assailant. Assailant grabs the vase, bashes him from the front. Vic's down and out, but he doesn't finish him. Maybe he's getting his tools and loot, maybe he rapes the wife again, maybe he starts cleaning himself up. Vic starts to come out of it, tries to get up. Then he finishes him."

She shook her head. "Stupid. If you're going to kill the guy, do it and get it done. If you're not especially interested in killing him, get your stuff and get the hell out. Wouldn't take fifteen minutes, unless you're stupid enough to have left everything scattered around in the first place."

"People are often stupid," Morris pointed out.

"They sure as hell are. Smart enough to get in there, slip right in the house during a dinner party for fifty with about a dozen staff. Unless he was a guest or staff. Vicious enough to beat and rape—made the wife strip, raped her in front of the husband—but not vicious enough to kill when the husband comes at him. Stupid or cocky enough to hang around for fifteen after—and he could have thought the guy was dead or dying—*then* finish him off. The way it looks, almost certainly took the time to cut the wife loose before he heads out."

"He released the wife?"

"She's got lacerations—she struggled against the restraints. Not as hard as the dead guy here, but she struggled. The shape she was in, I don't see her getting loose on her own, and there was no rope or tape left behind. Killer bagged it up, took it with him. Had to."

"Not only left her alive, but cut her loose. Can she identify him?"

"The devil, she says. She's a mess, but I figure that's how he looked. Mask or makeup. You go to that much trouble to disguise yourself, you probably don't intend to kill the targets. But now he has."

Eve studied Strazza again. "And they hardly ever stop at one."

5

WHEN SHE WALKED OUT, EVE SAW PEABODY WALKING TOWARD HER.

"I managed to contact all five of the delivery guys," Peabody began. "One of them whined a little, but they're all coming in. Two of them are roommates anyway."

"Good, saves times and trouble."

"I'd tagged Santiago and Carmichael for the party guests. So far, they're all checking out—times they left, arrived home. Nobody noticed anyone out of place, or felt anything off."

Peabody bundled back into her endless scarf as they swung into the car. "Olsen of Olsen and Tredway is on her way to Central now—just wants to talk it through. Tredway's actually in Philadelphia for a family wedding weekend. He'll be back tomorrow, and would come in today if you think it's necessary."

"It's not. If we don't beat Olsen to Central, I need ten to sort this out, take a quick look through the files. We'll set her up in the lounge."

She wanted to start her book, set up her board, but that could wait until they'd had their meeting with the detective. Still she wanted another good look at the files on the other attacks.

"We take the delivery guys one at a time, in interview. I want a consult with Mira first thing in the morning."

"Already set. She'll come to you."

"Appreciate it." Eve pulled into the garage at Central, zipped into her designated space. "Tag Nobel again, get an update on Daphne Strazza's condition."

Peabody made the tag as they rode the elevator. "Got v-mail, leaving a message."

"Try the nurse in charge." Still running it over in her head, Eve got off the elevator, strode into the bullpen, noted Baxter at his desk instead of being off-duty, and apparently entertaining a pale-skinned blonde in shiny knee-boots and a bold blue sweater over skinny black pants.

The woman turned, met Eve's eyes. In them, Eve saw cop.

"Detective Olsen."

"Lieutenant. Thanks for making time."

"Back at you. Can't get enough of the bullpen, Baxter?"

"Trueheart and I caught one, already wrapping it up so I sent him home. Nikki says you caught one, too—maybe connected to one of hers."

"Maybe. Detective Peabody will get you set up in the lounge, Detective. I need ten."

"I know the way. Whenever you're ready, Lieutenant. Later, David."

Olsen walked out, tossing a dark coat over her arm.

Eve lifted her eyebrows at Baxter.

"Nikki and I worked together a time or two back in the day." He smiled, and the quick gleam in it said they'd done more than work. "She's solid."

"Good to know." She left him with his wrap-up, walked back to her office.

Coffee came first. Once the mug was steaming in her hand, she sat at her desk, cleared her brain.

Then started at the beginning with her notes. Timelines, observations, facts, evidence, names, locations.

She skimmed the two case files, noted Olsen and Tredway appeared to be thorough. And yet nothing they'd unearthed connected the victims. No cross there but for the fact both couples were financially well-off, had a rung on the upper end of society.

She made more notes, added some questions—and decided her time would be better served by speaking directly with Olsen.

She walked out, signaled Peabody, who held up a finger as she spoke on her 'link.

"Thanks. We'll check in again later. Nobel," she told Eve as she rose. "Mrs. Strazza woke agitated and anxious—basically hysterical. He's given her another mild sedative. She begged him not to let the devil find her, to hide her. So far that's it. It's all she remembers. He's spoken directly with Mira—he's the proactive sort—and she's going in later today to do an evaluation."

"Good. Maybe Mira can pull something out of her."

They walked to the cop lounge were Olsen sat at one of the little tables working on her PPC while something steamed in a go-cup at her elbow.

She set down the handheld. "Coffee's better here than in my house."

"Then your house must have stupendously bad coffee."

"Oh, it does. Stan would be here, Lieutenant, but his niece's wedding's in Philadelphia—or was yesterday. A kind of family deal going on today."

"It's no problem. I skimmed your files, Detective, but why don't you walk us through?"

"Sure. July last year, Rosa and Neville Patrick returned home from an evening out—dinner and theater with friends. Newlyweds—had a big society wedding the previous June, and had lived in the residence on Riverside Drive since April. Three-story townhouse, solid security. They noticed the alarm was off, but Rosa admitted—as she had met Neville at the restaurant and left the house last—she couldn't remember if she'd activated it. In any case, they didn't think anything of it. EDD later confirmed the alarm had been compromised, the security cameras jammed."

She paused, sipped. "Rosa went straight up. Neville got them both a nightcap, and went up two or three minutes after her. Rosa stated a man in vampire garb—white face, black eyes, pointed incisors, black cape—grabbed her from behind, held a knife to her throat. He told her to be absolutely still, absolutely silent or he'd slash her. He snapped restraints on her wrists—behind her back—then punched her in the face. Rang her bell, LT. She was half out of it when Neville came in. He states he saw his wife, her nose bleeding, her eyes glazed. The assailant had the knife to her throat, ordered him to sit down. When Neville hesitated, the assailant gave Rosa a little taste of the knife. Neville sat, and the assailant held the knife to Rosa's throat, forced her to put zip-tie restraints on Neville.

"Neither vic resisted, both told the assailant to take whatever he wanted. He forced Rosa to tie Neville to the chair with a rope, then put the restraints back on her, ordered her to lie facedown on the floor while he added more rope, secured the rope with tape. Once Neville was fully secured, he beat him—black leather gloved fists, a black weighted sap. Then he dragged Rosa to the bed, tore her clothes off and raped her."

"Tore her clothes?"

"All but shredded them. He then restrained Rosa to the headboard, punched her a few times, and demanded the combination for the safes—he knew there were three. One in each of their closets for their personal valuables, and one in Neville's home office. They didn't hesitate, gave him what he wanted, but still he beat them both unconscious. When Neville came to, both he and Rosa were untied—she was still out. He called nine-one-one. The call came in just over two hours after they got home. All three of the safes were emptied and a few items—including one of Rosa's cocktail dresses, a pair of her evening shoes and an evening bag were missing. There's a list of the other missing items in the file. We haven't come across any of them being pawned or sold."

Olsen stopped, drank more coffee. "Questions?"

"Plenty, but finish it out."

"To wrap this one, for now, no DNA, no fibers other than from the rope and tape, no prints, no nothing. He's not stupid. Eventually Rosa remembered he'd whispered in her ear while he raped her. The best you ever had, over and over, and he choked her, told her to tell him he was the best she ever had or he'd kill her, then Neville. Neville stated while the fucker was raping Rosa, he looked at Neville, grinned, and laughed."

"Did they get anything from his voice?"

"Smooth, sophisticated, public school Brit accent. But he dropped the accent a couple of times when he raped Rosa, and Neville—who *is* public school Brit—said it was fake. They think he was a white guy, but neither are sure. His face was covered in makeup and a kind of mask—very theatrical, both claim, very authentic."

"More than his face was exposed during the rape," Eve pointed out.

"Exactly. He wore a black condom, covered the shaft, and his balls were white—painted white—stark white. He never took off his clothes or cape. Long black hair—they couldn't tell if it was a wig or real. Black eyes. Rosa thinks they were contacts, but that's not a hundred percent. We believe he had experience with theater or costuming, and has above average e-skills. And we've gotten nowhere."

Olsen paused, drank some coffee. "Okay. The second incident, last November. In this case, the couple—Ira and Lori Brinkman—return home after a long holiday—Thanksgiving—annual weekend in the Hamptons. The house droid takes their bags upstairs, doesn't come back. Ira goes upstairs, finds the droid disabled, and is assaulted from behind. He wakes up restrained to a chair, and his wife has a black eye and our assailant has a knife to her throat. He's outfitted as a kind of ghoul this time—gray face, cadaverous cheekbones, gray eyes, wearing an old-fashioned black suit. He tells Lori to strip or he'll gut Ira. When she does, he drags her to the bed, smacks her around, rapes her, chokes her.

"The assailant leaves her on the bed," Olsen continued, "takes some time to beat the crap out of Ira, then he goes back, rapes Lori again, tells her to scream 'You're the best I've ever had,' and when she doesn't, he cuts her until she does."

After a short breath, Olsen drank more coffee. "They have two safes, one in their dressing room, one in their library. The assailant demands the combinations, knocks them both around some more, leaves them alone. Ira is barely conscious, going in and out. Lori is in shock. The assailant comes back, gives her round three, this time telling her, repeatedly, it's the best she's ever had or he knows she wants it. He also watches Ira as he rapes Lori. When he's done, he strikes Ira on the back of the head with the sap. Lori doesn't remember if he hit her again, she's hazy, doesn't remember when he cut her loose. She called nine-one-one, couldn't give them any real information. Just 'Help us'. She thought Ira was dead. The responding officers found her curled up in Ira's lap, him still unconscious. The assault took two hours and about twenty minutes."

"What did he take?"

"Safe contents, some expensive bric-a-brac, a small painting, a bottle of high-end brandy and one of Lori's cocktail dresses, with shoes and bag."

"Voice?"

"Gravelly, hollow, deep-throated. He messed the second couple up more than the first, multiple rapes on the female on the second assault, used the knife—what they both believe was a medical scalpel—on both of them. Just shallow cuts and slices, but it's an escalation. We found no crossover between the victims."

Olsen rubbed her eyes. "Sorry, forgot. He had sound effects going. Howling wolves for Dracula, rattling chains for the ghoul. Lori and Ira say he did something to the lights. They're hazy about it, understandably, but they both said the lights were gray, dim and gray."

"To go with the costumes," Eve said. "The theme of each attack."

"That's how we see it. The first couple, Upper West—he's one of the owners of On Screen Productions—has his offices in their New York base. We looked at that—the costume, theater—but got nothing. Rosa's a, well, professional committee person, you could say. Society girl, does good works and shops a lot. Second couple, he's in international finance, she's a human rights attorney. And I want to add all of them are nice people. We didn't find any cheating or whoring or illegals or dastardly deeds among them. Rosa's twenty-six, Neville's, thirty. Ira's forty-four, Lori, forty-two. Rosa's Hispanic, Neville's Brit, Ira's Jewish, Lori's mixed race. Both women are stunners, Lieutenant, so that may play. Both are often featured in society media. Neville's in entertainment media, Ira's in financials. Rosa's into charity work, Lori's human rights, but she's done some script doctoring, some screen writing under other names. But they didn't have any mutual friends, didn't use the same vendors, doctors, gyms, housekeeping services, and so on. Nothing taken from the residences has shown up on the street."

Olsen shoved her cup aside. "And now he's killed someone."

Eve sat back. Even if Baxter hadn't verified Olsen as solid, Eve would have judged her the same. "Our surviving vic can't give us many details yet. She describes a devil."

"Vampire, ghoul, devil. I sense a theme."

"Follows," Eve agreed. "The basic MOs are the same. Slick break-in, waiting for the couple in the bedroom, the fists, the knife, the sap, the restraints. Escalation in violence, and a narrowing of his downtime. Our crime scene reads the male victim broke the chair, tried to attack, and the assailant downed him with a heavy crystal vase. Then there's a time gap—Morris," Eve said to Peabody. "About fifteen minutes before the two killing blows. That's something to think about. He cleaned out three safes. Other than that, we can't confirm what else he took, including potentially a cocktail dress with accessories—until the survivor is able to tell us. Dr. Mira is going to see her today."

"Nobody better," Olsen said. "Anyway I can talk to her?"

"I'm going to say no at this time. Not because you don't have a stake in this, and I intend to read you in as our case progresses, but she's in bad shape, emotionally. I don't want to add another face, another questioner."

"I get that. I want to say, if and when, Stan and I know how to approach a victim of rape."

"Understood, and I'll have Mira copy you and your partner on her reports. I'll give you what I've got, and expect the same."

"You'll have it."

"To begin, there's a variation. These vics were having a dinner party for fifty when, we believe, he entered the house."

Olsen puffed out her cheeks. "Christ, he's getting bold."

"The rest follows the basic pattern—up until the murder. We've got some people to talk to. We get anything, we'll pass it on. I'm going to check your files—you do the same—for Jacko's Catering and Loan Star Rentals. The last vics used both for this party, and have used them in the past. The caterer's coming up clean, but it could be a connection."

"I'll get on that. My take, if you want it?"

"I do?"

"He's a coward, but a lot of rapists are. And a sadist, and he likes drama. You've got to figure he's punishing them both. He wants the husband to suffer, wants him to feel impotent. Maybe daddy issues, who knows. I've got Mira's profile—we went to her after the second one clicked in. It's in the file."

Olsen got to her feet. "Any help we can give, it's yours. We can clear it with our LT." She hesitated. "You've got a rep—both of you," she said, with a glance at Peabody. "And that's rock solid. But I still asked Baxter for his take. He's not a bullshitter when it matters."

"Just all the rest of the time."

Olsen grinned. "And he's so good at it. He says you're the best LT he's ever worked under, and Peabody's as good as they get. So."

She offered a hand to Eve. "Thanks for making the time. Anything we can do to bag this bastard will have me doing my happy dance."

When Olsen left, Peabody preened. "I have a rep."

"That's what you got out of all that?"

"Just taking a moment to bask."

"Basking's done," Eve said as she rose.

"Good thing as I've got a notification Oliver Quint's just signed in. He's one of the delivery guys."

"Let's get him in interview."

"I liked Olsen," Peabody said as they headed out. "Do you think she and Baxter . . ."

"What is Baxter's middle name?"

"Horn dog. Yeah, that answer's that."

Quint was a skinny black guy with huge eyes and a tiny beard. He sat in the box with his narrow shoulders hunched and his dark moon eyes darting. Eve's first thought was nobody that jumpy could successfully shoplift a bag of soy chips from a 24/7 much less orchestrate a trio of break-ins, rapes, and a murder.

But you had to start somewhere.

"Nervous, Oliver?"

"It's Ollie, okay. My ma calls me Oliver when I'm in trouble. Am I in trouble?"

"Have you done anything to get you there?"

"Look, Chachie said how he found the wrist unit, and he needed some scratch, so I bought it off him cheap. Maybe I sort of figured he maybe stole it somewhere, but I didn't steal it."

Eve arched an eyebrow, studied the black, fake leather band and oversized unit on Quint's bony wrist.

"That wrist unit?"

"Well, yeah. See mine got busted, so—"

"So you're wearing what you believe is stolen property to a police interview?"

"I . . ." He looked sincerely baffled. "My old one got busted."

"We're not interested in the wrist unit, Ollie."

"Oh." His big eyes blinked. "Hey, I only went by that party to hook up with Marletta, and we didn't stay. Maybe an hour."

"What party?"

"Um. Lorenzo's party." He tried a sheepish, "aw shucks" smile. "Maybe I figured there maybe would be Zoner and shit there, but I didn't have any. I got a good job, and you could get bounced. Plus, my ma'd skin me."

Peabody smiled at him. "Your ma sounds like a good, smart woman."

"She ain't raising her boys to be criminals. Tells us all the time."

"That's good. You like your job, Ollie?" Peabody asked him.

"I like it fine and good. Pays okay, and Carmine, he's solid square. I got three years in, and I got a raise first of the year."

"You did a delivery and pickup yesterday," Eve began.

"Did five altogether yesterday. Weekends is busy. Five deliveries," he qualified. "Three pickups. Got another pickup I'm on tonight."

"The Strazza job," Eve qualified.

"Um."

But he brightened up when she reeled off the address.

"Sure did. Five ten-top tables, fifty chairs. Delivery and setup— that was for five sharp, and break down and pick up between eight-thirty and eight-forty-five. Big-ass house—you get to see a lot of fancy places with the job. We've done jobs at that place lots of times. The lady tips good. Some of them don't, but the lady there, she does. Always says thank you, too. Some don't."

"Did you see any of the guests?"

"Oh, no, uh-uh. We went in when they were in the dining room. See, they had this fancy before-the-dinner thing in the living room. Don't know why, but it's not my business. We just go in, and the lady who does the food—that's, um, Xena! Yeah, she's nice, too. She's cleared off the dishes and whatever, and we just go in, break down the tables, haul out the rentals. Quiet and quick like."

"So no one went in or out but you. You only saw the catering staff."

"Well, they had the valet guys outside—shot the shit with them a little. Then the entertainment."

Eve held up a finger. "Entertainment?"

"Yeah, I guess. I didn't really see him. Luca said how he must be the entertainment."

"What did he look like?"

"Luca?"

"No, Ollie, the entertainment."

"Oh, I only just caught like a glimpse when I was hauling out a table with Stizzle and this guy was going up the stairs—in the house. I said, 'I guess he's late for dinner,' and Luca he said how he must be the entertainment."

"How do know it was a man?" Peabody prompted.

Ollie's skinny eyebrows drew together in serious thought. "Um. I guess he looked like one. From the back. I dunno. I didn't think about it."

"White guy, black guy, anything?" Eve asked.

"I dunno. I think he had on a big black coat and a hat. I didn't really pay attention, you know 'cause we were humping it. Using the main 'cause it was the big tables and the double doors there made it faster. I just saw him going up the stairs."

"Between eight-thirty and eight-forty," Eve added.

"I guess about eight-forty-ish-like or like that. I guess we were in and out inside like twenty minutes, and we had the last table. Few more chairs left to go. So I figured he was late to the dinner thing, but Luca said he was the entertainment. Lots of times they have entertainment at the big-ass houses with the fancy parties."

"Okay, Ollie, thanks for coming in."

"I can just go?"

"Yeah." Eve rose to get the door. "And, Ollie, do yourself a favor and don't buy anything else from Chachie. One day it could come back and bite you in the ass."

"That's what my ma would say."

"Listen to your ma."

When he left, Peabody huffed out a breath. "The killer just walked right in and went upstairs."

"Ballsy," Eve said. "Plenty ballsy. And timed well. Valets taking a break, talking with delivery guys, delivery guys in and out, catering staff in the living area making sure it goes smooth. Everyone else in the dining room or the kitchen. Let's push on getting this Luca in here."

"Don't need to. He and his roommate just signed in."

"Luca first. Slim chance they helped this guy gain access, but it's there."

Luca DiNozzo wasn't a skinny black guy, but a ridiculously attractive Italian with a flirtatious smile and a gym-buff body in a snug black sweater and tight jeans.

Eve could all but hear Peabody's hormones humming.

He sat relaxed in the box, but then he'd been there before. Minor bumps, Eve thought, but minor often served as a gateway to more.

"What can I do for you ladies?"

"Lieutenant," Eve said. "Detective."

He just smiled his flirty smile.

"Tell us about the Strazza job."

"They're regulars. Dinner party last night."

He ran through the particulars just as Quint had done, matching the delivery, the timing, the break down. But he shifted as he finished up, and his jaw went tight. "They got a complaint? I supervised that job."

"A lot to supervise with your people moving in and out, a lot of pretty little things out in plain sight. Easy grab and go. You've had some bumps along the way, Luca."

Now his shoulders shot back, his jaw forward. "If anything's missing from that house, one of the guests pocketed it. Nobody who works for Carmine steals—and I know those guys. I know Jacko's crew, too. So if Dr. Strazza's making a stink, he should look to his own."

"About those bumps," Eve added.

"That was then, this is now. I did the stupid when I was drinking. Got into a program, stopped drinking and doing the stupid. And I never stole so much as a freaking gumball even when I was drinking. Carmine took a chance on me, and I don't forget it. I wouldn't do anything to mess him up, mess myself up. Like I said, the Strazzas are regulars. If we weren't trustworthy, they wouldn't use us, so if Dr. Strazza's got some bug up his butt, it's his problem."

"Strazza's dead."

Eve saw the shock—instant and violent. Luca's chiseled jaw literally dropped.

"What? What the hell? *Dead*?"

"Murdered. Take me through your night, Luca."

"I—wait." He closed his eyes, breathed for a minute. "Let me think. We had another pickup after the Strazzas'. Jesus. But that wasn't until eleven. We took the pickup back to the warehouse, stowed it, logged it, went out to get something to eat. Except Charlie went on home—didn't need him for the last job, and he's got a new baby, so I cut him loose. The rest of us did the pickup—way the hell down in SoHo. We hauled it back, logged that in—I know that was about twelve-thirty. We all went out for a beer—well, that's club soda for me. I guess Ollie took off about one, then Stizzle and Mac and me had another drink, got some bar food, just to hang. Stizzle and I went home—we're roommates—about two. Mac, he was making some progress with this brunette, so he stayed back.

"Jesus, we didn't kill anybody. You can check the pickups, the log-ins. Carmine's got security cams and the feed's time-stamped. I can vouch for every one of the guys. I can guarantee you Charlie went straight home to his girl and their baby. The baby's just two weeks old, man. We didn't hurt anybody."

"Okay. Tell me about the latecomer. Tell me about the person who walked into the Strazzas' residence while you were breaking down the job."

"The weird guy? Musician or something, right? Performance artist. I don't get that. Look, can I have some water or something? Jesus, somebody got murdered."

"I'll get it." Peabody rose, slipped out.

"Performance artist," Eve prompted.

"Something like that, I figured. He's all wrapped up in this coat, hat, shades—only assholes and entertainer types wear shades at night, right? He's carrying a case—I figure like a musical instrument or something."

"What did he look like—his face?"

"Couldn't really see it, but he was wearing like stage makeup. I could smell it. My cousin's an actor—done plenty of gigs off-Broadway. Well, an off-off, and one more off-Broadway. I could smell, like, the greasepaint. Just a weird artist type, I figured, and . . ."

Eve saw it hit, saw the horror come into the dreamy bedroom eyes. "That guy? He killed Strazza? But . . . he walked right by me. I let him walk right by me. I let him . . . He went right up the stairs in the house. Like he was supposed to. I let him in the house."

"Did you open the door for him?"

"I . . ." Breathing fast, he dragged a hand through his fairly magnificent mane of hair. "No, not exactly. I was by the door, I was holding it open—can't use a stop on the door when it's that freaking cold. The clients don't like it. So I was holding it open—Mac and Charlie had just carried out chairs and . . . Ah, yeah, Ollie and Stizzle were coming with a table, so I held the door. This guy, I saw him coming up the steps toward the door, talking on his 'link. And he walked right by me, and walked to the stairs, went up."

"On his 'link," Eve began as Peabody came back with the water.

Luca took the tube, cracked it. "Can I have a minute?"

"Go ahead."

He sat, drank, sat, drank again, then shot straight in his chair. "The lady. Mrs. Strazza. God, is she . . ."

"She's in the hospital."

"Oh, Jesus, Jesus. Is she going to die?"

"She's stable. She'll be all right. Did he say anything to you, this man who came in? Did you hear him talking on his 'link."

"He didn't even look at me, just breezed right on by. I let him breeze right on by. He was talking on the 'link, kind of pissy, you know? Like he was half pissed at who he was talking to. Said, like . . . 'I'm here now, okay? They're still eating.' Like that. He just came in, like he belonged, like he was supposed to be there. I never thought to try to stop him."

"How tall was he?"

"I wasn't paying attention. Truth? I was wondering if I'd have a couple minutes to hit on Xena. Can't get her to go out with me, and I wasn't paying attention. Not as tall as me," Luca said suddenly. "Shorter. Yeah. I'm six foot—or, okay, five-eleven and a half. He was shorter. Like a couple inches shorter, I think."

"Build?"

"Hard to say. It was a lot of coat. It had flounces! Like—"

He made wavy gestures with his hands.

"Theatrical, right? A big black coat with flounces or whatever they are, and a black hat with a big brim he had pulled down, maybe a scarf? I didn't pay attention. The shades, because I thought: Asshole."

"Race, age, anything?"

"His voice didn't sound old. I didn't really see his skin color—I think he had gloves. It was really cold. I didn't . . . you know, I think his face was kind of red. I didn't really see, it was like two seconds, but maybe red. That's weird."

Luca blew out a breath. "I just got an impression, that's all. I just figured they'd hired somebody to do a gig, put on an act. He walked in like he was expected, and I let him. Is it my fault?"

Eve met his eyes. "Do you think I'd soft-peddle it for you?"

"No." His voice wavered like a man on the edge of being sick. "No. God."

"I'm telling you it's not your fault."

Luca closed his eyes. Eve saw him press his lips together when they trembled. "It feels like it is."

"It's not. And what you're telling us may help us catch him, so take that away. Now let's go over it again. Did anyone else see him?"

"Ollie said something. And, yeah, Stizzle. They were heading my way, toward the door, as he went up the stairs."

"Peabody, bring Stizzle in." Eve looked back at Luca. "We're going to see if he can add any details."

6

It turned out Luca had gotten the best look, but his roommate confirmed the coat, hat, shades, and the height as shorter than Luca. And since Stizzle had noticed the UNSUB's boots—shiny black with short, stubby heels—they estimated five-eight.

Eve arranged for them both to work with a police artist the next day. If anyone could draw more details out, it would be Yancy.

With the rental crew interviewed, and cleared to her satisfaction, she headed back to her office to—finally—put up her murder board, start her book.

She found Roarke in her office, his boots (no short, stubby heels required) up on her desk—as she was wont to do—working on his PPC.

He wore black trousers, a black jacket, a steel-gray sweater. Roarke's version, she supposed, of casual office wear.

"Comfy?" she asked him.

"It'll do. I've been up in EDD with McNab, and wish there was better news on that front."

"I had a feeling."

He slipped his PPC into his jacket pocket. "You won't get a handy image of your suspect coming or going from the crime scene. He gutted, quite professionally, the security, and took the essentials with him. We can tell you the alarm wasn't compromised. It was shut down from inside, as were the locks."

"So you'd think an inside job. But it's not." Since it was there, she took the coffee he had set on her desk, drank it.

"Isn't it?"

"No, because we have three—potentially more when I speak to the valets—who saw the suspect walk right into the house at approximately eight-forty last night."

"Eyewitnesses? So your news is better. You'll tell me about that while we have lunch."

"I haven't had time to put my board and book together," she began when he swung his feet off her desk and rose.

"There's pizza in the AutoChef."

She stopped dead. "There is?"

"There is today."

"I'd have sex with you for that alone," she told him and smiled.

"I can lock the door."

"Later."

She started on her board as he programmed the pizza. The seductive scent of it struck her dead center when he pulled it out. That bubbling cheese, the spice of pepperoni.

She could have wept.

She ate one-handed—only one of the many advantages of pizza— while she arranged her board and filled him in.

"He's got big brass ones, doesn't he?"

"I think he likes the risk. It's part of the fun." Eve studied her board, grabbed a second slice. "He needed to know the timing, the routine. He had to know the targets were having a party. Figure there are, in addition to the hosts, forty-eight guests—and their staff, maybe hairdressers, and so on who knew. Add the caterer, and staff—and the people they might have mentioned it to, the rental place, and so on."

Nodding, Roarke passed her a napkin. "Potentially a few hundred people knew the time, the place, the basic setup."

"Not that hard to get the information. He plans. He gathers information on the targets. The first couple, out for the evening, he breaks in, disables security. Second couple returning from a few days away."

She sat down now, put her boots up, while Roarke settled for the ass-pinching visitor's chair. "His violence and lag time have escalated, but the Strazzas—that was the big one. Walking in while people were in the house, strolling right by staff and up the stairs to set the stage. I bet that added excitement. Possibly increased his violence due to same."

"The theatrics, the folklore monsters. There are easier ways to disguise yourself, but he chooses the elaborate."

"And it's a sharp angle," Eve agreed. "It's like a performance, right? And he's in character. He writes the script, sets the stage. But this time, he had to—what do you call it—ad lib. He didn't go in there intending to kill. But now that he has . . ."

"You expect he might write that ending for the next performance."

"I do. He will." Of that she had no doubt. "He likes causing pain, suffering, fear, humiliation. In every case he choked the female victim to unconsciousness. Sooner or later he'd have gone too far there, either by accident or design. Now he's crossed that line. He won't go back."

While he didn't doubt her, Roarke studied the board as she did. "Yet, every time he released his victims before he left—and even after he killed, he released Daphne Strazza."

"Yeah, well, show's over, right?"

"Mmm. If you take your theory to the next step, does he release her because he wanted a review? Someone who'd lived through the performance, as you called it, and would speak of it. Even—to his deluded mind—praise it."

"Like a critic?" Musing on it, Eve reached for her coffee, found the mug empty.

Roarke rose, got two tubes of water. "Switch it up," he suggested as he handed her one. "Like a critic," he confirmed, "or an audience review. Someone who'd relate how convincing his performance."

"I can see that." After gulping down water, Eve gestured toward the board with the tube. "Daphne Strazza's done just that because in her state of mind, she *is* convinced the devil attacked her."

"Surely there's no greater ego boost for a performer than having someone believe he was the character he portrayed. It's a terrible sort of praise, isn't it?"

"Ego," Eve murmured. "A need for praise. He made the women praise him while he raped them. Next to stupidity, ego's the thing that causes the most mistakes."

Again she gestured to the board. "Following a pattern's another. There's got to be some connection between the victims. Some linchpin. The SVU detectives are solid, they've been thorough, but there's something they haven't found."

"So you will."

She angled her head to look at him. He so rarely looked tired, so rarely showed fatigue, but she saw the first signs of it in his eyes. "So I will. And you should go home."

"Kicking me out?"

"For your own good."

"Come with me and work at home. After you have a nap."

"I've got the valets coming in—I have to cross them off. And some other things to deal with. Then I'll be home. And maybe take a nap in our big, fancy new bed."

He rose, came over to take her face in his hands. "Coming home as we did only yesterday—then going out again to the charity ball— we haven't yet slept or anything else in our big, fancy new bed."

"We'll make up for it. I like how it's turning out, the bedroom and all."

"And like even more that the bulk of the work was done when we were on the island."

"Goes without saying. I'll be home as soon as I can."

"I'll be there," he said, and kissed her.

And that, she thought as he left her, summed up the miracle of her life. She had a home with him, and he'd be there.

Swinging her legs off the desk, she started her murder book.

When they finished the last interview, Eve prepared to send Peabody home.

"Get some downtime. We'll pick it up tomorrow."

"Are you going home?"

Not directly, Eve thought, but . . . "Yeah. I want Mira's profile, another prod at the survivor when the medicals clear it, Yancy's sketch. None of that's going to happen now. I can comb through Olsen and Tredway's files at home."

"I can walk out with you," Peabody began, knowing her partner's methods.

"I've still got to grab my things," Eve began, then turned to the burly man with a visitor's badge clipped to his New York Knicks sweatshirt. "Can I help you?"

"I'm looking for a Lieutenant Dallas."

"You've found her."

"I'm Carmine Rizzo. My boys—Luca—he said Dr. Strazza's been murdered, and you talked to my crew."

"Yes. One minute. Go home, Peabody."

"I can speak to Mr. Rizzo."

"I've got it. Go." To solve the matter, Eve turned back to Carmine. "Why don't we go sit down in our lounge? I appreciate you coming in," she continued as she steered him out. "We didn't see any reason to interrupt your Sunday as your crew was cooperative."

"They're good boys. Men," he corrected. "All five of them on that job. I know them, their families. I want to make sure they're not in trouble."

"At this point, I'm looking at Luca, Ollie, Stizzle, and a valet—a Bryar Coleson—as witnesses."

"I know Bryar, she's a good girl, friends with my daughter. Witnesses, because they saw the one you think killed Dr. Strazza?"

"That's right." She led him into the lounge. "You want coffee?"

"No, no, thanks." He waved that away. "I'm cutting back."

"Take a seat, Mr. Rizzo."

"Carmine. Everybody calls me Carmine. Been at the game," he told her. "Whole family—doing the thing, so all day. I didn't hear about any of this until Luca finally tagged me. The boy's sick about this, half blames himself."

"He shouldn't. He's not in any way to blame."

Carmine nodded, blew out a relieved breath. "I told him the same. He said Mrs. Strazza was in the hospital. She's a sweet girl. Is she hurt bad? There was a news report when I tuned in on the way here, said how there'd been a murder and assault, but they didn't say how bad she was hurt."

"She was roughed up, but she's going to be okay."

"I don't understand the world most of the time. Don't understand the world. Now she's a widow, and at her age. Maybe we can send her flowers or something." Face grim, he stared down at the table.

"You knew Dr. Strazza," Eve prompted.

"I can't say I knew him all that well. Always paid on time, but he left the details of the order, the setup to Mrs. Strazza. She's a joy to work with."

"So I've heard."

"If there's anything we can do to help. You need to talk to any of the boys again, or talk to me, we're there."

"Would you know if you've done jobs for Neville and/or Rosa Patrick or Lori and/or Ira Brinkman during the past year or two?"

"I don't recognize the names right off, but I can sure check on that." He took out a notebook, keyed in the names.

"How about businesses, offices. Do you rent there?"

"All the time."

"St. Andrew's Hospital?"

"We've supplied some rentals for events, sure."

Now Eve took out her notebook, ran off the businesses of former victims.

"We've worked with On Screen, sure. Outfitted some sets when it made more sense for them to rent than to buy." He swiped through lists. "Oh, okay, that's Neville Patrick and Kyle Knightly. Sure, sure, we work with On Screen. We've done a couple of small jobs for Mr. Knightly at his place. I don't see the Brinkmans on here, or those other places. But I can check it back at the office. Memory's not what it used to be."

"It's working fine from my side of it. Thanks for this."

"Will it help?"

"It may."

"Then no thanks necessary. I don't stand for some man putting hard hands on a woman. I met my wife that way."

"You put hard hands on her?"

He laughed, and the tension he'd held in his face the whole time drained with it. "That'll be the day. I came out of a bar one night. In Jersey City where I was hanging out with a cousin, a couple of pals. I came out and in the parking lot this girl's fighting off this drunk. He's dragging at her and she's struggling, cursing him a blue streak. He smacks her right in the face."

"Ouch."

"Didn't slow her down, but, well, let me tell you, I don't stand for that. So I went over, shoved him off, told him to get going. Punched me, but he was too drunk to put much behind it. I wasn't near as drunk, and put him down.

"One year and three months later, I married the girl. That was thirty-three years ago."

"I'd say you pack a good punch, Carmine."

She went back to her office, added the interview to her book, considered her board. A connection, however thin, was a connection. One vic's business used the same rental company as the Strazzas. One vic's business partner had used that same company.

She'd see where it led her.

But now, she needed to go back to the beginning.

Eve stood outside the Strazzas' townhouse, hands in her coat pockets. She imagined the dark, and the thin icy breeze. The rental company van at the curb, cargo doors open, ramp down. A couple of valets in dark heavy coats by a portable heater making small talk with the rental crew.

Streetlamps send out their white pool of light. The door of the house opens, and its backwash of light silhouettes all.

He'd stride down the sidewalk—purposeful strides. Perception was reality, right? So he'd give off the perception of someone who knew where he was going, had a reason to go there.

Big, dark coat with theatrical flaps billowing some in the cold breeze. Dark hat, brim pulled low. A scarf—yeah, she'd bet on the scarf. Dark again, wound around the neck, arranged to cover most of the lower face. Add sunshades.

A flamboyant look, which was smart. People at a quick glance would notice the outfit more than the person wearing it.

Shiny boots with some heel. To add to the look, or because he was sensitive about his height? Or, again, to give the casual observer the perception of more height.

She let it roll around in her mind as she climbed the stairs. Main entrance, quicker in and out for the rental crew, and that had been client priority.

She broke the seal, mastered open the locks, then stood just inside with the doors open. She scanned the area from what would have been Luca's perspective.

Big, wide foyer that opened onto the living area. Two of the crew hefting one of the ten-tops. Supervisor's going to watch them.

Don't bump anything. Hurry it up, it's cold. Can't keep the damn doors open all night.

Glances back, sees the suspect sweep up the stairs, 'link to his ear. *I'm here now, okay?*

Smart again, give that impression of having the right to enter with attitude, words, a little impatience. Move fast, but not suspiciously fast.

Brisk. Move briskly. Straight in, annoyed, running late, and head right up the stairs. Like you belong.

Eve closed the door.

And walked in the killer's footsteps.

Had he known where to find the master suite, or had he walked from room to room until he found it? Either way, she thought, he'd done a little walk-around, a little hunt.

Plenty of time, plenty of places to hide if he'd heard anyone coming. Because the show didn't start until everyone but the Strazzas had left the house.

Plenty of time, she thought again. So he had the patience to wait— close to three hours. Had to set the stage, she mused as she went into the master.

She blanked out the bloodstains, the sweeper dust, the signs of struggle, let herself see the room as the killer had.

Rich, maybe a little on the hard-edged side, but rich.

"I bet you went through the closets." Eve moved to Daphne's closet as she spoke. "Sure you did. And you picked out the dress you'd take with you. I'd put money on that. Plenty to choose from."

He had set the stage, but he'd have waited. Just in case someone came in before showtime. He'd only have to keep the door open, maybe step a few feet outside the room to hear the guests over dessert, those saying their goodnights.

Excitement builds.

Check your makeup, adjust the mask. Set out the tools, set the lights.

Ease behind the door as you hear them coming up. Makes you hard. Curtain's going up.

They come in together. Take out the biggest threat. Sap the man, strike the woman. Restraints.

Haul the man to the chair you've chosen (bad choice on that). He's bigger than you, so you've got some muscle. Tie, restrain, use the tape to secure it all.

Turn on the strobe light.

She could see it. How he'd wait for the man to come around, hold a knife to his throat and demand the woman strip. Humiliation for both. Order her to the bed, give the man a couple whacks if she hesitates. Even if she doesn't.

Restrain her—wouldn't want her taking a swipe at you, getting any skin. Rape her, rough her up, choke her. Go back to the man, fists and saps. Maybe a few cuts because you need those combinations.

Yes, she could see it, a couple hours of brutality, fun times, and profitable.

Had he left them hurt, even unconscious—likely unconscious to clear out the safes, disable the house droids, dismantle the security system? Or . . .

Before that, Strazza breaks the chair, comes at him. Killer strikes him with the vase. Possibly believes he's dead. Then goes to clear out and disable. That would explain the time lag.

But why come back up, why not just get out?

Not finished yet? Maybe he wanted another round with Daphne, like an encore. Finds Strazza alive, struggling to his feet, ready to attack again.

Maybe he had to make sure Strazza was dead this time. That's exciting and new. The kill. Maybe he has that last round with Daphne, leaves her dazed, naked, possibly unconscious. Removes the restraints. Packs up and strolls out.

She could see it, and if Mira and Nobel could get through to Daphne, she could confirm, fill in gaps and movements, answer the dogging questions.

Eve left the bedroom, walked through the house again trying to imagine his movements.

Unlike the killer, she locked the door when she left. Added the seal.

She wanted to go home, wanted that nap on the new, fancy bed. But drove to the hospital. She needed to try.

This time she bypassed the desk, walked straight back to Daphne's room and the guard on the door, tapped the badge she'd hooked to her coat in case anybody along the way tried to stop her.

"The doc's in with her, Lieutenant."

"Anybody else go in?"

"Medical personnel only."

With a nod, Eve went in. She saw Del sitting on the side of Daphne's bed. Her hand gripped his as Del spoke in low tones.

She jerked when she saw Eve, then seemed to settle again as Del turned his head.

"You're back," he said.

"You're still here. Do you live here?"

"Feels like it half the time. But I went home awhile, got some *Zs*. Did you?"

"On my way there. How are you feeling, Mrs. Strazza?"

"Better, I think. It's Daphne. You can call me Daphne. I haven't remembered anything more. I'm sorry."

"No rush on it. Just wanted to check a couple of things, if you're up to it."

"I . . . Yes, all right?" Ending on a question, she looked at Del for confirmation.

"Anything you remember helps," he told her. "Even little things, things that don't seem to matter."

"That's right," Eve said. "You and your husband went into the bedroom together, is that accurate?"

"Yes, we went upstairs together. We were going straight to bed. He had rounds in the morning, and the party went a little longer than he thought it should—would. Thought it would."

"And you were attacked. At the same time?"

"I . . ." Her eyes went blank for a moment. "I think—it was so fast, so shocking."

"Take your time," Eve said as Daphne gripped Del's hand. "You went upstairs, into the bedroom."

"Yes, upstairs. I think I was, maybe, just a step behind my husband. He had my arm. I think. I think my husband had my arm, and was just a step ahead. And suddenly he fell forward. I think. I think he did, but something—someone hit me. In the face. Everything went gray. I just laid on the floor. And hit me in the stomach. Kicked me?"

Instinctively, Daphne wrapped an arm around her waist.

" 'Stay down'—I think he said that. 'Stay where I put you, bitch.' I think. And I did. I didn't move. I closed my eyes."

She did so now, and tears stood on her lashes.

"I heard grunting, and everything hurt, so I laid on the floor with my eyes closed."

"And when you opened them."

"It was the devil." She pushed up, eyes going wild. "The devil. I swear it. I swear."

"Easy now." Del took her shoulders, gently. "Breathe. Look at me, Daphne, and breathe. Nobody's doubting what you saw."

"That's right." Eve stepped closer. "It was makeup, it was a kind of mask. It was a man, Daphne, but he looked like a devil. He made himself look that way to scare you, and to keep you from being able to describe him."

"Makeup?"

"Theatrical makeup."

"But . . . He had horns, little horns, and the light was red and yellow, and I smelled sulphur."

"Sulphur?"

"I think . . . 'This is hell. I'm taking you with me to hell.' I think he said. I'm not sure. And his . . . penis. It was red. It glowed like fire. And it burned inside me. God, it burned inside me."

"He wore a condom, and makeup," Eve said, keeping her tone even.

"He used a novelty light that flashed the colors. All of it to confuse you, frighten you, and to set a kind of stage for himself."

Doubt, fear, hope, all ran across Daphne's face. "You're sure? You're positive."

"I am."

"You caught him?"

"Not yet, but I have some lines, some leads, and finding him is my focus. It's my top priority."

"Dr. Nobel says you're the best. That they wrote a book about you, made a vid."

Eve sent Del a sidelong look, got an easy shrug. "I wanted Daphne to know there's no way this bastard's getting through you, and me, the cop on the door, the kick-ass nurses on the floor. No way he can get to her."

"You got that right."

"He pretended to be the devil," Daphne said, as if to herself. "But he . . . Do I have to go back to the house? When I have to leave here, do I have to go back there?"

"No," Del began, but Eve touched a hand to his shoulder as she kept her eyes on Daphne's.

"Actually, it would help if, when you're released, you would go through the house with me. It would help if I knew what he took with him."

"Do I have to stay there? I don't want to stay there."

"You don't have to stay there. Just a walk through, with me, with cops right there with you."

"But not today."

"Not today. I'm supposed to tell you Jacko and Gula are thinking about you. He wants to send you soup."

"He's so nice. You had to tell him what happened."

"I did. And Carmine Rizzo, he and his crew asked how you were doing. You have people who care. If you want visitors—"

"No. Not yet," Daphne interrupted, pulling at the sheets. "Not like this. Please, not yet."

"Okay. Whenever you want, I can clear it."

Daphne's hands relaxed again. "Lucy and John came. They're doctors."

"I know."

"They were at the party. You had to tell them, too, and they came. They brought those flowers. They're so cheerful and bright. But they didn't stay long because I . . . I just can't."

"They seemed like pretty good doctors to me," Eve commented. "They understand you're not up for long visits yet. Have you seen Dr. Mira?"

"She was very kind. I was nervous because . . . But Dr. Nobel said she was kind and a good person for me to talk to."

"She's the best. She's in the book and vid, too."

Daphne smiled a little. "It's hard to talk to so many people, but she was easier. And you and Dr. Nobel, it's not as hard to talk to you."

"Good." Eve hesitated, stepped a little closer. "Maybe it's not as hard because you know we're on your side. If there's anyone else you want me to contact, you want to visit—"

"No, please. No one. No one else."

"That's fine. I'm going to be checking on you on and off, and if you remember anything more, or even think you do, you can contact me. Anytime. Day or night. You want me to tell Jacko to send the soup?"

"It would be nice."

"You got it."

"I'll walk you out." Del rose. "I'll be right back."

He went out with Eve, took a few steps away from the door. "She has anxiety attacks if she tries to remember any more, any real details. And every time she sleeps without aid, she has nightmares. Right now she trusts me, so I can calm her down."

"Mira will help there."

"I know it. Physically, she's healing well. Emotionally, it's going to be a longer road."

He glanced back at the door, toyed with the stethoscope hanging out of his pocket. "She won't give me permission to contact her family. Her parents were killed when she was a kid, but she was raised by friends of theirs, grew up with their daughter like a sister."

"I know. I'm a cop."

"But she won't budge on that. She could use family, but my hands are tied."

Eve lifted her eyebrows. "And you're implying mine aren't."

"I'm just saying that maybe, during the course of your investigation, you'd have reason to contact them."

"Actually, it's on my list. I'd prefer that she give the nod, but I've got some questions."

"Sooner the better. That's my medical and personal opinion. She'll have to be released in a couple days, even if I postpone it. She shouldn't be alone."

"I'll feel out the family, get a gauge."

"Great. Now, speaking as a medical professional, I advise you to go home, get some sleep. You look like hell."

"Good advice. Bill me," Eve said and walked away to take it.

7

Eve considered switching to auto, but decided to actively drive home. If she went to auto, she'd likely nod off, then end up sleeping in the car parked outside the house.

She'd rather be in bed.

She drove across town, cursing the traffic to help stay alert. Then let out a long sigh of relief when she drove through the gates.

Night had fallen when she'd done her second round in the crime scene, and low, sulky clouds smothered moon and stars. But the house, with all its turrets and towers, its dignified gray stone, glowed in welcome.

She wound up the drive, parked in front of the entrance, and let out one more sigh before grabbing her file bag. She stepped out of the car into the bitter wind and thought: Winter sucks. Pushed her way through the wind to the door, and stepped inside to warmth and light and quiet.

Where the bony figure of Summerset loomed in the foyer with the pudge of a cat at his feet.

Galahad trotted to her to slip and slide through her legs.

As she shrugged out of her coat, she eyed Summerset and thought of the ghoul costume.

"Where were you on the night of November twenty-eight?" she demanded.

He arched one elegant eyebrow. "I'll have to check my calendar."

"Never mind." She pulled off her hat, her scarf, tossed them on the newel post with her coat. "That asshole needed makeup to pull off the ghoul. You're a natural."

Ridiculously pleased she'd had the energy and brainpower for some decent snark, she started upstairs. The cat bounded up with her.

She thought of her newly redone office with its already beloved command center—with an AutoChef that would provide coffee right there. But calculated she didn't have the energy or brainpower to so much as set up her murder board, much less review her notes or add to them.

Instead, she aimed for the bedroom.

And there it was, the big, glorious bed.

She'd been fine with the way the bedroom looked before. Hell, a lot more than fine, she thought now, plus she'd gotten used to it.

But she couldn't fault the newly painted walls in their soft, relaxing gray, the deeper tones used on the thick molding of the ceiling to sort of showcase the height of it, the punch of the sky window. She could hardly bitch about the deep blue sofa in the sitting area— the longer, wider sofa.

She didn't know squat about floor plans and decor, really, but she couldn't dig up a complaint about the arrangement of chairs—and the rich tones of them—that all but insisted you sit down, relax, and let the world go somewhere else for a while.

Even she could appreciate the intricately carved doors closing off a slick little bar, including AutoChef and friggie. Maybe she thought the expansive closet/dressing room was over the top, but it didn't detract from the whole. And she knew both she and Roarke would enjoy the addition of a terrace outside of what the decorator called atrium doors.

But the real star of the room, in her book, was that big bed with its fancifully carved head- and footboard, all dressed in soft, smoky grays and mounds of fluffy pillows.

She didn't stumble to it, but it was close. Then fell across it, face-down, and dropped straight into sleep.

Galahad gathered himself, leaped up. He padded across the duvet, sniffed at Eve's hair. Apparently satisfied, he stretched himself across her waist as if to hold her in place. And began to purr.

Roarke walked in moments later.

"Down for the count, is she?" he said as Galahad blinked his bicolored eyes.

Shaking his head, Roarke moved to the bed, crouched, pulled off Eve's boots. She didn't so much as stir.

He lit the fire, sat to pull off his own boots. Snagging the cashmere throw from the foot of the bed, he tossed it over his wife. Waited for the cat's head to pop out.

Then he stretched out beside Eve, and slept.

Dreams broke down defenses. For hours she'd blocked out the echoes, the murmurs, the emotions. But sleep undermined boundaries.

She was a child, lost and frightened, bloody and broken. Though she kept it cradled against her body, the arm her father had snapped before she'd killed him jarred with every step, wept with pain. It burned where he'd raped her; her face throbbed where he'd struck her.

Yet it seemed she floated, like a ghost. Like the dead.

She feared the dark. Terrible things hid in the dark, waited there, watched from there.

Would they swallow her whole, would she fall into the bottomless pit where the rats and spiders would eat her as her father had said?

Everything around her looked like something she'd seen through a dirty window, all smudged and blurry. And all the sounds came from far, far away.

Was he coming after her? Would he find her and drag her back to that cold, cold room with the flashing red light?

He would hurt her, he would hurt her, he would hurt her. Kill her. Kill.

She wanted to hide, wanted to sleep.

She tried. But they found her. She couldn't fight, even when they made everything inside her scream at the pain, shriek with the terror.

Then the lights were too bright, burning her eyes, and the voices were too loud, banging in her head. Someone told her she was going to be all right, that she was safe. But she knew about lies.

Someone asked her for her name, but she had none to give.

There were hands on her, everywhere, and she smelled her own blood. Even as she screamed again, the dark came and took her in.

"Dreaming, just dreaming. You're home, you're safe. I'm here."

Roarke gathered her close, and his voice, his scent, broke the hold of the past.

"I'm all right."

He brushed his lips to her brow. "I wondered how long it would take. You held it back all day."

"I could see it in her face, in her eyes." Because she could, Eve burrowed into him while the cat bumped his head against her shoulder. "I know what she felt, I know what it is to be trapped in that kind of shock, to run with that kind of fear. It echoes inside me, all day, but I couldn't do the job if I listened."

"I know it." He held her close, held her tight. "I know it."

"You heard them, too. I can't let it break me."

"You haven't, and you won't." He tipped her face to his, met her eyes. "You won't. But it had to be acknowledged."

"It took me years to remember, and there are still blank spots. She's not a child, Roarke, but there's something defenseless about her. I don't know how much she'll remember, if she'll be able to give us details we can use."

"She's alive."

"Yeah, she's alive. Mira's already seen her, and Daphne seems okay with that. She trusts Nobel, that's clear, and seems all right talking to me. It helped her, I think, when I could tell her the man who did this wasn't a devil. It was makeup, a disguise. A false face."

"She'll know, as well as you and I, there was a monster under the false face."

"Yeah. Yeah, but she knows he's real. Flesh and blood." Steadier now, she reached back to scratch the loyal Galahad between the ears. "Did you get any sleep?"

"I'd say we both got a bit more than an hour. Or rather the three of us did."

"That's good. And it's one checked off."

"Checked off?"

"We slept in the fancy new bed."

"On more like, but check."

She brushed back his hair. "How about we check off number two?"

He smiled at her. "I'm always in favor of finishing off a checklist."

He continued to smile when she pressed her lips to his, as he stroked a hand over her. "You're still armed, Lieutenant."

She slid her own hand down, found him. "You, too."

He laughed as she rolled over, straddled him. Studying his face, she pulled off her jacket, hit the release on her weapon harness. "You know, the first time I walked in here and saw the bed—the other one—it was: Wow. This one's an even bigger wow," she continued as she tossed the jacket aside, draped the harness over the footboard. "But I liked that bed."

"It's still in the house."

"Is it?"

"In one of the guest rooms. I have very fond memories of that bed as well," he reminded her. "We can visit it whenever you like."

"Huh." Considering, she pulled off her sweater, tossed it after the jacket. "You know how they have those pub crawls?"

"I do, yes. Have participated more than once in my time."

"I've always been more find a bar, stay there, and do the drinking you came to do in one spot. But . . . One of these days we should have a bed crawl through this house. We'll see how you hold up, ace."

He laughed again. "Challenge accepted."

He drew her down to him.

And there it was, she thought, the real deal. Her place, her man, her heart, all right here. Wherever she'd been, whatever brutal the beginnings, however lost, however broken she'd once been, she'd found this. And this, and this, was worth every painful, bleeding step of the journey.

Overwhelmed by it, she cupped his face in her hands, poured herself into the kiss.

"Eve," he murmured.

"I'm alive." She pressed his hand to her heart. "I love you."

"You're everything. All. Only. Everything."

He shifted her so they lay facing each other, so he could glide his hands over her to soothe, to awaken. Gently, tenderly.

His only.

Every sigh, every murmur, every small tremble of response took him deeper into the beauty. The way she drew his sweater away to run warm hands over his skin, the way her mouth fit perfectly to his. He counted the pulse beats in her throat when he tasted there, felt the way her warrior's body softened.

How she looked watching him, with firelight in her whiskey-colored eyes.

He could make her want simply by existing. There'd been no one else who could ever hold her heart with no more than a look, a word. He'd given her a life beyond survival, beyond even the badge that had been her world, and the symbol of that survival.

He'd given her love when she hadn't truly believed in it, had never felt worthy of it.

And he'd made her believe, absolutely, she'd given him the same.

Now there was pleasure, pure and theirs. Flesh against flesh, hands and lips stoking that warm, glowing fire until it snapped and burned.

She arched when he undressed her, offering. She wrapped tight around him, giving. Her lips sought his, taking.

And when, as breath quickened, as pulses tripped, he slipped inside her, they shuddered together.

"Aghrá," he said, and her pounding heart melted.

With every rise and fall, it poured out for him.

When they lay quiet, bodies slack and tangled together, she sighed again. "It's official. I really like this bed."

He turned his face into the curve of her shoulder, brushing warm skin with his lips. "Here's to many hours of checking off both one and two on the list."

"I'm for that. But God, now I need a shower. It feels like days."

"A shower, some wine, a meal, I'd say."

"All over all of that." Lazily, she combed her fingers through his hair. "I need to set up my board. Not much more I can do at this point, but I need to do at least that."

"Wine and food in your office then. And you can fill me in on the details."

"I wish there were more of them, but I'd like your take."

It was amazing, she thought, what a solid hour's sleep, really nice sex, and a long hot shower could accomplish. And when you topped that off with a glass of really superior wine, a thirty-six-hour stint didn't seem too bad.

She let him choose the meal—it seemed fair—even resigned herself to eating whatever vegetables she found on her plate. And since he set it all up while she worked on her board, she drafted herself to the clean up.

Comfortable in flannel pants, a sweatshirt, and skids, she stepped back to study the board.

"You might wish there were more details, but that's a comprehensive murder board at this early stage."

"Maybe." Now she walked away from it, to the stylish new table by the new balcony doors. "What's for dinner?"

He lifted the warming domes.

Her heart sang a happy tune when she saw steaks, salted-skinned potatoes, and . . .

"What are those purple things?"

"Carrots."

"Carrots are orange."

"And purple." He didn't mention the turnips and cauliflower in the mix. He knew his quarry.

"Why would somebody dye a harmless carrot purple?"

"They're not dyed, they're natural. Have some more wine," he said, topping off her glass, "and try them out."

She went for the steak first, she was no fool, but cut off a small bite of the little purple thing. "It tastes like a carrot, herbed and buttered up or something, but carrot-like."

"Because it is one."

She shrugged, added enough butter for her potato to swim in. "I forgot. I brought you dessert."

"Did you?"

"Yeah, a cinnamon bun. It's in an evidence bag—in my file bag."

"Yum."

She shook her fork at him before dipping it into the pool of butter. "Trust me. It's from the caterer—Jacko—who did the dinner party."

"He has a fine reputation. Is he a suspect?"

She shook her head. "Alibied, and no way he fits or his wife or his daughter or any of the catering team I interviewed. Same with the rental company."

"That's a lot to eliminate in one day. So again, considerable progress."

"I guess it is." She glanced back at the board. "A lot of threads to be tied together or snapped off. I did find a connection."

"What connection?"

"Both the caterer and the rental company have done jobs for the first vic—or rather his company. The vic himself didn't use them, but it's a link from the company to the latest victims. And his partner used them personally a couple times. I need to see if I can make that link to the second victims. The SVU detectives didn't go there because there wasn't a there to go to then. Now there is."

"Wouldn't that un-eliminate the caterer and the rental company?"

"It's an avenue to explore," she admitted, "but . . . I just don't think so. Not directly. But somebody who's used them, done some work for them, knows someone—or more than one person on the crews. It also links to the hospital. Strazza was a big wheel at St. Andrew's, and

Daphne volunteered there for a time. I can link both companies to the hospital for events. So that adds hospital staff to the mix. I'm going to talk to the first four victims tomorrow, and something may shake there."

She applied herself to the steak. Sleep, sex, shower, wine, *and* red meat. It was enough to bring a tear to the eye.

"Daphne thinks she smelled sulfur during the attack. So did he add that—let's give them the full hell treatment. Or did she imagine it as he'd set the stage? Either way, this fucker gets fully in character—that's the term, right—he likes to *be* the monster he wraps himself in. So maybe he's an actor, or a wannabe actor. Actors connect to first vic's company."

"So they do."

"Actor, performance, reviews," she said as she ate. "Plus, if we go by the wit statements, the disguise is first rate, so he's either talented there or he's practiced a lot. Do actor types do their own makeup and costumes?"

"I imagine some do, and others might pick up some of the steps."

"That's how I see it. He had to do some stalking, some research on the vics, on the locations. The attacks went too smooth for him not to have planned them. He had to have known when to move in. Those are all upper-level neighborhoods, all the locations had solid security. Single-family residences, that's a key. Wealthy married couple, that's another. Seriously good-looking female vics, so he has a type. That could work a couple ways."

"He's jealous of the looks and wealth as he's had neither," Roarke suggested, "or he's of the same social strata and sticks to his own kind, so to speak."

Again, she wagged her fork at him. "Don't blame me for saying you think like a cop when you do."

"I think like a criminal—reformed. It's basically the same."

She couldn't argue with that. "He likes to steal."

"Well, now, I can relate."

Since she knew he could, she took it a step further. "Can you relate to taking valuables and not cashing in?"

Roarke thought it over while he drank some wine. "I can, to a point. If you don't need the money, or if profit itself isn't the goal, it's quite satisfying to have trinkets around that you've lifted from elsewhere."

"A kind of payback. I've got it now, sucker, you don't?"

"It could be. Still, people routinely collect souvenirs, after all, to remind them of a trip, an event, something they enjoyed. It may be just that simple."

"Nothing personal," she muttered.

"It's often not, even most usually not personal—from the perspective of the thief."

Something, he knew, the cop he loved would never appreciate.

"But as he's cleaned out a number of safes," Roarke continued as Eve brooded, "he'd have to make himself a kind of Aladdin's Cave for his spoils, wouldn't he? That's excessive."

Now she frowned. "Which guy's Aladdin?"

"Depending on the version, he's a young thief who stumbles across a cave filled with treasures—amassed by bigger, badder thieves, and acquires a genie in a lamp."

"Hmm. So hoarding, basically. That's an angle. Maybe this guy's hoarding all the loot, either because he's just a sick bastard or because he's a well-off sick bastard. And there was cash in every hit, so that would add to the well-off. Add e-skills, a risk-taker. And I'm betting he knew the layout of the Strazza house. He may have been inside previously. Maybe as a guest, maybe as some sort of worker."

"Or he might have accessed the floor plans."

"Those e-skills." She nodded. "He walked right in, right up the stairs. He waited up there for close to three hours. Patience, that he's got. But he's a coward. Comes in from behind, gets his prey restrained before he starts on them. Pounds on them even when they cooperate, so he likes to hurt people. But the rape, that's the main event. Raping the woman, making the spouse watch. Forcing her to say she likes it so the spouse can hear it. And terrorizing with the costume, adding that flourish."

Roarke waited a beat—she was in the groove. "Why does he untie them when he's done?"

"It only adds to how helpless they were, rubs their noses in the helplessness. Free them so they know he was always in control. Free them and they call for help—have to tell what happened. Reporting a rape, it's another level of humiliation. You have to go back over it, relive it to tell it. He likes that part, too.

"It's all part of it," she added. "Invade their home, where they feel the safest—their bedroom, their most intimate and private space."

Without thinking, she stabbed some cauliflower, ate it.

"Hurt them, take away their freedom, humiliate them, and make the male vic feel helpless, enraged, impotent while you violate the female. Stealing adds a layer. I can take whatever I want. Beat them unconscious before you release them so they wake in pain, in that shock and humiliation, and somehow worse, free again. It's a big mind-fuck, start to finish."

"And when you have him in the box, Lieutenant, you'll show him what it is to be mind-fucked."

"Damn straight, I will." She looked back at the board, at the victims. "Damn straight."

She refined her notes, wrote reports, studied case files. At the end of it, the best she could do was lay out her plans for the next day. She'd interview the previous victims, tug hard on those connections, start exploring possible theater angles.

She had to hope a night's sleep would help coalesce her thoughts enough to pull a solid theory out of them.

This time she got in the fancy new bed, and decided it was more than fine.

"Married couples so far, not cohabs. Does that matter?" She closed her eyes as Roarke's arm draped over her. "No kids in the house. I think that matters. No pets, no kids—or absent human staff."

"Let it go for the night."

"Except the Strazzas had a houseful. So . . ."

She didn't let it go so much as drop away.

When she woke just after dawn, it took her brain a minute to catch up with her eyes. New room, she reminded herself.

Roarke sat on the big sofa, fully dressed in one of his impeccable dark suits—apparently unconcerned about cat hair on the material as the cat had deserted her, and was now stretched out on his back beside Roarke.

Roarke absently scratched Galahad's exposed belly while he sipped coffee and watched the incomprehensible stock reports on screen.

They made a hell of a good-morning picture, she thought, the insanely gorgeous man in his emperor-of-the-business-world suit and the big cat riding on bliss at the touch of those skilled hands.

She could relate to the bliss.

He'd probably already had a couple of 'link or holo meetings, she mused. Might have bought Saturn for all she knew. But all in all, her biggest interest at the moment involved the fact that he had coffee, and she didn't.

"Good morning," he said when she pushed up to sit. "It's bitter out, and they're calling for snow—quite a bit of it—starting mid-morning."

She said, "Ugh," and stumbled her way to the AutoChef, remembered it wasn't where it used it be, stared blankly at the carved doors.

"Touch either," Roarke reminded her.

"Right." She slapped at one and both popped open, and the interior lights gleamed on. She programmed coffee—all that currently mattered—and waited to down the first heady gulp.

"You're going to have cat hair all over your million-dollar suit, pretty boy."

"It's easy enough to deal with, and it only cost a half million."

"Ha." She took the coffee into the bathroom, caffeinated and showered herself awake.

When she came out, wrapped in a red robe she'd never seen before—but it was as soft as a cloud, as warm as a hug—he'd already set up breakfast.

She knew, thanks to his handy weather report, she'd start the day with oatmeal.

At least it came with lots of berries and the crunchy stuff—and he'd added a side of bacon. Which explained why he'd banished the cat. Galahad now sat in front of the fire, industriously washing himself—and sending the human an occasional steely stare.

"It matters," she said.

"Does it?"

"That the victims are married. It matters. I just need to figure out why."

"Did you dream?"

"Just slept—and let me add another hot damn on that bed. Three assaults is pattern and purpose and profile. Typical escalation, and the murder comes off as of the moment. That wasn't planned. Next time it will be."

"Because there's no going back, only forward."

"Yep. Do you have any—trinkets—from back when?"

Walking his fingers down Eve's arm, Roarke ate some bacon. "Now that's a loaded question from a cop over breakfast. I did have a few, here and there," he said with a shrug. "But I passed them on, you could say, when a cop came into my life—as she wouldn't like it."

"She wouldn't have known."

"I would have. As a former thief, I'd say if your suspect is indeed keeping all his spoils, he's what you termed him last night. A hoarder. He doesn't need to liquidate, so it's not for the money—and a man can have plenty of that and enjoy taking more. Serials often take souvenirs, don't they?"

"Yeah, but it tends to be something specific to the victim, a memento. This is more . . . Aladdin's Cave . . . He'd need a place, and a private one. The jewelry alone is a serious haul. The dresses—he's taken a cocktail dress from each vic—though I haven't confirmed that with the Strazza hit. That's more a souvenir, but it's a weird one. A fancy dress, shoes, and an evening bag."

"Costume."

Eve poked Roarke's shoulder. "What I'm thinking. Not for him— different body types, so I don't think we're after a cross-dresser— but maybe for a woman or a droid or just one of those dead bodies the stores use to display clothes."

"Mannequins, darling Eve. Not dead bodies."

"They look like DBs. Anyway, he's got a lot of whacked-out layers to him. No pets, no kids, in-home safes, married couples, single-family residences with good security. They've got to be surrogates, it's too specific otherwise."

"You'll talk to Mira."

"Yeah, soon." She glanced back, frowned.

"Problem?"

"It's intimidating. The new closet deal."

"Some would find it efficient and convenient—especially some who don't care to ponder overlong on what to wear on any given day."

"Yeah, well." She rose. "I'm going for it."

"Good luck."

It was more a damn room than a closet to her eye. Sure, everything was set up in order, and that helped. All the fancy duds and the fancy stuff that went with them had their own area. She didn't even have to acknowledge their existence, and sure as hell didn't intend to use the closet comp to have them sliding forward on their magic rods, or to preview on screen how this sparkly dress went with those ridiculous shoes.

Intimidating, she thought again, and just a little embarrassing.

She stared at the line of jackets. Why did she have so many jackets? If you just had a couple, choosing wasn't a problem. But there had to be more than a hundred jackets, all arranged in color groups, the blacks leading to the grays, the grays leading to the blues and right down the line.

It could give a person a headache.

"Aim for warmth," Roarke said as he stepped in.

Plenty of room for him, she thought. Hell, they could throw a party in here. Serve drinks. Hire a band.

He pulled a jacket from the blue section. navy blue, she observed, no fancy work.

"Now if you used the comp, it would make suggestions on what to pair it with."

"How does it know?" But when he turned to it, she grabbed his arm. "No, it's too much for the first time in here. I have to sort of ease into it."

"I simply adore you," he stated, but stilled her hand before she grabbed navy trousers. "Then you'd have a sort of uniform, wouldn't you? These." He pulled out brown trousers, a kind of rusty brown, then shifted to vests, pulled one that had the same tone with navy blue buttons, added a crisp, tailored white shirt.

He handed her the lot, selected boots, brown and sturdy.

"I was getting the hang of it before everything got bigger."

"And you'll get the hang of it again." He kissed her cheek, left her to dress.

Maybe she would, she thought, but she didn't think she'd be making friends with the closet comp any time soon.

When she came out, strapped her weapon harness over the vest, Roarke gestured to the screen. "Reports and speculations re the Strazza assault/murder and the investigation."

"Then I'd better get to it." She pulled on the jacket, picked up her badge, her 'link, her comm, her restraints, added her clutch piece.

"You look completely competent."

"Clothes don't make the cop."

"But they give her an aura. Take care of my competent cop."

"Will do." She stepped to him, kissed him. Then left him to get to it.

8

As she fought her way downtown, Eve checked in with the duty nurse, learned Daphne had had a restless night, required a mild sedative. And that Dr. Nobel was already on his way in. The patient's physical condition had been upgraded to satisfactory.

The cuts and bruises would heal, Eve thought. The damage to the psyche took longer.

Put the past behind you—that's what people always said. But those people didn't get that the past was always behind you. Like a hound on the scent.

She pulled into Central, started toward the elevator, and spotted Jenkinson. You couldn't miss the tie, not even from space.

With his coat open, it glowed toad green with—perhaps not coincidentally—bug-eyed frogs of yellow and blue hopping over it.

"You could light a cave with that thing around your neck."

"Never know when you might end up in one. How was the time off, LT?"

"Quiet. Warm. Sunny. Everything winter is not."

"Nice." They stepped onto the elevator. "Cleared a couple while you were dancing on the beach."

"Junkie knifed by second junkie, woman bludgeoned by ex-boyfriend."

Jenkinson eyed her as the elevator stopped and more cops shuffled on. "Checking up on us from sun and sand?"

"I was in yesterday. Caught one yesterday morning, about two in the A.M."

"Well, welcome home." Then he frowned. "Strazza business?"

"That's the one."

"Getting play in the media. Bigwig surgeon, young fancy wife. She messed up bad?"

"Pretty bad."

"Still . . ."

"Yeah, always look at the spouse first. But this woman didn't rape herself, bust up her own face. Got two like crimes in the past year, just without the murder."

Though the elevator stopped again, added more people, she decided to ride it out.

"He dresses up."

Jenkinson, who'd been balefully eyeing the levels as they lit up, turned back to Eve. "What, like in a tuxedo?"

"Like monsters. Horned devil on this one."

Jenkinson shook his head. "People are fucked up."

A couple more cops came on. One of them studied Jenkinson. "That's some tie you got there, Jenks."

"Yeah, that's what your sister said when I put it on this morning."

That got a few snorts and made the crowded ride a little more entertaining.

When they shoved their way off, Jenkinson kept pace with Eve toward the bullpen. "Reineke and I are clear right now if you need more hands with this case."

"We'll see how it goes."

The minute they stepped into the bullpen, Jenkinson leaped forward. "Hey! Are those sticky buns?"

Santiago stuffed the last of one—from the box Eve had left in the break room—in his mouth, mumbled incomprehensibly over it.

Eve kept going toward her office, so whoever had already reported for duty could fight over whatever was left.

Eve hit her office AutoChef for coffee, tossed off her coat and winter gear and studied her board with rested eyes.

She had two police artist concepts of the first two costumes. Not Yancy's work, but more than decent. And still, she imagined, the victims' impressions, their fear, might have lent some drama to the looks.

She put in a tag to Yancy, left him a v-mail requesting he work with Daphne Strazza at the hospital in addition to the rental crew. She could use a good sketch of the devil.

Since Peabody hadn't reported in, Eve contacted the first victims, ran into a house droid that gave her grief. She geared up for a fight, then heard the click of Mira's heels heading to her office.

"We'll get back to you." She disconnected, held up a finger as Mira came in, and tagged Peabody. "Get your ass to work and contact the first two pairs of vics, arrange interview times. There or here. Make it happen."

She clicked off before Peabody could respond, turned to Mira. "Sorry."

Waving it off, Mira slipped out of her soft blue winter coat to reveal a rosy red suit. The clicking heels went with a pair of silver-gray short boots, with the combo showing off excellent legs.

"You want some of that tea stuff?"

"I'd love it, thanks."

"Use my chair. Seriously."

"I absolutely will. And welcome back. You look rested. Amazing what just a couple of days away can do."

"You should've seen me yesterday." Eve programmed the tea, and while its floral scent wafted through her office, passed it to Mira.

Mira sat, crossed those excellent legs, smiled at Eve out of her soft blue eyes. "I looked at Daphne Strazza's medical chart. You and Roarke may very well have saved her life." Sitting back, Mira brushed back a strand of mink-colored hair.

Eve cocked her head. "Did you and Mr. Mira head for the sun, too?"

"No, but that's a compliment. I decided to add some more high-lights, get through the winter doldrums. Actually, Trina talked me into it."

Eve goggled. "You're going to Trina now?"

"I am. My hairdresser moved to Brooklyn, and Trina—though I know she can be . . . opinionated—is excellent."

Opinionated, Eve mused. She'd have used *pushy*, *scary*, and *in-your-face*. And she couldn't believe she was talking about hair anyway.

"Okay, well. Daphne Strazza."

"I'll have a written evaluation for you this morning, and she's agreed to talk to me again. Physically, as you know, the attack was brutal, the beating and the rapes. Emotionally, only more so. She's blocking a great deal of it, and that's to be expected. Additionally, the blow to the head could be responsible for blank spots. She was tortured, terrorized, and I'm not telling you anything you don't know."

"Not so far." Eve sat on the corner of her desk. "Everyone I've spoken to about her describes her as sweet—that's a repeated word.

Personable, a perfect hostess, generous. It may be cynical, but some of my take-away on that is she's naive."

"I wouldn't disagree. She's young—even younger emotionally, I'd say, than her years. *Soft* would be another word I'd use. Malleable."

"Okay, that's the word." Eve shot a finger in the air. "*Malleable*. People don't speak of her dead husband in the same terms. Perfectionist, impatient, domineering, cold."

"And brilliant. I didn't know him personally, but I knew his reputation. Those in his field, with that reputation, are often cold and domineering. The classic God complex."

"Right. And often when an older, successful individual—with a domineering personality—marries a younger spouse, that individual goes one of two ways. Pampers or bullies. I vote for bully."

"I've only spoken with her once, for less than an hour, and was careful to keep it more on the surface. But my impression of their relationship matches yours. Small things. She refers to him as 'my husband' more than she uses his name."

"Yeah, I caught that."

"He was, I believe, more authority figure than mate or partner. His death frightens her more than grieves her. When I asked her about her routines, her interests, her friends—to try to make a connection—she spoke more of his expectations, his wishes, his social circle than her own. And there's a look," Mira added, "a look in the eyes, a body language, a tone, when someone's been bullied or abused."

"Yeah, there is. She's got all of that, but I can't be sure it's from the husband or a result of this attack."

In her pretty suit, Mira sipped her tea as if they sat in front of a classic work of art rather than a murder board.

"Are you considering, if she's been abused, she had a part in her husband's death?"

"I have to consider it, but a partnership doesn't fit. Not with what was done to her. Her injuries were brutal, and she wasn't playing it when we found her wandering the streets, naked, freezing, in the middle of the night."

Eve pushed off the desk, pace. "On the other hand, if there was some sort of partnership, you could consider the partner just went too far, damaged her more than planned. Plan is, mess her up to give her cover, kill the husband."

"I need more time with her, but my opinion at this point is Daphne Strazza is far too passive to have engineered any of this."

"It doesn't make sense anyway, for a lot of reasons.

"She fears violence, which may be yet another way her husband dominated her. She has several of the symptoms of an abused spouse, but as you say, it could be muddled with this assault."

"Okay, so more time there. Were you able to read the data on the killer?"

"Yes, reviewing the two open case files I'd previously profiled, and yours. Unlike Daphne, this man enjoys violence—perpetrating it, and even more so doing if to victims who are unable to fight back."

"A coward."

"Undoubtedly, but one who feels courageous by striking out when his quarry is helpless. Another sort of bullying. He may have been bullied, felt helpless as a child or young man. He's found a way to compensate. To punish, to humiliate, as he was once humiliated."

Mira set her tea aside. "He selects married couples. The third makes that a very clear pattern."

"Yeah, that's important."

"I believe it is, and I can add to the initial profile. Certainly his victims are surrogates, perhaps for his own parents. They may have, or one of them may have, bullied and abused him. Or brushed off and ignored those who did. He certainly had sexual feelings for his mother."

"His—huh."

"Possibly stepmother. It's possible his father remarried—younger woman, attractive woman, and he developed feelings for her. And he has a deep hatred for his father, or father figure. At the same time a deep envy of him. His father had authority, power over him, and, more, had a sexual relationship with the mother your killer wanted. If we follow this line, it's most likely the killer came from some privilege."

"Not that he envied that lifestyle, but had it." Eve eased back on the corner of the desk. "I lean there."

"I believe he grew up in a wealthy home, but never had what he most wanted. Power, control, physicality, and courage. He hides behind masks, elaborate ones, monstrous ones. They add to his sense of power, and probably theatrics as well. The stealing isn't beside the point. He takes the tangible as well. Strips things away from them."

"And keeps them—all. It's looking like he hasn't sold or pawned any of the jewelry or valuables, from—so far—the three hits."

"Hmm. I missed that. That's interesting, isn't it? Not just a souvenir, a token, a remembrance, but all. Greed. The theft isn't, even on a minor level, about profit. It's about having, holding, seeing, touching. He needs the tangible as well."

Pausing, Mira looked at the board. "He selects beautiful women—I believe they come first. He must find one, then find one who's married. The couple must be wealthy, privileged."

"No kids."

"Yes, that's another requirement. It may be because having children in the house adds complications to his plans, or—"

"He doesn't want the competition."

Mira smiled. "Exactly. I doubt very much he was an only child, and true or not, felt his sibling or siblings garnered the most love and attention—took what was rightfully his. He won't be married. If he's in a relationship it's a front. Another mask. He won't have children. He will be financially solvent, very likely successful. He knows how to become what's needed, even enjoys the false fronts, how he fools the people around him. His sex life is pedestrian if it exists. He needs to rape to feel true release. He needs to hear the victim praise him, to tell the father figure he's better, more virile, a better lover. By this time, he's impotent unless it's rape."

"How about jerking off?" Eve asked. "He takes an outfit from the female victims. Maybe dresses up a droid or whatever."

"Yes, he could achieve release by reenacting the experience, though that will become more difficult, more frustrating. He's probably between thirty and fifty. Old enough for control, for planning rather than impulse, for patience. He'll continue to plan—he has no desire to be caught, to be stopped. And he'll continue to escalate, to attack at shorter intervals."

"And he'll kill again now."

"Yes, almost certainly. He didn't plan on murder, but he will with the next. Eventually, he'll kill both mother and father figure."

"Not if I find him first. Thanks. I've got a picture."

"Will you tell me how you feel?"

Eve glanced away from her board, into those soft blue eyes. "What?"

"Eve. Clearly there are similarities between what happened to you and to Daphne Strazza."

"I'm dealing with it. It's not in my way." But she pushed up, stuck her hands in her pockets, paced to her skinny window. "Won't get in the way. I can empathize, sure. I'm not where I was a couple years ago. I don't shake as easy on things like this. It gave me some bad moments, and may give me more, but I can handle it."

"I don't doubt you can handle it. You're strong, and always have been. Even then, Eve, even at eight, you had strength or you'd never have survived it."

"Plenty of cracks. Less of them now." Eve turned back. "You get credit for some of that."

"I'll take it." Mira rose. "And tell you to remember that if you need to lean, need to talk, just need someone to listen."

"I do remember it. And if I start to shake, I'll come to you."

"Good." Mira rose, gathered her coat. "I've got an early session, but I'm available if needed."

"Thanks."

Eve turned back to her board, studied the hard, handsome face of Anthony Strazza, the bloody broken body she'd recorded.

She had a strong instinct that he'd been a mean son of a bitch. But he was her victim.

She wouldn't shake.

Moments after Mira clicked out of the office, Peabody clomped in.

"I've got Neville Patrick, at his office at his studio. I made a push to speak to his wife at the same time, and he balked about speaking to her at all. But given the choice of us going to his house, he's going to talk to her about coming into the studio this morning."

"That's one."

"Both Ira and Lori Brinkman prefer to address this in their home, want the privacy. They're juggling their schedules, and one of their admins will get back to me on the best time."

"Good enough." Eve grabbed her coat. "Let's go."

"Did Mira add anything we can use?"

"She says it looks like the killer has mommy issues."

"Mommy issues?" Scrambling to keep up, Peabody grabbed her own coat out of the bullpen.

"And daddy."

"I don't . . . Oh." Peabody's face scrunched up as she swung on her coat. "Mira thinks the vics are surrogates for the killer's parents. That's just beyond the ick."

"It gives us an angle." When the elevator doors opened, revealed the logjam of cops, visitors, support staff, Eve simply turned on her heel and headed for a glide. "All the elements are violations, deliberate humiliations, excessive violence. But the rapes are the centerpiece. Mommy may be stepmommy, but the surrogate makes solid sense."

"Daddy remarries—because marriage plays, too," Peabody said. "Younger, frosty new wife—probably—and this guy wants her for his own. Or at least wants to do her. Or . . ."

Peabody hoofed it as Eve switched glides. "What if mommy remarried? Killer's bent because he wasn't enough for mommy."

Eve angled her head. "Good. That's good. Either way. If Mira's right, we're looking for a schmuck with an Edison thing."

"Edison? Like Thomas?"

"Who's Edison Thomas?"

"I mean Thomas Edison. The inventor?" Peabody explained. "The lightbulb?"

"No, for Christ's sake, this isn't about lightbulbs. Like the sicko guy who married his own mother then whined about it."

After a moment's confusion, Peabody's own lightbulb went off. "That's Oedipus. I'm pretty sure that's Oedipus."

"Edison, Oedipus, platypus. Whatever."

Peabody huffed out a laugh, then realized the strange discussion had distracted her from hopping off yet another glide and hoofing it down two flights of stairs into the garage.

Peabody put on her hat, wound on her scarf.

"Plug in the studio address," Eve ordered, sliding behind the wheel.

Once Peabody programmed the address into the in-dash, Eve

glanced at it and bulleted out of the garage. As she fought downtown traffic, she gave Peabody the main thrust of Mira's profile.

"Same social/financial strata rings for me," Peabody decided. "Or he could have grown up in that world—say the son of live-in staff."

"You've got your thinking hat on, even if it is pink and purple. That road leads to maybe the employers are surrogates for mommy and daddy, and the vics surrogates for the employers. It's an angle. In the world, but not of it. Resentment simmers and boils, and to maintain requires a false face. Acting. It's not bad."

"The Patricks have to know a lot of actors, a lot of people in the industry. But then that falls apart with the Brinkmans and the Strazzas."

"Brinkman's international finance. A lot of people in the entertainment industry are rich. She's a human rights attorney. A lot of people in the industry get involved in causes. Strazza, hotshot doctor. There's going to be a cross in there, another common factor. And the first victims are always the launch point."

"The Patricks." Peabody pulled out her memo book. "What I dug up is they met through a mutual friend at a party on Long Island about three years ago. At that time she was involved with someone else. A few weeks later, that ended, but he was seeing someone else. Basically they knew each other for around ten months before they started seriously dating. They got engaged about a year later—big splash—bought a house and moved in with each other last spring. Got married—even bigger splash—last June. They honeymooned in Europe—a three-week deal—and had been back for just over a week before the assault."

"I'll bet there was a lot of splash, too, in the gossip and society blathering about their honeymoon."

"Yeah, I skimmed through some of it. They did Paris, Provence, Rome, Venice, London—"

"Not asking for their itinerary. They were specific targets. The assailant knew they were out of the country. If he'd just wanted to rob them, he'd have done that when they were gone. It just solidifies that the assaults, specifically the rapes, were the main objective."

The building that housed On Screen Productions had its own underground parking. She pulled in, veered toward the visitor's section and wound through until she found a slot.

Without a swipe card for other floors, the elevator took them as far as the main lobby. Security and Information held the center in a space ringed with coffee shops, sundry shops, snack shops.

The coffee shops had the bulk of clientele.

Eve headed for the central counter, took out her badge. "NYPSD. Lieutenant Dallas, Detective Peabody, to see Neville Patrick. On Screen Productions."

"One moment." The woman in an all-business black suit scanned the badge, swiped at a screen. "You're cleared for that. Twenty-second floor would be their reception level. Take any elevator in Bank B."

"Got it. Does Neville Patrick have a brother?" Eve asked Peabody.

"Two sisters." Peabody consulted her memo book. "Half sisters. One lives in New L.A., one in London. There's also a big family estate in the Lake District."

"Parents?"

"Father is a director—primarily episodic home screen. First wife died in a vehicular accident leaving him a widower with two girls. He remarried nearly a decade later. They produced Neville, and have been married for about thirty-five years. She was an actor, pretty much retired from that when she had their son."

"What about Rosa Patrick?"

"Half sister from father's previous relationship. Parents have been married for about twenty-five years. He's fourth-generation money— that's Hernandez money, which is substantial. He's an engineer, specializing in rebuilding areas after natural disasters. The mother's on the board of Give Back, which is an arm of the Hernandez Family Foundation."

"Lori Brinkman's a human rights attorney. Rosa Patrick's family is heavy into good works. Daphne Strazza's parents were killed in a natural disaster—nearly fifteen years ago, but possible cross there. Thin, but possible."

The elevator opened into a colorfully lush reception area just as a woman strode through a set of glass doors etched with the On Screen logo.

Her suit wasn't all business. A flowing jacket in bold red had a snatch of black lace beneath where impressive breasts swelled. The tiny skirt showed off long legs and skyscraper heels that matched the jacket. Her hair, shorter than Eve's, formed a golden halo around a face dominated by huge eyes so blue they read purple.

"Lieutenant Dallas." She had a smoky-room voice and a firm handshake. "Detective. I'm Zella Haug, Mr. Patrick's admin. I'll take you to his office. We'd like to keep this as quiet as possible."

"No problem."

They walked by a few offices, and a large area with a conference table around which about a dozen people all talked at once. A lot of people walked briskly while they talked on 'links or headphones or tapped on tablets.

Eve saw a man in an NYU sweatshirt with his feet on a big desk, watching a car chase on his wall screen. And another pacing his office while juggling three blue balls and apparently talking to himself.

"Writers," Zella said absently. "Show runners, project acquisitions."

She led the way to a corner office, knocked on the door, then opened it. "Neville, the police are here."

He turned from the trio of wide windows and a view grander than his office.

He seemed younger than his ID shot, Eve thought, and certainly less polished. He wore a dark gray suit, no tie. He had a curling mass of hair around a thin face. His frame was also thin, as if he'd lost muscle as well as weight.

His eyes, a few shades lighter than his suit, met Eve's, then shifted to Zella. "Thanks. I've got it. Send Rosa straight back if she comes in."

"Of course."

She eased back, shut the door.

"I spoke with Detective Olsen," he began. "She said there'd been another, but this time . . ." He gestured vaguely. "I'm sorry, please sit down. I can offer you coffee or tea, or my own personal vice? Pepsi."

"Don't worry about it. I'm sorry to put you in the position of revisiting a difficult experience, Mr. Patrick."

"Revisiting?" He shoved at his hair, sat on a chair that looked more comfortable than stylish. "We live with it every day. Every night. My wife . . . We sold the house we loved and are living in a fully secured condo neither one of us want. And still she can't be alone for more than a few hours during the day, has nightmares constantly. She was just starting to do better. We were starting to do better. And now this.

"Why can't you find him?" Neville demanded. "Until he's locked away, it'll never be over."

And not even then, Eve thought. "I wish I had a simple answer, and could promise you we'll find him quickly. What I can tell you is Detectives Olsen and Tredway have never stopped working the investigation. Detective Peabody and I won't stop, either."

"He's a monster. It wasn't just a costume."

"I know it."

"How do you catch a monster?"

"By understanding him."

Frowning, Neville leaned forward. "Yes. Yes. Understanding him. How do you do that?"

"We're working on doing that right now. It's why we're here. He targeted you and your wife, specifically."

"Why do you say that? Nikki and Stan never said that."

"I believe you were specific, as were Ira and Lori Brinkman, as were Anthony and Daphne Strazza.

"You represent something to him. Someone."

"Rosa's never hurt anyone in her life. You can't—"

"You did nothing. She did nothing." Because it mattered, Eve let her words simply hang for a moment before continuing. "It may be that the ones you represent to this individual did nothing."

Though he nodded, Neville rubbed his hands over his face like a man scrubbing away a film. "I did everything he told me to do, gave him whatever he asked for. And still he raped her, and he choked her, and he hit her."

"Because that's what he wanted. That was his purpose. The rest was incidental."

"What do you mean?"

"He violated your wife in front of you. That's what he wanted. You know him, Mr. Patrick."

Those words had him flinching back as from a sharp slap.

"You've done business with him," Eve continued, "he's worked for or with you, or with your wife. When we do find him, you may not recognize him immediately. But you will recognize him."

"Someone I know?" He had to choke the words out. "Why do you say that? How can that be?"

"He waited until you were back from your honeymoon, rather than breaking in when you were gone. Rather than taking what he wanted. And he waited until you were out for the evening, so he could ambush you both. He knew about the safes, he knew enough to deacti-vate your security, your house droid."

"You're saying he's been in our home. That he's spent time in our home?"

"Yes, I am. Considering that, I'd like you to think back. Did you have any arguments or disagreements, personally or professionally, with anyone?"

"Of course. We're in a creative and passionate business. We thrive on disagreements. It's how we refine any project. Kyle and I—my partner—give our people a great deal of autonomy, but at the end of the day, the decision to make or break comes from us. We started this company together. It's very personal to us."

"Did any of those disagreements lead to the termination of an in-dividual or project that left hard feelings?"

"Shelving a project always leaves hard feelings. But it's a business, Lieutenant. Anyone inside it knows how it works, has to work. And that they can always make a case to have the project revived."

"An actor," Eve pressed, "who wasn't given a part, or fired?"

"God, every project would have actors passed over for a part dur-ing the casting process. It's the nature of the beast. I honestly can't think of anyone who'd react to that with this sort of violence."

"In your statement you said he used a fake British accent. Upper-class Brit."

"Yes, he dropped it a couple of times when he . . ." Neville looked away. "He dropped it once or twice. I believe he's American, or Canadian."

"Could he have switched it up to make you think that?" Peabody asked him.

Struck, Neville frowned at her. "I hadn't considered that. But no. I'm nearly certain the English accent was fake."

"What about someone who had feelings for your wife?" Eve

suggested. "A former relationship, or someone who wanted a relationship with her."

"Rosa and I have been together more than three years. Her former relationship is now happily cohabbing in Florence, and has been for more than a year. Lieutenant, Rosa is beautiful, inside and out. If you didn't know her, you'd be struck by her looks. I'm fully aware men look at her, and look at me with some envy. I can tell you, without hesitation, I don't know anyone who'd hurt her the way she was hurt."

Eve changed tacts. "Your company has used Jacko's Catering and Loan Star Rentals."

"Yes, Loan Star. They're our go-to for renting a one-off. I don't know the caterer off hand. I'd need to check with Zella. Why?"

"We're exploring all avenues, any possible connections. Have you held any events at your home where you would have used a caterer or rentals?"

"No. We'd only moved in—in April, and were married in June. We had friends over from time to time, but small gatherings, informal. We'd planned to hold our first party as a married couple during the holidays, but . . ."

He looked over as the door opened, and Eve saw his face register love, grief, hope. He said, "Rosa."

9

SHE LOOKED LIKE A WOMAN IN MOURNING, EVE THOUGHT. BEAUTIFUL, tragic, resigned. She'd pulled her hair back so what were likely wild and wonderful ebony curls were restrained by a clip at the nape of her neck.

She wore black—a simple sweater and pants, with the pants tucked into knee-boots. Her eyes, a molten brown, showed signs of recent tears however clever the enhancements.

Neville hurried to her, gathered her in with an almost painful tenderness. Eve saw Rosa nod as he whispered to her.

"I'm all right. I wanted to come."

Before she drew away, someone called her name, came to the door.

"Rosa! Hey." Then he stopped, zeroed in on Eve. "Cops?"

As he spoke, the man touched a hand briefly to Rosa's shoulder, then flanked her. "Why are the Icove cops here?" he demanded, shaking his head at Neville's blank look. "Dallas and Peabody, Nev. The Icove cops."

"Yes, yes, of course. I was distracted, didn't put it together. My partner, Kyle Knightly. There's been another, Kyle."

"Another . . . goddamn it. Sorry, sorry, Rosie." Kyle shoved at his dark blond hair, then shoved his hands in his pockets. "Is there anything I can do?"

"Not right now. We'll talk later, all right?"

"Sure. I'll be in my corner. I'm always in yours."

With a last resentful look for Eve, he stepped out, shut the door.

"Let's sit down, Rosa. I'll get you some tea."

"Tea would be good. I'd like some tea." Rosa sat, rubbed her wedding ring. "I don't want to say it all again. I don't want to say again what he did."

"Okay. I'd like to ask you if, looking back now, there was anyone who made you feel uncomfortable. Anyone who said or did anything, however minor, you felt inappropriate?"

"No. I answered that before. It wasn't someone I knew." She said it quickly, almost desperately. "It was a stranger."

"Mrs. Patrick, there are similarities in all three attacks. Not only what was done, but who it was done to. We believe there's a reason for that."

"The second couple, they—they were older than we are, and married longer. And they didn't live in our neighborhood or . . ."

"Mrs. Patrick." Peabody interrupted gently. "We see a pattern, and that's a good thing. That's something we can use to identify him, to stop him, to put him away where he can't hurt anyone else. If we can help you see the pattern we do, you might think of something that gives us another piece."

"I didn't know him. His face was white, like the dead, and his eyes were black, and the light in the room was dim and gray."

She took the tea Neville brought her, but the cup rattled in the saucer, and she set it down.

"We're not going to ask you about the specifics of the attack," Eve told her. "The pattern, as my partner pointed out, is important. It's what we want you to think about. It may be someone you met in passing, or your husband met, someone who did some work for you, or was involved with one of your projects, your charities. As far as we can ascertain, you were the first couple attacked. We need to figure out why. Why you were first, how you were targeted."

"Sometimes a man might flirt a little, but nothing like you mean. It's like—you know, Neville—Boris always asks when I'm going to leave you and run away with him. Boris is gay. He's just being charming. And Micah, he's one of the show runners for *At Sea*, he used to say we should be each other's hall pass. That means . . ."

"I know," Eve said.

"He doesn't say it now, after this." Pausing, she pressed her lips together, hard. "People act differently now. But Micah, I mean to say, has been with Kate for ten years. They have two children. He's just flirting. Or was."

"I love that show." Peabody smiled. "*At Sea*. It always makes me laugh, and sometimes a laugh is the best part of a day. Does he work here, in the building?"

"He's been with *At Sea* since the beginning. He works here and at home."

"What about people who perform, who do makeup, costumes?"

"I know everyone who works in the studio." Neville sat beside Rosa. "Rosa knows most."

"Anyone you've had to let go in the last year?"

"No one. There are some who come on, of course, for a specific production, and that's a limited time frame. We're relatively small, privately owned. It's almost a family at the core."

"Mrs. Patrick, have you used Jacko's Catering?"

"On Screen's used them, and I recommended them to a friend who

was in charge of that area for a fund-raiser. She used them personally after that."

"How long ago did you recommend them?"

"Last year, I think . . . Yes, it would've been around this time last
year for a fund-raiser we were doing in March. She had food and bev-
erage, I was flowers and decor. They were very good, and she used
them for a dinner party later. We—I—we haven't done much social-
izing since the summer, so I can't say if she's used them again."

"How about Loan Star Rentals?"

"Several committees I've been on use Loan Star. They're reliable
and have a diverse catalog. I don't understand."

"It's details, that's all," Eve said easily. "Every detail can matter.
Could I have the name of the friend who worked with Jacko's?"

"Marlene Dressler."

"Did you have much interaction with the staff of either company?"

"Some, but Marlene's so efficient. And the rental company, I
wouldn't have been in charge there, either. I'd have helped with
the setup if I was around. You think someone from one of those
vendors—"

"We're going to look at everything, everyone. St. Andrew's
Hospital."

"I chaired a committee for two of their fund-raisers, and have
served on the committee for others."

"Who did you work with, from the hospital?"

"Oh, the first was more than two years ago." As she rubbed her
temple, Rosa looked a little lost. "At least two. I don't— wait, I do
remember. It was for the pediatric wing. I worked with Daphne
Strazza. Her husband's a surgeon there. I liked her so much."

"So you've kept in touch?" Eve prompted.

"Actually, no. We had lunch a couple of times, then, well, she could

never make it. Then Neville and I got engaged, and there were wedding plans, and finding a home. We lost contact."

"Happens," Eve said. "You haven't seen or spoken to her in a while?"

"At least a year. Probably more. When the committee contacted
me again for the annual event, I asked, and they told me she wasn't
involved any longer. It's a shame. Some people have a knack for this
kind of work. I thought she did."

"Did she ever come here?"

"No." Frowning, Rosa picked up her tea, her hands had steadied.
"We wouldn't have had any reason to. We met at the hospital, or at
my home or hers. And a couple of times in a restaurant. There were
twenty or so of us involved in the project. We were cochairs that year,
so we talked and met more often."

"Can you give me the names of the others on that committee?"

"I'd need to check my book on it. I don't remember everyone. It
was two years ago, more. And I used to do a lot of this sort of work.
I haven't been as involved since . . ."

"Why?" Neville spoke up. "Why does this matter?"

"It's been released to the media, and reported by same, so I'm able
to tell you that Daphne Strazza and her husband were assaulted in
their home Saturday night. We believe by the same individual who
assaulted you and the Brinkmans."

"Daphne?" Shock and sympathy echoed as Rosa clutched at
Neville's hand. "Like us?"

"Yes. She was more severely injured, physically, but is recovering.
Her husband was killed during the assault."

Color leeched from Rosa's face. "He's dead?"

"This individual is escalating. Let me say that I believe, absolutely,
he's done with you. He has no reason to ever come back. And what
you've been able to tell us here gives us that other piece. You're going
to have helped us find him."

"Are you sure it wasn't her husband who hurt her?"

Eve kept her eyes and voice cool even as the bell rang in her head. "What do you mean?"

Rosa picked up the neglected tea again. Her fingers trembled, that steadiness fleeting, but she drank. "I've worked with abused women. Not as a counselor, I'm not trained. But I've done work in shelters. I recognized signs. I know I'm not a therapist or a professional, but I *know*. If she wasn't physically abused by her husband, she was emotionally abused. I know she was afraid of him. I saw it."

You're not the only one, Eve thought.

"We have no evidence supporting the suggestion Dr. Strazza assaulted or raped his wife on the night of this incident. I'm not doubting your instincts or observations, Mrs. Patrick. But Anthony Strazza was, as was Daphne, attacked by an intruder."

For a moment, Rosa turned her face into Neville's shoulder. Then she straightened her own, sat straight. "Can you tell me where she is?"

"I can't release that information."

Rosa nodded. "Would you tell her if she wants to talk to me or see me, to contact me. It helps. Lori and I have been talking. Lori Brinkman. I know it can help."

"I can do that. I will do that. She could use a strong shoulder."

"I'm not strong."

"You're wrong," Eve said as she rose. "You came here, you asked to help someone who needs help. You're no weak sister, Mrs. Patrick, and he can't make you one."

When Eve and Peabody stepped out, Eve saw Kyle Knightly leaning against a doorway, talking to someone inside the office. and clearly waiting for her to come out of Neville's.

He shot a finger at whomever he spoke with, started toward her.

"I'm going to take this. Find wherever they do the makeup, the costumes, see what you can find out."

"I got that. More fun than you'll have," Peabody added as she veered off.

Eve walked up to meet Kyle. "Mr. Knightly. Problem?"

"You could say that." He looked down the long corridor toward Neville's closed door. "Neville and Rosa are just starting to come out of this nightmare, and now you're in there going at them. I don't want to see them twisted up again."

"Understandable." She noted people wandering about, loitering— and obviously hoping for a tidbit. "Maybe we can talk about that, somewhere private."

"Sure."

He gestured, began to lead the way. Another open area with casually dressed people at comps or in huddles. A few called out his name, or hopped up to start toward him.

He signaled them off, addressed a few.

"I'll be back around, Jen. I really need to see that report, Bry."

They moved into a small reception area where a man in a turtleneck and jeans manned a workstation.

"Hey, Kyle," he began. "Myra Addams from SAR wants a 'link meet about—"

"I need a few, Barry."

With that he walked into his office, closed the door behind Eve.

Neville had the corner spot, but Kyle's office boasted almost twice the space. Vid posters lined the walls, mementos and what she took for awards crowded shelves. His workstation, a wide semicircle of slate gray faced the far wall and its enormous screen.

He gestured her to a chair, walked to a bar area, opened its cold box. "Got your Pepsi. Neville and I share an addiction. You want?"

"Sure."

"Need a glass?"

"Tube's fine."

He brought two over, dropped into the facing chair in the sitting area, cracked both. "I get you're doing your job." He handed her one of the tubes.

"I get you're protective of your partner and his wife. I take it you go back."

"All the way back. Neville and I are cousins. Our mothers are sisters."

"Is that right?"

"Yeah. His mom did the exchange-student thing, fell for London, and up and moved there when she was like eighteen. Went to college— well, *university*, got married. Neville's dad lost his first wife—car wreck. Anyway, we'd go over and visit them, they'd come here. I spent some summers there. Nev and I, we loved the vids. His dad's a direc- tor so we'd get to go on set. Anyway, we started planning when we were kids how we'd start up our own production company, our own studio."

"And now you have."

"We made it happen." Kyle leaned forward. "I'm saying this, lay- ing it out so you'll understand. Nev's not just my partner, he's my family. My best friend. What happened to him and Rosa . . ."

He sat back again, gulped from his tube, stared hard at the wall. "If I caught the bastard who did this—"

"That's my job."

"Yeah?" His eyes locked on hers. "It's been seven months. I haven't seen you getting the job done."

"You will," she said simply. "Your cousin suggested I ask you about a couple of vendors you've used professionally. Jacko's Catering, Lone Star Rentals."

"You having a party? Sorry," he said quickly, and rubbed his temple. "Seriously, I'm sorry. I'm just pissed off. Rosie looks so damn fragile."

"You're close to Rosa, too?"

"She's family. Hell, I was with Nev the first time he laid eyes on her. I told him then and there to make a move, but she was with somebody else, and Nev's no poacher. Worked out though. Anyway." He shook his head. "We've used Jacko's—office parties, a couple of private screenings. Same with Loan Star. What's that have to do with what happened to my family?"

"Dotting *i*'s. Have you used either personally?"

"Rented from Loan Star once . . . maybe twice? I used Jacko's once. Basically, I don't do a lot of entertaining at home. I'm more the wine-and-dine guy—pick a restaurant or club that fits the guest, pull out the stops."

"I'm sure it's in the file, but could you tell me where you were when your cousin and his wife were attacked?"

"Yeah, the other cops checked it out so I don't have to look it up." His jaw tightened, then he visibly relaxed it. "I know you have to ask, but it's still insulting. I had a dinner meeting—a director we wanted to pull onto a project, his wife, the female lead we'd signed, the male lead and his date. It went from about seven-thirty until about ten. Got the director," he added with a smile. "I went home, settled in with a stack of potential project reports."

"Did you see or speak to anyone?"

"Nobody but the house droid. I had it bring me warm cookies and a vanilla shake about midnight. It's a weakness. I'd already gone to bed when I got the tag from Detective Olsen. It was about three A.M. I went straight to the hospital."

He pushed up, walked to his windows, circled the room. "Sorry, it still gets me right in the gut. Seeing them that way. Nothing like that, *nothing* has ever happened to somebody I love. We make vids with some nasty shit, but that's make-believe. It's not real. All the director says is 'Cut,' and it's done. I don't know if this will ever be.

"This monster took their lives—their everyday lives, their normalcy. How do they ever get that back?"

"Knowing the person who did this is locked in a cage can be a good step toward that."

Kyle came back, dropped into the chair again. "Whatever I can do to help put him there, consider it done."

"You make a lot of the vids here?"

"In New York? Yeah, we have our own studio. Neville and I built the company on the idea of starting small, being self-sufficient. We've got the studio right here, and now another soundstage in Brooklyn. Our team of scouts, production teams, our own writers for original productions and series."

"Makeup, costumes."

"Sure. Our girl copped an Emmy, two years running now, for makeup in an original series. *Planet Plague*. Christ, don't cops watch screen?"

"I've been known to."

"*Planet Plague*'s the number one original series, two years running. Zombie apocalypse never goes out of style." He jerked a thumb behind him at one of the posters, depicting a tough but beautiful woman, armed with a crossbow, and a hard-bitten yet handsome man with a katana surrounded by what certainly looked like walking corpses.

"Last year, it took makeup, original score, best guest appearance and capped it off with best actor, original series."

"Nice."

"Oh, yeah. Awards aren't just shiny, they can translate into ratings and funds, and ratings and funds translate into more creative productions. And don't get me started."

On a half laugh he swiped a hand in the air. "We're building something solid. We're doing what we always dreamed of doing. Neville's been shattered and shaken, and he's just coming back. It's been a hard road. Having him hit, seeing Rosa hit, with more cops, more questions, it can't help him."

"Reality doesn't wrap up when the director says cut, or the screen goes to black, Mr. Knightly. What you do may give people a break from reality, and that's all good. But we've all got to come back to it."

She pushed to her feet. "I appreciate your time, understand your concerns. Now we both better get back to doing our jobs."

He rose with her. "We put in a bid on the Icove project."

"Sorry, what?"

"Nadine Furst's book. We tried to get the rights to it, but it was above our reach. Congrats on the Oscar noms."

"Okay."

"They announced them this morning. It's up for seven Oscars— best actress, best supporting actor, best director, best adapted screenplay, best editing, best sound, and the holy grail of best picture. You didn't hear?"

"I'm a cop, Mr. Knightly."

"Kyle. And you're the Icove cop."

"No, I'm the NYPSD cop."

She stepped out, headed in the direction of the main reception, tagging Peabody as she walked.

"Where are you?"

"One floor up in Makeup. Jesus, Dallas, I met Adrianna Leo. I *talked* to her while she was getting hair and makeup for a scene. Then Joe P. Foxx just strolled right in, and I could've passed out!"

"Do I have to come up there?"

"What? No, I covered it."

"And your face? What's on your face?"

"Um. Makeup."

"Get your made-up face down to the garage." Eve clicked off, reminding herself she'd been the one who sent Peabody into the damn candy store.

She rode down on the elevator, ignoring other passengers who seemed buzzed on Oscar talk, until one of the women stared at her.

The woman's eyes popped. "Oh my God, you're Marlo Durn!"

"No, I'm not."

Obviously undeterred, the woman continued to chatter while digging in her rhino-sized bag. "Oh, I'm such a fan. I just *have* to have a picture with you."

"I'm not Marlo Durn."

'Link already in hand, the woman frowned at her."Are you sure?"

"Absolutely."

"You could so be her stand-in for the *Icove Agenda*. I mean you look *just* like her Eve Dallas character. Are you her stand-in?"

"No."

Eve escaped the elevator, took another down to the garage.

She got in the car, began a run on Kyle Knightly. And sent Peabody a long stare when her partner climbed in.

"Why do you have blue eyelashes?"

"They make my eyes pop, and it's just a hint of blue. Mags gave me a professional daytime look."

"That's so special."

"It was for me," Peabody muttered. "Plus I got to meet one of my favorite screen stars, *and* interview two of the top studio makeup artists. One of them also does the specialty work—like on *Planet Plague*."

"Zombies."

"Yeah, I love that show. Scares the crap out of me, but I love it. They have everything our UNSUB would need, right in studio. I've got a handful of names to run. Plus, Mags's good friend Uma in Ward-robe half-dated Hugh—Jacko's nephew—a few months ago."

"Half-dated?"

"They went out a couple of times, but it didn't click. She clicked more with his friend Anson—bartender at Jacko's—and they're semi-dating now."

Eve concluded semi-dating was more serious than half-dating. "Maybe it was worth the blue lashes."

"I'm buying this lash color, you can bet on it. And did you hear? Our vid's up for major Oscars!"

"Peabody."

"It's mega, Dallas. Nadine has to be zooming out of orbit. She could win a fricking Oscar. I've got to text her."

"Peabody."

"Later. I'll text her later. Run the names now."

"Good plan."

"It was exciting, sitting there getting my makeup done right next to Adrianna Leo, and she was really nice. Mags said she's total earth. Just like Wendy Rush is a total bitch—and she always plays a sweet thing, but she's completely not. And how Joe P. Foxx is not only frosted cream, but is always showing off pictures and little vids of his kids. Devoted family guy, which makes him frostier."

"Mags like to gossip."

"Which is how I got the data on the wardrobe pal dating two of Jacko's crew, and a lot of info on makeup, who does what, where they get it, how accessible it is. Mags is strictly in studio, but they have several artists who work location shoots or travel with the crew for exterior shots. Some are freelance and move from project to project, company to company, but some are contracted to On Screen."

Peabody shook her head as she studied her handheld. "And my top choice isn't going to fit. Mags said this Max Bloombaum was the ace at monster makeup and prosthetics, which is why they contracted him to create the makeup for *Planet Plague*. He's sixty-three, height six-two, married, three kids, two grandkids."

"Too tall, too settled for the profile. Finish my run on Kyle Knightly."

"Does he ring for you?"

"He's connected to the first vics, has used the caterer and the rental company, has access to the necessary makeups and effects. His alibi is a house droid."

Eve drummed her fingers on the wheel. "He comes off as sincere, concerned, emotionally attached to the Patricks. But he runs about five-eight, knows their house, would easily know their plans. Not married, lives alone."

"I'm on it—wait." She switched to her 'link. "Detective Peabody. Yes, Mr. Brinkman, thanks for getting back to me. That would be fine. We'll come to you now. Yes, sir, we will. Thank you."

Leaning forward, Peabody programmed the Brinkmans' address in the in-dash. "They're home now, ready to talk to us."

Eve took the next turn, and headed uptown.

"Knightly, Kyle," Peabody read. "Caucasian, age thirty-one, height five-eight and a quarter, weight one-fifty-two. Born Greenwich, Connecticut, to Lorinda Mercer and Quentin Knightly, no sibs. Good education," she added. "Private schools, prep schools, majored in cinema art and science—at Juilliard, two years, with another two in London. No marriage, no cohabs on record. Got a few minor producing credits—England, France, New L.A. Formed On Screen Productions with Neville Patrick (cousin) in 2055. Some links here to various articles on that."

"Later."

"Their first production was a low-rated but critically acclaimed home-screen series, *Urbanites*, canceled after its first season. Several other productions, more successful also listed. No criminal that shows. Net worth estimated at sixteen-point-five million—that's personal. Company is estimated at just under five hundred million, largely due to the success of *Planet Plague*, *At Sea*, and the big-screen production of *Camelot Down*. Do you want me to dig deeper?"

"Not now. Run the others on your list. And we'll see if the Brinkmans bring any of this into focus."

10

THE BRINKMANS' HOME HAD A DIGNIFIED LOOK OF WEATHERED BRICK AND creamy trim. It wore its age gracefully, and that age and grace contrasted with an obviously new security system. She counted three cams, imagined there would be more on the sides, the back. Another trio—sharp, silver-toned police locks—bored into the thick front door. A palm plate, with scanner, had been installed in the rosy old brick beside it.

The minute she hit the buzzer, the security comp demanded her name and her purpose.

"NYPSD. Lieutenant Dallas, Detective Peabody. We're expected."

Please hold your identification up to be scanned and verified.

She did so, as did Peabody.

Thank you. Your identification has been verified. Please wait.

Moments later the door opened. The man who answered wore what she thought of as a Summerset suit. Unlike the bony butler, this one had shoulders like an arena ball tackle, and a subtle bulge at his side under his jacket where he wore a weapon.

"Lieutenant, Detective. You're cleared to enter."

Second line of defense, Eve thought as they stepped into the foyer. A tall mirror, a long table, a dreamy painting of a water lily gave the narrow entrance the illusion of space and depth.

"Maxine will take your coats."

Eve eyed the woman in black. She might be a housekeeper, but she looked like she could kick some ass. Eve shrugged out of her coat, passed it over.

The man said, "Follow me," and led them into the living area off the foyer.

A fire simmered in a room where everything sparkled, nothing seemed out of place. Eve would have termed the room stylishly elegant, a long way from cozy.

The Brinkmans sat together on a gel sofa where bold red birds flew over a deep blue background. They sat so close they might have been fused at hip and shoulder.

Though it had started out black, Ira Brinkman had allowed his hair, like the bricks, to age so wiry strands of silver sprang through it, reminding Eve of Feeney. His eyes, a clear blue, stayed steady on her face even as he took his wife's hand in his.

Lori's heritage had gifted her with pure mocha skin, with eyes caught between blue and green under sharp, dark brows. Eyes fringed with long, thick lashes, eyes that held nerves and fatigue.

Ira squeezed his wife's hand, released it, got to his feet.

"Lieutenant Dallas, Detective Peabody, my wife and I are very sorry to learn there's been another, even more tragic incident."

"Yes, sir. We appreciate you taking the time to speak with us."

"It's difficult."

"Understood. We'll do what we can to make it less so."

"Please sit down. Can we offer you anything?"

"Please don't bother." Eve and Peabody took chairs facing the sofa. "My partner and I have familiarized ourselves with the details of the investigation into what happened to you. We're coordinating with Detectives Olsen and Tredway."

"Are you sure it was him?" Lori Brinkman's voice was like silk, smooth and soft. "Are you sure?"

"All evidence at this point indicates that, yes. The details of this latest attack are too similar to yours, to the Patricks', to believe otherwise."

"But he killed someone. He could have killed us. We were helpless. He killed the husband. He could have killed Ira."

"He didn't." Ira took her hand again. "I'm right here."

"He kept hitting him, even when Ira gave him the combination, kept hitting him even when I . . . I said what he told me to say. I thought he would kill us both." She closed her eyes, breathed in. "But he didn't. I know it wasn't our fault. I've gotten through that part."

"No, nothing that happened was your fault."

"But it happened to us. At first you ask why—why did this happen to us? Then you realize, and try to accept, there is no why." Lori leaned her head to Ira's shoulder. "An evil person does evil things. There is no why."

"There can be enough of a why, though it makes no rational sense, to help us find him."

"Enough of a why?" Ira echoed.

"Why the Patricks, why you, why the Strazzas? Married couples, childless married couples, who live in single-resident homes in good neighborhoods."

"Three makes a pattern," Lori stated. "I write screenplays."

"My information is you're a lawyer."

"Yes. I write on the side—under other names. It's more than a hobby, less than a job. In any case, I've script doctored several thrillers. Three makes a pattern. We're . . . a type."

"We believe there's a pattern, yes, and that helps us. We believe he selected you as he did the others. And that he's done with you," Eve added when she saw fear leap into Lori's eyes. "If he continues pattern, he's already selected his next victims. You may be able to help us stop him."

"We agreed to talk to you," Ira said, "because we would do anything, *anything* to stop him, to know he's locked away. I wanted to kill him. I've never been a violent man, but I wanted to kill him with my bare hands. I've dreamed of it, of getting free, and beating him to death right there, in our bedroom."

Even as he said it, Ira's eyes glittered with retribution.

"He struck Lori, again and again, raped her, again and again. And he watched me while he raped her. Grinned at me. I could do nothing."

"He wanted to humiliate you, Mr. Brinkman," Peabody told him. "As much as he wanted anything, he wanted that. He's a coward, and he's weak, that's why he threatened your wife. He threatened her to disable you."

"He used me to hurt Ira, used Ira to hurt me. Yes, he's a coward, but you haven't stopped him."

"We're adding details that may help us do that."

Lori looked back at Eve. "You said *selected*. He selected us. What do we represent to him?"

"We're working on that. You had no connection with the Patricks before this?"

"No—at least we didn't know them," Ira qualified.

"I recently learned I'd script doctored a screenplay, one that had been shelved. On Screen acquired the option when the previous one expired."

"When was this?" Eve asked.

"It was just last month, early last month. I haven't met or discussed it as yet with the producers. The last thing on my mind the last months has been the fun, and that's what this is for me. We met with the Patricks, with Neville and Rosa a few weeks ago. Nikki—Detective Olsen—arranged it when I asked if we could. It helped, just talking, the four of us."

She glanced at Ira. He smiled a little, lifted her hand to press it to his cheek.

"It's helped," Lori repeated. "And Rosa and I have talked several times since. She's younger than I am, and they were just married when . . . Just starting their lives together. I think it's been harder for her."

"She struck me as strong."

For the first time Lori smiled. "I think so, too. So am I. So are we," she said, looking at Ira. "Ask what you need to ask."

"Can you tell me if you've ever used Jacko's Catering?"

"Catering?" Lori sent Eve a puzzled look. "No. We've used First Class for years. My friend Rhia raves about them, but—"

"So you've been to events they've catered?"

"Yes."

"How about Loan Star Rentals?"

"I couldn't say. Ira?"

"No, it's not familiar. Why?"

"Just some details we're exploring. Do you entertain here often? Personally, professionally?"

"I'll bring clients and associates here for dinner occasionally," Ira said. "It's more usual to take them out to dinner, or lunch. Certainly we have friends over."

"Ira actually likes to cook, so if we're hosting a couple of friends or a small, intimate group, he makes the meal. For larger groups, Lilia sets it up with First Class."

"Lilia?"

"Our border collie—and I mean that in the best way. Ira's fiercely organized, and I'm not. I'm a failure when it comes to times and dates, even checklists, particularly when I'm inside a case. So Lilia handles it all. We'll just say, we're having a party on this date, and she takes care of the details—and makes sure I remember to stop work in time to actually shower and dress."

"And that's been a close call a time or two." More relaxed, Ira lightly pinched Lori's arm.

"Lilia Dominick?" Peabody asked, consulting her PPC.

"Yes. She's been with us for about eight years. She makes Ira's fierce efficiency look like chaos." Watching Eve, Lori rubbed a hand just above Ira's knee. "Do you think we've had the person who did this in our home? Invited him in?"

"We're going to explore every avenue, Mrs. Brinkman. Whatever we find, you'll remember: You didn't invite him in that night. You didn't invite his actions that night. You aren't responsible, in any way, for what happened."

Because she wanted to keep them from dwelling on that possibility, Eve changed gears. "Detectives Olsen and Tredway indicate neither of you met or knew the Patricks before the attacks. How about the Strazzas?"

"Actually, when Rosa and I were talking—she contacted me before you got here—we realized we'd all attended some of the same events. We'd just never connected."

"What events?"

"Well, ah, the Celebrate Art Gala last April. And the Winter Ball— that was the year before last. Neither of us attended this year's. And a few others, I don't remember now. Which is why I need Lilia. Rosa actually helps organize the art gala. It's a lovely evening. We'll go this year," she said to Ira.

"Of course we will."

"Oh, and, I remember another. Wait." Lori tapped two fingers to her temple. "I just had it. The Have a Heart Ball. It's a Valentine's Day event, a charity ball in association with St. Andrew's Hospital."

Another link in the chain, Eve thought. "But you never met the Strazzas?"

"I met Dr. Strazza as it happens," Ira told her. "Just met, as in we were introduced briefly by a mutual acquaintance. At one of these charity events. I'm nearly certain it was the Celebrate Art Gala. I only remember at all—it was that brief—because of all this."

"You spoke with him?"

"Really no more than 'How do you do.' I'd gone to one of the bars with an acquaintance, and Dr. Strazza was passing by. You'd gone off with Rhia and Lilia, one of your safaris to the ladies' lounge," he said to Lori. "I headed to the bar with Chase."

"Chase Benson," Lori expanded. "He knows everyone, and drops names like they are seeds for the garden."

"Now, Lori."

"Did you meet his wife?" Eve probed. "Daphne Strazza?"

"No, she wasn't with him at that moment—and it was only a moment. Chase intercepted the man, gave him one of his patented hearty handshakes. I believe he did ask about Strazza's wife. Something like 'Where is that gorgeous creature you stole from the rest of us?' That's how Chase talks. I think Strazza said something about her powdering her nose."

"Stupid expression," Lori muttered.

"That may be, but when I think of it, I'd say Strazza looked a bit annoyed. Chase can have that effect. In any case, Chase introduced us,

Strazza nodded and left. It was brief. Abrupt, really. Chase said something about Strazza being a dick with a young, sexy wife. That was it."

"How many ladies' lounges?" Eve wondered.

"The one main," Lori told her. "You can hoof it to others, but the main's big and beautifully appointed. It means something, doesn't it, that we were all there—the six of us—that night?"

"It may." Following a hunch, she took out her notebook, scrolled through to Daphne Strazza's ID shot. "Maybe you noticed her there."

Lori took the handheld, stared at it. "She's so striking. It's not a face you'd forget. And, yes, I saw her, saw her in the lounge. It was the Celebrate Art Gala. I even spoke with her. She'd been crying— was doing her best to hide it. I asked if she was all right, the way you do. She said she had a headache, and had taken a blocker. She was wearing a fabulous white dress with hints of sparkle, beautifully fitted, cut low on the back, an off-the-shoulder bodice with thin black chains draped on each shoulder."

Ira let out a laugh. "Lori can't remember the day of the week, but she never forgets an outfit."

"And I don't forget she had a bruise here." Lori touched her left biceps. "Just a little bruise, but still showing some red. A fresh bruise, like she'd been pinched hard. I remember her because she was a strikingly beautiful woman in a strikingly beautiful dress who looked unbearably sad and was trying to hide it."

Lori drew a breath. "I wonder if you could tell her, ask her, if I could go see her. If she'd want to talk to me, talk to me and Rosa. She may not be ready, but you could give her my contact information. Whenever she is . . ."

"I will. I don't want to take you through that night again, but I wonder if you'd let my partner and me see the bedroom."

"It's not the same." Lori looked at her husband, waited for his nod. They rose together. "We'll take you up. We've made changes," she explained as she led the way. "We couldn't live here at first. We went to our house in the Hamptons, even talked about selling this house."

"We've lived here all our married life," Ira added. "In the end we decided we'd make some changes, add more security. We'd try, and if either of us felt we needed to sell, we would."

"It's a great house," Peabody commented. "You can feel the history of it just like you can feel the, well, settled aura. It reflects you both, I think."

"So do we." On the second floor, Ira moved to a pair of double doors, opened them. "We can secure these, and did for the first few weeks."

Eve stepped inside.

In the file, the walls showed a strong, tropical blue. Now they held a warm, quiet taupe. The bed with its elaborate chrome posts had been replaced with something more simple with a high padded headboard. Everything in the room spoke of the simple, the streamlined, all the tones read soft, soothing.

Eve noted the motion detectors, the alarms, the locks on the windows.

"The en suite also serves as a safe room," Lori told them. "We can secure the door from the inside, bring down a steel panel over it. It has its own alarm and communication system. It's a little over-the-top, but—"

"Nothing that makes you feel safe in your own home is over-the-top." Eve responded.

Despite the changes, she could see it as it had been.

Just another pattern, she thought now. He worked on patterns.

"Do you still have the house droid?"

"No. After the police released it, we had it reprogrammed and sold it." Ira draped an arm around Lori's shoulders. "We hired a security team, and a live-in housekeeper with a background in security."

"Okay. Thanks for the time and the access. Do you have any problem with us talking to Lilia Dominick?"

"Not at all," Lori said. "Will you remember to give my information to Mrs. Strazza?"

"I'll give it to her today."

"Find him." Ira tightened his hold on his wife. "Put him away."

We will, Eve thought, but could only say, "We'll do all we can."

C ontact the border collie, see if she'll come down to Central." Because the predicted snow had started during their time inside, Eve dragged on her snowflake hat. "We're going to go by, have another talk with Daphne, then we need to put this together."

"All the victims in the same place, the same time, the same event? That means something."

"Yeah. The killer was there, too. No way he wasn't there. As staff, as a guest. He saw these people, and something started the wheels turning in his fucked-up head."

As the snow fell thin and fast, Eve slid behind the wheel. "He's going to be one of them," she said as she pulled away from the curb. "That's what my gut tells me. He's one of the privileged—or he was. One or the other. He knows the lifestyle."

"The caterer, the rental company."

"Not a coincidence, because there aren't any. He's used them, or has been to events they worked. He knows someone—or someones—who work there. Well enough to pump one or more of them for information on his targets, which they give either inadvertently or incentivized by—"

Eve rubbed her thumb and fingers together.

"No matter how, we've connected the victims. They're linked. It's not random, never was. They're specific targets who meet his specific requirements."

She lapsed into silence, thinking, thinking, while Peabody talked to Lilia Dominick.

Peabody muted the 'link. "She says she'll come in, if we need her, but couldn't get there until after five today. She's swamped. But her office isn't far from here. If we can go to her, she'll juggle things around. Sounds cooperative," Peabody added. "And a little harassed."

"Tell her we'll be there within the hour."

Eve pulled into the hospital lot while Peabody arranged the interview.

"She's out of her office now," Peabody reported. "She'll be there within thirty."

They made their way through the hospital to Daphne's floor, passed the desk. Eve nodded to the uniform on the door. "Officer."

"Lieutenant. Nobody but medical types in or out. She got some soup delivered from a place called Jacko's. The doc said you'd cleared it. Big vat of soup. She said to send me out a bowl of it. Damn good, sir."

The uniform shifted. "She asked me to come in a couple of times this shift, Loo. Wanted me to check the bathroom, under the bed, in the closet. Laughed about it, but the laugh was put on. You know?"

"Yeah."

"It was after one of the nurses said something about how well she was doing and how she could probably go home tomorrow. She got freaked over it, but tried not to show it."

"Okay. Take a break, Officer. You've got fifteen."

Eve stepped in.

Daphne sat in a chair by the window, listlessly swiping a tablet. Her long hair lay in a simple braid over her left shoulder. The beauty the beating had masked shined through despite the bruises.

Daphne managed what passed for a smile.

"How are you doing?" Eve asked.

"Better. I've been up and walking, and it hardly hurts at all. They said I could sit here, or even go down to the indoor garden. I think I might do that. Go down there. But—"

"But?"

"Dr. Nobel said he would fix it so I could stay longer, but they're saying I could go home tomorrow. I can't go back there."

"You don't have to go back there."

"I don't know where to go."

"You could stay with a friend."

"I . . . I don't have anyone I could stay with."

"Your family," Eve began. Daphne went stiff.

"No. No, they're not here."

Since the mention of her family had put that look back in Daphne's eyes, Eve let it go.

"You could stay in a hotel. We'd keep a police officer with you. You're going to need some things from the house."

"I . . . I could get things from the store."

"Yeah, you could." Eve sat in the facing chair, gesturing for Peabody to sit on the side of the bed. Casual, she thought, nonthreatening. "We can take care of that for you, if you give us a list. Or we could bring you things from the house, your own things."

"I—maybe. I need a few things, and, well, I don't have any way to pay right now. They gave me a basic kit. For the bathroom, but—"

"A girl wants her own hair and face products," Peabody pointed out. "Maybe your makeup, some comfortable clothes. Those are nice pajamas."

"Jilly—one of the nurses? She got them for me. She said they'd just add the cost onto the bill. I . . ." Her eyes filled. "I don't know how to pay the bill. There's insurance, but I . . . I don't know how it works, or what I would owe over that. I talked to Del—Dr. Nobel—and he said not to worry about it yet, and that when I was ready I should talk to the lawyer, the one in charge of my husband's—Anthony's estate."

"That sounds sensible. As a matter of fact, I was planning to contact the lawyer today, just to discuss some details."

Relief visibly flooded her face. "Oh, then maybe you could ask him what I should do. How to pay the hospital, and for a hotel if I have to leave."

"I'll talk to him. That's Randall Wythe, right?"

"I think—yes. I signed papers before my husband and I were married. The legal papers, but after that my husband handled all the legal business."

"Okay. Daphne, you know there are two other couples who were attacked, who've been through what you're going through."

Daphne pressed her lips together, nodded.

"You met them. You worked with one of them on a committee. And met the other at an event once."

"I did?"

"Rosa Patrick."

"I'm sorry. I don't remember. I can't remember anyone with that name. I'm terrible at remembering things." Her breath began to shorten. "I have to try harder. It's rude and embarrassing to forget someone's name."

"No, it's not," Eve said. Daphne just blinked at her. "She wasn't married when you worked together. So she was Rosa Hernandez."

"Oh, of course. Yes, I remember. I remember Rosa. She was so smart and very patient. I make so many mistakes, but she—"

"Really? Because Rosa told me she thought you were great at the work."

"Oh, she was just being kind."

"No, she wasn't. She said she'd hoped to work with you again, and had even asked about you when it was time to put together that event again."

"She did?"

"Yeah. She was very clear on that."

"I thought . . ."

"What?"

"Nothing. Nothing." Lowering her eyes, Daphne stared at her hands. "I'm sorry we lost touch."

"She feels the same about you. The other woman. Lori Brinkman. You didn't exchange names, so you won't remember her that way. You just happened to run into her at an event. Last spring, the Celebrate Art Gala. Do you remember attending that?"

"Yes. I was to wear the white Delaney gown with the black-and-white Rachel Carroll evening shoes and the Joquin Foster evening bag—the black one with the pearl clasp."

"That's funny. The woman I'm talking about? She's terrible with dates and times, but she never forgets an outfit. You sure remember yours, too."

"It's important to dress appropriately, to present the correct image—and not to repeat in the same venue."

"Right. You and Lori Brinkman were in the ladies' lounge together at the same time. You'd been crying."

"I—I don't remember that." Daphne's gaze cut away. "She may be mistaken."

"You told her, when she asked, you had a headache."

"Oh. I sometimes get headaches. It's a weakness."

"I get headaches. Anybody calls me weak, I'll kick their ass. But that's just me."

"I . . ." It seemed to hit her, all at once. "They were attacked, like me? Rosa was hurt, like me?"

"Rosa was the first."

"Oh, I'm sorry. I'm so sorry." Her eyes, a striking green against her tawny skin shimmered. "I liked her so much. She's so smart and funny and kind. Is she—is she—"

"I saw her today. She's holding her own. It's been hard, you know it's hard. But she's going to counseling, and she's talking to Lori. It's helping them to talk to each other. They'd both like to see you, talk to you."

"Oh. Oh, I don't know. I don't know if I can, if I should." As she spoke, her voice hitching, she looked all around the room.

"He's not here to tell you what to do, what not to do."

Daphne's hands stopped pulling at her pajama top, clutched together in her lap. "I don't know what you mean."

"We'll leave that for now. What I'm saying is: Both these women understand, and they want to reach out. Because it could help you, and because it helps them. Peabody's going to leave their contact information, and you can decide if and when."

"Are they ashamed?" Daphne whispered.

"Not anymore, because they know they didn't do anything to be ashamed of. They survived, Daphne, like you did. This man— Look at me, okay? Look here. Anyone who preys on someone they see as weaker, who hurts them, violates them, traps them— Are you hearing me?"

Eve waited until Daphne nodded.

"Anyone who deliberately makes someone else feel less, feel helpless? That person is a coward. They're the weak ones, the shameful ones. What's not weak, not shameful, is taking help that's offered.

You said Rosa is smart and funny and kind. Lori struck me as the same. We can all use the smart, funny, and kind. So think about it.

"Peabody?"

"Already done." Peabody hit print on her PPC, took the printout, set it on the table by the bed. "When you're ready."

"Maybe I'll talk to Del, and to Dr. Mira, ask them."

"That's a good idea. Is there anything else before we go? Anything more you remember?"

"I'm sorry. Every time I try to think about it, to remember, I can't breathe. His hands are on my throat, squeezing, when I try to remember."

"It's okay."

"I—I have a question."

"Go ahead."

"How can it be all of us, all, were at the same place before? That I knew Rosa and met this other woman? How can that be?"

"It's a good question. I'm working on the answer."

Eve stepped out, spotted the uniform chatting up a couple of nurses. Eve signaled her back before they left.

"She shows the signs," Peabody commented. "Submissive, self-critical, unwilling or unable to make decisions without directives. Appears to have been cut off from family and friends."

"Classic battered spouse," Eve agreed. "Contact the lawyer. We need a conversation."

"Do you think she'll contact the other women?"

"I think when her doctors nudge her to, she may. She was happy to see us. She's in that room basically alone. I think she's used to being alone, being grateful to have anyone to talk to. I'm contacting her foster family, and we'll see where that leads."

She checked her wrist unit as they rode the elevator down. "Do this. Let Dominick know I'm on my way, then go back to the crime scene. You'll know what she'd want or need better than I would. Put it together, snag a uniform to send it back. I'll either swing back by and get you or you meet me at the border collie's or the lawyer's."

"I can do that. She doesn't even know if she has the funds to pay her hospital bill or to get a hotel room."

"We're going to see what the lawyer says about that. It might be she's got enough to buy a damn hotel."

"It's not what she's after, Dallas. I know you always look at the spouse or the partner—at whoever has the most to gain. But there's no way that sad, scared woman put some ugly plot together to kill her rich, abusive husband."

"No. She's victim, not villain. I doubt she has a clue about the terms of her husband's will. But we need to find out." As they hit lobby level, Eve dug in her pocket. "Take a cab."

"Thanks—really—but with the snow? Subway or hoofing it'll be faster and easier. I might just beat you to the border collie. I sent the address to your PPC."

"Don't play with the damn makeup," Eve called out as they went their separate ways.

11

Eve found a street slot—small miracle—and decided it was worth a two and a half block hike in the snow. She imagined some cheery optimist would call the wind bracing.

She hated cheery optimists.

She stuck her hands in her coat pockets for warmth, was surprised as she nearly always was to find gloves. Deciding it was a day for miracles, she pulled them on.

A woman—college aged, small stature, Asian—in a snug blue ski jacket, a blue hat with a long tail ending in a bouncing pom-pom, and fuzzy-topped blue boots jogged by with a couple of spotted dogs on the leash jogging with her, like it was summer in the park.

Eve just bet the woman was a cheery optimist—the dogs also had that gleeful, slightly mad look in their eyes.

Bella got that look, Eve thought picturing Mavis's little girl. Kids and dogs, who knew what they were thinking?

Plotting.

She preferred the middle-aged, beefy woman stomping toward her in scarred and simple black boots while huddled in a thick black coat with a sour sneer on her face.

You *knew* what she was thinking: Fuck the snow, fuck the city, fuck everybody.

It made things as simple as the old black boots.

She passed a glide-cart smelling of boiled soy dogs, hot chestnuts, and bad coffee where the vendor scowled up at the sky as if the snow was a personal insult.

There, too, she could relate.

She joined the jam of pedestrians at the intersection waiting for the Walk sign.

Bits of conversation swirled around her with the snow. One woman told her companion some guy named Chip was hopeless. A man in a cashmere topcoat, with a clipped Asian accent, steadily fried whoever was on the other end of his 'link over a bungled report. A man who gripped the handle of a small rolly muttered to himself: "Gonna be late. Fuck it. Gonna be late."

She caught the subtle move of a guy in an oversized, many-pocketed coat toward a trio of women loaded with shopping bags, clucking like chickens about the bargains they'd just scored, about where to have lunch, about how *pretty* everything was in the snow.

As their purses dangled like offerings to the god of street thieves.

She shifted between, pulled out her badge, wagged it in the street thief's line of vision.

He sulked. "I ain't do nothing."

"Go do nothing somewhere else." When he opened his mouth to protest, she smiled. "Or I'll do something with what you've already got in your pockets."

He said, "Cops is wheeze." And he took off.

"Yeah, 'cops is wheeze.'" Whatever the hell that means, she thought as she crossed the street behind the oblivious shoppers.

She'd expected Lilia Dominick's office to be in an office building, but the address turned out to be a four-decker with three levels of apartments over a swarma joint and a shoe repair.

The *suite* in Suite 201, Eve thought as she pressed the buzzer on the residential door, was obviously an upward spin.

The voice came tinny through the tinny speaker. "Yo."

"Ms. Dominick?"

"Another yo."

"Lieutenant Dallas. You spoke to my partner, Detective Peabody."

"Right. Good timing."

When the door buzzed, Eve pushed in, climbed the narrow stairs in the skinny entrance to the second floor.

Lilia Dominick wasn't what she'd expected, either. She leaned on the doorjamb of her apartment, a woman about the same age as the cheerful optimist with the gleeful dogs. Strands of red hair bundled in a messy topknot over a friendly face slipped free as she gave Eve a casual sizing up out of pale green eyes.

"Mag coat. It shows off in person even better than on screen. I've seen you do interviews and media conferences. Come on in. I'm just back from yoga—was just heading back when your partner tagged me to tell me you were on your way."

Which explained the sunburst skinsuit covered by a flowy green topper. "I like to get a couple of real practices in every week when I can manage it."

She gestured Eve inside a multipurpose living area cleverly sectioned off for each purpose by the arrangement of furniture. Screen-viewing area on one side, conversation area on the other, office in the back, and every inch rigorously neat.

"I appreciate you agreeing to talk to me so quickly," Eve began.

"I've considered committing a crime to get a meet with you, but murder seemed extreme. I'll get it out of the way by saying if you ever need someone to organize and coordinate for you, your calendar, your social engagements, your bookings—personal, not arrests—or assist with your entertainment obligations I'd be all over it."

She talked fast, a *rat-a-tat-tat* that came off as energetic as her smile.

"And with that, would you like some coffee? I have a small stash of real to go with the cookies my grandmother just sent me. We'll never tell my yogi about either."

"Sure."

"Why don't you come on back?"

Graceful in skids, Lilia walked back to where the living area became the office, made a jog to the left into a tiny kitchen.

"My grandmother bakes the best chocolate chip cookies in the tristate area. She could make a living," Lilia continued as she programmed the little AutoChef, pulled out a couple of snowy-white mugs, crisp blue cloth napkins, a white dessert plate.

She put together an artistic-looking tray in about forty-five seconds.

"Before we sit down and dive in, I want to tell you I spoke to Lori. My first loyalty is to her and Ira, and if she'd asked me to evade, obfuscate, play dumb, even lie, I would have. But she didn't. She liked you and your partner, and told me to give you full cooperation. So I will. She's not just a client, Lieutenant Dallas."

"Understood."

"Okay, we'll settle into the parlor, and have some coffee and cookies to help this very difficult subject go down easier."

She carried the tray to the conversation area, set it on a table painted a glossy red in front of a pair of light gray chairs.

"Lori told me you've connected the murder of Dr. Strazza, and the attack on his wife to what happened to her and Ira."

"We're pursuing that angle."

Nodding, Lilia picked up her coffee, settled back, and actually slowed down a little. "I heard about what happened yesterday from my grandmother."

"Your grandmother."

"She's addicted to the Crime Channel. She's going to go crazy when I tell her I had coffee with you. She's a big fan. And that's my way of postponing talking about this. I'm not as fond of crime talk as my grandmother, and what happened to Lori and Ira, it's still . . . It's hard. How can I help you?"

"Do you know Rosa and Neville Patrick?"

"I've met her several times—before all this. I organize and coordinate for a few people. I don't work for her, but I've worked for or done specific events and tasks for people she knows, and for groups she's involved with."

"I imagine you've done business with Jacko's Catering and Loan Star Rentals."

"I have. They both have excellent and well-earned reputations. They're on my preferred vendors list. Lori uses First Class, and that's also on my list."

"What about Loan Star? Neither of the Brinkmans could be absolutely sure if they've used the company or not."

"They haven't. I can double-check my files, but I remember details. It's possible Ira's company has, dealing with them through his admin, though I can't think of any specific event where they'd have needed rentals."

"Okay. How about the Strazzas?"

"I was at her wedding." Lilia lifted the dessert plate. "Come on, try one. You won't regret it."

"You're friends with the Strazzas?"

"No, not at all. They hired a friend and associate of mine, Darcy Valentine—real name—of Valentine Event Coordinators to do their wedding. Darcy pulled me in to help. Huge, splashy deal at the Roarke Palace."

"Really?" Intrigued, Eve bit into the cookie, decided she had no regrets.

"It is *the* place for huge, splashy society weddings in the city. So I worked with Daphne for a few weeks, though Dr. Strazza ran the show."

She shrugged slightly, crossing her strong, athletic legs. "I didn't work much with him—he met primarily with Darcy. Daphne was a spectacular bride, absolutely fairy-tale time, and the wedding was perfect. Believe me, Darcy and I weren't working with Bridezilla on this one. Darcy had Groomzilla to deal with, and I had Dream Bride."

"So you worked more directly with Daphne."

"As it turned out, yeah. Darcy had her hands full with the groom. Dr. Strazza was very clear about what he expected, and while there's nothing wrong with that, he was, well, let's just term it *unpleasant*. Darcy—and I know this is talking trash about the dead—nicknamed him Dr. Dictator, and actually gave her entire staff a combat bonus after the wedding.

"On the other hand, Daphne wrote Darcy and me each a personal thank-you when they got back from the honeymoon. She had a quiet class, the sort my cooking-baking grandmother would say comes from a good upbringing."

With a fresh smile, Lilia polished off her cookie. "I liked working with her—and she had good ideas. She had event-planning experience and it showed, but he most often either vetoed her ideas, or turned them into his ideas. Made it seem like he'd thought of it. I hate that. Don't you hate that?"

"As a matter of fact."

"Yeah. Frankly, I didn't like him. Sorry he's dead and all that, but I'm glad she's not."

She blew out a breath. "So three women I know and like have gone through something horrific. I'm not my grandmother, but I can figure out there's a connection somewhere. You asked about those vendors. I'm pretty well acquainted with the people who work at both companies, even tight with a few of them. I would swear, without hesitation, none of them could do what was done."

"You probably shoptalk with the people at both companies, what jobs you've done, what you've got coming up, what the clients are like and so on."

"Sure. You can spend considerable time together, going over menus, decor choices, stemware, linens, coordinating schedules, itineraries, agendas. What worked for Client A, didn't work as well for Client B. And war stories. Oh." Lilia flopped back. "Oh, I get it. We talk. I just told a yoga friend about this new client who tagged me yesterday because she'd decided she wanted to go to Borneo, to this specific resort and book this specific suite. And she wanted to leave today. That's one day to arrange travel, bookings—and the spa treatments she reeled off. Plus, it's a popular resort, especially this time of year, and the suite's booked, and—never mind."

Lilia batted it away with both hands. "But if it's not confidential, you talk. Now I'm not going to tell somebody in the local market that Clients Smith and Jones on Second Avenue are leaving for Europe tomorrow and will be gone for two weeks. That's just careless and asking to have the clients' house broken into. But I may tell Darcy just that if we were talking and there was something interesting about it, or if we both knew the clients."

"Anyone ever try to tap you for information?"

"Sure. Gossip and society reporters mostly, and that's a line you don't cross. Unless the client wants you to, and sometimes the client wants you to. Shit." She put her head in her hands. "Oh, God. Could I have said something about Lori and Ira's trip, any of the details? I don't know. I wouldn't have used their last name, because they're Lori and Ira, but could I have said something? I don't know."

"You set up the trip for them?"

"Yes, I booked their transpo to and from, had the car they keep there serviced, had the house opened, linens changed, flowers ordered, and the kitchen stocked for the arrival. I checked the guest list—who was coming to dinner, who was staying for the whole long weekend. Worked with First Class for the catering for Thanksgiving dinner. They have a branch in the Hamptons. I even made a list for the house droid on what to pack for Lori so she wouldn't have to think about it. It's what I do."

"How do you do it all?"

"Comp primarily, so there's a record of everything."

"They've taken this trip before?"

"Every Thanksgiving. It's their tradition. I can't go as I have my own—my family in New Hampshire. It's a lovely tradition for them, close friends, their families. I book what needs to be booked—including some of the guests' transpo, hotel rooms or rentals, as not everyone can fit in the house. I make reservations, appointments. Ira loves to golf—there's an indoor nine-hole, and he likes an early tee time. Things like that. And I work with the house droid on wardrobe, book Ira's haircut for three days before the trip, Lori's cut and color for the day before. I—"

"I bet they have a usual salon for that."

"Ira goes to this fabulous classic barbershop. Lori's used Arthur at Serenity for years."

"And being comfortable there, they'd probably talk about their plans, how much they're looking forward to this trip, to having that time with friends and family."

"Yes, I'm sure they do." More red strands fell as Lilia pushed at her hair. "You're saying it didn't have to be me."

"It didn't have to be you, or them. It could have been a friend, an associate who mentioned something about them being off on their annual fall trip. One or both of them could have been stalked by this attacker before they left. People who worked for Ira knew he'd be away, when he'd be back."

"That's true. That's true. But now I want a good slug of wine instead of coffee."

"Let's try this. Lori stated she'd met Rosa Patrick prior to the attacks."

"Yes. They didn't really know each other, and Lori didn't put it together as Rosa hadn't yet married Neville when they met—very casually—a couple years ago. She was using her maiden name. It was after they started talking, after what happened, that they realized they'd met before."

"And Rosa knows Daphne, as they'd worked on the same charity function. Lori spoke to Daphne at a function last spring."

"She did? I didn't know that."

"The Celebrate Art function. You were there."

"Yes, I sat at Lori and Ira's table, with Rhia and Marshall Vicker. I didn't see Daphne. I would have recognized her."

"You were in the ladies' lounge together."

Lilia looked baffled, then doubtful, then gave Eve a firm shake of her head. "I'm sure I didn't see Daphne Strazza. I don't forget names and faces, and she has a really amazing face."

"Lori spoke to her. Daphne had been crying."

"Now *that* I remember. That's who it was? Lori said she'd spoken to a beautiful woman in a beautiful dress who'd looked miserable, had tears in her eyes and a fresh bruise on her arm. I'd been sitting on the sofa, gossiping with a couple of women I knew. I never saw her."

"Looking back, did you notice anyone paying too much attention to Lori? Anyone who made you uncomfortable?"

"I don't remember anything like that, and believe me, I've gone over and over it in my head since Lori and Ira were hurt. It was a fun night, and there was a *lot* of wine going around. A lot of competition in the silent auction, celebrity guests, dancing. I danced a lot. I didn't take a date so I could mingle—I can always use more clients. And I danced a lot."

"You'd have made the bookings for the Brinkmans soon after that night."

"Yes, I start the setup for Thanksgiving first week of May. You think that's important?"

"It's a line to tug on."

"I can send you all the e-mails, the itinerary, everything. I sent it to the detectives before, but—"

"I know. I have it." And would study it again now. "That's the third time your 'link's signaled since I've been here," Eve pointed out. "You're not going to answer?"

"I'll catch up."

"Do you usually answer?"

"Not when I'm with a client—or talking to the top cop in New York. And I always return contacts quickly."

"But otherwise. Say you're working with a vendor or setting something up, helping coordinate an event."

"Sure."

"And say if the tag was to confirm a booking, switch something, add something, you'd deal with it right then."

"Usually."

· "Or if you're out with friends, on a date?"

"A date, I'd excuse myself, take the tag if I felt I needed to. Out with friends, I'd check the readout, take it if I needed to. So I might have easily said something about this trip, at least some of the details, in front of someone else." She pressed her hand to her belly. "I feel sick."

"None of this is your fault or responsibility. Even if the information got passed to the assailant in this way. Any more than it would be Ira's for mentioning his plans when he was in the barber's chair or Lori's if she talked about it over a lunch date with a friend. He had an agenda, and he found a way to get the information he needed."

The buzzer sounded. "That I should get."

Lilia rose, went to the intercom. "Yo."

"Ms. Dominick?"

"Another yo."

"This is Detective Peabody."

"Tell her I'll be right down," Eve said.

"Detective, Lieutenant Dallas says she'll be right down."

"Thanks. I'll wait."

Eve got to her feet.

"Is there anything else I can do?" Lilia asked. "Anything?"

"You move in the various worlds. The client, the vendors, the staff, the friends, the events, and the parties. Give it all some thought, see if anything or anyone starts to float to the surface. Something out of step, a little off, anyone just a little bit too curious."

"I will. Believe me, I will."

Eve went downstairs, found Peabody on the sidewalk, face upturned to the snow with a goofy smile. Jesus, a cheerful optimist.

"Don't make me hurt you."

"Hey. It's so pretty."

"It's cold, it's wet, and it makes many, many people behind the wheels of vehicles behave like morons." She jerked her thumb. "We're this way."

"How'd it go with the border collie?"

"She's smart, personable, efficient. And she's really fond of Lori Brinkman. It came through. She also worked behind the scenes on Daphne's wedding."

"Oh, boy, that's a big bell ringing."

"They talk," Eve continued as they walked. "The vendors, the co-ordinators, the servers, and so on. Shoptalk. Easy, so easy for little details to get passed along. When and where, how many and like that. He knows how to listen, knows how to pick up tidbits. Maybe he was smart enough to stalk Lilia, too, and pick up those tidbits. Maybe he hacks her 'link or comp—he could have those skills. No real security on her building or apartment. Basic stuff. He could've gotten in there, gone through the files, found what he wanted that way. Lots of ways."

"Do you think he knows her—she knows him?"

"I think she brushes up against an awful lot of people doing what she does. I think it's a pretty good bet he was there at Celebrate Arts Gala, and he started selecting his targets."

"All three."

"Oh, I don't think he stopped at three. All those women. Plenty of remarkably beautiful women, I'm damn sure, who happened to be married. Plenty of very rich couples who fit his requirements. And however many he might have earmarked that night, he's had other nights, other opportunities. One way or the others, he moves in that world."

When they reached the car, she got behind the wheel. "Either nobody notices him—staff—or he's one of them. Either way, he's in a position to select targets and pull out the information on them that he needs."

She glanced in the rearview before pulling out, watched a car take the corner too fast, fishtail, barely miss spinning into an oncoming car, which swerved and spun as its driver overcompensated.

"Snow," Eve grumbled, pulling out. She glanced at the address Peabody plugged into the in-dash. "That's Roarke's building."

"Aren't most of them?"

"Ha ha. That's his HQ."

"Oh, right. It's the lawyer. I didn't put it together. I just think of it as the big, black tower looming powerfully over Midtown. And woo! Underground, VIP parking for us!"

Eve considered opting for street parking, just to be contrary, scowled at the thickening snow. Might as well take what made the next stop easier.

It did loom, she admitted as the sleek black tower came into view. And looked dramatic and important, especially rising up against the white sky.

The man did enjoy making an impact.

"What did you find out about the bartender?" Eve asked as she maneuvered through the increasingly deplorable road conditions.

"A couple of bumps, but nothing major or violent. Arrested twice during animal-rights protests, went peacefully, charges dropped. He's worked at Jacko's for just under three years. Lists his height as five-eight and a half. Interestingly, he's a member of the East Side Community Players, and though most of his income comes from bartending, he lists his profession as actor."

"That is interesting. We're going to want to talk to him."

"We can try bringing him into interview today, but this storm's now predicted to dump fifteen to eighteen inches in the city, and the wind's going to take it into blizzard territory before evening."

"Who decides that?" Eve demanded, sorely irked at having the weather interfere with procedure. "Who decides this is the blizzard line, or fifteen to eighteen. Why not sixteen to nineteen?"

"The weather wizards?" Peabody suggested.

"Wizards, my ass. A real wizard would say you're getting hammered with fifteen-point-six inches because I say so."

"It's going to be worse in the 'burbs—and I don't know why," Peabody said quickly. "But they're already advising people to stay off the roads barring emergencies."

"They can say whatever the hell they want. Nobody listens to them."

Annoyed, she pulled into the garage entrance. The gate lifted as it scanned her license plate. Gate security flashed green as the computer engaged.

Good afternoon, Lieutenant Dallas, your priority parking is Level One, Slot Two. Please turn right, proceed thirty-two feet.

"VIP," Peabody said, executing a little shoulder bump.

Eve said nothing, simply drove into the slot. "What floor for the lawyer?" Eve asked.

"Wythe, Wythe, and Hudd have the entire eighteenth floor."

Eve headed for the closest elevator. Before she could call for it, she noted the quick scan. This security comp spoke silkily.

Welcome, Lieutenant Dallas, Detective Peabody. You are cleared for all levels in express mode.

The doors opened, as did Peabody's mouth until Eve shot a finger at her.

Peabody followed Eve into the elevator, mouthing *VIP* and doing the quick shoulder bump behind her partner's back.

"Eighteen," Eve ordered, and the elevator immediately began its smooth, rapid rise.

Law offices of Wythe, Wythe, and Hudd, the elevator announced, and seconds later, the doors opened.

A single female, with hair piled high and white like the snow outside, manned a long counter of all-business black. There were two empty stools flanking her, along with slick data and communication centers.

A standard, upscale waiting area spread on one side of the room. The other side held the surprising choice of potted dwarf trees, fruiting with little oranges and lemons, around a pair of black stone benches.

"Good afternoon." The woman offered a quick, professional smile. "The traffic must be horrendous."

"It isn't good." Eve laid her badge on the counter. "Lieutenant Dallas, Detective Peabody, to see Randall Wythe."

"Yes, Detective Peabody arranged for an appointment. Just let me check with Mr. Wythe's office."

She tapped her earpiece. "Yes, Carson, the police officers are here for Mr. Wythe. Of course." She tapped it again. "Mr. Wythe should be available shortly. His administrative assistant will come out to escort you back if you'd like to take a seat."

"Okay. Where's everybody else?" Eve gestured to the empty stools.

"We sent some of the staff home. This storm's supposed to be a bruiser."

"But you're sticking it out."

"I grew up in Wisconsin," the woman said with an easy smile.

"I guess you see pretty much everyone who comes in. Have you met Daphne Strazza?"

The woman's smile faded. "I haven't, no. It's terrible what happened. I hope she's going to be all right."

"She's improving. You've met Dr. Strazza?"

"Yes, I have. He's been a client for a very long time. Was, I should say."

"Can you remember the last time he was in?"

"Not offhand, no. Some time ago. He and Mr. Wythe often meet at the club rather that here. Here's Carson."

Carson—skinny, long-necked, with short brown hair meticulously side parted—stepped through a wide doorway.

"Lieutenant, Detective, I'll take you back to Mr. Wythe's office. Ms. Midderman, Mr. Wythe said to tell you to switch to auto on the desk anytime you want to leave today."

"Thank you, Carson, I'm fine for now."

They followed Carson's long, somewhat gawky strides down a wide corridor of offices, hushed as a church, past a meeting room or law library where a couple of young staffers huddled over laptops and talked in reverent whispers.

They turned beyond a break room, complete with kitchen and Vending, and continued down to glossy wood doors.

Carson knocked, waited for a quick buzz before pushing the pocket doors open.

"Lieutenant Dallas, Detective Peabody, Mr. Wythe."

"Yes, yes. Carson, get us some lattes, then cancel anything I have the rest of the day. I'm damn well going home."

"Yes, sir."

Carson went through a side doorway. Wythe leaned back in the big leather chair behind his massive desk, and sizing up his visitors.

12

HE HAD A SCHOLAR'S MANE OF SHINING SILVER HAIR AROUND A RUDDY, lived-in face with sharp, hard blue eyes and a beak of a nose. He wore his lawyerly suit—deep, dark blue with gray chalk stripes— with a precisely knotted red tie and the corner of a red handkerchief peaking out of his breast pocket.

"I knew Anthony for more than twenty-five years," he said in a voice that seemed to hover on the edge of a boom. "I was just trying to calculate, and believe I actually liked him about ten days out of that time. That said, I'm appalled by what happened to him, and to his wife."

Wythe gestured, a flick of his hand, to the visitors' chairs—leather, the color of port—facing his desk. "You might wonder at a lawyer volunteering that sort of information, but I knew him for nearly a third of my life, have no motive, and was in Miami—a friendly, annual golf tournament—from Thursday until Sunday evening. It's easy for you to verify."

"We will, if we find it applicable."

Carson stepped back in with a tray holding three oversized cups. He served them competently, even as he sent sidelong glances toward the snow falling outside the window wall.

"Now cancel those appointments, Carson, and go home. Then you can cast worried glances out your apartment window instead of out of mine."

"Yes, sir." Carson stepped out, shut the doors.

"Why did you dislike Anthony Strazza?" Eve began. "Except for those ten days?"

"The short answer would be: He wasn't a likable man. Surely someone with your skill and experiences has already gleaned that. However, when I broke my leg and shattered my elbow several years ago in a skiing accident, I had myself airlifted to St. Andrew's, and Anthony's OR."

Wythe lifted his arm, bent and unbent his elbow. "Not just good as new, better than. Same with the leg. I'd like to inquire about Daphne. I'll need to speak with her before long, as the trustee and executor of Anthony's estate."

"She's in good condition at this point, under a doctor's care. I can tell you she has no desire to go back to her residence."

"Understandable."

"She'll be clear to leave the hospital by tomorrow or the day after. At that time she'll require funds."

"Require funds?"

"She indicated she has none."

"But . . ." He caught himself, sipped his latte. "I see. I can, of course, authorize that."

"Why do you suppose Mrs. Strazza finds herself without the means to pay for a hotel, or whatever medical expenses she's incurred over her insurance?"

"I can't speak to how Anthony set up his household finances, Lieutenant."

"But as his lawyer, the trustee and executor of his estate, you can speak to the terms of his will and his wife's inheritance."

"If she's close to being released from the hospital, she should be well enough to speak with me."

"I can clear that from my end, but you'd have to go through her doctors. Physically she's improving. She's young, healthy, and—though her injuries and trauma were severe—she's gotten excellent care."

"Anthony may be dead, but there remains a matter of privilege and confidentiality. And I have a responsibility to look out for the welfare of his surviving spouse as well as his estate."

Eve's gaze remained as cool and direct as his. "We can sit here and talk about privilege and court orders while the person who killed your client, beat and raped his wife is snuggled in somewhere planning who he's going after next. We can keep doing that while the traumatized spouse of said client adds to her current anxiety as she is apparently without funds, resources, or a credit line. Or we can cut through it."

Wythe frowned, drummed his fingers, then rose, walked over to a small putting green on the side of the room. "Do you play?"

"No," Eve said. Peabody shook her head.

"Helps me think." He sank a ball, scooped it out, set it back on the narrow green, sank it again. "I'm going to give you some broad strokes," he said. "Some, we'll say, hypotheticals. Clients who come to me for estate planning generally have complex finances, so the paperwork is rarely simple and straightforward. Still some want just that."

He walked back to his desk, picked up his latte. "You'll also have those who, sometimes for spite, sometimes for good reasons, wish to disinherit a family member, or set aside that inheritance with restrictions. Some wish to leave the bulk of their estate to an organization or a charity. It might be, we'll say, the hospital where they've been attached for a number of years, and the bequest might be on the terms it's used for a specific purpose, with specific naming instructions from the benefactor."

"I see."

"Yes, I'm sure you do. The client may have a spouse or partner. He may, if there is real property, such as a home, leave that property to the surviving spouse, along with gifts given during their marriage or partnership. Jewelry, for instance, clothing, furs. It may be this client is very exacting, very precise in his bequests, naming pieces of art, furnishings, and so on that may be left to the spouse or partner, or must be sold at auction to benefit the charity the client has already designated.

"As a lawyer, one who handles a great many estates, I would advise, of course, that a trust be established for the spouse or partner, at the very least to help this individual maintain the real property, certainly to pay off any existing liens on same. My advice is sometimes dismissed."

"Okay."

"Let me also point out that even expediting, an estate like this hypothetical example would take up to two years to settle. This real property could not be sold until that time, in the event there were any challenges to the terms. If you speak to Daphne before I'm able to do so, will you ease her mind, tell her this office will advance her what she needs?"

"All right. You did their prenup."

Now he sighed—a sound almost like a bull snorting. "I did. Again, I can't discuss specifics. I will say that while I strongly advised Daphne to engage her own attorney to vet the agreement, she didn't do so. And the period of time it took to write the prenup to Anthony's specifications was not inside the ten days I liked him."

"What would you say if I told you there's evidence coming to light that Anthony Strazza abused his wife? That the abuse was emotional, verbal, physical, and potentially sexual."

Wythe shoved away from the desk, stared hard at his putting green. "That's not going to do it this time."

He turned his back, looked through the glass at the curtain of snow.

"I didn't socialize with Anthony, though we belonged to the same club—stuffy, old-fashioned place I'm fond of here in the city. We had very little in common otherwise. I wouldn't have been surprised if you'd said he bullied her—verbally—domineered, pressured her to be and behave in a certain manner. But you're saying he used violence?"

"I can't discuss the details."

"Touché," he countered. "I only met her a handful of times. Young, fresh, ridiculously lovely. I never expected the marriage to last, frankly. I assumed one or both of them would become bored and walk away from the marriage. But I never, even saying I didn't like the man, I never suspected he'd be violent with her. I'm not sure what I'd have done about it if I'd known."

He came back, sat again. "I have a daughter. She's the second Wythe in the firm. She married about three years ago and is about to give me my first grandson. I think the world of the man she married. Absolutely the world. And if I learned he'd raised his hand to my daughter, I'd break both his arms. I don't know what I'd have done if I'd known Daphne was being abused. No, I'm wrong."

He sat back, nodded. "I have a son. Our black sheep as he opted not to follow me as I followed my father, my grandfather into law. Instead, he's one of you." Wythe smiled as he said it. "If I'd known, I'd have gone to Nelson, asked him to look into it."

"Detective Nelson Wythe," Eve said, "under Lieutenant Mercer. He's a good cop."

"That's my boy."

"What about the first wife?" Eve asked.

"I didn't know her well. As I said, I didn't socialize with Anthony. I didn't handle the divorce, but passed that to one of our associates. It's my understanding Anthony's ex-wife accepted a monetary settlement and moved out of the country."

"Okay."

"Tell Daphne that I and this firm are at her disposal, and that I would like to speak with her at the earliest opportunity. As for her medical bills, those can be paid out of the estate. I can work that, and we can and will advance her what she needs for lodging and living expenses.

"Now, unless there's more, I'd very much like to go home and have a very large whiskey."

He was pretty okay for a lawyer," Peabody commented as they left. "And that was a really good latte."

"Another check mark in the Disliked Strazza column."

Stepping out into reception, Eve noted the woman still manned the desk. And was currently being charmed up to the eyeballs by Roarke, who leaned casually against the counter.

He turned his head, aimed that killer smile at Eve. "And here's my cop, and our own Peabody."

"What's the deal?" Eve demanded.

"As I was just telling the delightful Donna, we're closing down most of the operation for the day, and I'm here to hitch a ride with my wife."

"I'm not going home."

"I'll still take the lift, wherever you're going. You mind your step out there, Donna."

"Oh, I will. I like the snow."

Eve moved straight to the elevator, gave Roarke the hard-eye when the doors closed. "She's old enough to be your mother."

"Your point?"

Eve only shook her head, ordered Level One Garage. "Did you actually track us to Wythe's office?"

"It was easy enough. How are you, Peabody?"

"I'm all good. I like the snow, too. I'm thinking of hitting the market when I get home, getting the makings for a pot of soup, maybe some beer bread 'cause it's quick."

"Beer bread?" Roarke asked, apparently fascinated.

As Peabody explained—God knew why—the details of making beer bread, Eve ignored the conversation, considered what she knew, didn't know.

And what came next.

"Go home," Eve said as they reached their level. "Make the soup and bread of beer."

"Seriously?"

"Write up what you have on the bartender, write up the interview we just had with Wythe. Check with Santiago and Carmichael on the rest of the guest list, and get me that, and for the thorough, confirm Wythe's alibi for Saturday night through Sunday morning."

"Can do."

"I can get a car to drive you home," Roarke said.

"Thanks. I'd take it, but I can catch a subway a couple minutes from here, and get downtown without the crazy drivers. I can stick, Dallas."

"I'm going to work from home myself. It's desk work for now anyway. We've covered the field for today."

"I'll cover my list. See you tomorrow. Snow day!" she added, almost dancing away.

"You drive," Eve told Roarke. "I need to check a couple things."

As Roarke worked through miserable traffic, she checked her incoming, read the lab report.

"All the blood on the DB and the surviving victim was his and hers. No blood from the assailant. None of his blood in the room, so if Strazza got in a shot, he didn't draw blood, or none ended up on the crime scene."

"What does that tell you?"

"Potentially . . . Strazza breaks out of the chair, charges. He's probably still tangled up some, and he's hurting from the beating. Killer grabs the heavy object, spilling water and flowers as he bashes Strazza with it. She may still be restrained and/or unconscious. Maybe just dazed, in shock, but I lean toward restrained or out as Morris estimates about fifteen minutes between the initial blow to the head, and the killing blows."

"That's quite a gap."

"Yeah." Fifteen minutes could equal a lifetime, she thought. "Potentially. Killer thinks Strazza's dead or dying, Daphne is out of it or restrained. He leaves the room to clear out the safes, select what he wants, clean up. He'd have blood on him. Or he took the time to rape the female again. Potentially, one more time, he comes back to get his zip ties, his rope, his tape, his light, whatever else."

Everything into the case, she thought. The case he'd carried in with him, in front of witnesses.

"Now Daphne's unrestrained—he released the other vics, so pattern indicates he'd release her. But Strazza comes to, not dead, gets up, starts to. Killer bashes him again and again. Daphne tries to stop him, or to just run. He gives her a knock, hard enough so she cracks her head on the footboard, and she's out. She crawled through some of the blood—Strazza's, her own. It was on her hands, on her knees.

We've got smears of it on the floors from her feet where she walked through it."

She left it there, checked something else, stared out at the snow.

"He abused her in the will. Even dead he's slapping at her."

"What do you mean?"

"The lawyer had to circle, use hypothetical, but was a lot more cooperative than I expected. He didn't like Strazza."

"Did anyone?"

"Not so far. In any case, Strazza left the bulk of his estate to the hospital—with strings. They use it for whatever purpose he designated, and name it after him."

"What of his wife?"

"She gets the house, her clothes, her jewelry—which was stolen— and whatever's left in the house he didn't earmark to be sold to go to the hospital. No financial trusts or whatever toward her maintaining the house, or paying it off. I got the impression he didn't own it free and clear. And since you showed up, you could check on that."

"I could indeed."

"And a good dig into the rest of his finances."

"Now it's a happy day for me. I feel giddy as Peabody in the snow."

He would, she thought. Roarke wasn't—thank God—a cheerful optimist, but he had his moments.

"You saw the house, just an educated guess on what it's worth."

"Double townhouse, that neighborhood, well maintained? Twelve to fifteen million. Unless he's heavily mortgaged or borrowed against it, she'll be more than fine."

"She doesn't want to go back there, and the lawyer says she can't sell it until the estate's settled. At least a year, more like two. He didn't want her to just be able to walk away, not with his money, if he popped first. I couldn't wrangle any details on the prenup, but clearly Wythe felt Daphne got screwed over there. He says he advised her to get her own attorney, but she didn't."

"Neither did you, it turns out."

She aimed a look at him. "Did I get screwed over?"

"No, but . . ." He lifted a hand, let it fall. "We settled that, didn't we?"

"Add this: He worked things so she needed him for money. No job, no family—and I'm contacting them when we get home, because I want to know *those* details—no friends. It's classic. She was completely dependent on him, and he structured the will so she gets a house and her own damn clothes, plus the baubles he gave her. She nearly always calls him 'my husband,' rarely actually uses his name."

Eve shrugged it away. "Not the issue, it just pisses me off in general. I don't know if it applies. I can't see how it would, except the killer might have targeted her because he saw and recognized it, saw her as weak. An easy target. He may have seen Rosa that way, too. But Lori doesn't come off as soft or easy."

She brooded about it as he turned through the gates, then reached over, laid a hand on his arm. "Stop a minute."

When he did, she slid her hand down, linked fingers with his. "I hate winter mostly. It's cold, wet, messy, and inconvenient. But that? That's a hell of a visual."

Some droid, she supposed, had cleared the long, winding drive and the steps leading to the house. All else stood white and perfect with that house rising up from the snowy carpet, the stone laced on the rooflines. Trees and shrubs, wrapped in white mink, shimmered in the lights.

"I'm glad we came home," she told him.

He leaned over to kiss her. "So am I."

He drove the rest of the way as more lights flickered on inside the house. When they stepped inside that light, Summerset and the cat waited.

"Early and together," Summerset observed as Galahad pranced over to slither between two sets of legs.

"I expect the city will be shut down in another hour or two," Roarke told him. "You shouldn't plan to go anywhere."

"I don't. I'd hope the two of you will also do the sensible thing and stay inside."

"Easier to reschedule a ghoul party than a murder investigation." Eve tossed her coat over the newel post. "But I'm working from here until I'm not." She started up the stairs, stopped. "Don't go outside. It's cold, windy, and slick." And continued up.

"Was that actually a concerned directive?" Roarke asked as he walked up the stairs with her.

"Sure. His bony ass slips in the snow, we've got to deal with it. It gets buried in the snow, I've got an unattended death to wade through. Just trying to avoid the mess."

"Of course." He swung an arm around her shoulders.

"I need to contact Daphne Strazza's foster family. She's indicated she doesn't want anyone contacted, but I want a better sense of who she is, and what they—the family—might know about her relationship with Strazza."

"How will that help you?"

"Details." She shrugged. "It could give me—or Mira—a clearer sense of how to help her to remember the attack."

"I'll leave you to that, and give myself the entertaining time of digging into Strazza's finances."

"Speaking of." It didn't apply, Eve thought, but . . . "The first wife probably got a financial settlement. See if you can find that."

"The fun never ends."

"Glad you see it that way. Catch you later."

She went into her office, Roarke into his. The cat debated, then opted for her sleep chair.

Eve nearly headed into the kitchen, then remembered she had the ability to program coffee from her magalicious command center. Then remembered she now had the addition of a fireplace.

Why not use it?

She ordered it on, stood studying the simmer of flames, wondering why the hell she'd ever bucked Roarke on his idea of updating her office.

She sat, programmed coffee while watching the snow fall outside the window, fast and steady.

Getting to Central in the morning would be a bitch. But, that was tomorrow.

Now she opened the file with Daphne's data, and contacted the number for the couple who'd been her guardians.

The woman who answered, bouncily, was far too young to be Daphne's guardian. Mid-twenties, Eve judged, hair an improbable shade of red streaked with an improbable shade of blue. A line of multicolored hoops—ala McNab—ran down the lobe of her left ear while a single red stud punctured her right. She looked almost fiercely bright and happy.

"I'm trying to reach Mr. or Mrs. DeSilva."

"Sorry, they're not available. Can I take a message?"

"It's important I reach them." Eve held up her badge. "I'm Lieutenant Dallas, NYPSD."

"New York." That bright and happy froze, turned to fear. "Daphne? Something happened to Daphne? Tell me! I'm her sister. I'm Tish DeSilva. What happened to Daphne? Is she— Oh my God, oh God, is she—"

"She's all right. How can I reach your parents?"

"They're in Fiji—vacation of a lifetime. Please, tell me. I'm staying here while they're gone, watching the house, the dog. Please. I'll give you their contact information, but please."

No need to keep the woman tied in knots, Eve thought. And Minnesota was closer than Fiji. Pretty much.

"First, I'm telling you Daphne's all right. She's in the hospital, but—"

"Was there an accident? It's snowing something fierce out east, right? I saw the reports."

"No, she wasn't in an accident."

"Then what—did he—" She broke off again, held up a hand studded with rings. "Wait, just give me a second to settle down. I won't interrupt again."

"Late Saturday night Daphne and Anthony Strazza were assaulted in their home."

"Both of them?" Tish's eyes narrowed. "Both of them were hurt? Sorry, I said I wouldn't interrupt again."

"Daphne was seriously injured but her condition has been upgraded, and, in fact, she could be released tomorrow or the day after. Anthony Strazza was killed during the attack."

Tish DeSilva didn't so much as blink at the death notification. "He's dead? You're sure he's dead?"

"Yes, I'm sure."

Tish nodded, slowly, then let out a long breath. "But Daphne's okay? She's all right?"

"Yes."

"Where is she, please? What hospital?"

"She's currently in St. Andrew's."

"You said they were both attacked. Who did it? Why?"

"That investigation is ongoing."

"You don't know yet? But didn't Daphne tell you? You said she was okay, so why hasn't she told you? Look, you can be straight with me. I'm not the hysterical type—this just—it's upsetting and it's terrible to know she's hurt and we're not there. I'm going to contact our parents as soon as I get off with you. I want to be able to give them the truth, the facts."

Eve considered. "You say 'our' parents."

"Daphne's mom and dad died when she was only nine, and she came to us. That's what her mom and dad wanted. It's not just blood that makes family. *We're* her family. She's my sister. Do you have a sister?"

"Not through the blood."

"But you have a sister," Tish said, eyes keen. "So you know. Please, tell me what happened to my sister."

"She and her husband were assaulted physically. Daphne was assaulted sexually."

"She was beaten and she was raped." Tish's eyes filled, a few tears spilled over, but she stayed steady.

"Yes."

"She's in St. Andrew's Hospital, in New York, in good condition?"

"Yes."

"Is she able to speak, to talk?"

"Yes."

"And she asked you to contact us?"

"No, she didn't."

Tish closed her eyes, nodded, swiped at tears. "Okay, got it. I'll give you my parents' contact information, but I'd like to talk to them first. It's going to— They love her, so much. Let me talk to them first, so they don't hear this from a stranger. From the police."

"Why do you think she didn't ask me to contact you?"

"He poisoned her. It's like he infected her, God knows he controlled her. There wasn't anything we could do, or . . . we couldn't figure out the right thing to do. Hang a second, will you?"

The screen bobbled, then settled on a tilted image of a ceiling, a corner of a wall. Eve clearly heard the sound of a nose being thoroughly
blown, then two, quick, hitching breaths, a longer, smoother one.

The screen shifted again. Tish's face, eyes fierce, glittering wet,
came back.

"I'm glad he's dead. If I knew how, I'd be doing fucking cartwheels.
I'm glad because now we can do something, do something, to bring
her back. He killed my sister, he turned her into a droid. I have to tell
my parents. I have to get to New York."

Eve wrote down the contact info as Tish rattled it off.

"She's under police protection and medical care, Miss DeSilva. I
can't say if she'll agree to see you. And we're in the middle of a blizzard."

"You don't know from blizzards," she said with frank and amused
derision. "I'll get there, and she'll see me."

Eve simply raised her eyebrows as the screen went blank.

She weighed the idea of contacting the parents immediately, decided to let their daughter relay the situation first. Thinking through
the conversation, the reactions, she rose to update her board.

She added all three DeSilvas, connecting them to Daphne.

She wrote up the conversation, added it to her case notes. She
sent a copy to Mira as she wanted a shrink's take on the sister's reaction and statements.

Poisoned, infected, controlled.

Clearly, the foster family had been cut loose, cut off. And, yeah,
she could believe Strazza had manipulated that. Why? Likely for the
same pathology as the killer. For control and power over another.

Though she'd set Peabody on the task, Eve took a good look at the
bartender/actor. No violent incidents on record didn't mean he didn't
have violence under the mask.

When Roarke came in, she was adding him to the board.

"You have a suspect?"

"I have a person to look at harder. Actor—that's what he lists as his profession, though he makes his living tending bar at Jacko's. He hits a couple notes."

"So you'll push buttons, see if he plays the whole tune."

"Yeah. Nice colorful metaphor. I spoke with Daphne's sister—the guardians' daughter. She clearly despised Strazza, clearly blames him for them being out of touch with Daphne. Parents are in Fiji on a big vacation. I'm letting her contact them, tell them. If it wasn't for the severity of the attack on Daphne, I'd actually look closer at the sister. Taking a look anyway."

"As you will at the parents."

"Yeah. Gotta cross the *i*'s, dot the *t*'s. I know it's the other way around," she said before Roarke could correct her. "But that gets boring."

"Speaking of boring, Strazza's financial didn't present any challenge at all. He's a cautious investor, has a few pet charities, though he's a bit stingy even there. The house itself is worth what I estimated, but it's mortgaged for a bit more than half of that."

"So she won't exactly be rolling in it."

"Well now, it's better than a poke in the eye—though a spouse might see it as one. His first walked away with five million, which—as I thought you might want to know, and I certainly did—she used to purchase a sheep station in Porongurup—that's Australia."

"Why do sheep need a station? Are they catching trains? Where are they going? Why do they have to go there?"

"I imagine they find themselves herded onto trains from time to time, but a sheep station's a ranch."

"Then why do they call it a station?"

"Blame the Aussies. In any case," he continued before she could take him further into the weeds, "she invested a bit more than half of the settlement in the property and the sheep. Appears to be making it work well enough. I also found no travel out of Australia for her in more than three years. Absolutely none to New York."

Because visuals always helped, Eve called up the first wife's most current ID shot.

Attractive, Eve thought, an attractive, outdoorsy-looking female in her late forties. Someone who looked both competent and content.

"She doesn't fit as a part of the attacks. She's just part of the puzzle. From important New York doctor's wife to sheep in Australia. That says to me, she got as far away from him and the life she had here as she could."

"You think he abused her as well."

"It would fit," Eve said, then shrugged. "She got out, and I can't see her in this. Any more on his financials?"

"He has considerable art insured. Perhaps that's included in what he's designated to his widow. Upward of eight million there, and the jewelry, which is now missing, about the same. He has a luxury vehicle—with a lien, again about half its worth—and pays a garage fee."

Roarke wandered over, selected a bottle of wine. "I'm in the mood for a glass. You?"

Eve glanced at her board, at the snow. "Yeah. Might as well."

"There's nothing in his finances to indicate affair. No jewelry purchases, for instance, not listed under his insurance, no odd trips or hotel expenses, no secondary residence where one might keep or entertain a sidepiece."

"No hidden accounts?"

"None. All quite aboveboard and, as I said, boring." He poured two glasses, brought Eve one. "He lived well within his means. In fact, he could have afforded to live more lavishly. I'd say he spent considerable on wardrobe—his and hers."

"Appearances were important."

"Agreed. The house, the car, the furnishings, the art—all on the flashier side. Aside from that, he strikes as a bit of a miser. He liked having the numbers rather than the things. Two vacations per year, as a couple. Like clockwork. Two additional trips for him—golf trips that appear to check out. Relatively short jaunts. Two days at most, as were any professional trips for medical conferences or lectures. Never more than two days away from home without his wife. And occasionally she joined him on those as well."

"Didn't want her on her own for long. Not discounting your particular skill, wouldn't it be relatively easy for a decent e-man to get the information you just got?"

"Ridiculously simple."

Thinking, she swiveled side-to-side in her chair. "So the killer knew there'd be jewelry and cash in the house, which gave him the cover for the attacks—the excuse. The purpose remains the rape and beatings. He'd just as likely know when the house would have been empty, but that's not the way he wanted it."

She turned to Roarke. "How long would it take you to get the guest list from the Celebrate Art Gala last April?"

"About as long as it took me to select, open, and pour this wine." He gave her a playful poke. "How about finding something more interesting for me to play with?"

"Get me that data, and I will."

"I'll do that. And since we have a long, snowy night ahead of us, how about we have dinner somewhere other than your office?"

"I can agree to that."

"Give me a couple minutes." He tapped his glass to hers, strolled back into his office.

13

IT DIDN'T TAKE HIM MUCH LONGER TO STROLL BACK OUT.

"The list is on your comp," he told her.

"Great. Maybe you'd find it interesting to split the list with me, cull out married couples—first requirement. Married couples in the upper-class strata—second requirement. Married couples with no children—at least, none living at home. Married couples where the wife is a serious looker. And last, single-family residence. He doesn't do apartment buildings or duplexes. Not yet anyway."

"I can follow that. Have you considered same-sex couples? It isn't pattern, as yet, but isn't it possible he'd target a beautiful woman whatever her orientation?"

She jabbed a finger at him. "Damn good point. I'd put that as a lower probability because I think it's a mom-and-dad deal, but it's definitely a possibility. So . . . don't discriminate."

"What does the sign say in your bullpen? 'No matter your race, creed, sexual orientation or political affiliation, we protect and serve. Because you could get dead.' "

"Even if you were an asshole. We added an addendum."

On a half laugh, he jabbed a finger back at her. "Well done."

"Okay. So all of that, just pushing the married and the money. And the looks."

"I believe I'll work in here with you, on your auxiliary. That way we can coordinate more easily."

"Pull up a chair. You start at the top, I'll start at the bottom."

"You should know there are more than eighteen hundred names." And considering, he tugged off his tie, shrugged out of his jacket.

She huffed out a breath. "They won't all be married. We'll back-track for legal cohabs, put them in another lane. But we're starting with married."

Nodding, he rolled up his shirtsleeves. "You should know Mavis and Leonardo are on here, as are the Miras."

Her sister, she thought. Mavis Freestone stood as her sister in everything but blood. "Mavis lives in an apartment building, and has a kid. Mira's a looker, but she's not his type—so far. She's older than any of his vics thus far. I think he'll stick to pattern."

It wasn't a fast job, and it was mindless, which wasn't always an advantage. Eve worked split screen, the list on one side as she did quick runs on the names, making a note when she hit one that fit all requirements.

She slogged through a hundred, switched back to coffee.

They worked in near silence, even when Galahad gave up the sleep chair to leap into Roarke's lap, curl there.

At the halfway point, Roarke sat back. "Let's take that dinner break before our brains melt."

"What?" She looked up, distracted, then realized a low-grade headache had already started to brew. A short break wouldn't hurt as she couldn't do anything about whatever she put together tonight anyway.

"Sure. Yeah. Good. But maybe—"

He watched her eyes shift to the table by the terrace doors. "A deal's a deal, Lieutenant."

"Yeah, yeah. You want to eat down in the dining room?"

"I had something else in mind." He got up, took her hand and pulled her to her feet before she found some excuse. He glanced at the cat as he drew Eve to the elevator. "It's a table for two tonight, my friend. You'll find your dinner down in the kitchen."

He tugged her into the elevator, kissed her between the eyes— where he'd already diagnosed that low-grade headache. "Roof terrace," he ordered.

"Going fancy?"

"I expect the view will be."

As usual, he was right.

It was like being in a reverse snow globe, Eve thought. Outside the glass dome, in the streams of the exterior lights, the snow fell fast, as if shaken from the sky by an angry hand. Winter winds swirled and tossed it into dramatic sweeps, and through the sweeps, the lights of the city gleamed and sparked. The great park spread in a study of black and white. The streets rayed in stark lines, empty of traffic with only a scatter of emergency vehicles trudging through the thick carpet of snow.

He lit candles on a table already set for two with silver warmers over the plates.

"How'd you manage this?"

"I gave Summerset an ETA." He poured rich red wine for both, took her hand so they looked out the wide glass together. "We're lucky, you and I. To be up here, warm and safe, without the worry of keeping that way. I remember being neither as a boy in Dublin when winter hit hard."

"I don't think I ever actually felt the snow until I was maybe nine or ten. Even then I sort of remember thinking: It's cold and wet. What's everybody so excited about? But from up here it looks pretty spectacular. Nice choice for dinner, ace. Very nice."

"Let's see what you think of the meal."

He lifted the warming lids. Some sort of pasta deal, she noted, which was never wrong in her book. Not spaghetti, but the tube things in sauce with cheese melted all over it.

And the smell added more warmth and some spice to the air.

Reminded her stomach it wanted food.

"Looks great. What is it?"

"Baked penne, I believe." No point in mentioning the spinach.

They ate it with a colorful little salad, a baguette to be torn apart and dipped into herbed oil. And more wine.

"Whatever it is," Eve said between bites, "it's pretty good. You snuck spinach in it."

"I didn't personally prepare it," he reminded her.

"Ha. Still, it works. Will you keep your HQ shut down tomorrow?"

"I've advised anyone who isn't essential to work from home, arranged for some to house on site tonight. If you need to go into Central or into the field, take one of the all-terrains. Your vehicle can likely handle this, but you'll be better off in an A-T."

"Yeah. I might end up doing some of the interviews from here by 'link, possibly holo. I want a face-to-face with the bartender, so I may push for that, and I want another with Daphne. The more she sees me, I think, the more she'll open up. Anyway, I'll need to get into Central at some point. I'm the boss."

"That you are."

"You, too. You'll take an A-T?"

"I will."

"How many do we have?"

"More than enough," he said, and smiled. "How many couples have you noted out of your portion of the list?"

"Six that meet all. That's out of nearly two hundred and fifty people. A couple more that skim the margins. How about you?"

"Nine, that's out of about three hundred. So we've made some progress."

She told herself it didn't matter he'd cleared through more than she had. It wasn't a competition. Exactly. "So that's fifteen, plus two marginal. Even if we triple that before we're finished, it's a workable number."

"And how will you work it?"

"Talk to all of them. Cross-check any who use the caterer, have used the hospital, the rental company. Even any who socialize with any of the other vics. Look for a connection, put them on alert. Maybe one of them has had an incident—something. A thwarted break-in, an altercation, or the female will have had an encounter with someone who made her uncomfortable. I think the Patricks were the first, but that doesn't mean this guy hasn't practiced. Maybe he did the Peeping Tom deal, or broke into a house or two, stole a cocktail dress. Maybe he just got pushy with a female. Something."

She shrugged. "It's fishing."

"You tend to catch what you fish for. One of my nine is a same-sex couple."

"One of mine, too. I might have dismissed that."

"I doubt it, once you dug in." Lifting his wine, Roarke studied her over the rim. "You realize we fit his pattern, you and I."

Eve shook her head. "I'm not his type. He goes for the killer looks, leaning or nailing glam."

When Roarke raised his eyebrows, she shook her head again, ate more pasta. "You've got a blind spot."

"I'd say the blind spot is yours. In any case, he'd never—however skilled—get through the security."

"Jamie Lingstrom did once," Eve reminded him. "A teenage kid."

"A remarkably talented kid," Roarke added, thinking of Feeney's godchild. "And he didn't get through, as the alarms alerted us, and we dragged his talented young ass inside. Plus I've added to security since—and asked Jamie to try to circumvent it."

"I didn't know you had him try another break-in."

"Because it failed. Twice. He's determined to conquer it. If and when he does, I'll use that to add more layers." Reading her face, he sat back with his wine. "I didn't mention us and the pattern to give you ideas about being bait. It wouldn't work for one thing. He'd be stupid to try for a cop, especially you. Or to try to get into this house. I expect he's too careful for that sort of challenge."

"He's too much of a coward," Eve corrected. "But a trap . . . not us, not here. If he considered trying for us, he'd want weeks of planning—and he'd want Summerset out. When does Summerset go on his winter vacation deal?"

"I thought it was marked with glittering stars and dancing fairies on your calendar. Soon."

"Just wouldn't work. But if I can refine the list, try to suss out who he might be targeting, I might be able to talk a couple into letting us bait the hook. Gonna think about that."

"Let's think about that later, top off our wine, and drink it on the sofa there, watching the snow fall. That's a fine way to round out the dinner break."

"Can't argue with it."

She settled down with him, actually put her feet on the table in front of them.

"I believe you're relaxing, Lieutenant."

"For a minute." Since she was, she leaned into him. "It's taken me a while."

"To?"

"To get used to being here, living here, having this. You built it all over years. I dropped into it. It's taken a while to adjust. To relax. I wonder if it was the same with Daphne. She comes from solid middle—edging toward upper middle—class, had a job, and was building it into a career. Rich doctor comes along, pays attention. I imagine he was charming at the start of it all. She's dazzled. Big important house, probably fancy dates, expensive gifts, and I'll bet on a romantic proposal. The whole swooping off the feet."

"Sweeping."

"Nobody in their right mind sweeps feet."

"But they'd swoop feet?"

He had her there. "Anyway, she's dazzled, swooped and swept and married inside a few months."

Amused, he tapped the diamond she wore on a chain around her neck when she tugged it out from under her shirt. "I worked up to giving you expensive gifts."

"You sent me coffee, real coffee, right off. Nailed that in one."

"I did, yes. And still, I don't believe you were ever dazzled, swooped or swept."

"More appalled, I guess, but I got over it." As they sat, shoulder-to-shoulder, the snow and the city it fell on providing a breathtaking view, she turned her head to look at him.

Another breathtaking view, she thought.

"I might've been slightly swooped."

"And I, darling Eve, a bit appalled—a cop, after all—but completely swept."

She gave him a little shoulder bump. "But the thing? You and me?

Experienced cynics and ass-kickers. Daphne's young, relatively in-experienced, has—by all accounts—a soft sort of nature. He plays on that, chips away at her self-esteem, begins to limit her activities and interests, starts distancing her from friends and family. It's how it works."

"Claims to cherish," Roarke said, "even as he diminishes."

"You got it. He probably didn't seriously smack her around until he'd accomplished most of that. Then he'd apologize, lost his temper. Forgive me. But—here's a key—but you, little lady, did, said some-thing or behaved in such a way to make me lose control. So it turns, it becomes her fault he clocked her."

She sipped more wine. "It really doesn't have anything to do with the case."

"It has to do with those echoes you spoke of. Did he apologize when he first hit you?"

She didn't have to ask who. Richard Troy. And, yes, the echoes grew louder, grew longer with every step she took into the inves-tigation.

"I honestly don't remember the first time he hit me. Couldn't say whether it's buried or blurred, or if I was just too young to retain it. But I remember how he sometimes brought me something, some toy. He'd say things like I had to be good, had to do as I was told—always—so he wouldn't have to punish me. Then he'd take it away or break it because—he said—I'd done something wrong."

Idly, Eve rubbed a hand on Roarke's leg. "Did Patrick Roarke do that with you?"

"He didn't, no. No toys or rewards. Neglect was his style, followed by beatings. Perhaps a grunt of approval now and then on a day I'd had particularly good luck with picking pockets or lifting locks. It's crueler, I think, the reward and punish than the neglect. What sort of toys did he bring you?"

"The only one I clearly remember, probably because I really liked it, was this little music box thing with this ballet girl inside who'd twirl around when you opened it. Sometimes if I couldn't sleep, I'd open it up, listen to it, watch the girl. Sort of, I guess, imagine being happy enough to twirl around. And one night he came in, raging, busted it to pieces, whaled on me pretty good."

And because he could see it so well, the young, trapped girl dreaming, then brutalized, it broke his heart. Simply shattered it.

Eve drank again. "Reward and punish. Praise and denigrate. It's how it works. Daphne's not a child, but she's got that softness so she'd have been a pretty easy mark. She's not me, but I understand her. And I should get back to her."

"Another minute," he replied gently.

Because she'd made him sad, Eve realized. Because she'd put the image of that scared and helpless little girl in his mind.

So she leaned in a little more. "We got an early enough start on things, so maybe if we plow through it, we can watch a vid. I feel like something fun, where the good guys and bad guys are over the top, and lots of things blow up."

"I think it's time to introduce you to *The Avengers*."

"Who are they? What are they avenging?"

"Your vid and graphic novel education is pitiful, darling. They're classics." Smiling, he turned his head to brush his lips to hers.

"Classic what?"

"Superheros who band together to save the world."

"Do they kick ass doing it?"

"Is there any other way?"

Now she smiled. "I'm in for that." And kissed him back.

Decided she could absolutely take a minute—or two—and added some punch to the kiss.

He set his wine aside so he could slide his arms around her.

No sadness, she thought, no harsh images. Now, only heat and pleasure for both of them.

She caught his bottom lip between her teeth, gave it a sharp little nip before she swung her leg over, straddled his lap. Then easing back, studying his face, she drained the rest of her wine.

"Should probably work off the alcohol."

She bowed back, lean and agile, set her empty glass beside his. Then flowed up, fast, latched her mouth to his, gripped his face with her hands as she plundered.

She rocked him to the core. She always could. That aggressive mouth lit lust's short fuse so he hardened like steel under her, so the hands digging into her hips shot up to close over her breasts.

"This time it's you wearing too many clothes." His fingers flicked open the buttons of her vest.

"We'll work around them because this has to be fast." she used her teeth on the side of his throat. "Hard and fast. Got me?"

"I've got you, and I'll be keeping you."

He dealt with her shirt, managed to tug the tank out of her waistband despite the weapon harness. And found it acutely arousing to possess her breasts with her weapon still strapped to her side.

He had a dangerous woman in his hands, and yes, he'd keep her.

She rocked against him, tormenting them both, and as if starved for the taste, ravaged his mouth.

Candlelight and snowfall provided a romantic backdrop, a soft contrast to the greedy lust they spurred in each other. New York gleamed, a frozen city through the glass, as she dragged at his belt.

"Fast and hard," she reminded him, her breath already tearing as she struggled to help him yank her trousers down past her knees.

She didn't wait, but took him in, muffled her own moan against his mouth.

She rode him like a stallion, spurred into a mad gallop that left him no choice but to race with her.

The world blurred. There was no world but her and that strong, glorious body, those wild, pistoning hips. She came like lightning, a snap and flash that bolted through him like a current.

Melting from it, she dropped her head on his shoulder. "Just need to catch my breath."

"You'll find it later."

Half mad he dragged her jacket down her arms, trapping them, shoving her back to open her more. Now he rode.

She couldn't free her arms, couldn't grab hold. Couldn't stop as the fresh orgasm built fast and brutal over the first.

"Roarke. I can't."

"Take. Just take."

He watched her, all but drowned in her. The crisp, professional clothes disheveled from his hands, the weapon at her side as much a part of her as a limb.

Her face warmed by sex and the candlelight alive with the crazed pleasure they brought each other.

And he watched as those eyes, those sharp and cynical cop's eyes, went blind from it.

He dragged her back, wrapped tight around her. Let himself break.

She shuddered against him, quaking aftershocks. Then fighting for breath, went lax.

"There you are." He pressed his face to the curve of her neck, simply overwhelmed by her. "Relaxed again."

"That was more than a minute."

"Time well spent. I adore you beyond reason, Eve."

"Who needs reason? But I guess we'll remember at some point to get naked first."

She eased back, laid a hand on his cheek. "I have to get back to it."

"So we will."

"I think I'm going to stop off, change clothes. Might as well get the comfort on."

"Another fine idea."

She swung off him, hitched up her trousers. "Was it hard? Not that," she said when he laughed, "because, obviously. I mean adjusting to me. The cop thing."

"Shockingly easy."

She shook her head as he rose, took her hand. "I never can figure it."

"Who needs reason?" he reminded her.

She changed into flannel pants, an ancient hooded sweatshirt and thick socks. She noted Roarke's choice wasn't so different from hers, but he somehow looked stylishly casual while she knew she just looked sloppy.

In her office she programmed coffee while Roarke strolled into the kitchen. He came out with two slabs of chocolate cake.

"Where'd you get that?"

"I just popped off to the cake factory." He set the dessert plates down on her command center. "Your AutoChef, Lieutenant."

"I had chocolate cake?" She took a bite, made a sound not dissimilar from one she'd made during sex. "I had really amazing chocolate cake?"

"Apparently. Now we both do."

"Excellent." And stuffing in a second bite, got back to work.

It took a couple hours, and more complications than she'd expected. What about the couple who'd been married in April but were divorced as of September? Or the couple who hadn't been married, but were now, like the Patricks?

She opted for different columns, and quashed the automatic annoyance when Roarke completed his half before she did.

He didn't interrupt her, simply got himself a brandy, then sat in front of her office fireplace, swirling and sipping and toying with his PPC.

She only had ten left, considered asking him to take half. Found the idea even more annoying so slogged through on her own.

She swung around. "I've got nine more," she told him. "That includes a married couple who attended, divorced shortly thereafter, and the male's already remarried. And two couples who weren't yet married, but now are married. According to the guest list, one of those couples attended with people who were set to but didn't end up getting married."

"I had eight, and that included a couple now newly married. It would fit, wouldn't it, as the Patricks were newly married at the time of the attack?"

"Exactly. So we'll assume he keeps up. Either because he's in that circle, or he uses the society and gossips media. Maybe all of that. One on my list is on the edge, age wise, as they're both into their fifties, and he's gone younger on the females. But, and this could be a connect, she's an actress. Mostly theater, but some screen, too. Nothing with On Screen that's listed."

"What's her name?"

Eve swung back to her list. "Gloria Grecian. Do you know her?"

"Of. I've seen her perform. Musical comedy."

"Makes sense. She's been married to Maurice Cartier, a choreographer for twelve years. We'll start making contact with the thirty-odd couples on the list tomorrow."

She looked toward the window. Had the snow thinned or was that just her own version of cheery optimism? "Nothing much we can do tonight."

"Are you still in the mood for a vid?"

"Yeah." She looked at the list, her board, accepted she'd just be turning in circles to keep at it now. "Yeah, I am. What's it again?"

"I thought we'd dive right in to *The Avengers* rather than take you through the individual vids establishing the characters."

"Superheroes."

"Exactly." He went to her, took her hand. "Ironman, for instance."

"Like Cal Ripken, Jr.?"

"Sorry?"

"Ha—got you on one. Cal Ripken, Iron Man Ripken—late-twentieth-century baseball player, Baltimore. Third base, shortstop. Still holds the record for most consecutive games played."

"You often amaze me," he said as they started out.

"Well, it's baseball. Ironman, but not like Ripken." Her eyes narrowed. "Is this porn?"

He laughed. "It isn't, no."

"Ironman sounds suspicious to me. What are the others?"

"There's Thor, the Hulk," he began.

"Sounds like porn."

"You'll see for yourself."

"I want popcorn," she decided. "It'll probably make me sick, but I want it."

"The way you saturate it with butter and salt, there's no doubt you'll be sick."

"I still want it," she said, also wanting to find out who the hell Ironman was if it didn't apply to sports or porn.

While she stretched out with Roarke—eating popcorn, watching the Hulk smash—a solitary figure walked the snow-covered sidewalks.

He was nearly as entertained at that moment as the woman hunting him.

No one would anticipate he'd perform again so soon, and he loved the idea of surprising the public. It was a perfect night for this opening. The blanketing snowfall, the whizzing wind, the empty streets while the city hunkered down inside their cozy mansions, their chilly cold-water flats, their flops, their gleaming towers.

He did love the city, and in these moments it felt as if it was his alone.

He wore a long black coat with a deep hood, for warmth and protection, and to conceal his face. No point in scaring any innocent bystander he might happen upon.

But the night and the city were his—the blizzard a kind of bonus, providing a wonderful atmosphere—he saw not another soul.

He'd done his research, of course. He was a professional. He drew out his jammer as he approached the lovely old brownstone. He'd admired it numerous times, its classic lines. its stately veneer.

Naturally he'd been inside as well. He always took a tour of the theater, planned his staging.

The house sat dark, his audience tucked into bed by now.

The five minutes it took him to bypass the alarms and the locks only added to the anticipation.

He opened the door. Death walked into the house, and chuckled softly in its throat.

14

Eve woke with a start, sat straight up, stared blankly at the simmering fire.

"All right?"

She turned her head to where Roarke sat with his coffee and his stock reports.

"Yeah. Just a weird dream."

"About?"

"*The Avengers* and that jerk Loki and his weird-ass army, and I'm trying to help them. Then I see this devil grab this bystander. Why are bystanders always standing by when they should be running and hiding somewhere?"

"A question for the ages."

"Right. So the devil—and I know in the dream it's the killer—is dragging the woman off, and she's screaming and crying instead of trying to kick his ass and get away. So I have to leave the aliens and gods and whatever to the Avengers and pursue. I'm chasing him, and buildings are toppling, debris is falling like an avalanche. New York's a frigging mess with more idiot bystanders running around screaming and waiting to get pancaked. And the devil, he jumps into this pit, just jumps right in. I put on the brakes, because it burps out some fire—the pit—and I'm trying to decide do I go in after him, try to save the woman, catch the killer, or try to keep New York from becoming a big pile of rubble.

"And I woke up."

"They could make an excellent vid if they could record your subconscious."

"They had swarma—the Avengers—after the whole battle of New York. I did an interview yesterday in an apartment over a swarma place. It's just weird. I need coffee."

She rolled out of bed, walked over to get her first cup, looked out the window. "It's going to take a couple days to dig out from under this."

"Better snow than avaricious gods and aliens."

"Yeah."

She grabbed a shower, came back to find breakfast. Not oatmeal but scrambled eggs, some bacon, toast with jam and the berries she thought nearly as good as candy.

"I'd figured stopping by to see Daphne, but I'm going straight into Central," she told him as they ate. "Not only to see who I can pull in for these interviews, but some people consider a blizzard a fine time to bludgeon, knife, or strangle somebody. Add in your accidentals and unattendeds, we could be busy."

"There'll be an A-T out front when you're ready."

"Thanks. Pretty quick actually." She shoved in the last of the eggs, stood to walk into the closet.

She wasn't the comp, or Roarke, but she could damn well dress herself. Especially since she was going for black—straight black— and warm.

She grabbed trousers, a sweater, a jacket, and because she'd likely be trudging through snow, black boots that rose to her knees.

When she stepped out, Roarke arched an eyebrow. "Black Widow couldn't look more dangerous or alluring."

"She could handle herself."

"See that you handle any bad guys who come at my cop."

"Dallas smash."

Pleased she'd made him laugh, she bent down to kiss him. "It was good, coming home together, and everything after. Makes it hard to be annoyed with the snow."

He tugged her down for another. "Mind the roads. They're bound to be an unholy mess."

"You, too. See you later."

She jogged downstairs, swung on her coat, wound a scarf around her neck for warmth, pulled on the snowflake hat, stuffed the gloves in her pockets.

And pulled them out and put them on when she stepped outside into the bitter.

The burly A-T in sober gray waited, already warm inside. She decided if she couldn't get downtown—or anywhere else—in this machine, she'd need a damn tank.

She drove down the perfectly cleared drive, through the gates and onto the god-awful mess of the street.

She didn't blame the road crews—or not much—as the snow had still been coming down when the Avengers beat the snot out of Loki and his team. The good part was the streets were nearly deserted. She spotted the road crews, a couple of emergency vehicles. Considering that, she tagged Peabody on her wrist unit.

"Can you get into Central?"

"Yeah. The subway should be running. Man, it's so pretty out there."

"Get in as soon as you can. If you need transpo, I've got an all-terrain."

"I'll check with Transport before we leave, make sure the trains are running. If not, I'll tag you. Only official and emergency vehicles allowed on the streets until oh-nine-hundred, so no cabs or buses."

"Yeah, and that's what I call pretty."

Eve clicked off and made her way downtown, easily breezing through blinking lights and empty intersections. Maybe, possibly . . . probably, she'd get bored with this kind of quiet, but for one morning's commute, she'd take it. Halfway downtown, she realized not a single ad blimp had drifted across the sky to blast its hyperactive news about sales on something, somewhere.

She'd definitely take it.

She noted when she reached the garage her level held only a scatter of vehicles. And the elevator carried no more than a handful of cops, several with snow melting off their boots, all the way to Homicide.

Maybe it was just a little spooky.

When she walked into her bullpen, she saw Baxter at his desk—kicked back in his chair, feet up, eyes closed. He wore one of his slick suits with an unknotted tie draped around his neck. She walked over, punched him in the shoulder.

He shot straight up, one hand slapping his weapon.

"Nap on your own time."

"Jesus. What time is it?" He looked blearily around the empty bullpen. "Where is everybody?"

"They'd better be en route."

"Right. Right." He scrubbed his face with both hands. "Trueheart and I caught one last night. Couple of guys decided it would be lots of fun to have lots and lots of drinks, smoke lots of illegals, and blast music loud enough people in apartments two floors down were complaining. Across-the-hall neighbor, who'd also done some copious drinking, decided, after several attempts to get them to knock it off, to bust in there and smash their player with a baseball bat. This action was cheered by many other occupants of the building, condemned by others.

"Violence ensued. Numerous injuries and one fatality."

"Snow makes some people crazier than they already are."

"Tell me. By the time we wrapped it up, it was too late and too bad out there to go home. We bunked in the crib. Might as well sidewalk sleep," he complained, trying to work kinks out of his neck and shoulders. "My boy's in the shower."

"But you wrapped it up?"

"Yeah, wrapped and packed. Report's in your box."

"Okay then. I'm pulling in you and Trueheart to conduct interviews."

Baxter's sleepy eyes cleared with interest. "The Strazza murder? The serial rapist Nikki's working?"

She glanced over as Trueheart came out of the locker room, his hair still showing damp from his shower, his young, earnest face all but dewy.

"Loo's drafted us, pal. Come on and get briefed."

"I'll copy you on the file," Eve began. "Basically, the suspect targets wealthy married couples, childless, in single-family residences. He possesses the skills to bypass their security, enter the residences. In the first two incidents, he laid in wait until the couple came home. In this last, he entered the premises during a dinner party, walked right by outside contractors and up the main stairs. He disables the male, restrains him."

She punched her way through the details, the connections, the theories.

"Using the guest list from this charity event all known victims attended, we've extrapolated most likely future targets. It's probable he's attended other events and functions, earmarked targets there, but it's a decent bet there'll be some cross. I'm going to give you five. Arrange face-to-faces, walk them through what they need to know, find out if they use the caterer, the rental place, know or socialize with any of the other vics. You know the drill."

"We'll get it covered, boss."

"Um, Lieutenant?" Trueheart half raised his hand. "Our usual vehicle probably won't handle the current road conditions."

"Requisition an all-terrain."

She glanced around as Jenkinson came in, snarling, his blinding white snowflakes on a fiery red background tie leading.

"Didn't they *know* it was coming?" he demanded of his partner as Reineke, smirking some, came in with him. "Didn't they?" He threw out his arms to the nearly empty bullpen.

"Problem, Jenkinson?" Eve asked.

"Yeah, there's a problem. Damn straight there's a problem with the basic infrastructure and maintenance of this city we serve and protect."

Reineke slapped Jenkinson's arm. "I'm gonna get us come coffee, partner." So saying he walked toward the break room, giving Eve a wild eye roll on the way.

"Weather guys all say the storm's coming. Hold on to your asses, boys, it's gonna hit. But are we prepared?" Jenkinson demanded, arms out like an evangelist preaching to the flock. "No, we are not."

He tossed his coat on his desk chair, stomping that way on boots crusted with snow.

"I was fucking prepared. I tag my kids, tell them to get over to the skinny-ass garage I pay my left nut for every month, clear the snow from the door so I can get my vehicle in there. And they do, my kids do the job, so I get home, parked it up. And what do you think happened? I'll tell you what happened," he ranted, before Eve could respond. "I come out this morning, wade down there over sidewalks nobody's cleared along streets the crews have half-assly cleared, and see they've shoved a couple feet of that fucking snow right in front of the garage door. What the fuck, LT!"

"Bastards."

"Damn straight. Ends up, I flag down a black-and-white to haul me in, pick up Reineke. And my kids are bitching—can't blame 'em— that they've got to go back over, dig me out a-fucking-gain."

"Requisition an all-terrain."

He opened his mouth, more raging on the tip of his tongue. Then angled his head. "Yeah?"

"Yeah. You might as well have one on tap in case, and do it now before everybody else gets the same idea and we're out. Meanwhile, you and Reineke hold down the fort."

Reineke came out with coffee, shoved one at Jenkinson. "Tell him it's not going to do any good to call and bitch at the mayor, Dallas."

"It's not going to do any good to call and bitch at the mayor."

Jenkinson's face settled into a haughty sulk. "It's the principle."

"It's the politics," Eve corrected. "I need you holding the wheel if I don't make it back in from the field today. Remember?" She gestured to the squad slogan posted over the break room wall. "That holds for before, during, and after snowstorms and shitty road-crew work."

Jenkinson sighed, gulped coffee. "Yeah, but I bet nobody blocked the mayor's car in."

"Five'll get you ten the mayor's buried under irate 'link calls, e-mails, v-mails, and texts this morning."

The idea had Jenkinson brightening. "Yeah. Yeah, that's something."

"If Peabody comes in, tell her to keep her coat on. We're heading out in ten."

Eve escaped to her office, got her own coffee. At her desk, she sent the list to Olsen and Tredway, to Baxter and Trueheart, earmarking names for each team to contact. She sent Baxter and Trueheart a copy of the case file, put a brief update together for Olsen and Tredway.

She skimmed Baxter's report on the case they'd closed, found it—as expected—competent and thorough. Noted Carmichael and Santiago had caught one at roughly six-thirty that morning. Bludgeoning with a snow shovel.

Yeah, snow could make some people crazier than they already were.

She walked out to see Peabody, and a couple of uniforms who'd just logged in, listening while Jenkinson ran through his rant again.

"Peabody, with me."

Peabody trotted to catch up. "Jenkinson's on a tear."

"I know. He already ripped through it once. Do I need to catch you up?"

"I read the update on the subway. No problem getting a seat this morning. Lots taking a snow day or working at home."

"I sent our share of the list to your PPC. Start plugging in addresses when we get to the garage."

"Do you want me to contact the couples first?"

"Let's just do drop bys, see how it goes. Plug in the bartender/actor. We'll pay him a visit."

"Anson Wright—changed his name from George Splitsky when he turned eighteen. I ran through his education—average student, except in drama, theater, and stagecraft. There he excelled. Performed and participated in all the school plays, and even got a couple of walkons and minor parts on and off Broadway as a child and young teen."

When they got to the car, Peabody took out her book, began transferring addresses. "Hit a dry spell, took a bartending class, joined the community players. He's got an agent, and apparently goes out for auditions. Gets a part now and then. Nothing he could live on, and he lives pretty close to the top line of his income. When I worked my way through the maze, I found out he's the nephew of the step-mother of the head waitress's cohab."

Peabody ordered the in-dash to list the addresses in order of distance. "Looks like our closest is Dana Mireball and Lorenzo Angelini, both artists, Tribeca."

Roarke's A-T laughed at shitty road-crew work, and muscled its way over the snow-crusted ice with a smooth, satisfied hum. The sun decided to bust out—which brought out the carts, the street vendors with scarves, caps, gloves, shovels, gray-market boots, and window scrapers.

Pedestrians began to pick their way along sidewalks. Kids, busted out of school for the day, raced, airboarded, and generally looked maniacally happy.

By the time they'd worked through the first five on the list, the traffic was back in force. The air blimps boomed out the thrill of the Blizzard of '61 sales.

Eve hated to admit it, but it all felt more normal.

They moved from arty loft to dignified townhouse, from slick converted warehouse to ultra-modern residence.

She didn't feel a real buzz until number seven on the list.

Toya L'Page and Gray Burroughs lived in what had once been a church in Turtle Bay. The tall, arched doors opened directly onto the sidewalk. The stained-glass window over it gleamed color in the winter sun.

Eve gave her information and her badge for screening to the door comp, waiting until that door opened. A teenage girl with short, spiky, plum-colored hair peered at Eve with enormous brown eyes.

"Are you really cops?" she demanded.

Eve held up her badge again, and the girl sniffed.

"Like you can't buy fake ID."

"Lieutenant Dallas, Detective Peabody. Check with Cop Central if you're worried about it. Otherwise we'd like to speak to Toya L'Page and/or Gray Burroughs."

The kid cocked her hip—bodily snark. "Maybe they're busy."

"Why don't you find out?"

"Gemma, you're letting the cold in. You need to . . . Oh, sorry."

Eve had seen a slice of beautiful women on this investigation. Toya L'Page towered over the rest.

She easily hit six feet in her skids, and all of it willowy and perfect. Her skin appeared poreless, without artifice, a rich, deep brown smooth over knife-edged cheekbones. Her mouth, full, sharply sculpted curved slightly. Large, tawny eyes showed caution and curiosity as she moved quickly to the door. Subtly draped an arm around the girl's shoulders, putting herself between Gemma and Eve.

"Can I help you?"

"She says they're cops," Gemma announced, with ripe skepticism.

"Oh. Could I see some . . ." She trailed off as Eve held up her badge again. "Yes, of course. Can I ask what this is about?"

"We'd just like to ask you, and your husband if he's available, some questions in connection with an investigation."

"No way Toya or Gray did anything illegal. They're totally equidistance."

"We're making inquiries," Eve continued, "hoping for assistance in an investigation. Can we come in, Ms. L'Page? We won't take up much of your time."

"Of course. I apologize."

"You don't have to let them in without a warrant."

"All right, Gemma." Toya leaned down, brushed her lips to the girl's temple. "My sister-in-law is very protective. Please come in."

"You live here?" Eve asked the girl.

"I could if I wanted."

"Gemma's just hanging, right, Gemma? We're going to try for some skating and sledding later. Will you go tell Gray to come down?"

Gemma shot Eve a warning look, then dashed to a staircase on the side of a spacious, open-concept entrance and living area. Light from the stained glass scattered over old wooden plank floors like jewels.

"This is a beautiful home, Ms. L'Page," Peabody commented, head swiveling to take in the high ceilings, arched windows, massive fireplace.

"Thank you. We just love it. We're still tweaking a few things. Please sit." She gestured to high-backed chairs near the roaring fire, settled herself on a curvy sofa with carved wood trim.

"It was a church pre-Urbans. A nondenominational church and a community gathering place. It served as a shelter and a hospital during the wars, and was abandoned after for some time."

"You were able to save some of the original features."

"Some, and some we reconstructed. My husband's an architect, and he simply fell in love with the building. His father had bought it, mostly for sentiment as he'd worked here, as a medical, during the Urbans."

She was trying, Eve observed, to be polite, not to show nerves. So Eve let Peabody chat her up.

"My father and my brother are carpenters. They'd really appreciate what you've done here. How long have you lived here?"

"This is year three. We don't count the year before that as it was full of workers and we only stayed occasionally. Sort of camping out.

Gray." Toya got to her feet when her husband came in, Gemma all but glued to his side.

He was tall like his wife, gym-fit, with a striking face with features that made Eve think of exotic islands with grass skirts and tiki huts.

"Is there a problem?"

Eve stood. "We'd like to ask you a few questions in connection with an investigation."

He gave his sister a narrow stare. "Gemma."

"I didn't do anything! And it was a scavenger hunt. I wasn't *stealing*. Plus, they're Homicide. I looked them up before I went to get you. Somebody's dead, and we sure as hell didn't kill anybody."

"Homicide?" Toya wrapped her long, elegant fingers around Gray's arm.

"Anthony Strazza."

"Oh, God. We heard about that. It's terrible. Just terrible."

"Did you know Dr. Strazza or his wife?"

"We never met his wife. Sit down, Toya." Gray tugged her down on the couch, glanced at his sister. "Gemma, go ask Pauline to make coffee."

"You're just trying to get rid of me."

"I am getting rid of you. Go ask Pauline to make coffee."

Gemma rolled her eyes, but stomped off.

"She'll have heard any way," Gray said, "or she'll look it up. I don't know how we can possibly help your investigation."

"You knew Dr. Strazza?"

"He operated on my great-grandfather," Toya told them. "Last winter after he fell and broke his hip, and his wrist. He was out walking the dog, in weather much like this, and he slipped and fell. Late at night, and no one heard him calling for help for more than an hour. I absolutely believe Dr. Strazza saved his life. I met him at the hospital— or we did. and I took Poppy in for follow-ups a few times."

"You've never socialized?"

"Not really. I realized we'd attended some of the same events and functions. And, it turned out we have some mutual acquaintances."

"Could you give me those names?"

"Did she read you the Revised Miranda?" Gemma demanded as she rushed back in. "She's supposed to, and if she hasn't—"

"Look, kid," Eve interrupted. "Nobody here is under arrest or under suspicion. A man's dead and a woman's in the hospital recovering from a brutal attack. My job is to find out who did that to them. I'm going to do my job, so stop showing off."

Gemma sulked, but she shut up and sat down beside her brother who disguised a laugh with a cough. "You should go on upstairs, sweetie."

"I know what happened. I looked it up. Besides Junie's mother was there that night."

"Who is Junie, and who is her mother?" Eve demanded.

"I don't have to say."

Eve shifted back to the adults. "If I could have those names," she began.

"Junie Wyatt. Her mom's Catherine Frummon. You guys don't know her mom," Gemma said to her brother and Toya, "Junie mostly lives with her dad."

"Abbott Wyatt," Toya supplied. "They've been divorced for years, as far as I know."

"Okay. Anything else?" Eve asked Gemma.

"Junie said her mom went whacked after it happened because Oh My God! She was *there,* and she could've been attacked or *murdered.* Like that. It's always all about her mom with her mom. And she said how Dr. Strazza's wife probably did something stupid so Dr. Strazza got killed because she thinks his wife is stupid and a gold digger and a trophy. Junie's mom is a bitch."

"Gemma!"

Gemma looked around her brother, and her sister-in-law. "If you knew her, you'd say the same. I'm not going to lie to the police. That's a crime." So saying, she smiled. "Right?"

"I can't argue."

Toya let out a sigh. "Off the top of my head—and you may have others, Gray—the mutual acquaintances would be Junie's dad, Abbott Wyatt . . ."

The housekeeper or cook or whatever she was rolled in a cart. To Eve's surprise, Gemma hopped right up. "I've got it Miss P, thanks." And began to pour and serve while Toya ran down a list of people.

"Okay. Can you tell me if you've ever used Jacko's Catering?"

"All the time. We're terrible cooks, and don't mind staying that way," Toya said. "Pauline will often make meals for the AutoChef before she goes home for the evening, or we'll do local delivery or take out. And we eat out a lot. But Jacko's is a favorite if we've having friends or family over. Not to serve unless it's a bigger party, but they have a terrific menu and they deliver so I can set it up as if I've fussed for hours."

"Nobody's fooled," Gray reminded her.

"No, but it's all in the presentation."

"How about Loan Star Rentals?"

The quick amusement faded out of Gray's face. "I've used them for staging a project, and we used them when we were working on this house, staying here occasionally. We didn't want to furnish it until we'd made real progress. How does this apply?"

"We're connecting dots," was all Eve would say. "According to our information you both attended the Celebrate Art Gala in April of last year. Is that correct?"

"Yes. We missed the year before because Gray was on a project out of town, and I didn't want to go alone. It's no fun without him."

"I'd like you to think back to that night. Who you met, who you spoke with. There was dancing. You probably danced with other people."

"We had a table of friends," Toya recalled. "It's a lovely evening, really one of my favorite events. We spoke to so many people . . . I couldn't begin. Gray?"

"It's a social evening," he continued. "We had a lot of friendly competition in our group and some others we know on a couple of items in the silent auction."

"Anyone who stands out for any reason. Anyone who bothered you or made you uncomfortable?"

"Mavis Freestone was there—talk about a standout. I actually stalked her into the ladies lounge and begged an autograph and a selfie for Gemma."

"You a fan?" Eve asked Gemma.

"Anybody who isn't is wheeze. She's the ult."

"Yeah, she's pretty much the ult."

Gemma eyed Eve, considering. "You're into Mavis?"

"You could say that."

"She was so sweet about it," Toya added, "even later when I stalked her husband, who's one of my favorite designers. They're such a striking couple, and I loved meeting them. It was the high point of the night for me."

"Every time I turned around Toya was off trying for another sighting."

"I wasn't that bad." Batting her husband's arm, Toya laughed. "And I stepped out a few times so Gemma and I could text our mutual excitement. That was when—" She broke off, frowned.

"When?" Eve prompted.

"Oh, nothing. Just a minor annoyance. Not worth mentioning."

"I'd like you to mention it."

"Well, it's nothing, really, but it did bother me at the time. I was in this little nook, texting Gemma, and this man sort of blocked me in."

"What?"

"It was nothing," Toya repeated, rubbing Gray's arm when he reacted. "Honestly. I said, 'Excuse me,' or something along those lines, and stepped forward. But he didn't step back right away. He said he'd noticed I was alone, and said I should join him for a drink. I said I was there with my husband."

"That was it?" Eve asked.

"That's the gist of it."

"So he backed off when you told him you were there with your husband."

Now Toya shifted. "Not immediately."

"Damn it, Toya, why didn't you tell me?"

"Because you'd have confronted him, and it wasn't really anything. I just didn't like . . . He blocked me for just a few more seconds, it was deliberate, I guess, and I didn't like the way he looked at me. But then he just smiled and walked away."

"Did he touch you?" Eve asked.

"No. No, he did not. He invaded my space, absolutely, and it was a narrow opening to the little nook so I couldn't have gotten past him without touching him, and I didn't want to. He didn't say anything offensive. He thought I was alone, asked me to have a drink, I said no, I'm with my husband. He didn't say anything else. But it was the body language and the look in his eyes that, I guess, insulted me, and intimidated."

"Can you describe him?"

"Oh, I don't really think so. It was nearly a year ago, only about half a minute at most, and it was a little dim there. Ah, he was white, I'm fairly certain, and probably in his thirties? But I'm not altogether sure."

"You're about six feet, right?"

"On the money."

"Glam event like that, you'd be in heels."

"Absolutely. I love a good shoe."

"Was he tall, like your husband?"

"No. Shorter than me, by far. But a lot of men are shorter than me, especially when I hit six-four in heels."

"Build?"

"Average?" Toya posed it like a question. "I'm sorry. That's pathetic, but I didn't pay attention. I just wanted him to move away."

"Okay. If any more details come to you, I want you to contact me."

"Why is this important?" Gray asked.

Eve turned her head, gave Gemma a cool stare. Gemma just shrugged.

"You can send me out, but I know where to go to listen. Plus, I'll get it out of Toya. I have ways of making her talk. She's my sister," Gemma added, reminding Eve of Tish DeSilva. "We look out for each other."

"We believe the man responsible for the attack on the Strazzas, and two previous attacks, attended that gala. We've been able to discern a certain pattern to this individual's selection of targets. The two of you fit that pattern."

"How?" Gray spoke more steadily than she'd expected. He slid an arm around his sister, took his wife's hand, but spoke steadily. "We need to know."

"Wealthy married couples who live alone in single-family residences. No children. Good security that is, nonetheless, compromised. In each case, the wife has been particularly attractive. Beautiful, striking. You fit on every point.

"You should know," Eve continued, "we've spoken with several others who fit this pattern, and have several more to speak to. However, to this point you're the only ones who knew one of the other victims personally, and use the two vendors we discussed. And the only one who's mentioned, when asked, any sort of incident or uncomfortable situation at this event."

"What should we do?" Toya managed.

"I'm staying." Gemma said it fiercely. "Live alone, no kids, I can cross off two of those, so I'm staying. You can't make me go."

"Oh, yes, I can," her brother corrected.

"If you make me go I'll find a way to get back. I will!"

He poked her between the eyes. "I'll hire security. Private security. We'll have professional security in the house, around the clock, until you find this maniac. I'll arrange that right away."

"That's a good precaution. If you go out, don't leave the house unattended. He may do test runs—may enter the empty house to get a feel for it. Let the security you hire make themselves known. They shouldn't be subtle about it. Sorry."

Eve pulled out her signaling communicator. "Dallas, text only," she ordered.

Dallas, Lieutenant Eve, see the officer at 2751 Morton. Reported double homicide. Male and female, possibly connected to current investigation.

"Acknowledged." Eve got to her feet. "You've been helpful. If you remember anything else, or if you see or hear even feel something that concerns you, contact me. Peabody, give them a couple cards. If she talks you into letting her stay here?" Eve gave Gemma a glance.

"I *am* staying."

"Okay. Don't be subtle about that, either. He's a coward, he attacks from behind. He's not going to want to try for you when you've got a teenager and a security guard in the house."

When they stepped outside, Peabody glanced back. "We've got another."

"We've got another."

Peabody gave the house a last glance before trudging to the car. "I think they're going to be okay. They're forewarned, they'll take precautions."

And, Eve thought, there are two dead who weren't forewarned, hadn't had the chance to take precautions.

15

EVE PULLED UP TO THE PRETTY BROWNSTONE, DOUBLE-PARKED, THEN engaged her On Duty light.

"They're on the list," Peabody said. "Ours. We were circling back this way, would have hit them after one more stop."

"I know it." Eve shoved out, strode through the slush, kicked through a mound of piled snow to get field kits from the back.

She asked herself a dozen times on the drive downtown if she'd opted to go crosstown, hit the East Side first, would it have made any difference?

No point in asking, she told herself as they moved across the slippery sidewalk.

"Front steps are clear," she noted. "Let's find out if the occupants handled that or hired it out. The snow didn't stop until close to midnight."

She studied the security cam over the door—off—then the locks.

"No palm pad. This is a voice recognition system. Two locks, good ones, and a swipe. Get EDD down here to go over this. Record on."

Before she could press the buzzer, a beat droid opened the door.

"Identification, please," he said.

Eve held up her badge so the droid, broad shoulders, nonthreatening face, could scan.

"Lieutenant, Detective." The droid stepped back to admit them.

"Report."

"Sir. My partner and I received instructions from Dispatch at thirteen-twenty-four to see the woman at this address. Nina Washington, identified as the housekeeper for this residence contacted nine-one-one from this location at thirteen-twenty-three and reported two bodies she discovered in what appears to be the master bedroom on the second floor. We arrived on scene at thirteen-twenty-seven and verified this information. The deceased—one male, one female— have been unofficially identified by Nina Washington as Xavier and Miko Carver, of this address."

"Where is the witness?"

"Sir. Ms. Washington is in the kitchen area of this residence with my partner."

"Tag your partner, inform him Homicide is on scene. Keep the witness contained. EDD is on the way. Until such time as I clear it, no one else is to come in, go out."

"Yes, sir."

She sidestepped him, scanned the long, narrow entranceway. Caught the scent of . . . oranges.

"Does the housekeeper live in?" she asked the droid.

"No, sir. Ms. Washington states she arrived at ten this morning."

"Ten, and the nine-one-one came in at thirteen-twenty?"

"Thirteen twenty-three to be precise, Lieutenant. That is correct."

With a nod, Eve walked to the stairs—narrow and straight—started up.

"She comes in—does she notice the cam's not on? Maybe not," Eve said. "She just comes in as usual, and starts work on the main level. You can still smell the cleaner—citrus type—and the flowers in the entrance look fresh. She might have brought them with her."

"Does the cleaning, the polishing," Peabody agreed.

On the second floor, they glanced in doorways. Guest room, home office, a kind of office/sitting room, another guest room. Eve noted someone had brushed a few swipes of different color paint on one of the walls.

"Thinking about redoing the room," Peabody commented. "Testing wall colors."

They wouldn't pick one now, Eve thought as she turned, looking into the master directly across the hall.

Xavier Carver remained bound in a chair. His head slumped toward his bloodied chest. Blood pooled beneath the chair, soaking the soft seagreen of the carpet, and streaked over the walls where his severed jugular had streamed and spattered in mad patterns.

What she could see of his face was blackened from a beating.

He wore only plain black boxers.

She took the can of Seal-It Peabody held out, coated her hands, her boots. Taking off her coat, scarf, hat, she left them in a pile outside the room.

The bed nestled in a wide nook with white pedestal tables on either side, sleek silver pendant lights spearing down from the ceiling. Hands bound, secured above her head to the fancy work of the headboard, Miko lay naked on bloodstained sheets.

The flesh of her torso showed slices where he'd cut her in random patterns, as well as discolorations from blows. Her eyes, filmed over with death, stared out of a face battered by violence. Dried blood smeared the sides of her mouth, her chin, streaked her thighs.

The cord used to strangle her dug viciously into her throat.

She'd been beautiful once, Eve thought. The killer had taken her beauty as well as her life.

Was that part of his need?

"Take the male," Eve ordered, and approached the bed.

She followed procedure, step-by-step, cleared her mind of pity, of outrage. "Female is identified as Carver, Miko, age thirty-three of this address."

"Male is identified as Carver, Xavier, age, thirty-three, of this address."

She left Peabody to add the details for the record, focused on adding her own. "Shallow cuts, primarily on the torso, evidence of blows, also to torso, to breasts. More violent blows to the face. Victim bit through her own lip. Lacerations and bleeding evident on the wrists around the zip ties used to bind them, the cord tied over that to secure her hands to the headboard. Further lacerations and bleeding on the ankles indicating binding at some point during the assault. Blood and bruising on the inner thighs indicate probable rape. A cord around the victim's throat, used to strangle. Hemorrhaging in the eyes indicate strangulation, probable COD. ME to confirm."

Eve stepped back. "Let's turn her, Peabody."

"He broke the vic's fingers." Peabody straightened, walked to Eve. "It looks like he smashed them with something heavy."

Eve glanced back. "The last vic got loose, came at him. Break this one's hands, he's not going to be able to use them in a fight, if he gets loose."

"Miserable coward bastard," Peabody muttered as they turned Miko's body over. "Oh hell."

"Sodomized her," Eve said flatly. "That's new. No other injuries to the back."

Eve stepped away, nodded at the red pajamas on the floor. "Pajamas. And the male is wearing boxers. He didn't break in while they were out this time, and if they had people over, he didn't break in and wait for them to come upstairs."

"They'd gone to bed," Peabody finished. "They were in bed, probably sleeping, when he broke in. He hasn't done that before."

"He's trying new tricks. He's escalating on all his elements, getting bolder. Only days between assaults now. And two deliberate murders. Not his usual rape, torture, beatings, and an in-the-moment killing. Two deliberate murders."

She walked back to the doorway, studied the scene.

"He waits until late, until they've gone to bed. It's a great night for it. Empty streets, empty sidewalks, people holed up at home. How did he get here? Couldn't drive unless he got his hands on an official vehicle. Subway, possible. Let's contact TA, find out how late the subways ran last night. Walk? Would it be so sweet to him he'd be willing to walk?"

"Unless he brought a change of clothes, he'd have been covered with blood when he left."

"He'd be prepared. He came here to kill, and messily. He circumvents the alarms, the locks. Did his research. They live alone. Daytime housekeeper.

"He walks upstairs. It's exciting, walking in the dark, in a house where people are sleeping. It really adds something . . . fresh. He'd take out the male first."

She walked back to the bed, to the far side. "*Whap-slap* with the sap—that's what I'd do if I didn't have a stunner. He's out, no threat. Does she stir—even if she does, he's on her. He has the knife, the cord. Bind her up while she screams. Give her a couple of slaps to show her who's in charge."

She moved to the male victim, lifted one of his bare feet out of the congealed blood. "Drag marks on the heels. He doesn't have enough muscle to carry the husband to the chair, but enough to drag him, haul him into it. Bind him up. Now he gets to play."

"He wants the husband conscious before he works on the wife," Peabody said.

"That's right. Wants him awake and aware for that, and before he breaks his fingers. No fun causing pain if nobody feels it. But he's got plenty of time."

She could see it, could see all of it.

It played through her mind while she walked to the closet.

"Check the bathroom, Peabody. Big shared closet, and a safe, open and empty in here."

"Bathroom's clean, Dallas. It looks like somebody took a bath. There's bath oil, a bottle of it, by the tub, and a towel, unfolded, draped over the rack.

Curious, Eve moved to the bath, scanned. "He wouldn't have done that." Eve opened the bottle, sniffed. "Very girlie. Most likely the female vic took a bath, or possibly took one with the male vic, but only one towel, no drying tube, so likely just her. Morris may be able to confirm. Pull the sweepers in. They'll check the drains anyway. And get the morgue team in."

She stepped back out. "Why don't you go through the rest of the rooms up here, see if there's anything? Then take a look at the third floor. I'll start with the housekeeper."

"Back stairs down the hall probably lead to the kitchen."

Peabody checked her 'link. "McNab. He and Feeney are on the way."

With a nod, Eve took the back stairs.

The kitchen area had been modernized. The working kitchen itself spread bright and shining clean, a bowl of glossy red apples piled in a white bowl on the main counter. The majority of space flowed for entertaining. A long dining table painted a soft, faded blue was lined with chairs covered in a cheerful floral print. Another table, tall and narrow served as a bar. Its deeper blue surface held fancy decanters and bottles. Shelves behind it displayed stemware.

A female officer sat at the table with a middle-aged woman. The woman's eyes, swollen and red-rimmed, still leaked tears.

"I'm going to be close by, Nina," the uniform said as she patted the woman's hand and rose. "Lieutenant."

"Thank you, Officer. If you and your partner would begin the canvass, I'll speak to Ms. Washington."

"Yes, sir."

Eve sat. "Ms. Washington, I'm Lieutenant Dallas. I know this is difficult. Can you tell me how long you've been employed here?"

"In this house, five years. For my Miko? I worked for her mother since Miko was ten, and I came to work for Miko when she and Xavier moved into this house."

"You were close."

"I have two children. Miko was like my third. And Xavier. I loved him, too. Who would . . ." She shook her head, pressed her fingers to her eyes. "I know there's evil, I know. But this? They were so young and so *good*, so happy. So happy. Miko was pregnant."

Eve sat back, felt her stomach twist. "You're sure?"

"Only a few weeks. She told her mother, and they told Xavier's parents, and me. Only last week. Only last week, and we were so happy."

"I'm sorry, Ms. Washington. I'm very sorry for your loss. And I know it's painful, but I need to ask you some questions."

"I know. I told Officer Aaron some. She said I'd have to tell you, and more."

"Did you work here yesterday?"

"No."

Nina drew air through her nose, brushed both hands back over the hair she wore in a single thick braid. After knuckling a tear away, she clasped her hands together on the table.

"No, I didn't come in yesterday. Miko said the snow was coming, and it was supposed to be very bad. She said I should stay home, and everything was fine. She was at her work. She helps at a homeless shelter. She does good work. She said she was leaving early, and Xavier was coming home early, too. She said they were going to come home and stay home."

"Is that the last you spoke to her?"

"It was in the morning, about eight, and she texted me in the afternoon, when she got home, and Xavier got home. Just so I knew. I think it was around three-thirty. She said not to come today early, and not to come at all unless it was clear enough." Nina's voice wobbled again. "She took care of me, too."

"So you didn't come here today until ten."

"I usually come at nine. Sometimes Miko's here until later, and sometimes she goes to the shelter to help earlier. I thought they'd gone to work. I thought . . ."

"So you started your work."

"Yes. I cleaned off the steps outside. It was only a couple inches, and I thought Xavier cleaned them off before they went to bed, but it snowed more. I cleaned them off so it wouldn't be slippery when they got home from work, and then I started in here. I picked up the apples and some flowers on my way here, so I washed the apples, and put the flowers in the vase. She likes fresh flowers. I cleaned the kitchen, and put away the dishes from the dishwasher.

"I'd have gone upstairs sooner, because I do laundry on Mondays and Fridays, but I wasn't thinking. I wasn't here to do the laundry on Monday, but I wasn't thinking, so I didn't go upstairs to get it."

"Okay. You're doing fine."

Nina pressed her lips together. "I cleaned the dining area, and the sitting room. Scrubbed the powder room, and changed the guest towels, and all the things I do. I—I had an apple and some yogurt, and sat there, over there at the counter and watched a show I like on my break. And all that time, they were—"

"Ms. Washington."

"Nina. Everyone calls me Nina."

"Nina, you were taking care of them. Let me ask you if, when you were cleaning down here, did you notice anything missing or out of place?"

"Miko's Daum dragon. It's not in the living area, but sometimes she puts it upstairs. And in the sitting room, the old nested wooden boxes Xavier's grandfather made years and years ago. But I didn't think—"

"That's okay."

"I turned the droid on to vacuum down here, and I thought, all of a sudden: For God's sake, the laundry. I was annoyed with myself, went right upstairs. I always change their sheets on Mondays and Fridays and do the laundry. I walked right into their bedroom, and— I saw them. I saw Xavier and my Miko."

She began to weep again, fast, fat tears.

"Did you go into the room, Nina, did you touch anything?"

"A few steps in, because I wasn't thinking, and I saw them and I screamed. I screamed and screamed, and I fell down. I just fell. I couldn't stand up at first. I couldn't get up again. There was so much blood, so much, and I could see they were gone. I could see I couldn't save them. I had to crawl away because I couldn't stand up. I was going to be sick, but I *wouldn't* be sick."

Anger slashed through the grief-thickened voice. "I had to get help, but I couldn't stop shaking. I dropped my 'link because my hands were shaking, then I made myself stop, and I called for help. The person who answered said help would come, and she'd stay with me. She kept talking to me even when I couldn't stop crying. And when the police came she told me to let them in, so I did. I—I have to call her mother. I have to tell his parents."

"We're going to take care of that." Eve glanced over when Peabody came in. "This is Detective Peabody. She'll contact someone if you want someone to come, be with you."

"I don't know. I don't know."

"Think about it. Give me just a minute."

She gestured Peabody, stepped out of the room. "She holds up, and so does her timeline. She thought they were at work, didn't come in yesterday as the female vic told her not to because of the snow. They were tight. A couple of things missing from down here. She cleared off the steps this morning."

"Might be some missing items from the second floor. Third floor's like a media room/lounge deal. It looks like the vics settled in up there, watched a couple of vids, some dishes—looks like movie snacks. A glass—I think juice. Only one wineglass. Maybe the killer had some wine."

"No, more likely the male vic. Female was pregnant."

"Oh hell. Goddamn it." Peabody hissed out a breath. "The paint. Probably going to make that the nursery, the room right across from the master."

Peabody shook it off, but her jaw stayed hard. "McNab and Feeney just got here. They're on the door."

"Stick with the witness."

She walked out, found McNab and Feeney running a diagnostic on the alarms. "Didn't expect the boss."

Feeney, his magic coat open to reveal his rumpled shit-brown suit, scrubbed a hand over his wiry silver-threaded ginger hair. "I was going stir-crazy." EDD's captain and Eve's former partner turned his basset-hound eyes to her. "Took out both of them this time?"

"Both, and did a lot more damage first. Did he jam the system?"

"He did that." McNab jiggled his skinny, plaid-covered hips while he worked. "Slick job, too. It's a solid system, not the best, but solid. One of the troubles is, for convenience, the owner or tenant can set or turn off the system remotely. From in or out of the house. That's the kind of gap, unless it's extreme top line, a good B and E man juices over."

"How many times do we tell people that?" Feeney said to McNab.

"Infinity, boss. Infinity."

"Well, let's see the setup. Where is it?"

"I haven't gotten there," Eve told Feeney. "Kitchen area has a utility room off it from my quick glance. Maybe there. Peabody's in there with the housekeeper. She found them."

"Tough luck all around."

He nodded when Eve opened the door for the morgue team, directed them upstairs.

"Yeah, tough luck all around. Here come your sweepers."

In minutes, cops and techs were spread over the crime scene. The uniforms completed the canvass of the neighbors, reported no one—who was now home—had seen anyone or anything.

Hardly surprising, Eve thought as she watched the morgue team bring down the bagged bodies. People hunkered down in a snowstorm, drank, had sex, watched vids, read books, whatever.

Then again, some couldn't resist heading out in it, playing around in a city gone white and still. Maybe, just maybe, they'd still find some of those. Just one witness who'd seen someone around this house.

Once the morgue team left, Eve went back to the dining area, sat again.

"Nina's just given me her brother's contact information." Peabody nudged the glass of water closer to Nina's hand. "I'm going to have him come and pick her up, or stay with her until she can go."

"Good. You can go pretty soon. I have something I need to ask you to do. A hard thing for you to do, but it will help us."

"It'll help you find the son of a bitch who hurt my kids?"

"I think so."

"Nothing's too hard, not for that. I'll do anything."

"I need you to come upstairs with me." Eve kept her gaze steady as the color drained out of Nina's face. "I need you to look at Nina's clothes. Her closet. Her cocktail dresses and outfits especially. Would you know if one of them is missing?"

"I know her clothes. I'd know. I'd know. Is she—are they still up there?"

"No. They're not upstairs now. They're going to someone who's going to take care of them. He's the best."

"Can I go where they are and see them? After? Miko's mom, especially, Miko's mom, she'll need me with her."

"Yes. We'll let you know when you can do that."

"Okay. Okay." She squeezed her eyes shut, then rose. "I can go up with you and look."

They started up the back stairs.

"I want you to do what I tell you. I want you to look down, keep looking down when we go in. I don't want you to look at the room. There's no need for that."

"I'll see it in my head until the day I die."

"Just look down," Eve repeated, taking Nina's arm to steer her inside and into the closet. "Okay, now take your time, take a good look through."

"I don't have to. Her new red cocktail dress is gone. She hasn't even worn it yet. She bought it special for a Valentine's Day party, and it was right here—you see? She said I should take this other red one for my girl. They're near the same size. And the one that was on the other side of it, the dark pink one? It's crooked on the hanger, like somebody hit it, knocked it some when they pulled the new one out."

"Red cocktail dress. Short?"

"Short—she has beautiful legs. With a sweetheart neckline." Nina drew the top of a heart in the air. "Three layers of flounces on the skirt, and a little silver bow in the back at the waist. Shoes are missing, too. Silver evening shoes with tiny red metallic bows on the backs."

She moved deeper into the closet, a woman on a mission now. "He took her jewelry, from the safe back here. That evil bastard took their things from the safe. She had her great-grandmother's ruby pendant in there. She was going to wear it with the dress, and the earrings Xavier gave her for Christmas, just this past Christmas. Diamond drops with ruby hearts. Xavier's grandfather's watch. Xavier's grandfather gave it to Xavier's father when he turned twenty-one, and he passed it to Xavier. Xavier prized that watch."

It was pure rage flooding Nina's face now. "That evil bastard can't have it, you hear?"

"I hear."

Nina swiped at tears that fell despite her anger. "Miko's favorite evening bag's gone. It's silver with a red bird flying over it. She likes red."

"Okay. Nina, when we go back out, I'd like if you can look through the other rooms, see if you find another else missing. Then we can sit down and you can try to describe them for me, in detail."

"He might try to sell them or pawn them, and that'll help you find them." She turned to Eve, face ravaged, eyes hard. "I can look in their bedroom. I'd know if anything was gone. I can do it. Let me do it."

"Okay. If it's too much, we stop. You're going to see people out there, in white protective suits. They're looking for evidence."

"I watch screen. I know about sweepers and such. I can do this."

She could, and did, though her color was gray by the time they left the room. Still, she went with Eve through the rest of the house, sat and gave descriptive details on every missing item.

"Nina, I want you to know that you're about the best witness I've ever dealt with."

"You're going to find him, stop him."

"We're going after him with everything we've got. What you did gives us more. I'm going to have an officer stay with you until your brother gets here."

Eve stepped out, and Peabody stepped up.

"Feeney and McNab are loading up the electronics. They'll go through all the 'links, the comps, and tablets. The killer took the hard drives, the discs, smashed the hell out of everything he left, but they'll take what's left, try to piece something together."

"We need to work this. Contact Baxter and Olsen, pass the rest of the names to them."

"Already did. I let them know the situation."

"Good." Eve rubbed the center of her forehead.

"You okay?"

"Headache. Sometimes it's harder to go through this with some-body who's holding on instead of someone who falls apart."

Peabody pulled an energy bar out of her pocket. "Emergency food. May help."

"That is in no way food."

"It's crap, but it helps." Peabody broke it in half, held a portion out to Eve.

"Fine. Thanks. Let's see what Morris can tell us." As they headed out, Eve took a bite. "It's terrible. What is it?"

"Honey Nougat Cluster Pop."

"Now it's somehow even worse."

But thinking of what lay ahead, Eve choked down the rest.

16

Eve found Morris completing his Y-cut on Miko Carver, while a voice that sounded like an angel soared through the room.

Xavier Carver lay on a second slab, cleaned and prepped for autopsy.

"I'm sorry to see you again so soon." Morris, his midnight-blue suit protected by his cloak, deftly spread Miko's ribs.

Eve heard Peabody swallow hard, snapped, "Suck it up."

More tolerant of the reaction, Morris gestured to the friggie tucked away near the cold drawers reserved for the dead. "Water, fizzies, and our Lieutenant's Pepsi. Have something cool. Music volume decrease to three."

As Peabody gratefully headed to the friggie, her gaze averted from the slab, for now, the angel's voice lowered to a loving murmur.

"I know I'm pushing it," Eve said, "but I wanted to see what, if anything, you have before I go into Central."

"I'll be able to tell you more in an hour or two. My initial exam on the female confirms she was pregnant at the time of her death. Five to six weeks. The cuts along her torso are shallow, most likely inflicted by a thin, sharp blade."

"Like the others."

"Yes, like the others. She was raped, multiple times. Sodomized. I need to complete my examination to confirm, but I believe the sodomy was a single incident. And postmortem."

"He sodomized her after he killed her?"

"I need to confirm, but that's my preliminary opinion. We could consider it a blessing she had passed before that final, ugly act, but I also believe her death was slow and painful. I'll need to confirm your on-scene evaluation of strangulation as COD, but at this point I agree with it."

He gestured her forward. Peabody stepped up, offered Eve a tube of Pepsi.

Distracted, Eve stuck the tube in her coat pocket, leaned closer to examine the neck wounds as Morris did.

"Even without the goggles or the comp enhancement, you can see several wounds that are distinct and of varying degrees."

"Choked her, let her revive, choked her, let her revive. Repeat."

"Yes, until he increased the pressure and the length of time, depriving her of air, and crushed her windpipe."

"He's good at it." Peabody sipped from her tube of ginger ale, bearing down on the queasiness. "Good and controlled enough not to go too far, to keep her coming back until he decided to finish it."

"It's part of the rape," Eve said. "Her body convulses, she struggles for air, her eyes roll back. It's an orgasm to him. The postmortem anal rape, that's new. Maybe he wanted to try the new, or maybe he wanted another bump, or maybe it had something to do with the show."

"Show?" Morris repeated.

"Whatever stage he'd set, whatever costume he'd chosen. She

fought, struggled, tore her wrists up fighting the restraints. She'd have told him she was pregnant. It would be at the top of her mind. 'Please, don't. I'm pregnant.' What did he think of that?"

She looked over at the male victim. "Can you confirm he died first?"

"Yes. About ten minutes before. And, again from a visual exam, there were gaps in time between several of the injuries, on both victims. It appears—I stress *appears* for now—the male victim suffered a blow to the right temple, the initial attack. The rug burns on the heels appear to have been incurred around the same time. And this?" Morris laid a sealed finger, gently, on the bruising beside Miko's left eye. "Again, in that same time frame. This isn't as violent, this blow, but would have disoriented, debilitated."

And hurt like hell, Eve thought.

"His hands next?"

"If you want opinion rather than confirmation, yes."

"Okay." It all jibed with what she'd seen, felt, observed on scene.

Give pain, create terror—the terror was every bit as important as the pain. Control, perform, humiliate.

"We'll get out of your way. Anything that jumps out—whether you can confirm or not—let me know. Anything."

As she walked out, she heard Morris order the volume up. And the angel sang.

She thought about detouring to the lab, but accepted it was far too soon, a waste of time. Instead she checked addresses, then drove to do the notifications of the next of kin, and shatter more lives.

When they finished, Peabody put her head back, shut her eyes. "It's always harder than you tell yourself it will be. It's always harder."

"You helped Miko's mother."

"I hope. Some. It'll help more when Nina goes to her. And maybe, when the shock wears off some for her, for Xavier's parents, they'll remember something. Some details that adds to this."

"Have the bartender brought in," Eve ordered as she pulled into Central's garage. "I want a look at him, and I want him to have a look at me. In the box."

"How about I send Uniform Carmichael and whoever he picks? He can be smooth and persuasive."

"Do that. Then check with Baxter and Olsen, see how far they've gotten on the list. Anything buzzes, we need to know."

They started up in an elevator that quickly grew crowded. "I've got to make a stop. Get this started." Eve shoved off, switched to glide aimed for Mira's office.

Mira's admin, her personal dragon, sat in the outer office busily keyboarding.

"I need to see her."

"Dr. Mira is in a session."

"Don't fuck with me on this." Eve felt all the anger and frustration she'd shoved down through the day rising fast, like hot vomit in the throat. "This directly concerns her."

"Is Mr. Mira—"

"No, it's not that." Reading the genuine fear in the admin's eyes, Eve fought to throttle back. "But it concerns both of them, and it's important."

"She *is* in a session, and specifically asked not to be interrupted barring emergency. She'll be done in forty minutes. I can get you in directly after and shift her next appointment."

"I'll get back if I can. She doesn't leave here today without seeing or speaking to me. Clear?"

"Absolutely."

With a curt nod, Eve strode out. She chose glides again to give herself time to settle down, then pulled out her 'link.

Another admin answered, but Roarke's sort of magnificent Caro usually proved more flexible.

"Good afternoon, Lieutenant. What can I do for you?"

"Hey, sorry, but is there anyway I can speak to him, or that he can tag me back as soon as possible?"

"Give me a minute." So saying, the screen went to a waiting blue.

It took that minute, and a little more, but Roarke's face came on screen.

She heard a babble of voices in the background, and a number of *whooshes*, thuds.

"Lieutenant?"

"Where are you?" she asked.

"At An Didean, just outside what will be the recreation center."

She thought of the shelter he was creating for disenfranchised kids—and the dead girls they'd found sealed inside the walls of the building the previous year.

"I need a favor."

"All right."

"Can you work in a stop by the Miras sometime today?"

"What's wrong?"

"Nothing, and I just want to keep it that way." Stupid, she told herself. Overreacting. But she couldn't stop it. "I thought you could take a good look at their security, maybe do what you do to beef it up, or add a couple layers. He hit again last night, killed both of them this time. I know the Miras aren't on the list—she's outside his age preference, and they're not seriously wealthy, exactly, but—"

"I'll pick up a few things, go by before I come home tonight. Will that work?"

"Yeah." Ridiculous relief flooded her. "Thanks. Mavis and Leonardo and the kid are in New L.A. for a couple of days. Some fashion thing for him, some gig for her. They're not really in the pattern either, but I don't have to think about them right now. The Miras . . . I just don't want to risk it."

"Then we won't."

"I'll let her know you're doing this. I . . . I can't talk now, but thanks for this."

"They're mine as they're yours. Tag me if you're going to be delayed, more than usual, getting home."

"I will."

She clicked off as she turned into Homicide.

"Carmichael's on the way with the new uniform to scoop up Anson Wright," Peabody told her. "I just got off with Baxter. He and the other detectives are coordinating, and they can handle the rest of the list. One of the couples he and Trueheart talked to are friends of the Patricks, and were at their table the night of the gala. No connection to the vendors, but the wife's done numerous vid ads, and is currently one of the stars in one of On Screen's projects in development. Baxter says she's: 'Ooh-la-la.'"

"Other than him getting a woody over an actress who's someone else's wife, any more buzz?"

"Neither of them remember anything unusual about that night. The wife admits she gets hit on pretty regularly, just part of the package, but doesn't recall anything that night, or anything period that's gone beyond her expected hitting on. Oh, and some mildly creepy and suggestive fan mail. They asked if we can take a look at that."

"Take a closer look at her, send me what you get."

In her office, Eve updated her book, her board, wrote detailed reports on the interviews. Then meticulously wrote up the report on the double homicide.

Rather than take the time to return to Mira's office, she wrote out an e-mail, read it, fiddled with it, sent it.

It would be harder for Mira to argue the need for Roarke's visit if Eve didn't give her a way to argue.

She flicked over to an incoming, read Peabody's quick, additional run of one Delilah Esterby.

Eve remembered the name, the face—husband of ten months (only dating at the time of the gala), Aidan Malloy, of the really, seriously rich Malloys.

Both stupidly good-looking, ages twenty-seven and twenty-six respectively. Young, rich, beautiful, and living in a classy house on the Upper West.

Fit like a glove.

Eve opened the vid attachment to the report, lifted her eyebrows as she watched a montage of Delilah's ads.

Selling with sex, she thought. Wear this, buy that, use this, and every man—or woman—alive will want to bang you the way they want to bang me.

Considering, Eve studied her board, all the other victims. Stunners, with faces and bodies gifted from gods.

But this one added straight-out fuck-me sex to the mix.

So why hadn't he gone there? Why pick the soft, the submissive, the busy professional, or the happily devoted wife and daughter instead of the bombshell who made her living selling sex?

Fitting another piece into the twisted puzzle of the killer's mind, Eve replayed the video as Peabody came in.

"Makes me want to run out and buy that entire line of bath and body products," Peabody said.

"Why?"

"Well, ah—"

"Serious question."

"Because it makes me think—absolutely illogically and unrealistically—that I'd end up looking like that, sounding like that, and being just, I don't know, aware how iced and powerful I am."

"And that's why she's not on a slab in the morgue."

"What? I don't follow."

"She intimidates him." Eve rose, paced the stingy confines of her office. "She's saying wouldn't you like to have a taste of this, and you know I'd let you. She's overt, available, and, yeah, totally confident in her sexuality and appeal."

"So . . . she's too much for him?"

"He goes for the soft, the vulnerable, the . . . more subtle. He may be working his way to her level, but he couldn't start there. What's the point—for him—to rape a woman who's inviting him to have a bang?"

"Well, but she's not. Not really."

"No, she's not, but that's the image. That's what he sees. She comes off strong and fearless. Yeah, she—types like this—intimidate him. I want to see those creepy fan contacts. Maybe he approached that way. Maybe he dipped a toe in the pool that way, but she doesn't fit his . . . mold."

She turned back from the board. "We're going to go through the list again when we have interviews with all. Look at them from the angle of the more vulnerable, the more subtle, the more . . . traditional," she ended, finally finding the word that had eluded her. "The vics, they all run on that track, in most ways," Eve continued. "Married, and they all took their husband's name."

"I never thought about that," Peabody admitted, frowning at the board. "Never noticed."

"Only one of them had a career outside volunteer work, charity work, that kind of thing. Why does that break the pattern, why is that?"

Eve paused, stared at Lori Brinkman's photo. "Is it her job's acceptable? The human rights lawyer who writes on the side? Or is that just something he discounted?"

Something there, she thought, and she needed to pull it out.

"It's not coloring, body type, even age," she concluded. "It's looks, yeah, but also, maybe, his perception. And his perception of the woman or couple they're substituting for. I want to get this to Mira, see it from her take."

"The bartender came in, no fuss. Carmichael's with him in Interview A."

"All right, I'll take that. You get this to Mira. You understand where I'm heading?"

"Yeah, yeah, I get it. I'll put it together."

Eve took the slim file they'd put together on Wright, walked to Interview A.

She stepped in, nodded to Carmichael. "Thank you, Officer."

When he stepped out, Eve engaged the recorder. "Dallas, Lieutenant Eve, entering Interview with Wright, Anson, for the purpose of routine questioning, ongoing investigation."

She read in the case files of all the attacks as she sat across from him.

He sipped from a tube of some sort of health drink that had broccoli and carrots dancing over it.

"Thanks for coming in, Mr. Wright."

"No problem. Word came down straight from Jacko: Anybody who works for him gives total co-op to the police. This is about the Strazzas, right?"

"Before we can talk about that, I'm going to Mirandize you."

He said, "Whoa," and looked a little excited.

"It's procedure," Eve continued. "Before we talk about an ongoing investigation. So. 'You have the right to remain silent . . .'"

Gaze riveted on her face, he appeared to cling to every word until she'd finished. "Do you understand your rights and obligations?"

"Yeah, sure. You gave that a crisp reading."

"All right. How do you know the Strazzas?"

"They came into Jacko's a few times when I was on the bar, and I tended bar at their house a couple times for parties."

"You didn't work the dinner party on Saturday night?"

"No. Last time was . . . yeah, they had a party in December, big holiday bash."

"You weren't on-shift at the bar at Jacko's Saturday night, either. Can you tell me where you were?"

"Sure. I worked the lunch shift that day, got home by five. Easy by five. I had a big audition on Monday, so I stayed home, rehearsing, getting into character, did a purge, and—"

"A purge of what?"

"Of my body." He waggled the tube. "My character's a health nut. Abso obsessed, starts a commune—really more like a cult—so they grow all their own food, close themselves off from society because, you know, germs."

"Okay. You stayed at home Saturday night."

"Right through until I left for the audition yesterday morning. It was a callback, and I think I nailed it."

"Was anyone with you over the weekend?"

"No way. I did the total blackout because I had to saturate in the solitude. See, the scene for the callback's a monologue, and it's—"

"So no one was with you," Eve interrupted. "No one came by, contacted you?"

"I put the word out: DND—Do Not Disturb. Let me tell you, the last thing you want is someone banging on the door or buzzing your 'link when you're, you know, purging."

"No one can verify your whereabouts from five Saturday evening until Monday morning?"

"Well, like I said, I had to—"

"Saturate in the solitude and purge."

A little dimple flirted in his left cheek when he smiled at her. "You got it. My character's a true believer, and he's on a mission, you get me? It gradually drives him over the edge. It's a journey, an evolution leading to a kind of metamorphosis. It takes a lot out of you."

So, Eve thought, does a purge.

"Tell me about your relationship with Daphne Strazza."

"Mrs. Strazza?" Shifting, he laid his forearms on the table. "I hope she's doing okay now. Gula said she was really hurt bad. She's okay— Mrs. Strazza, I mean. Good to work for. Good tips."

"A beautiful woman."

"And then some." He waggled his eyebrows. "Never could figure why she'd hooked up with a guy like . . ." His face sobered quickly. "That's a crap thing to say about a dead guy. I just mean she looked like somebody who could have anybody. And he was, like, your dad old. Plus, he wasn't exactly Mr. Personality, you dig?"

"You didn't like Dr. Strazza?"

"Hey, a gig's a gig, and like I said, she tipped good."

Eve leaned back. "Do you do a lot of private gigs like that? Big house parties, that kind of thing?"

"Sure. I'm a hell of a bartender. It's a kind of theater, too, right?" He edged closer to make his point. "You've got to figure out your audience, play the role. It's not my mission in life, right, but it pays the bills, and gives me a lot of grist for the old mill. You gotta *observe* life, you know it? Listen to people, cue in. For the day job, and for the art."

"When you're going into one of these big houses, working the bar for all those rich people, I guess you cue in there, picture yourself living that way, maybe as master of the house, having that beautiful woman in bed."

"Sure. You gotta put yourself into it. But say, if I had a gig like that tonight? While I'm immersing in Joe Boyd—my character? I'd be more disdainful of that lifestyle, of all those people pumping alcohol and rich, processed food into their systems. In my head," he added. "I wouldn't let the disdain show because, hey, tips."

"Did you ever do a gig for Neville Patrick?"

"You mean On Screen's honcho? I got some juice through On Screen, a solid shot in *Triple Threat*. Nailed that death scene, too. A couple of other, smaller bits. Theater's my first love, but the screen gets you more exposure."

"I guess you've met Neville's wife, Rosa."

"Never actually met her or the main man."

"Lori and Ira Brinkman?"

"Ah . . ." He sucked thoughtfully on his juice. "I don't think so."

"Miko and Xavier Carver?"

He shook his head. "Don't hear the bell ring. Man, are they suspects?"

"Toya L'Page and Gray Burroughs?"

"I don't— Wait." He closed his eyes, brow furrowed. Then he shrugged, opened his eyes. "Nope."

"Where were you last night, Anson?"

"Home, man. Barely made it home, had to hoof it for five blocks in the frigging blizzard."

"You didn't go to a friend's, have a friend over?"

"A couple pals had a blizzard party, but I couldn't get there. Wanted the girl I'm sort of seeing to head over, but she was holed up, too. It was, like, whiteout time."

"Did you talk to them, to anybody, say after midnight?"

"Went to bed about then, I think. I'm hoping my agent tags me soon saying I got this part. I should know by the end of the week. They said end of the week. It's a long time to wait."

"Tell me where you were July twenty-second of last year."

He let out a quick laugh, which that ended in a puzzled smile. "You're kidding, right?"

"Do I look like I'm kidding?"

"I guess not, and, man, I'm so stealing that approach if I ever play a cop. But I don't know the answer."

"Don't you keep a calendar? For work shifts, for dates, for auditions?"

"Sure. But that was *last* year. You gotta wipe the slate, get down on the now."

"How about November twenty-eight?"

"Who keeps track? I was in workshops for three weeks running in September, then the backing fell out. I remember that. Man, I was *this* close. Second lead."

He brooded into the distance.

"Do you do your own makeup, Anson?"

"For theater, sure." He gave a little sigh, likely over being *this* close, then seemed to cue back into the moment. "It's part of the immersion. Screen's different. You need to put yourself into the hands of the artists there."

"I bet you're good at it. Doing your own."

"Took some courses to hone the skills. A lot's just practice, experimentation."

"And doing the makeup, that helps you, what, become the character?"

"That's exactly right." Earnest, he leaned forward. "I'm already immersed, right? Then, once I'm in makeup and costume I *am* the character. The character is me. No separation. It's exhausting, but it's the only way."

"Have you ever played any violent characters?"

"Oh, man, that's part of the *fun*. You get to cut those inner demons loose, baby. Joe Boyd, as he descends into madness, he kills a member of the commune he thinks is infecting the crops. Accidentally, but that act pushes him over the edge. He sets fire to the storehouse after that, blames the guy he's killed. Then—"

"I get it. How do you immerse yourself for the violence?"

"You have to *believe* it. I mean the staging's all set, and the cues, the lines, all of that's around it, but *inside*, you have to believe you're going to shove this guy over a cliff to his death."

"And tap into your own inner demons."

"We all got 'em, right?"

"How about horror? Ever done a vampire, a ghoul, an actual demon?"

"I was a zombie, an extra on *Planet Plague*—that got me the audition for the spot on *Triple Threat*. Man, I would totally kill for a continuing role on *Planet Plague*." He caught himself. "Not kill-kill, you get me?"

"Right." She tried another avenue. "When you're bartending, I imagine you talk to a lot of people."

"It's part of it. You've got to talk, but even more, to listen."

"Do people ever ask you about your outside jobs, the fancy parties?"

He frowned. "The customers? How would they know about them?"

"At the theater, or if you get a screen part, maybe you'd mention the parties you've been to. Do a little name-dropping, or talk about what you've . . . observed?"

"I guess. Maybe."

"And maybe if you've got one coming up, you chat about it."

"Maybe."

"Anybody specific you might chat with about it?"

"I don't know. Like I said, it's just the day job."

She worked him another half hour, then cut him loose. She stayed in Interview A, brooding into the distance.

Peabody poked her head in. "How'd it go?"

"Either Wright's an oblivious moron or a hell of an actor."

"He gets solid reviews."

Eve frowned, turned her head. "Does he?"

"I did a search on that, and more than one said he was the best thing in some crap play. Authentic's what comes across."

"He's got no alibi for any of the attacks. Claims he doesn't remember and has no record of his whereabouts on the night of the first two, and claims he was home alone for the last two."

She rose, scowled at the two-way glass. "He's white, and L'Page thinks the guy who pushed at her at the gala was white. He's the right height. But, Jesus, he doesn't ring. Not for the killer, not for somebody who'd pass information to someone, except in rambling conversation—but that's a factor. He connects to the Patricks through On Screen, and he's worked in the Strazza home, but he doesn't ring. Yet."

"Baxter and Trueheart just logged in. Olsen and Tredway are coming in."

"Let's try for a conference room."

Something had to shake loose, she thought. But right now the big-ass tree she beat her head against seemed immovable.

"I figured that, so I grabbed Room B."

"Good. We'll set it up now."

Maybe the act of creating a new board, arranging photos, evidence, reports would help shake the damn tree.

17

As Eve finished setting up the board, Peabody stepped out of the conference room. She came back with a couple of pita pockets that smelled iffy at best.

"I'm fading," Peabody confessed. "I need something more than half an energy bar. You do, too."

Eve eyed the offered pocket cynically. "What's in it?"

"Veggie ham, nondairy American cheese, and shredded spinach. Everything else in Vending looked worse. At least it's sort of hot."

"Why is there always spinach?" Eve wondered, tried a bite. "It's terrible."

Peabody sampled. "Yeah, but still, sort of hot. I've lost six pounds."

"Depend on Vending, you'll whither away to nothing."

"That'll never happen, but I've lost six and kept it off for eighteen days and counting."

"I thought you weren't going to obsess about the numbers?"

"I like obsessing about the *good* numbers, and my currently loose pants. It motivates. If I'm not motivated, I'll eat a bunch of brownies." She closed her eyes a moment. "Mmm, brownies. Then I obsess about packing on enough to crush McNab's skinny ass whenever I'm on top."

Eve slapped two fingers to the corner of her twitching eye, noted Peabody's innocent smile. "That was on purpose."

"Just breaking the tension." Peabody took another bite of the pocket. "But now I so really want a brownie."

Shaking her head, Eve decided if she had to eat a revolting fake sandwich, she might as well top it off with the terrible cop coffee in the conference room AutoChef.

She was scowling over the first sip when Baxter and Trueheart came in.

"What is that smell?" Baxter demanded.

"Vending lunch," Peabody told him.

"There ought to be a law." He walked to the board, stood, hands dipped into his pockets, studying. "L'Page and Burroughs—possible targets?"

Eve forced down more coffee. "That's right."

"We've got two of those."

"Put them up."

Trueheart stepped up to do so while Baxter took a harder look at the most recent crime scene shots.

"Having a real party now. Escalating from target to target, but killing Strazza's opened up a whole new world for him. He killed the male first?"

"ME has confirmed, yes."

"Bigger threat—and having Strazza get loose, to go at him? Spooked and pissed. But if he can work up the balls, he'll do the female first next round."

Eve nodded, following Baxter's reasoning. "Watch me kill your wife. You can't stop me, can't protect her. I'm a bigger, better man than you."

Trueheart cleared his throat—his substitute for raising his hand. "Slitting the male's throat? It's quick, eliminates any potential threat. But it's also messy. I think he liked the mess. It desecrates the bedroom. The victims' private space."

"And adds to the staging," Eve agreed. "We can—"

She broke off as Olsen came in with her partner. Something tugged at her memory when the male detective—narrow shoulders in a tired-looking glen-plaid sport coat, lanky legs like skinny pipe cleaners in brown trousers—walked in.

His dark hair was cropped close to his skull, and his eyebrows formed sharp, inverted Vs over hazel eyes. He wore a single gold stud in his left earlobe.

Then it clicked.

"Tredway. It's been a while."

"It has. What, six, seven years?"

"About. Detective Tredway and I worked a murder together some back," Eve explained.

"Back when Feeney was your LT. Vic was one of my weasels, so Feeney brought me in. We got the bastard."

"Still in a cage."

"And now you're the LT." He crossed to the board, shook his head. "Better you than me. These potential targets?"

"So far."

"We have two couples to add to that," Olsen said.

"Put them up," Eve told her, "and let's get down to it."

She had Peabody run them through the interview with L'Page and Burroughs.

"This guy who put the moves on her at the gala deal. Any chance of a sketch on him?" Tredway asked.

"Next step. She says it was dim light, and almost a year ago, but we have detective artist who's got a way of refreshing memories and getting details."

"Is that his work?" Olsen gestured to the devil sketch on the board.

"Yeah."

"It's worth a shot." Tredway considered, drank cop coffee as if it didn't burn the stomach lining. "Course some guys—most, really—are likely to put the moves on a frosty-looker. We're either assholes or optimists, depending how you look at it."

"Me, I'm an eternal optimist."

Olsen snorted at Baxter's comment. "World champ."

"Worth a shot," Tredway continued. "What are the odds some random asshole or optimist puts *those* kind of moves on her at *that* event, and she and the guy she gets married to fit the target requirements down the fricking line?"

He took notes as they talked—actual notes in a little dog-eared book with a stubby pencil. Though she knew better, Eve would have sworn it was the same book, the same pencil he'd used seven years before.

"I tagged Yancy on this," Eve said. "He'll take his first pass with L'Page today. If this is our guy—and though the world is full of assholes, I'm with Tredway on the odds—she's the only one we know of who's seen the suspect's face."

"Maybe that face?" Tredway gestured toward Anson Wright's ID shot.

"I've just completed an interview with him."

Eve ran them through it.

"To sum it up, there's some weight there. He's been in the third vics' home, has a second connect with them through the first male vic's studio. He knows how to do makeup. No alibis, lives alone. He's the right height and build, and if L'Page is correct, the right race. On the other side, he made no attempt, whatsoever, to come up with an alibi, and seemed oblivious as to why I asked. Not stupid, but oblivious and self-absorbed."

"An actor," Baxter added.

"Yeah. Apparently a good one. So I want to keep eyes on him the next couple days."

"We can take some of that." Olsen glanced at her partner for confirmation, got his nod.

"The boy and I can run shifts with you. That work, boss?" Baxter asked.

"I'll clear it. Set it up. Who are your picks up there?"

"Take it away, Detective," Baxter told Trueheart.

He ran through the bombshell's data, her husband's.

"My angle on that," Eve began, "she doesn't fit."

"My angle is, she'd fit anywhere."

Eve sent Baxter a cool stare. "Keep it in your pants, horndog. She doesn't fit his type," Eve continued, and laid out her theory.

Tredway took his notes, nodded through her explanation. "He's looking for his dream girl, and his dream girl doesn't bang out the sexy."

"Unless it's for him," Olsen agreed. "But the get-'em-up-big-boy on screen doesn't fit the image."

"Too much competition," Baxter added.

"That factors. They should take precautions," Eve added, "but they're low on the list. Who's next, Trueheart?"

"Jacie and Roderick Corbo, both age thirty-one. Married three years with main residence Upper East. Additional home in Oyster Bay, and an interest in a family estate—her side—on St. Lucia."

"Big-time trust-fund babies," Baxter put in. "Both of them."

"They've used both vendors," Trueheart continued, "and Mrs. Corbo has used On Screen twice to record and broadcast infomercials for a line of skin-care products one of her family's businesses repre-sents."

"She's the face," Baxter explained. "It's a hell of a face. She also states she received a couple of overtly suggestive 'link calls a short time after the last infomercial hit the screen."

"You got her 'link?"

Baxter shook his head. "She said she lost it. Husband confirms she loses her 'link about once a month."

"The infomercial initially aired in November, Lieutenant," True-heart continued. "She thinks the calls came in right after. Two of them."

"Describe 'overtly suggestive,'" Eve said, and Trueheart flushed.

"I'll take that and spare the boy. A male, blocked video, told her he was going to fuck her and fuck her right and she'd beg for more. He claimed he was watching her. The second time he called, she thinks maybe a week after the first time, it was more of the same, but he added he liked her in green, how that tight skirt hugged her ass. But he was going to like her naked, tied up, and begging for it even more."

"Did she report any of this?"

"No, sir." Trueheart cleared his throat again. "She said she just considered it an annoyance at the time. She didn't even tell her husband, didn't relate it to us until she began to get nervous during the interview."

"When would the suspect have been able to see her in green? Could she pinpoint?"

"She checked her closet records, gave us two dates. The first was a family Thanksgiving dinner, which included some close friends, the second was an anniversary party held at the Corbo mansion, and catered by Jacko's. We verified that as she wasn't a hundred percent on it. The first event had about seventy-five people, the second more than two-fifty."

"We'll need the guest lists."

"Working on it. We're expecting the one from the first shortly," Baxter said. "The problem with the second is the Corbos' social secretary is currently on vacation. Some sort of meditation camp—no communications. And apparently nobody else seems to know where to find the guest list."

"Christ's sake."

"We're pushing." Baxter shrugged. "The rich really are different. The social secretary has an assistant—and if that isn't excessive enough, the assistant has an assistant. Neither of them are allowed to access her files. Even if they were, the woman's so paranoid she took it with her. She works on a portable. We're running down where she is because nobody there seems to know. We're on it, Loo."

"Stay on it. Your two," she said to Olsen.

"Gregor and Camilla Jane Lester. Ages forty-eight and twenty-nine respectively. Married two years. His second time around," Olsen added. Gregor is chief of emergency medicine at—drumroll—St. Andrew's. He knew Anthony Strazza well. He parsed his words, but clearly, no love lost there. He met Daphne Strazza, briefly and casually at a few events, such as the gala. They have used Jacko's. Camilla Jane *loves* to entertain," Olsen added with an eye roll. "But she likes to mix it up, surprise her guests, and Jacko's is so, you know, conventional."

"Bimbo." Tredway circled a finger in the air, then tapped it at his partner. "Her word."

"Well, Jesus, if you did a search on the word, Camilla Jane Lester's picture would pop up. She's gorgeous, incredibly silly, and her husband adores her. Indulges her. It shows."

"Guy's got a face like a hamster, and he lands somebody who looks like that? Why wouldn't he? Interesting fact," Tredway continued. "As Camilla Jane, prior to the marriage, she made a living acting. Bit

parts, stage and screen. Very bit from the sound of it. And supple-
mented that living as, we'll politely call it, a dancer."

"She was a stripper?"

"Ah, you say tomato. She had some work as an extra on a couple
of serials—the daytime sort—played a dead girl once, and so on."

"Connection to On Screen?"

"Auditioned for a couple of productions there, didn't get the parts.
Did shoot a pilot for them, but it didn't get picked up."

"Connects," Eve stated. "A lot of connections."

"She hasn't worked since the marriage—her choice, she says."
Olsen shrugged. "She met Lester when she was further supplement-
ing her income as part of the entertainment on Burlesque Night, a
fund-raiser."

"The kicker? Why they're up there?" Tredway lifted his chin
toward the board. "She swears somebody was in the house last month,
and went through her underwear. Took a matching set. Since nothing else was missing they dismissed it. But when she was shopping
a few days ago, for more fancy underwear, she says she got a text
telling her to buy more purple. It was a good color for her."

"Her 'link?"

Olsen fluttered her eyelashes. "Well, she got *so* upset, so angry,
she threw her 'link right in the recycler and bought another. *Bim* with
a big *bo*. We got the name of the boutique, went by. Any security re-
freshes every twenty-four, and no one could recall a man loitering in
the shop."

"Your number two?"

"Anna-Teresa and Ren Macari, twenty-eight and thirty. Married
eighteen months. More trust-fund babies and these two don't much
pretend to work at anything."

"Now, Olsen, he has his magic," Tredway reminded her.

"Right. He's a magician. That's his passion. Daddy bought him a magic club where he can perform. A quick check on that shows he's driving it into the ground playing Houdini, he doesn't actually do anything else there. Neither have used the vendors, but her mother's used Jacko's for events, and both the Macaris have eaten there. His father is a major donor at—*buzz*—St. Andrew's, and helped defray the costs for a fund-raiser. A masquerade ball last May. At that event, Anna-Teresa was accosted—her word—by a man dressed like the Phantom of the Opera."

"Wait," Eve interrupted. "How does anybody dress as a phantom? Aren't they invisible. Isn't that the whole stupid idea?"

"It's a character, sir," Trueheart explained. "An actor who was burned and disfigured in a theater fire, and went insane. He's obsessed with a young actress, and kills people he blames for his accident."

"Pretty much," Olsen agree. "He was, according to the wit, wearing black cape, a white mask obscuring half his face, and what she thinks might have been a wig—longish, black, curling."

"Where did it happen?"

"She'd gone outside." Tredway picked up the report. "To get some air, she claimed, how it was crowded and stuffy. There's a garden area, and eventually she confessed she'd snuck out and found a dark corner because she wanted to smoke an herbal. So the Phantom comes along, tells her they have to dance, grabs her. At first she figures drunk and obnoxious, and starts to pull away. But he clamps on, grabs her ass with one hand and he's got an erection. Now she struggles, and he laughs. Tells her it's going to be the best she's ever had. As she's gearing up to scream, he shoves her down, swirls his cape and runs away."

"She went right in, told her husband, and they told security. They didn't find him." Olsen looked back at the board. " 'Best you've ever had.' That's the magic phrase."

"There's going to be more," Eve said. "He'll have accosted more, harassed more. Doing that helped him fill the gap between break-ins, rapes. Guest list for the party?"

"Not an invite deal. You bought tickets. A cool grand a pop. Twelve hundred plus tickets sold. You could buy a table," Olsen added. "Plunk down ten large for a table, and bring guests."

"People don't pay cash for that sort of thing, so there'll be a paper trail. Peabody."

Peabody added the task to her handheld. "I'll start heading down the trail."

"And let's see if Wright can verify his whereabouts on the night Macari was accosted. Have EDD go to the underwear shop, dig into the security. If necessary, have them get a warrant, confiscate and bring it here to work on. The four couples added should be advised to add to their own security."

She glanced around the conference table. "Thoughts, complaints, remarks, comments?"

Trueheart started to raise his hand, caught himself. "I think he's been inside several more houses, Lieutenant. Taken other personal items the homeowners haven't noticed. Or if they did, put it down to their own carelessness. Lost it, left it somewhere, that kind of thing."

"I agree. Small, intimate items belonging to the female is most probable. No valuables—that could be reported. He can fantasize, imagine, plot, and plan."

"He has to know when to go in. He has to watch them," Olsen added.

"Somebody with plenty of free time," Eve agreed. "Either has money enough he doesn't have to work every day—or at all—or has a job that allows him to go out of the office or place of business. Or a job or position that gives him access to their schedules."

"They broadcast a lot of it." In a world-weary way, Tredway shook his head. "Through the society channels, and on their own social media. Fricking invites a break-in, you ask me."

"I wouldn't argue," Baxter said, "but even bimbos aren't likely to broadcast they're going to buy panties today. A combo of watching them virtually and otherwise, I'd say."

"It started in earnest in April of last year at the Celebrate Art Gala." Eve rose, paced to the board. "He may have harassed women before that time, and likely did. May have broken into their homes and taken panties to sniff. But what we have points to this night. Every victim on this board attended that gala. So did he."

She closed her eyes a moment, let it circle in her mind, turned back.

"Mira profiles him between thirty and fifty. I think forty is top age. He's younger, but old enough to have control and patience. Not as much patience as we previous thought as he's clearly used other avenues to satisfy his needs. Between thirty and forty, most likely white. Around five feet, eight inches tall. Average build. He's either one of this social group or he knows how to blend with them."

She gestured to Anson Wright's photo.

"That doesn't take the bartender out. An actor knows how to inhabit a role—and that's pretty much what he told me in interview. In fact, made a point of it. He won't be married, won't have a cohab or a serious relationship. He hoards. He has to have a place where he can keep all the loot he takes from his hits as there's no evidence he disposes of it."

She walked from one end of the board to the other. "He takes surrogates. Married couples only, exceptionally beautiful woman. Rape is the primary goal. And it *is* about sex as much as power and causing fear. Violent sex, the sort that eases—temporarily—his frustration at not having the true object of his desire. At not being able to punish and humiliate her for rejecting him, to do the same to the male for having what he couldn't have.

"The 'link calls, the texts, the . . . putting moves on, even the break-ins to steal underwear, that's all foreplay for him. Adds excitement, anticipation. But since he killed Strazza, everything changed, opened, expanded. He doesn't need that kind of foreplay now—a grope in the dark, a voice over a 'link. He needs the kill, the climax. Now when he chooses his costume, does his makeup, goes in to set the stage, he knows those first performances were just—what do you call them—dress rehearsals. These are the real shows. And he just can't fucking wait to step onstage again."

"He won't wait long," Tredway agreed. "Maybe a couple of days."

"Then we'd better find him first. We're all going to go over the guest list, the list of staff and support staff for the gala. We're going to cull out every man between thirty and forty, white—but it was bad light, so we need to consider mixed race. We have his approximate build. Unmarried males, no cohabs. He's going to live alone. And when we have those, we're going to look at his mother, a stepmother, or an older sister maybe. She's going to be exceptionally beautiful."

"Lieutenant?"

She gave Trueheart the nod.

"It could have been a teacher—the person he's fixated on. I just mean to say I, ah, had a pretty hard crush on my English Lit teacher in high school."

"You dog," Baxter said with a laugh.

"I got over it, but for a few weeks there, it was pretty intense in my head. Or it could have been a friend's mom, a neighbor, or—"

"Christ, you're right. Someone he saw regularly, had a connection to, a relationship with. Enough to stick in his twisted brain. She'll be married, and upper middle class at least. Start with mothers. We'll work down the list of possible others. Look for any sort of

complaint—even juvie. Dig in, maybe his parents sent him to therapy or rehab. Work the levels.

"Peabody, divvy it up so we're not stepping on each other's feet.
He could be a little taller or a little shorter," she considered. "Make it
five-seven to five-ten. Let's not let him slip through because we re-
stricted too much."

She glanced at her wrist unit. "I want to take another pass at Daphne
Strazza. Send my list to my home office, Peabody. Anybody gives
even the shortest buzz, contact me. Any questions, any new avenues
to try, the same. That's 'round the clock."

She headed out, walking briskly toward the bullpen. She'd grab
her coat, get to the hospital, maybe pull something else out of Daphne,
then head home, drop straight into the work.

She should check and see if Roarke—

Her brain took a detour when she saw Rosa Patrick and Kyle
Knightly step off the elevator.

"Mrs. Patrick, Mr. Knightly."

"Oh, thank God! You're right here." Rosa all but launched herself
at Eve. "He sent me a text, with a picture from . . . Oh God."

"Hold on, Rosie." Kyle wrapped an arm around her waist as he
looked at Eve. "Is there a place we can sit down? She really needs to
sit down."

"Come this way." She considered the lounge, but Interview A
wasn't in use, and closer. More private.

She showed them in. "Have a seat. Tell me what happened."

"My 'link. I answered my 'link, and— Here." She dragged it out
of her purse, shoved it toward Eve.

"Here." Kyle took it, gently pressed Rosa's thumb to the security
pad. "I'll bring it up, okay?"

"Yes. Sorry."

He called up a text, handed the 'link to Eve.

An image of Rosa, bound, naked, unconscious on tangled sheets came on screen. Above it, the text read:

Wasn't that fun? The best you ever had. Let's do it again!

Eve read the time sent: thirty-five minutes earlier.

"You can trace it." Rosa clutched her hands together, knuckles white as she pressed them between her breasts. "You can do that. Can you do that? Please. You can find him."

"Give me a second." Eve rose, stepped away from the table, tagged McNab.

"McNab, e-whiz."

"Interview A. Now."

"I'm there."

Eve came back, sat across from Rosa. "Is this the first communication you've received like this?"

"Yes."

"Think back. Before the assault did you receive any kind of communication from anyone that was suggestive, overt, threatening?"

"No. I swear. Why would he do this now? Why? It's been months."

"He got stupid, that's why." Kyle gripped her shoulder. "They'll trace that text, Rosa."

"The picture. He—he recorded . . . It's like it's happening again."

"Mrs. Patrick, where's your husband?"

"He's on his way. He was uptown, in meetings, but he's coming."

"Where were you when you received this text?"

"We were—we were in the West Village."

"We're doing a location shoot there next week," Kyle explained. "I wanted to take another look, walk the streets we're using. I asked Rosa to come along, give me her perspective."

"He wanted to give me something to do. I have a hard time getting out, alone. Staying home, alone."

"You're doing better."

Rosa managed a smile at Kyle. "I was. I will. But . . . Kyle convinced me to go downtown with him and the assistant director. I was enjoying it. It took my mind off everything, and then this happened."

"You, Mr. Knightly, and—"

"Karyn Peeks," Kyle supplied. "The AD on the shoot. We were standing on—God, I think it was Charles." He rubbed his forehead. "Mind's a little scrambled. Karyn and I were discussing some angles, and Rosa answered her 'link. She went white, absolutely white. She nearly dropped the 'link. I caught it, and I saw . . ."

"I wanted to run. I don't even know where, just run. Kyle said we needed to bring it to you, right away. To bring it to you, and you'd trace the transmission."

"That was the right thing to do."

McNab knocked briskly even as he opened the door.

"This is Detective McNab, with EDD. I need your permission to give him your 'link."

"Yes, yes. I don't care if I ever see it again."

"Give me a second." Eve stepped out with McNab. "Incoming text with image, came in about thirty-five minutes ago. Get me all you can, fast as you can."

"Done. I can do this in your office if that's okay. Save time."

"Save time."

She went back in. "He's one of the best," she told them, "I want to reassure you. I've just come from briefing a team of detectives working on the investigation. It's my top priority, and theirs."

"Do you have any leads?" Kyle lifted his hands. "Everyone asks that, but there's a reason they do."

"And there's a reason I can only tell you this investigation is open and active, and we're pursuing any and all leads. And we are," she said, looking back at Rosa.

"I went, or, Lori and I went to see Daphne last evening."

"That's good."

"It was hard, for all of us, but I think it is good. Lori and I know what she's feeling right now, and I hope we showed her she's not alone, and that it will get better. It was better, and now—"

"This isn't going to change that or you. You're not going to let him violate you again."

"If I'd been alone when . . ."

"You weren't." Kyle took her hand. "You're not."

"I just . . . Neville. I wish he'd get here."

Giving her hand a squeeze, Kyle nodded. "How about I go out, get you some coffee, tag him and let him know we're talking to Lieutenant Dallas, get his ETA?"

"Would you? I'd just feel better."

"Sure."

"Skip the coffee," Eve advised. "It's as bad as it gets. Tea's a better bet."

"Thanks for the tip. I'll be right back."

"Rosa," Eve began when they were alone. "I know you've been through this countless times. I know you're feeling vulnerable right now. I'm going to ask you to think, and carefully. Before the assault, in the time after, but particularly before, was there any incident—however minor—when someone approached you, touched you, or . . . you know what I'm saying. Moved on you?"

"No."

"Rosa, you're a beautiful woman. It's hard to believe you haven't had someone hit on you."

"Not in an ugly way. A flirtation, an attempt? I mean you're in a bar or a club waiting for friends and a man offers to buy you a drink? Sure. You say no thanks, and he may try to chat you up for a minute. You can judge if it's harmless or if he's going to get pushy, and you handle it accordingly."

"And there's never been one of those times anyone approached you that way, frightened you, made you feel threatened."

"Honestly, no. Annoyed, yes. But since I've been with Neville, not much of that. I almost think—well, one of my friends said it's like I have this aura of 'Don't Bother' around me. I knew the first time I saw him. I was with someone else, but my heart just . . . *Thud*." She let out a half laugh. "And when I managed to work my way up to him, to start a conversation, I was sunk. I knew it, felt so guilty because the man I was with was a very, very nice man."

"Was he angry?"

"Who? Justin? Oh, no. He didn't know for one thing. Honestly, I thought of Neville as a lovely fantasy. The looks, the accent, the manner, the chemistry. I was sure it was only that when we ran into each other again. I was free, but he was with someone else. Missed that chance, that's what I thought. Then, third time's the charm. We met again and we were both single, and it turned out he'd felt that same thud. And that's been that. The Don't Bother aura descended."

"Did you ever have the feeling someone had been in your home when you weren't? Notice something missing?"

"Not really."

"Underwear," Eve said and watched surprise flicker over Rosa's face.

"I . . . It's odd you say that. I bought all new lingerie before the wedding, didn't wear any of it. Neville and I lived together in the house since the spring, and I wanted everything new when we were married. So I put it away, but didn't wear it. When we got back from the honeymoon I'd have sworn a couple of sets were missing. I took some with me on the honeymoon, but I was so sure I'd bought and put away these others."

"They weren't where you'd put them."

"They weren't anywhere. I just chalked it up to all the wedding chaos."

She stopped, rubbed a hand over her heart. "He'd been in the house?"

"It's something we're looking into."

"It feels like it's never going to end," Rosa murmured.

McNab opened the door, let Kyle walk in ahead of him.

"Lieutenant?"

"Give me a minute." She stepped out with McNab.

"Drop 'link."

"I figured."

"But I've got a location. Where the text originated, and where the 'link—still active—is now. It's half a block from the Patricks' building. I checked the file."

"Get your gear, you're with me. Garage, five minutes, so move your ass."

"It's never still."

Simple truth, she thought as he rushed off on his tartan airboots and she went back into Interview A.

"As I suspected, the text came from a drop 'link."

"What does that mean?" Rosa demanded.

"They can't identify it, Rosa," Kyle explained. "It's not registered."

"Oh, but—"

"We do have a location. I'm going there now. I can take you down to our lounge to wait for Mr. Patrick."

Kyle checked his wrist unit. "Damn it. He's still about ten minutes out. Don't wait. Go. I'll tag him back, and we'll meet him downstairs. He's nearly here, Rosa. We'll go meet him."

"Yes." Rosa stood up. "Hurry," she said to Eve.

Eve hurried to her office, barely slowing her stride when Peabody sprang from her desk in the bullpen. "McNab said—"

"Work the list. McNab's enough for this. We get anything, you'll know."

Eve grabbed her coat, arrowed down to the garage. McNab loped up half a minute behind her.

Eve simply bulleted out of the slot, hit the lights and sirens, and sped out of the garage.

"Yee-haw," was McNab's reaction, but he tightened his safety harness. "Not to dampen down, Dallas, but he's not going to be there."

"I know it."

"Okay then. This sucker moves. So this fuckhead escalates to murder on one hand, devolves to taunts on the other."

"Why 'devolve'?" she asked as she swerved around a sedan whose driver obviously decided sirens meant nothing to him.

"It's small time, right? Sure it keeps a former target on edge, or brings back that edge, but he's onto bigger now."

"Ask yourself why this target? Why this woman? The first."

He asked himself as she hit a clear stretch on Tenth, and the city blurred by. "She's still important. She, especially, means something to him."

"He didn't include the husband on the text—it wasn't a couple thing. He didn't threaten violence. He taunted, yeah, but it's let's do it again. The sick part of him that twists this into actual sex wants to do it again. With her. That's my conclusion until and unless the rest of the victims get the same."

McNab thought it through. Nodded. "That's why you're the LT."

"Fucking A. Still in that location?"

"Hasn't budged. I got a lock on it." He studied the read on on his PPC.

He guided her in as they got closer, then cursed.

"Shit, fuck, damn, it shut down."

"Turned off?"

"Shut down," he repeated. "Vanished. I've got the lock on the location, but the 'link's shut down. Left here, half a block. Shit. Ten feet, south side. Stop. We're right on it."

Eve cut the wheel, double-parked. And saw the blueprint of it all the minute she stepped out of the A-T into the blast of angry horns.

"Recycler." She pointed, jogging to it. "It's still humming, goddamn it."

"Smash-and-churn schedule's right on it." Frustrated, McNab kicked the bin. "Started up five minutes ago. Not just shut down, Dallas. Crushed and shredded."

18

SHE WAITED WITH MCNAB, CLEARED THE PROPER PAPERWORK, AND STOOD by while a city drone unlocked and opened the bin.

And looked into the open bin at the god-awful, compacted mess.

"Well." McNab shoved at his purple and green earflap cap. "I like a challenge."

"You've got one. Take it in, do what you do." She considered the logistics of him carting a big bag of compacted trash and garbage on the subway, dug into her pocket. "Cab it back." She shoved money into one of his many pockets as his hands were currently busy working with the city drone to transfer the contents of the recycler to a large green bag.

"Thanks."

"What are the odds?" she asked him.

"Pretty much zilch, but you never know. Maybe it gets lodged in a little pocket, and just gets compressed instead of shredded."

"Good luck with that." She started back to the car.

"Ten minutes sooner, I could've jammed the sucker, and we'd have it whole."

She nodded as she climbed into the car because that had already struck her as a very interesting point.

Heading toward the hospital, she used her wrist unit to shoot off a quick text to Roarke:

Got a little delayed. I'm heading toward the hospital to check on Daphne Strazza. Home after that. I've got a long night coming—sorry.

Even as she asked herself if she was taking time here better spent elsewhere, she navigated the now-familiar route to Daphne's room. She found her—white pajamas and robe, hair groomed—standing with Del Nobel.

"Lieutenant. Jacko's keeps sending food. I'm trying to convince Dr. Nobel to take a share of today's chicken Alfredo. It's wonderful."

"You look good. Stronger."

"The nurse—Rhoda—she convinced me to, well, clean up a little. I do feel better. They said I can leave tomorrow, but—" She pressed her lips together, looked pleadingly at Del.

"I can stretch it another day, but it'd be good for you to get out of here."

"I just don't know where . . . My husband's lawyer came by to see me. He was very, very kind. He gave me a debit card, for expenses until . . . until everything's settled. I just can't go back to that house. I just can't go back there."

As if her legs had given out, she sat.

"I can sell the house whenever Mr. Wythe says I can do that, but I can't go back there."

"Do you remember anything else?"

Daphne shook her head, but her fingers twisted together, and her eyes cut away.

"Do you remember walking outside?"

The fingers untwisted. Daphne looked at Eve. "No. I don't. Not even like a dream. Dr. Mira said she'd come here tomorrow. If I'm not here—"

"She'll come wherever you are," Eve told her. "Mr. Wythe told me you're allowed to get a hotel, and whatever you need. I can get you a room at the Palace. I can make sure you're safe and secure there."

"But . . . will you come there?" she asked Del. "If I have to go, will you come there and talk to me?"

"I can do that."

"I'm not sure. I just don't know what . . . What should I do?"

Before he could answer, Eve caught the sound of raised voices outside the door. She stepped back, opened it to see the on-duty uniform blocking a furious woman in a long red coat with a huge bag slung over her shoulder.

"You are *not* going to stop me from seeing my sister. Nobody is going to—"

"Officer. She's clear."

Tish shoved past the uniform, shouldered by Eve, then stopped dead, dropped the bag on the floor with a *thump*.

"Daphne."

Daphne pushed to her feet, froze. "Tish."

"Daph." Tish flew across the room, threw her arms around the pale, rigid Daphne. "Oh, Daph, Daph, Daph."

"How did you— Why are you—"

"Why?" Tish pulled back an inch. "Don't be an idiot. Daph," she said more gently, cupping her sister's face in her hands. "It's going to be all right now." When Daphne just shook her head, Tish gripped tighter. "Yes, it is. I swear, it is. Mom and Dad will be here tomorrow. They couldn't get a flight out any sooner because of the blizzard, but—"

"No!" Daphne struggled free and looked, to Eve's eyes, absolutely terrified. "They're not supposed to come. You're not supposed to be here."

"Why the hell not?"

"He said. You need to go. You need to go *now*. He'll be so angry. He'll be furious if he knows you're here."

"He's dead," Tish said flatly, laying her hands on Daphne's face again when Daphne flinched. "He's dead, Daphne, so that's done. It's done, and you're not pushing me away. You're not pushing us away again. Daphne, we're your family."

Tears swirled into Daphne's eyes, spilled over. And broke with sobs as she clung to Tish.

"It's all going to be okay," Tish murmured. "I promise. I'm here now. I'm here."

"Let's give them a minute," Nobel suggested, gesturing to the door.

When Eve stepped out with him, he let out a long sigh. "That's a very good thing. Those are the first tears she's shed that weren't from fear or pain. You contacted the sister?"

"Yeah."

"I couldn't. Patient says don't, I can't. I'm damn glad you could. She'll start healing on the inside now. It'll take time, but it'll begin."

"She's looking to you to tell her what to do."

"I know it, and I'm not going to. I think she's had enough of being told what to do, what to wear, what to say." He shrugged. "She talks to me. She's careful, and more than that, she's pretty thoroughly brainwashed. But, hey, I'm a professional."

"So am I, and she's remembered more. She lied just now."

"Maybe. If she did, it's out of fear. She continues to have nightmares, flashbacks, even some mild hallucinations where she says the devils were in the room."

"Plural?"

"Sometimes. After the episodes, she's ashamed, apologetic. She's very fragile yet, Lieutenant. Her emotions are a thin piece of glass already cracked. Too much pressure, they'll shatter. Putting them back together will take a lot longer."

"I don't believe I'm putting undue pressure on her."

"You're not, and believe me I figured I'd have to put on the stern-doctor face with you. But you're good with her, so she's responding. If she lied, it's because she's not ready. I may be projecting, but I don't think lies are her fallback or go-to."

He glanced toward the door. "Having her family here is going to help her mend and, frankly, it takes a load off my mind. I could've stretched her stay here another day, maybe two using the Strazza's widow pressure, but she's ready to be an outpatient, physically."

"I need to go in there. I have to get back to work, and I need to know where she's going to be when she leaves here."

"Yeah. I want to see if she'll agree to me arranging for a cot in here for the sister. I'm hoping she'll stay with her tonight."

Eve went in to see the two women curled together on the bed, with Tish, still in coat and boots, stroking Daphne's hair and soothing her.

She lifted a finger of that stroking hand to hold Eve back.

"I'm going to make some arrangements, and let Mom and Dad know I'm here."

"Don't go."

"I'm not. We're going to have a pajama party tonight. Remember how we'd do that? I'm just going to take care of a couple of things, just outside the room, then I'm putting on my party pj's and we're getting some ice cream to go with a vid marathon. Pizza first, right? Pizza, then the ice cream, then the bellyache. Don't start without me."

"I'm sorry, Tish. I'm so sorry."

"Shut up."

Tish eased out of bed, walked toward the door. She gestured with a jerk of her head, strode outside.

"I'm so pissed off I may not be coherent, but—" Tears sprang to her eyes so she pressed the heels of her hands against them. "No, no, no, not going there. Couldn't get a flight because of the damn blizzard, then finally got a standby when the transpo centers opened. I should've been here."

"You're here now," Eve said, and Tish dropped her hands.

"You're the cop who contacted me."

"Dallas. Lieutenant Dallas."

"Thank you." Tish offered a hand, then turned to Del. "You're the doctor who's been taking care of her."

"Del Nobel."

"Thanks." She offered him her hand, too. "I want to talk to both of you in a lot more depth, but I don't want to leave her alone long right now. I'm staying in there with her tonight."

She issued it like a challenge.

"I'll have a cot brought in for you."

"I don't need it. You can bring it if that's a rule, but the bed's big enough. I want to know when she can get out of here."

"She can be released tomorrow. She'll require some follow-ups as an outpatient, and there are some instructions she—and you—will need to follow."

"Whatever it takes. I need to get a hotel. I need a good, secure hotel where she'll feel safe. A two bedroom, for when my parents get here, with a sitting room or whatever. We'll need a place to sit together, talk together."

"I was about to arrange a room at the Palace," Eve told her. "It's very secure. I can make it to accommodate what you need. Your sister has a debit card for—"

"From him?" Tish's damp eyes went hard as stone. "From Strazza?"

"From the lawyer in charge of his estate."

"We don't want it. We won't take anything from him. I'll use my card to secure the room. Fuck him—not the lawyer, though if he's Strazza's lawyer he probably deserves a few fucks. We'll pay our own way."

"I can secure the room," Eve said evenly. "Just give my name at the desk along with yours."

"I appreciate it. I appreciate, very much, what you've done for Daphne, both of you. I'm glad he's dead. I'll be glad he's dead for the rest of my life."

She glanced toward the door. "There's one more thing. Is there a way I can get her another pair of pajamas? He made her wear white." She turned back, face set. "I'd like to get her another pair to wear tonight. I don't care what color, I don't care if they're covered with pictures of three-headed sheep. Just not white."

"I'll see what I can do," Del told her.

"Solid. Oh, yeah, one more thing. Pizza and ice cream. Anyway to make that happen?"

"There's absolutely a way to make that happen."

"Mag." Tish took a long breath. "Good start. We're going to take care of her. We're going to get her through."

When Tish went back in, Eve thought, yes, they would.

Tired from the marrow out, she drove home. She'd recharge, she promised herself. Coffee, lots of coffee would pump her right back up.

She had items checked off her list. The Miras' security—thanks to Roarke—was beefed up. Daphne Strazza and family had rooms waiting for their arrival the next day. And she had a theory to follow right down the line.

Multiple theories, she admitted, and felt fatigue fall over her as she drove through the gates.

Can't let up, she thought, not on this one. So many reasons she couldn't let up, reasons she wasn't sure she could adequately explain to anyone.

She left the car, went in the house. Found annoyance on the heels of relief when neither Summerset nor the cat waited. Where the hell were they? She'd have dug up a decent insult. She was tired, not brain dead.

She walked upstairs, decided to go straight to her office. If she went to the bedroom first, that big, wonderful bed might tempt her to take a nap.

No time for naps.

She heard Roarke's voice coming from his adjoining office, turned that way.

He'd snazzed his space up, too, and right now had the dual-sided fireplace he shared with her snapping. He sat at his own command center—sleek, powerful black, talking on an ear-link while a holo of some sort of . . . mechanical-like thing circled slowly and his wall screen ran with numbers, figures, maybe equations.

Galahad sprawled over one of the legs of the command center, tail switching as he eyed the holo.

She gave Roarke a half salute, stepped back into her own space.

For a moment she just stood, staring at her board, staring at the dead, the blood, the cruelty.

Grimly, she tossed her coat aside, the scarf and cap with it, and began the work by adding the last victims to the board. Then the crime scene photos, the ME's findings, the lab results—no hair, no fibers, no DNA.

She expanded the board—a handy new feature—and put up ID shots and data of the couples interviewed that day. She looked over as Roarke walked in, the cat padding ahead of him to greet her with body rubs.

"You looked busy," she said.

"Just a few final touches on the meeting I was in when you contacted me earlier."

"I'm sorry to add more stuff to your day."

"Why? It all gets done, doesn't it? Dennis was a bit baffled and more than fascinated with the new toys I added to their system. Our Mira was initially annoyed you'd—add stuff to my day and your own—but she came around.

"And you, Lieutenant," he continued as he went to her, skimming a finger down the dent in her chin, "look tired."

"It's not that kind of tired."

She surprised them both when he drew her in for a kiss by clinging to him, by the tears that spilled.

"There now. What is it?"

She shook her head, clung tighter. "I can't explain. I can't. Just, just hang on, okay? Hang on. I have to let go. I just have to let go."

He picked her up, carried her to the sofa, cradled her on his lap. "Let go then, baby. I'm right here."

The words, the way he held her, stroked her hair, had the grief, the exhaustion from fighting it, the sheer sorrow pouring out.

"I can't explain," she managed when the tears slowed.

"We'll worry about that later."

While her head banged from the crying jag, it was a comfort to rest it on his shoulder. "I have so much to do."

"And you'll do it. You'll tell me how I can help."

"If I'd caught this case three years ago. February, three years ago, right before you? I think it would have broken me. I think it might have been the end of me. Now it just . . . Maybe it bruises some, but it won't break me. It won't because you hang on when I have to let go."

"Tell me what you can."

"There's a lot. Starting with the victims this morning. What he did to them . . . Well, it's right there, on the board. Reveled in it, I think. More than before, even more. Because taking those lives, that was the grand finale—isn't that the term—he'd missed that before. He didn't realize he'd missed that, and now he knows."

She started to get up, settled back when he held her against him. Yes, she thought, stay for now.

"He's made moves—virtually and face-to-face—with other women. Before the first assaults, between assaults. It fed the beast just enough."

She ran it through for him, through to the trip with McNab to the destroyed drop 'link while she sat in his arms with the fire crackling.

"He may be able to salvage something," Roarke said. "But isn't the question: How was it all timed so very well?"

"Yeah, that's the question. It's arrogance. It's finding himself in the spotlight, feeling invincible. He likes to taunt—and that taunt was for me—for the cops, but I think for me. Female cop."

"All that's difficult, but it's not altogether what tied you into knots."

"The finish was Daphne Strazza."

She closed her eyes, told him.

"Nobel's right. She's dangerously fragile right now, struggling just to get through one day to the next. She's so damaged she doesn't know how to make a decision, is so indoctrinated she can't make one without being told. I know what it's like. I remember what it's like when you're so terrified of making the smallest mistake you do nothing. And still it's not right. I saw her face when her sister came in. Her first reaction was raw fear. Not *of* her sister. Maybe *for* her, not sure."

"You think Strazza threatened to hurt her family, used that as another level."

"I think it's possible—probable. The fear was the first reaction, instant, ingrained. Then she flinched, jerked back like she'd been slapped when the sister said Strazza was dead. Period. It's almost as if she didn't completely understand it or believe it until that moment. Then she let go. What I saw in the sister was someone who knew how to hang on, to hold on."

She turned her face into his throat. "I saw myself, and you. What it is to have that, to be stunned you do. I saw love, and a chance to heal.

"It took brutality to give her that chance. It took brutality to give me mine. Fighting that understanding, that mirror I see when I look at her, is exhausting."

"Why would you fight it?"

"I have to be objective to do the job, and if I don't do the job, do it right, another couple could end up on that board."

"Darling Eve." He stroked her hair, pressed his lips to it. "It's the blend of your objectivity, observations, instincts, and your empathy for the victim that makes you what you are. It's that very blend that'll lead you to the answers, lead you to him."

"I hope to Christ you're right. Because they're leading me. In a couple of directions, but they're leading me."

"Then we'll follow. But first, you'll eat."

She started to dismiss that as a matter of course, then realized she felt steady again. And surprisingly hungry.

"Actually, I could. I had the worst pocket of something earlier." She eased back, smiled at him. "I could eat actual food of pretty much any kind."

"That's quite an opening. I'll surprise you." He shifted, pulled a little case out of his pocket, flipped it open. "Take a blocker for that miserable headache, and don't be a baby about it. Then, half a glass of wine, I think, to smooth out the edges. You'll work better for it."

She took the blocker, deciding to reserve judgment on the wisdom of the wine when he wandered back into his office.

And came out with a box wrapped in silver paper.

"I think this is the right time."

She looked at the box, at him. "Come on. Wasn't it just Christmas?"

"No. And this is something, like the blocker, I think you could use at the moment."

She could hardly bitch at him when she'd just blubbered all over him, so she took the box, lifted the wrapped lid. And nearly blubbered again when she saw the little music box.

When she looked at him, just looked at him, with her exhausted eyes stunned and filled with emotion, Roarke knew he had chosen well.

She lifted out a young girl's music box, not a fancy, important one. Just a sweet little white box with some gold swirls. And the dancer, twirling on one leg, arms curved over head as the music played.

"It's a common thing," Roarke began.

"No, it's not. It's not. Shut up a minute." She fought back tears, even if they were hot with gratitude, full of the miracle that she had someone who loved her just this much.

"It's not common," she managed. "It's beyond special. Not my style, right, not cop-style. But . . ."

"Even when I bought it I wasn't sure if it was for you or for me."

"For us then. It made you sad when I told you about it. You could've bought something slick or fancy or glittery, but you knew it wouldn't be right. It would've looked important, but it wouldn't be special. You took some . . . you took an ugly little memory, and you turned it into love. I'll never . . . I can't tell you . . ."

She took a long breath, watched the dancer twirl. "What's the song?"

"A twentieth-century classic. 'Tiny Dancer'."

"Fits. Thanks." She moved to him, wrapped around him. "It means . . . I can't begin. I'm going to put it in here. Not cop-style, but it fits in here."

She drew back, walked to the shelf where she'd put the silly stuffed Galahad he'd once given her, set the box beside it. "It'll remind me there's room for the sweet. No matter what, there's room, and you need to take it. "

Gently she closed the lid. "And when I need the sweet, when you're not right here for me to grab on to, I just have to open it."

"He didn't break you," Roarke said.

"No, they didn't break us. That's why it fits in here. It's why *we* fit in here. And the way we do, Roarke, the way we fit? Nothing's ever going to break us."

Touched by her reaction, steadier in his own heart seeing the little box on her shelf, he smiled at her. "We are what we are, and what we've become together. I'll see to that meal."

When he went to the kitchen, she gave the music box a last brush of her fingers. Then she went to her command center, brought up the list the dependable Peabody had sent her, skimmed an e-mail from Mira thanking her for Roarke and telling her she shouldn't worry.

"I forgot," Eve called out. "The resident corpse wasn't in the foyer. What gives?"

"Summerset, alive and well, is off meeting a group of friends for drinks and dinner."

"Do corpses have zombie groups or friends or—"

She swung around at the unmistakable scent.

"Pizza?"

"There are times," Roarke said as he carried it to the table, "you need it."

She sat a moment, afraid she'd become overwhelmed yet again.

Then she rose, went to him. She slipped her arms around him, kissed him softly, brushed her lips over his cheeks, then again to his mouth, still soft, but deep.

"You make me question why I don't offer you pizza every day. Several times a day."

"Just the right amount." She hugged him, swayed with it. "Just one thing?"

"Which one?"

"Tell me there's no spinach anywhere in that pie."

"There is no spinach anywhere in that pie."

"That's perfect. I think wine's a good thing. I'll get it."

She looked back at him as she chose a bottle with a name she actually recognized. "It doesn't matter."

"What doesn't matter?"

"How hard it gets with the job. It doesn't matter if you're pissed at me or I'm pissed at you, or we're seriously pissed at each other. Because we're always going to come back to this."

"To pizza and wine," he said a smile.

"To that. To each other." She carried the bottle to the table, poured him a glass, poured herself half of one. "And that's enough sloppy stuff. Let's eat."

19

SHE COULD TAKE A HALF HOUR, EVE TOLD HERSELF, WITH HIM, PIZZA, AND wine. And talk about anything but murder.

"So the youth center, it's coming along?"

"It is. We should do a walk-through, you and I. You may have some ideas on the finer details as we move in that direction."

"They won't care about that—the kids who come there. They'll care about having a roof over their head, and a decent bed to sleep in, a decent meal."

Which should include pizza regularly, Eve thought.

"I know it's more than that," she added. "The counseling, the education, and the training, the chance to become something other than a punching bag or an addict or a petty criminal. They're not going to care what color you paint the walls, or the shape of a sofa or table."

"Perhaps not, but by living in a space that surrounds them with care in those details, they may be more inclined to care how they live, to take care of where they live."

He brushed his hand over hers. "And some," he continued, "might make the connection that someone cared enough about them to add the little details."

"That's a point. It's a good point," she decided. "I can guarantee they are going to care about the size of the screen in the community room, and what vid games they're allowed to play." She smiled as she bit into pizza. "And they'll bitch about the classes, the assignments, the chores."

"Which would make them normal, wouldn't it?"

"That's exactly right. And that's what you're doing. Giving them a chance for normal. It's big, Roarke. I'd like a walk-through."

"Good, we'll set it up. I want, very much, for you to see what it's becoming."

She thought of the girls they'd found there—those long-dead girls. And knew he'd always think of them, too. "When do you figure you'll open?"

"We're planning for spring. May, if all continues to go well. We've already contracted some of the key staff, and we're interviewing and vetting others."

"You move fast, ace."

"If I didn't, we might not be sitting here now, having pizza and wine."

"Sure we would." She ate another bite. "You'd have caught up with me eventually."

He laughed, took a second slice. "Your headache's gone."

"Yeah, it is."

And because it was, because of all she had—right here—she added another dollop of wine to her glass and embraced the moment.

After the meal, she went straight to coffee. The work, the job, the hours ahead would be long and tedious. The conclusions her instincts pointed her to had to be set to the side.

Facts and evidence, she reminded herself. The gut wasn't enough.

"What's my assignment?" Roarke asked her.

"We've culled out names from the gala's guest and staff lists. Males that fit the elements of Mira's profile, with a little refining. The probability, given current evidence and statements, runs more than ninety percent he was there. It's possible he crashed, isn't on either list, but that's where we start."

She ordered the list Peabody'd sent her on her wall screen. "This is my share. I've cut down Mira's age bracket. I'm reasonably sure he's closer to thirty than fifty, otherwise, these individuals run on what she profiled. We're going to dig down, every name. Family, education, travel, finances, any criminal however small—including traffic violations. Medical that we can get—and for now, no hacking."

"Lieutenant," he said with sorrow. "You spoil my fun."

"For now," she said again. "We get this list down, I'll wrestle out a warrant for deeper, for any sealed files, for the works. Connections to theater or screen—anything involving the level of makeup and costuming the UNSUB uses, that's a big bonus if found. Same with any major interest in e-work."

"As both of those may simply be a hobby, something that wouldn't show in the data."

"That's it. I'm going to give you the first five."

"It seems a lot of names for the profile."

"Some of them were married or cohabbed at the time of the gala, and now aren't. We're checking them. Some are staff who, while not assigned specifically to the gala, would have easy access. Peabody added those, and she's not wrong."

"I'll start in my office. I need to multitask for the next hour or so. Then I may join you in here."

Eve settled into it. It was routine—tedious, but routine—with a rhythm she knew well. Within thirty minutes, she'd eliminated two names, one as she could confirm he'd been in Rio on the night the Patricks had been assaulted, and the second who'd been involved in a vehicular accident the day of the Strazzas' attack, and was still recovering from a fractured ankle and other injuries.

She moved on, discarding, earmarking for a yet deeper search.

When Roarke came in, she'd just programmed more coffee as she studied the next subject.

"This guy went to clown school. Why is there a school for clowns? Why are there clowns?"

"Someone has to make 'em laugh."

She slid her gaze to his face. "Seriously?"

He shrugged. "While some fear the clown, many more are vastly entertained."

"This guy supplements his income in food services by dressing up in weird getups for parties and benefits. Or his income in food services supplements his clown gigs. Hard to tell. But there you have makeup and costumes and a propensity to scare the shit out of people."

"Some people."

Sincerely shocked, she gaped at him. "You *like* clowns?"

" 'Like' is a strong word in this context." He helped himself to her coffee. "I assume the clown goes on the suspect list."

"You bet your ass."

"I have one out of my five that bears a deeper look. The others I've eliminated, for reasons I've detailed in my memo back to you."

"Good. I've got three out of nine."

Roarke lifted an eyebrow. "You're quicker at this."

"I'm the cop." And a human being, she thought, who could use a little smugness. "Want another set?"

"All right." He sat at the auxiliary, hair tied back, sleeves rolled up.

She sent him five more, settled back into the rhythm.

At one point, she sat back. "I don't think this guy's a killer—or not ours anyway—but he's sure as hell into something hinky."

"Hinky as in supporting a sidepiece, travel and gifts for same—I've had a few of those—or hinky as in criminal?"

"Both actually. But I think the sidepiece is also a partner. A lot of travel for her, a lot of suspicious deposits—smallish, that added together aren't smallish. Sixty to eighty large every six weeks, when she travels to Argentina—no relatives or business there on record. The deposits disappear, except for an exact ten percent."

"Or end up in another account," Roarke said. "Money laundering, and the ten's her fee."

"I get that. I don't have time for that." But she earmarked the name to send to those who would, and should. Caught Roarke's grin.

"What?"

"The poor bastard has no idea of the good news/bad news heading his way. 'Sir, you're clear of any suspicion of murder, and are now under investigation for money laundering, probable fraud, and so on'."

"He should've thought of that before he got so greedy."

She moved on, frowned when her 'link signaled.

"Dallas."

"Hey." McNab's pretty face came on screen.

"You're still at it?"

"Got sucked into the puzzle, you know? She-Body's up here in the lab working on her stuff, so it's all smooth. Got pizza and fizzies. But we're calling it pretty soon so I wanted to let you know I've got some pieces. Man, you would not *believe* what people throw in a recycler, and in that ritz neighborhood."

"Pieces of the 'link?"

"Yeah. Only some of it got shredded—we lucked out. It's crushed to shit, so it's going to take a while. I can't say a hundred percent, but what I'm putting together I'm going to say it looks homemade. It looks

like somebody made it out of spare parts. It's not all from one manu-
facturer or from the same model—that I can say for a hundred."

"That's good. That's good work. Put Peabody on."

"Hang a mo. She-Body, Dallas wants a jaw."

"I don't want a jaw," she muttered. Roarke shook his head, made
a talking gesture with his hand. "Why doesn't he say *talk*?"

The screen bobbled as McNab passed the 'link. Peabody came on.

"We're making some progress—McNab told you his. I've got one
good possible out of the first eight."

"Good. Send it. We've got . . ." Roarke held up a finger, signaling
he had another. "Nine out of the first twenty-nine. I'll copy you."

"How'd you get through twenty-nine? I've been at this since—"

"Roarke's working some."

"Oh. Okay, that's better. He's really fast with comp work."

"I'm beating his total," Eve said before she could stop herself.
"Doesn't matter. Stop at ten, go home. Both of you."

"Twenty," Peabody said. "I've got twenty in me."

"Twenty. Send me all potentials before you leave. We'll pick this
up tomorrow."

Eve clicked off, pressed her fingers to her eyes.

"You can take a break," Roarke pointed out.

"No, not yet."

"A pick-me-up then. Milk and cookies."

"I'm not drinking milk. Do you know where it comes from?" The
idea made her shudder.

"As does the cheese on the pizza you're so fond of."

"Entirely different. Cookies, maybe. After I do another five."

"What about soy milk?"

"Soy milk, soy milk. Say that a few times running and tell me it
doesn't sound revolting."

"I fear I can't." He glanced at his wrist unit when it beeped. "That's

Tokyo. I need to deal with this, then I'll be back. For cookies and something other than milk of any kind."

She went through the next five, painstakingly. Moved on to another three before she pushed away from the command center, moved around the room, circled the board.

Her gut wasn't wrong, she thought, and her head was in line with it now. But she still had work to do, the routine, the eliminations.

She went back, brought up the names of the possibles the other team members had sent her. And lined them up.

Seventeen so far. Seventeen who had enough in their backgrounds, histories, routines, lives to be considered potential rapists, murderers.

Eighty more eliminated, by herself and people she trusted to do the job right.

Another forty-plus yet to be put through the intrusion of a police search.

And every inch of the cop she was knew what he hid behind his mask.

She went back, set aside the current work, pushed down the avenue where her gut, her head told her to go.

"Took longer than I'd hoped," Roarke said as he came back. "You really should take that break. Five minutes to rest your eyes, your brain."

He paused when he glanced at the wall screen, at the list of names.

"You have more."

"I put up what the other team members sent. We're more than halfway done with this first pass. We'll need those deeper runs on what we cull out. I'm going to want to take a look at the ones the others have listed, but if they pulled them out, there's something."

He looked back at her. "You're a cop to the bone."

"No surprise there."

"And the love of my life. I know all sides of you. You found something. Someone."

"I can't say that. More than one someone up there."

"What did you find?" he persisted.

"Cheats, liars, some shady dealings, embarrassments, mistakes, good deeds, broken hearts."

"Eve."

"Life's full of all of that." Then she sighed. "You have a respected, high-skilled doctor—not much liked on a personal level, but respected. A BFD in his world. His bad luck isn't just being dead, but that the investigation into his murder will expose him as an abuser, possibly a sadist. A cruel, domineering son of a bitch who preyed on a vulnerable, much younger woman and essentially made her a prisoner of his will.

"I might say she was old enough to get out, she had people to run to, but she didn't. And we may never know how he managed to wrap the chains around her that kept her with him."

She got up now, let herself move.

"That woman, cowed, fragile already, is brutally, viciously attacked, raped, beaten, choked by an assailant that uses staging to terrify *his* prey. Who humiliates her—and this woman had already suffered, no question, constant humiliation. During the long, brutal, and humiliating assault, her husband's struck down, and in turn, she is struck down. Blow to the back of the head. When she recovers, she's in such deep shock she ends up wandering the streets naked in the middle of a frigid night."

She looked toward the board and Daphne's battered face.

"She wanders outside because the assailant released her, as he had with previous targets. Other couples, with similar lifestyles, social and financial standings. A pattern. Murder changed the pattern, expanded it, so the assailant pushes his escalation, in time frame, in violence."

She could see it—God, she could feel it. All of it. All sides of it.

"It was always going there," she said. "Always. From the first time he tried to intimidate a woman, to push himself on her and was rejected. From the first time he fantasized about a woman he couldn't have, it was going there. This?" She gestured to the board. "This was always in him, no matter what mask he wore to hide it. He couldn't have this woman. Might have made some overture, was rejected. Maybe simply kept it to fantasy, but the fantasy kept cycling, deepening, darkening."

She walked back to her comp, opened a file, ordered an image on screen.

The man and woman stood with their arms around each other's waists, laughing. An ocean flowed behind them. She wore a short, billowing dress that the breeze blew high on her thighs. Her hair lifted in it, swirling dark, wildly curling around a singularly beautiful face.

While the man was handsome, fit, appealing—leaning toward distinguished—she dominated the image.

"This was taken about twenty years ago, for a profile on the couple, published in some glossy mag."

"Who are they?"

Eve held up a finger, called up another image.

Now two couples stood together, formal wear, jewels, glamour. Along with the glamour was an ease, a look of enjoyment.

"Are the women related? There's a resemblance, though the one on the left is . . ."

"Exceptional. Stunning. The object of his desire."

Roarke nodded, came to lean against the curve of the command center. "His mother?"

"No. His mother's on the right. His aunt's on the left. He spent a lot of time with his aunt and her family. Visiting, spending school breaks."

She called up a picture of the woman, just the face, then split-screen it with another.

"Do you see it?"

Roarke glanced back at Eve, then looked more closely at the two images. "Both have dark, curling hair, both are extremely beautiful."

"It's more," she insisted. "The shape of the face, the shape of the mouth. Not exact, but very similar. The way their eyes are set—I did a comparison. They don't resemble each other, but they do, on a kind of subliminal scale. It's the balance of their features, the almost perfect symmetry. He may not have understood it, not consciously, but there, suddenly, the woman he'd fantasized about most of his life. There she was, young, beautiful, available. But—"

Eve reached for her coffee. "She didn't want him. She wanted his cousin."

"You believe . . ." He had to look at the board to read the name. "You believe Kyle Knightly attacked his cousin, beat and raped his cousin's wife. Stole from them, tormented them, shattered them because he lusted for his cousin's mother?"

"I know it. I felt something off, just off, when I talked to him at the studio. Something about the way he talked about Rosa—not the words, so much. But he did say that he'd seen her first, like he was joking, but his eyes weren't joking. He said he'd told his cousin to make a move, even though she was with someone else. But today, she told me she'd made the move. It's a small thing, but it's going to matter,

I think. And I think when I talk to her alone, she's going to tell me Knightly approached her, she'll tell me she had to brush him off."

"Rejected him."

"She wouldn't have seen it that way. She'd have barely seen him at all because she'd already seen Neville. She told me today that the minute she saw him, that was it."

Pausing, Eve turned to Roarke. "I know what she means. That's another echo for me. The first time I saw you—that was in a crowd, too, the funeral for one of my dead—it hit, and hard. I didn't like it one bit. It pissed me off, but it hit."

"On both sides. One look." Without thinking, he slid a hand into his pocket, rubbed his fingers over the button he'd carried ever since, one that had fallen off her truly ugly suit the day they'd met. "So, she barely saw him because all she saw was his cousin."

"And, oh, that festered. He wants what he wants. He's rich and powerful, actors and screenwriters and industry people come to him, and *she* says no? The others say no? His cousin thinks he can steal what should be his? First his cousin's mother flaunts herself, makes him want, but won't let him have. Now his cousin takes the fantasy that's standing right in front of him, young and fresh. They have to pay for it, they all have to pay, these fucking people who remind him, over and over of what he's denied. Because he's the best those bitches have ever had, and he can make them admit it."

She let out a breath. "His second victim—the female—writes screenplays, like his aunt. That fits, and it solves the puzzle for me of why Lori Brinkman when none of his other female targets had any kind of career. He's never been married, never officially cohabbed or unofficially that I can find. He has a rep as a ladies' man: dating beautiful women, never sticking according to gossip rags. And—"

She broke off, took another hit of coffee. "He's got a sexual assault hit, charges dropped, right after his eighteenth birthday. And I went back, took a look, noted that right about the same time a cool mill was transferred from his parents financials to the complainant, the twenty-year-old woman who recanted.

"I think I'm going to find more payoffs, from him, that didn't get as far as formal charges first. He dabbled in school plays, but hit his stride performing in and producing vids, high school, college. One of his highlights—self-proclaimed in an interview—was the restaging of *Dracula*, in which he also starred, his freshman year in college. He said, in the interview, he saw Dracula as romantic as well as sexual, and that by seducing and taking his female victims, he was giving them sexual release during a time when repression was the rule. He . . . released them. Bound them by his power, then released them from their own inhibitions."

"That's one way to look at it," Roarke conceded. "And now I want a drink."

"I can't prove it, yet. But I will. He took e-courses, but everybody does. He excelled, but didn't pursue them. I'm betting when we ask, we're going to find he's one of the go-to guys when somebody has a comp issue. I bet Kyle can fix it."

She frowned when Roarke offered her a small glass of wine.

"I guess so," she considered, and sipped.

"I knew, Roarke, everything in me knew, today when he sat across from me, an arm around his cousin's wife. Her shoulder to lean on. He set it all up. His cousin's uptown on a shoot, he's downtown, and he talks Rosa into going with him, has a director type there for cover, too. He's right there to support her when she gets that text."

"Easily sent by remote, or scheduled to send at a certain time."

"I got that. And it's dumped in a recyler half a block from the Patricks' building—to add more fear—and that bin just happens to do the crush and shred before we can get there. Previous crush is eight A.M., giving him a big wide window to dump it, head into work. No way we could've gotten to it before the scheduled crush—he even checked the time to be sure when we were at Central. I went hot all the way, and we were still too late. He had it all worked out.

"He's smart," she said, pacing again. "Reckless—that's arrogance. He didn't have to take another swipe at his cousin and Rosa, didn't have to put himself in the position of sitting across from me. He just wanted to."

"The Patricks will be grateful, will feel grateful he was with her when that text came. That he took her to you, stayed with her. All of it designed to make them grateful to the man who brutalized them."

"He's a damn good actor." She stared at Kyle's ID shot. "Damn good at setting the stage. I've got to write it up. Write it all up, every detail, then I have to convince Reo to get behind it, get me a search warrant. He's got that hoard he's stolen stashed somewhere, and somewhere he can bask in it whenever he wants. We still have to finish vetting the list. If I'm wrong—"

"You're not." Roarke recalled the images of Knightly's aunt and Rosa onto the screen. "You're not wrong. I'll start working on the other names while you write it up. But you're not wrong."

It took her an hour to write up the report in such a way that utilized only facts, only available data, making the connections in a logical point by point.

Then she let it simmer while she updated her lists or eliminated more possibles before going back and reading it all again.

When she felt it would stand, she sent it to APA Cher Reo with a request for a face-to-face meeting at the earliest possible time the next day; to Mira, asking for a consult if the profiler felt one necessary; and to her commander.

She copied the other members of the team on all.

When she'd finished, she sat back, closed her eyes.

"You need sleep."

"I know. I have to be on top of things tomorrow. If I do it right, he won't have the chance to do this to anyone else. He's got the next targets, he's got the costume, the props, everything. He's dreaming about it. He'd never stop."

"No, and eventually, he'd kill his aunt and uncle."

Eve opened her eyes, turned to Roarke. "Yes. His full circle. He'd have to. I requested access to his full medicals. His parents paid off the woman he assaulted. Maybe they did that on the condition he get help."

"He's close to his cousin. His cousin may know."

"Yeah, I may have to go there."

She turned back to view an incoming text.

"From Reo—that was fast."

I'm staying with a friend tonight in your area. I can come to your place when I leave. Out of here by seven-thirty. Due in pretrial meetings at ten. CR

"That works," Eve muttered, replied with the same, then sent a message to Peabody.

Report here, by eight for full briefing and

"Wouldn't you want to brief everyone at once?" Roarke interrupted.

"Crap. She added the others on, continued . . .

meeting with APA Reo.

"Will provide breakfast."

"Uh-uh."

"Eve. You're asking them to come here after working until near midnight. It's a small thing."

"Crap and more crap." But she added it on. "Satisfied?"

"With that, well enough. Altogether, the way you're drooping other satisfaction will have to wait. Come on then, it's time to put it away and sleep."

"I'm not drooping," she grumbled. "Besides," she added as he pulled her to her feet, "it's male drooping that postpones other satisfaction."

"Very droll."

Maybe she was drooping, a little, by the time they got to the bedroom. And there lay the cat, stretched out on his back in the middle of the bed.

"That's where he went." Eve shrugged off her jacket, unhooked her weapon harness. "He likes the big fancy bed, too."

"He has exceptional taste."

"Well, he's going to have to make room." She sat, pulled off her boots. Just sat. "I don't want to dream. I can feel dreams circling around in my head, just waiting until I close my eyes. I don't want them."

"Do you remember our last night on the island?"

"I remember there was a lot of non-drooping satisfaction."

He smiled, lit the fire. "We spread a blanket on the beach, and we had a bottle of wine, a loaf of bread, cheese, fruit."

"Those little eclair things."

"And those. We ate, drank, watched the water, watched the sun go down until the water took it. And the moon came up."

"We did more than sitting and watching," she recalled as she rose to undress.

"We did, but we did sit and watch and it was quiet and lovely. It was the world right then."

"If I'd known you owned an island, I might have married you for it. It was a nice bonus."

He just kissed her forehead. "Dream of that," he said, and led her to bed.

He slipped in beside her, drew her close, rubbed her back in the way he knew helped her drift away. "Dream of that tonight. Only that."

And she did.

20

THE NOW, THE WHAT CAME NEXT, PUSHED AT THE EDGES OF HER BRAIN AND brought Eve out of sleep. In the dark, she reached for Roarke, the comfort and solidity. But he wasn't there.

She sat up, then just curled into herself, knees to her chest, as the weight, the fresh misery of what she had to do fell over her.

She'd get her warrant, and she'd pull Kyle Knightly into the box. She'd break him. She knew how to break him. And then . . .

God, then.

In the dark, the cat jumped on the bed, padded to her, butted his head against her shins.

Eve picked him up—Christ, talk about weight—clutched him to her as a child might a teddy bear. The cat purred in her arms, rubbed his wide head against her shoulder.

"You always come through, don't you?" she murmured, easing her hold to stroke and scratch. "Pretty smart of me to haul your fat ass home that day." She rubbed her cheek against the top of his head. "Yeah, I'm pretty smart."

She let out a sigh. "Lights, ten percent."

In the faint glow, she called for the time. Oh-five-twenty-one.

"Might as well get started."

After giving Galahad a last cuddle, she rolled out of bed, headed straight for coffee.

As she lifted the mug, the cat eyed her. Steely, unblinking.

"You wouldn't tell me if Roarke already fed you."

Those bicolored eyes seem to harden, and never wavered.

"You, pal, would be a challenge in the box. I've got to respect that."

She ordered him up some kibble, added a salmon chaser. And when he pounced on it, took the coffee with her to shower.

No point in thinking about it, she told herself as she let the jets pummel and steam. She'd take the first steps, then the next until it was done. Case closed, move on.

When she came out again, Galahad—bowl empty—sat washing himself industriously.

She walked into the closet, stopped herself as she reached carelessly for the closest jacket at hand. She glanced back, reminded herself the cat couldn't help her here. Besides, she wasn't an idiot. Though she'd never buy that what she wore mattered in the day-to-day of cop work, today . . . Image, perception, presentation? It wouldn't hurt to keep those things in mind regarding breaking Knightly.

Normally she avoided red for the job as it struck her as too female, too deliberately bold. But that might be exactly what the day called for.

She mulled over the section of red jackets, their various hues and tints, until she annoyed herself, so grabbed one at random.

Not bright so much as strong, she decided, and the fact it would hit just below her waist added another subtle point. Unbuttoned, it would show part of her weapon harness.

Because her mind wanted to swim when she scanned trousers, she grabbed a pair of straight-legged, simple pants out of the gray section.

She opted for a sweater rather than a shirt—easier movement, in case she got a chance to . . . or, rather, was required to physically restrain Knightly.

She dressed, grabbed boots the same shade as the pants as it seemed easiest, and considered the most aggravating portion of her day complete.

She stepped back into the room as Roarke walked in.

"Good morning. I'd hoped you'd sleep longer."

"Long enough. What?" Her brow furrowed as he studied her. "Are you going to tell me there's something wrong with this?" She waved her hands down her body.

"Quite the opposite, Lieutenant. I was just thinking you look strong, capable, and in charge."

"Good. I am."

He crossed to her, lifted her chin. "Then why do your eyes look sad?"

"Not sad, just working things out. What time did you get up to lord over the known universe?"

"A bit before five. I had a brief 'link conference." He lifted her chin a little higher, kissed her. "Did you dream after all?"

"Not bad ones." He saw too much of her, she thought, and evaded by shifting away to gather her things from a table. Restraints, 'link, comm, badge, loose credits.

"Is that all you have?"

"Of what?"

"Money."

Annoyance rising, she shrugged. "I just need to go by the machine, pull some out. I'll hit an AutoBank when I get to Central."

He took a money clip out of his pocket, pulled off several bills. "Take it. It'll save you time." When she made no move to do so, he felt his own annoyance rising. "Christ Jesus, if it troubles you so much, you can pay me back. You've more important things to do and think about today than stopping by an AB."

She took it, stuffed the bills in her pocket. "You're right. Thanks." But she said it stiffly.

"Would you feel better if you signed an IOU? Perhaps I should charge you interest."

"I said you were right." When he only lifted an eyebrow, she fumed. "I didn't pay for anything I'm wearing."

Now he angled his head. "I don't believe I bought those restraints, your weapon, your 'link."

"Goddamn it, you know what I mean."

"I do, just as I know you hate to shop for clothes. For anything, actually, while I enjoy it."

She started to snarl back at him, hissed out a breath instead. "I'm looking for a fight." Cursing herself, she pressed her fingers to her eyes, dropped them. "I can't explain it."

"All right. Should we have one now," he said, very pleasantly, "or schedule it for later?"

"It's not you and me. I'm just using you and me so I don't have to think about everything else. I want it done, I want it over. I want to close this door."

"This door opened so hard on the heels of the last investigation. It's hardly a wonder you're scraped raw."

"Yeah. Time to hope for a nice, straight murder. Greedy bastard shoves business partner out the window. Brother stabs brother over the last bag of soy chips. Spouse bludgeons spouse over sidepiece. You know, the fun stuff."

"I have no doubt you'll get that wish. After all, there's never a dearth of greed or sidepieces in the world, but only a finite number of soy chips."

"That's the damn truth. We okay?"

"Of course we are."

"I want to go ahead and finish up the rest of the names, just check that box off."

"I've one or two things to see to myself."

"I fed the cat," she said when they started out together.

"That's a coincidence. So did I."

"I knew it!" Glancing back at Galahad, she would have sworn he smirked.

Roarke smirked right back at him. "What he doesn't know is he's now eating low-calorie kibble."

"He is?"

"By Summerset's decree after a vet checkup where the vet advised that our boy should lose three to five pounds."

"I gave him a little salmon," Eve confessed.

"I went with tuna."

The laugh felt good. Then she walked into her office, saw the long table already stacked with plates, flatware, cups.

"Oh, hell."

"People need to eat," he reminded her, and walked into his office.

She sat, got more coffee, and diligently worked her way through the remaining names. She barely noticed Summerset rolling trays of heat-domed dishes out of the elevator. Or did her best to ignore it.

She heard someone coming—not Peabody, wrong stride, wrong sound—swiveled in her chair as Reo came in.

"Look at this! You redid your office. It's fabulous. You have a fire-place. I'd *kill* for a fireplace this time of year. I love the colors, and your workstation—"

"Command center," Eve corrected.

Reo went, "*Oooh,*" and walked over on boots with high, thick heels. "Very impressive. And whatever's for breakfast smells wonderful."

"Didn't your friend make you breakfast?"

Reo sighed, took off her coat. She wore a slim dress, short jacket, both in deep, dreamy green. "No, he had an early shuttle to catch. It's someone I've been seeing for a few months, semi-seriously the last few weeks. And now he's leaving for Sierra Leone for sixteen months."

"Where the hell is Sierra Leone?"

"West Africa. Can I have coffee?"

Eve tapped the AutoChef in the command center.

"Okay, now I'm seriously jealous. He's a teacher, part of an or-ganization called Literacy Warriors. He's going there to teach, to educate. It's noble, admirable, and really crappy timing for me, per-sonally. But." She shrugged, took the coffee. "That's how it goes."

Now she walked to the board. "Your report was detailed, thorough, and largely based on circumstantial."

"I'm right."

Reo sipped, studied. "A sexual obsession for an aunt—she is a knockout—leads him to rape, torture, and eventually murder?"

"A sexual assault on his record at eighteen."

"The complainant recanted."

"And, gee, a million dollars shows up in her bank account."

"That does add interest. It's still a thin net, Dallas."

"He fits the profile."

"He does. He certainly does. But so do others as you've very aptly illustrated."

"I've eliminated all but a handful from the gala. You want to tell me it's just strange coincidence that every victim up there attended that gala and the assailant didn't?"

"No—that's a defense ploy. You honestly think you're going to find the things he took from these people—the jewelry, the valuables, the clothes—right in his home?"

"Yes, I do. He needs them close, and he needs them private. He lives in a converted loft, has the whole building. It's not huge, but it's plenty big enough. He doesn't do much entertaining—according to his own statement. Prefers to take people out. He knows makeup, costuming, staging. And the last victims, hit on the night after the blizzard? Under four blocks from his place. He could've walked it, Reo. He targeted them because he could get there, because after Strazza's death, he wanted the blood. He had to get a kill."

"How sure are you?"

"Truth? All the way. I got an itch the first time I talked to him, but I knew when he came in yesterday. We'd already started on the list of potential males, and he came in. I knew. We still ran them, dug in. And he fits like a fucking glove, Reo."

She nodded, brushed back her frothy mop of blond hair. "I'm going to get you the warrants. It's going to take some tap dancing, but . . ." She turned back, smiled. "I've got the talent."

"You get me the warrants, I'll take him down."

"You take him down, we'll put him away. Okay if I grab some food? I'm starving. A night saying bon voyage eats up the calories."

"Go ahead. Here come Peabody and McNab," Eve added, recognizing the clomp and prance.

Peabody clomped into the doorway, stopped. Her mouth fell comically open. "Wow! I mean mega-wow. This is—when did you— wow. You have all kinds of— Oooh, a balcony!"

"Command center extreme!" McNab bounced straight over.

Eve should've figured an e-geek would know what really mattered.

"You got holo, and multiscreen." He wedged himself in the U with her, bending down to study controls and babbling in geek, apparently about available bytes, streaming, functions.

"Don't touch anything," she ordered, but got out of his way because he looked, well, aroused.

"It's mag, Dallas." Peabody wandered, letting her fingers skim over a chair back. "It's a really good space, and it really, really works. For you, for the house."

"It worked fine before."

"Yeah—the work's the work, right? But, jeez, the new board's awesome ult, and it just all fits with the house instead of being, you know, sort of separate. Got some power vibes going in here." She looked over at McNab, grinned. "He may start crying over that command center."

"Get him, go eat. That'll dry his tears."

Since Eve didn't want to tangle with McNab, she went to the buffet table for more coffee. Then had to deal with the reactions of the others as they filed in.

Baxter looked around, nodded. "Nice. Oh, yeah, very nice. This is what I call a home office. You ought to hit your office at Central like this, Dallas."

The thought actually had a chill whipping down her spine. "Don't even go there."

"Swank, but not fussy," Olsen said, taking a long scan of the room. "Serious work space with just enough pizzazz."

"Priorities," Tredway interrupted. "When we got the word on breakfast, I figured some half-assed Danishes, but . . ." He lifted the dome on a warming dish. "Holy pig meat."

"Dig in," Eve ordered. "We've got a lot of ground to cover."

She let them mill, stuff faces, and when Roarke came in made herself a plate because otherwise he'd make her one.

When, as she'd expected, most went back for seconds, she got the ball rolling.

"Kyle Knightly, prime suspect. If you haven't read the report, do so." Since she had the kick-ass wall screen, she used it, ordered Knightly's ID image up. The suspect is . . ."

She trailed off when Mira came in.

"I'm sorry, Dr. Mira, I didn't know you planned to attend."

"I thought I might be able to answer any questions regarding your suspect's pathology." She looked around as she spoke, started to speak, then stopped herself. "Don't let me interrupt."

Eve continued, detailing Kyle's basic data while Roarke moved to Mira, whispered in her ear. Mira shook her head, patted his arm, then moved to take a seat.

"As detailed in the report, we believe the suspect's fixation and fantasy regarding his aunt escalated into a need to fulfill that fantasy through rape and violence. We are requesting the full incident reports and statements from his arrest at the age of eighteen for sexual assault, and any legal documents that may have been generated to persuade the complaining party to recant."

"A million macaroons are pretty persuasive," Baxter put in.

"Damn right, and the payment casts suspicion on the recant. Considering the length of time between that incident and the assault on the Patricks, it's probable there were other incidents, possible payoffs, possible treatment for the suspect for his behavior. We are requesting access to his medical files, in full."

"I can add weight there," Mira put in.

"Any and all would be appreciated. The suspect lives alone, has never married or by all accounts had a serious relationship. He has a connection to, experience with, and a talent for the theater and screen, with access to professional makeup and costuming, as well as stage props. He is of an upper social and financial rung. Mira's profile fit him like one of his tailor-made suits. Am I wrong?" she asked Mira.

"No. I would conclude Kyle Knightly developed an unhealthy attachment to his aunt—the sister of his own mother. A sexual desire for her. But she belonged to his uncle. He may have merely fantasized, or may at some point have made an advance, and been rejected. Whether gently or angrily, or any point in between, it wouldn't matter. The rejection became as intense as the desire. They're connected for him, and therefore to achieve that desire, that release, he must use force. Must negate any chance of rejection."

"When he sees a woman who brings him that same, or very similar desire," Eve continued, "and she rejects him. More, she prefers his cousin—the son of the woman he wanted."

"It's enough to fuck up the already fucked up," Tredway commented.

"Having this woman," Mira put in, "the one he wanted, the one who would, at the very least, serve as a surrogate for his obsession, choose his cousin? I believe that would have been the psychic break. While he may have raped others, such as the incident when he was eighteen, he likely considered those assaults merely bending the female to his will. Giving her, in his mind, what she truly wanted. He may have used LCs—and if so, they would resemble the aunt. But when Rosa Patrick chose his cousin, forced or rough sex was no longer enough. Assaulting the female, no longer enough. The couple had to pay, the man dominated and humiliated, the woman taken sexually and—vitally—forced to give him validation."

" 'Best you ever had,' " Eve finished.

She paused, noted that Roarke brought Mira a cup of tea. "We know who he is, what he is, where he lives, and where he works. APA

Reo will secure the necessary search warrants for his residence, his studio. Peabody, find out the suspect's schedule for today. Use whatever ploy works."

"Can do."

"McNab, request from Captain Feeney an e-team, including uniforms to secure, to be deployed on my go to the studios. All of the suspect's electronics in that location are to be confiscated."

"You want me there?" McNab asked.

"No, I want you at the residence where it's more likely he keeps any records of his crimes, of his victims and his plans. Should the schedule indicate the suspect will be at the studio at the time of the go, I want Peabody, Tredway, and Olsen to take him in for questioning. Should the schedule indicate he'll be at his residence, we all hit it."

"That's a lot of cops," Olsen pointed out.

"This started with the Patricks, and that's your case. You're going to be there for the takedown."

"Sir," Trueheart began. "The suspect may be in another location, on a shoot or in a meeting."

"Should that be the case, it's Peabody, Tredway, Olsen. You, Baxter, McNab, and myself hit the residence wherever the fucker may be. If he's there, we serve the warrant and proceed. He will be held and brought in for questioning. I'm taking the lead there."

"No argument," Tredway told her.

"I'll break him."

"As long as we can watch," Olsen added.

"Mira, I'd like you to observe as well."

"I'm planning on it."

"The rest of you, remember: He's a coward, and cowards can be more dangerous than the cocky."

Reo circled a finger in the air as she studied her 'link screen. "You'll have your warrants within thirty because I'm just that good. Go get him."

"Peabody, get me his location."

Peabody rose. "Let me just . . ." She wandered off into the kitchen. "Oh, man, the kitchen, too!"

"Focus, Detective."

"Give me a couple."

"Getting a last hit of real coffee before the wars." Baxter strolled back to the buffet.

Roarke pulled Eve aside. "Tag me, will you, when you bring him into Central."

"Sure, if you want."

"I do. I want to watch you work him."

"You must have a couple million things to do."

"I did at least a million of them last night and this morning. Let me know. I'd like to be there. I saw what he did to Daphne Strazza firsthand."

And because he believed, very strongly, his cop might need him before it was done.

Peabody hurried back. "He's slated as working from home until noon today."

Eve thought: Perfect. "By noon he's in a cage. McNab, give Feeney the go. And let's move out. Reo, nice tap dance."

Reo executed a quick, snappy time step, complete with jazz hands. "Keep me updated."

The A-T waited. She decided Roarke had ordered it with the idea she'd have more than Peabody in tow. "Leave your ride," she told Baxter. I'll get you back to it."

He and Trueheart climbed in the back with McNab. "You figure he'll try to rabbit?"

"He's arrogant, so that won't be his first impulse. Insult, fury, threats—lawyer, blah-blah. Might be he'll try the rabbit when he realizes we're going to find his cache—because he damn well has one."

"Don't want to be a downer," Peabody began, "but what if he keeps the trophies in another location? A storage locker we don't know about, another residence we haven't uncovered."

"He needs to look, touch, bask whenever the mood strikes. He needs them with him."

"I've got a basketball trophy from high school." Trueheart smiled at the idea. "My mom keeps it on a shelf in the living room. And the team picture from that year, too."

"I've got first place comp science awards from elementary school," McNab added. "I like looking at them."

"Not sick, but sweet—ever the geek," Baxter commented. "Still, same thing. How about the boy and I do a walk around the building while the rest of you serve the warrant? Just in case he tries to climb out a window."

"That'll work."

She grabbed a street spot, watched Olsen pass and circle as she hunted up a place to park.

Eve got out, studied Knightly's building. Square and substantial on the corner, with the bricks painted a silvery gray, the windows privacy screened, the double entrance doors heavily secured.

"Let's take a walk, my man." Baxter slapped a hand to Trueheart's shoulder and they strode away.

Though everything inside her revved—get this done, get this done—Eve waited until Olsen and Tredway rounded the corner on foot.

She pulled out her PPC, checked, then printed out the warrant.

"Here we go."

"Bet he recognizes us," Tredway said to his partner, then glanced at Eve. "We interviewed him after the Patricks. Never got a buzz, and I'm pretty pissed about that now."

"You didn't have enough."

"Coulda, shoulda, woulda," Olsen said under her breath. "But we've got it now."

"Record on." Eve pressed the buzzer.

"Dallas? I'm betting that cam goes to a screen in most every room in the place." McNab stood casually, orange earflaps over his bedecked lobes, kept his back to the cam, and his voice low. "Audio, too."

"Hmm. It's a good thing we're cleared to enter whether or not the resident is home." Eve didn't keep her voice low. "I'm going to give it another buzz or two, in case he's a late sleeper. Peabody, you can get the battering ram out of the vehicle if the occupant doesn't answer."

It took less than thirty seconds more for the locks to click. Kyle opened the door, casual sweater, pants, skids. Because she knew him—she *knew* him—Eve watched him paint a mask of fear over his face.

"Neville and Rosa. Something happened. God, what—"

"Nope." Eve held up the warrant. "We are authorized to enter this building and search same. Please step back."

"What? Wait a damn minute."

"You need to step back," Eve said when he tried to block the door. "Now," she added, shoving her shoulder against it as he started to slam it shut.

"You can't just break in here," he began.

"Warrant, read it."

"I don't give a god*damn* about some ridiculous warrant. This is private property. This is my home. Get out."

"Mr. Knightly." Tredway's voice stayed cool as ice. "You don't want to interfere with a duly executed warrant."

"Fuck you and your warrant." Rage stained red over his face; insult glittered in his eyes. "We'll see what my lawyer has to say."

"Yeah, you see what your lawyer has to say. Peabody, take this first area, McNab, all electronics."

Kyle shouldered Olsen aside, pushed his face into Eve's. There was the pure, hot, violent fury, unmasked, she'd waited for. "You touch anything, you so much as lay a finger on an inch of my home, I'll have your badge, you arrogant bitch. You touch nothing!" He dragged his 'link out of his pocket. "My lawyer will deal with this, and you."

"Peabody, Olsen, Tredway," After each name, Eve pointed in a direction. "You're in my way, Mr. Knightly."

"Get out of my house. Marco, get Wesley on the 'link. I don't give a fuck who he's talking to! Get him now!"

"You need to move, Mr. Knightly."

"You need to move," he snapped back, and shoved her.

Eve signaled the others to stay back with a hand held down at her side. Oh, yeah, she knew him. And just which buttons to push.

"You may think you're in charge here, but you're wrong. I'm in charge. You're going to do what I tell you to do and step back. You don't want to lay a hand on me again."

"You don't tell me what to do! Get out of my house." He backhanded her. She could've dodged it—he telegraphed the move—but she wanted the hit, wanted the taste of blood in her mouth.

She heard four weapons slap out of their harnesses.

"Stand down," she said easily. "I've got this."

As she lifted a hand to wipe the blood from her mouth, she shot her foot out, swept it, and took his legs out from under him.

He fell hard, as she'd meant him to.

She pulled her restraints, pressed her knee into the small of his back, yanked his arms behind his back as he struggled, and spat obscenities. "Kyle Knightly, you're under arrest for assaulting a police officer." She leaned down closer. "Believe me, other charges will follow. Peabody, send for a couple of uniforms in a black-and-white to take Mr. Knightly into Central for booking. No rush," she added.

She pulled her comm. "Baxter, he's not going to rabbit. Come on in, give us a hand."

Tredway hauled Knightly to his feet. "I've got him, Dallas. Why don't we have a seat?"

"Take your hands off me. Get these things off me. Do you know who I am?"

"I know exactly who you are," Eve said.

She watched his face, his eyes as she wandered the large, open, sleekly furnished main level. Plenty of rage—he shook with rage—but no fear, not yet.

Then she saw it, watched it leap through the rage as she started up the first curve of open iron steps.

"Up here, isn't it?"

His bedroom, an office area both opened onto the wide balcony that overlooked the main level. But beyond, snug behind a jog in the wall, was a large door, closed and locked.

She tapped on it, heard the ring of metal.

"McNab."

"Yo." He came double time.

"Can you bypass the security on this?"

"Wowzer. As much as he's got on the exterior. It'll take some time, but I'll get you in."

"Let me know."

She walked back to the bedroom, and Trueheart came upstairs. "Baxter said you might want some help up here."

"Take the office, Detective. Let's be thorough."

She found porn—no law against it—some sex aids for solo flights. He wouldn't bring women here, she thought. No need for women here.

McNab had been right about the security screens in every room—and the audio.

She stepped out again when she heard Kyle shouting.

He looked up as two uniforms gripped his arms. "I'll make you pay."

"You know what we're going to find when my e-guy gets through that door, Kyle. We both know. You'll be the one paying for the rest of your miserable life."

When the uniforms hauled him out, Olsen shut the door behind them. "Whew, listen to the quiet."

"McNab, how much longer?"

"Nearly got it! This bitch is slick, she is crazy slick."

"Peabody, the battering ram, and this time I mean it."

"Come on, Dallas!" A kind of panic hit McNab's voice. "It's a matter of pride now. Five minutes. Five more."

It took ten, but he let out a war whoop. "She's down."

He glanced back as Eve walked to him. "Could be booby-trapped inside."

"He's the best, remember? He'd never believe anybody would get this far. But . . . stand back."

Eve eased the door open, shoved it clear, stared into pitch dark. "Lights on full," she ordered.

The dark remained.

"Probably cued to his voiceprint," McNab told her. "I can fix that, but—"

"It'll take a minute."

"I've got a flashlight." Tredway stepped behind her, turned on his flash, swept the area slowly.

Eve thought: Aladdin's Cave.

21

WHILE MCNAB WORKED, PEABODY HANDED EVE ANOTHER FLASHLIGHT from a field kit. Eve walked into the room.

Larger than the master bedroom and bath, she noted on her first scan. More a priority, she supposed, as he'd spend the biggest chunk of his time in this space. The long work counter of comps and comms and screens and other e-toys would likely give McNab a small orgasm—and whatever EDD dug out would surely add to the prosecution's case.

She might not understand the geeky wonders of electronics, but she damn sure knew a stack of hard drives and motherboards when she saw them tidily stored on shelves.

She'd bet her magic coat they'd find the victims' security equipment among them, waiting to be stripped for parts or used in builds.

She left that for the time-being, angled her light to the left. She heard Peabody's quickly indrawn breath, understood it. The droid looked very human, very beautiful. It wore the red cocktail dress and sparkling shoes, carried the red bird evening bag Nina Washington had described after the last murders.

Miko's jewelry as well, Eve observed. Then she shined the light on a square-cut diamond and diamond encrusted band on the third finger of the droid's left hand.

All of the victim's wedding rings had been stolen, but none matched this set.

"He put those rings on her finger. In his head, he married her. Replicated his aunt," she said, "played dress up, and God knows what else with it. McNab once you get those lights on, see what you can do with this droid."

"Kept it all." Tredway shined his beam over a large display table holding jewelry, three open cabinets carefully arranged with objets d'art and expensive dust-catchers.

"Not only organized, boss," Baxter pointed out, "but labeled. By victim. Jesus, the PA's going to have a cakewalk."

"Why walk in cake when you can eat it?" Eve queried, then lowered her flash after the lights snapped on.

"Trueheart, do a three-sixty record of this room before anybody touches anything." When he didn't respond, she turned toward him. He stood, staring at the droid.

"Detective Trueheart."

"Sir. Sorry. I was just . . . It's going to come out. How's she going to feel when it comes out he used her to do all this? She's probably a nice person, and it's her own nephew. How's she going to feel when all this comes out?"

"She'll have to accept it had nothing to do with her. She's as much an object to him as the stuff on those shelves. Get the three-sixty."

As he did, Eve walked to the display table. He'd designed it in sections, with room for more. And had brass plates made. Every section, filled with shiny, glittery things bore a name.

Rosa, Lori, Daphne, Miko.

Curious, she opened a drawer, found a collection of other plates, recognized several names of women on the list they'd created.

Future victims, she thought. Safe from him now.

"Dallas. Special little table over here."

Eve crossed to Olsen. Under the glass top of a small, ornate table, one polished to a high gloss, a few pieces of jewelry rested on deep blue velvet. A single earring, a slim bangle bracelet, a pair of small hoop earrings, a necklace formed with multicolored beads.

"This is the sort of jewelry I can afford," Olsen pointed out. "Every day stuff—and the necklace is like something a clever kid might make. Like for his or her mother for a birthday or Mother's Day."

"Hers, the aunt's. Maybe things he pocketed, during visits, things she'd think she lost or misplaced. Just a few tokens, probably from his childhood."

"That's my take. I recognize some of the things on the shelves from the stolen items, the insurance photos, and descriptions."

"And here's a little dresser full of women's fancy under-wear." Baxter gestured to a drawer he'd opened. "All labeled and organized. Got those little sachets in here with them." He took one out, sniffed. "Nice."

"You can bet that'll be the aunt's signature scent." Peabody walked over to look. "And it'll match the fancy perfume atomizer he's got in the wardrobe area. All the cocktail dresses and shoes and bags on our list, Dallas. Along with perfume, a fancy hand mirror and brush set, a case of high-end droid cleaner."

"Make sure it goes on the record." She moved beyond the little table. "His dressing area. Let's back up the record here, make sure we get it all. Costumes, makeup, work counter, wigs."

"It's a pro setup," Peabody said. "It's almost as good as the one at the studio. That tub there? It's what they use for making prosthetics, like noses and—"

"Devil horns?" Eve suggested.

"Yeah."

"Let's pull in the sweepers. He'll have had whatever he wore during the attacks cleaned, but there may be trace, may be blood." As she spoke, she stepped over to a long black coat with hood. "Give me the UV light from the kit. I can fucking smell blood on this."

Peabody dug it out, switched it on. "Holy shit," she said as the black coat lit up with spatters and smears of harsh purple.

"Didn't get it cleaned yet. Busy boy. Tag it, bag it, for the sweepers. I want this into the lab and tested asap."

"Dallas?" McNab gestured her over to the droid. "She—was programmed to respond only to Knightly's voice and command. Pretty simple bypass. You can ask her questions now."

"What is your name?"

The droid smiled. "I'm Astra. I'm so happy to see you, Kyle. I missed you, Kyle."

"It's the bypass," McNab explained.

"When were you programmed?"

"I don't understand."

"Who programmed you?"

"I don't understand. Do you need to punish me?"

Eve took a breath. "Who do you belong to?"

"I belong to Kyle. Only to Kyle. Do you want to fuck me now?" The droid rubbed her hands over her breasts. "I want you, Kyle. You're the only one I want. You're the best I've ever had. Tie me up, Kyle. Make me scream. Make me—"

"Enough. Shut her down, McNab, and start on the comps."

She turned away, noticed Trueheart wasn't blushing. Instead his eyes were hard as flint, all cop.

"All right, boys and girls, let's see what else we can find so we can all eat cake."

By the time they'd finished, Peabody chugged the water from the tubes McNab passed out. "This has to set a record for us. Most evidence ever bagged. Logging it's going to take hours."

"Won't that be fun for some bored drone?" Eve glanced at her comm. "Knightly is booked—on the assaulting an officer charge—and already talking to his lawyer."

"Not a lawyer in the history of lawyers who could spin this one," Olsen said.

"They'll try to make a case for insanity. We're not going to let them. Baxter, I'll get you and Trueheart back to your ride."

"Don't worry about it, boss. Trueheart's got a buddy who'll run us back to my baby in a black-and-white."

"Even better. This was good work, everyone. Good, solid work. McNab, you buffed your e-creds today."

"Thanks."

"Keep buffing. Once the droid and the rest of the electronics are loaded for transfer, go with them, and keep digging."

Hands rubbing together, McNab bopped his hips. "What's it make me that I can't freaking wait?"

"Top geek of the day. Olsen, Tredway, see you back at Central. Peabody, with me."

"I want him in a cage," Peabody began as they walked to the car. "For the rest of his life. Then I want him reincarnated as a slug and put in a tiny box for the rest of that life. Then he can come back as a cockroach. You get the idea."

"It's a really good idea."

"But." Peabody huffed as she settled into the car. "Don't you figure he's totally crazy?"

"He's so bat-shit crazy he should come back as bat-shit in one of those lives. But he's not legally insane. Not even close. He knew what he was doing, Peabody, every step of the way. Mira's going to say the same."

"I wonder if you can come back as bat-shit. It's organic. Are there maybe fizzies in your vehicle AutoChef? I seriously need a boost."

"I don't know, try it."

"You want?"

"Not one of those oversweet bubbly things that look like dyed slush." She started to opt for coffee, then realized she needed something cold. She already had too much heat in her throat. "Pepsi."

"Cherry fizzy, score! We're going to have to tell the Patricks. The rest of the victims and survivors, but the Patricks . . . It's almost as bad as when we had to tell Mr. Mira about his cousin."

"Makes you wonder about cousins."

"I've got dozens of cousins. Pretty great cousins." She passed Eve the tube of Pepsi. "I don't have to play good cop with Knightly, do I?"

"No, you don't. We don't need a confession. I'll damn well get one, but we don't need it. We're going to hammer him, Peabody, give him a good taste of what it's like to be trapped.

"Tag Reo, tell her we're coming in. Mira, too." Though she wished now she hadn't said she would . . . "And Roarke."

She hit lights and sirens. "I want to get started."

When she strode into the bullpen, Jenkinson waved a hand. "Your asshole's lawyer's squawking about having a sit-down with you."

"He'll have to wait. Peabody, get the record of Knightly's trophy room and workshop set up in Interview, and get the asshole and his lawyer brought up once you do."

She walked to her office, decided coffee wouldn't hurt after all, then sat to put together a big, fat file of photos and documents.

In the end, she used fat files for each set of victims, finishing the last as Reo came in.

"Do you want me in the box or in Observation?"

"Observation. I don't want to get hung up on lawyer back-and-forthing right now. No deals on this, Reo."

"So you said before, and what you showed us, briefly, from the suspect's residence leaves no room and no need for any. I spoke with Mira. Her current analysis is the suspect is legally sane. Should that fall apart—"

"It won't."

"Should it," Reo continued, "he'll still spend the rest of his life caged."

"I'll get what you and Mira need. Then you'll wrap him up. Max security, off-planet, consecutive life sentences." She rose, hefted the files.

"Interview A," Peabody said when Eve came out. "The commander had it held for us."

"Handy."

"They're in there. Lawyer is Wesley Drummond—high-end celeb mouthpiece. I gotta say, Knightly looks really smug."

"Not for long."

Eve moved toward, and into Interview A.

"Record on. Lieutenant Dallas, Detective Peabody entering Interview with Knightly, Kyle, and his attorney, Drummond, Wesley."

She paused, just a beat while she studied Drummond—ignoring the client.

Drummond looked slick and winter-tanned, wore a pin-striped suit she figured Roarke would approve of, a trim goatee, and a small silver hoop in one ear.

"Mr. Drummond, would you like to make a comment or statement before I read the charges into the record?"

"Thank you, Lieutenant, I would. I hope we can dispense of this matter without undue time or fuss on anyone's part. While I concede you were authorized to enter and search my client's home, we will dispute the reasoning used to obtain said warrant. My client was, naturally, shocked and upset by the intrusion and this invasion of his privacy. And given the strain of the assaults on members of his family, the threats on a family member only yesterday, his emotional state was and is, naturally, fractured. He acted rashly, however, he was arguably provoked and simply trying, as anyone would, to protect his rights and properties."

"Uh-huh." She tapped the bruise on her jaw. "By striking a police officer in the course of performing her duties."

"I understand there was a scuffle. Surely all parties can admit tempers were high, and step back from this, avoid the negative media attention this will bring to your department."

She said, "Uh-huh," again. "So your only concern, at this time, is the initial charge of assaulting an officer? You're not worried about the other charges?"

"What other charges?"

"Aw, Kyle, you didn't tell him? I'll just read them into the record so we all know where we stand, and who'll be stepping back. Kyle Knightly, you are currently under arrest for assaulting an officer, with additional charges of resisting arrest—"

The lawyer made a *pfft* sound. Eve simply held up a finger.

"You are further charged with breaking and entering, illegal entry, theft, and possession of stolen goods."

"Just one minute," Drummond began.

"Oh, I'm not close to finished. Haven't even got to the meat. To continue, you are charged with assault, assault with intent to cause bodily harm, enforced imprisonment, the torture of Neville Patrick and Rosa Patrick, with the additional charges of sexual assault and rape on the person of Rosa Patrick."

"This is bullshit. Take care of this Wesley."

"What possible proof—"

"Not done," Eve said again. "You are further charged with . . ." She repeated all, naming Ira and Lori. Then she continued on to the Strazzas. "You are additionally charged with the murder of Anthony Strazza. To wind it up, you are hereby charged with—"

She detailed the lesser charges in the case concerning the Strazzas.

"You are charged with rape and sodomy on the person of Miko Carver, and the murders of Miko and Xavier Carver. Did I miss anything, Peabody?"

"It's a lot. It's a whole cavalcade."

"Further charges may be brought by the people of New York. But we'll work with these for now. Peabody, just to keep the bow tidy, read Mr. Knightly his rights again."

"Happy to."

Eve could see the lawyer's wheels turning as Peabody recited the Revised Miranda. She didn't bother to sit.

"I would like some time to consult with my client."

"Sure. Dallas and Peabody exiting Interview. Record off."

She opened the door, looked back at Kyle with a wide smile, tapped her files. "Got it all."

"He didn't tell his lawyer?" Peabody shoved a hand through her hair. "Did he actually think we wouldn't go into his locked room?"

"He's a coward, and he was stalling. Trying to figure the way out, telling himself his pricey legal suit would get him out. We're not finished with him, Peabody, and I don't mean just here and now. We're going to find the other women he molested or raped, document how he scared or bought them off from pressing charges. We're going to hand that to Reo, too."

Eve glanced at the door, shrugged. "They're going to be a while. See if you can find and contact the woman his father paid off—the first one we found. Convince her to tell her story."

"Can I tell her he's been arrested, and the charges?"

"Not the charges, not in detail."

Eve went back to her office, sat and studied her board. Then just closed her eyes until the lawyer sent word they were ready.

"I got her, Dallas. She relocated, married, took her husband's name, but I got her. She says she's put it all behind her, has nothing to say. But, my take? When we can tell her the charges, when we can tell her he's going away? She'll talk to us."

"Good enough for now. Dallas and Peabody reentering Interview. So?" This time she sat, let the files drop with a weighty *thump*. "All set?"

"My client refutes all charges."

"Seriously?"

"Lieutenant, this is no joking matter. These crimes are heinous, and even if the hint of them leaks into the media, my client's reputation will suffer irreparable damage. Should this occur, you will have opened yourself and this department up to a civil suit."

Eve began opening files, removing crime scene photos. "Neville and Rosa Patrick suffered irreparable damage. Lori and Ira Brinkman suffered irreparable damage."

"None of those victims can identify my client as their attacker. I know Neville and Rosa personally and well. They would be appalled by these accusations, the outrageous and heinous accusations you've made against a member of their family."

"I expect they will be. Did your client tell you about his treasure trove, his personal souvenir room? We got in, Kyle, in case you're wondering. You've got some e-skills, but I had a master geek with me. He slid through your security like butter. Want to see what we found behind a locked door in your client's residence, Mr. Drummond? On screen, Peabody."

"Record of search, Knightly, Kyle's residence, cue mark 33.42.6, on screen."

Trueheart's slow and steady three-sixty showed all.

"We've got your girlfriend up in EDD. She's already talked to me."

"Bullshit," Kyle muttered, but was silenced by a sharp look from the lawyer.

"Owning a droid, having a private room, the equipment I see, the personal items, is hardly a crime. Is hardly evidence pertaining to accusations of this nature."

"Zoom in, Peabody. You see here on this display cabinet, the names of the female victims, and in each compartment so labeled are *their* personal items of jewelry taken from their homes on the nights of the attacks. You see here on the shelves . . ."

She waited for Peabody to adjust. "Other items listed as stolen on the nights of the attacks. The dresses—including the one the droid is wearing—were stolen from the female victims on the nights of the attacks. You see here, the costumes and professional makeup and the props used by Mr. Knightly on the nights of those attacks, including the black coat tagged in this recording, and these black leather gloves on which we found blood, blood that has been matched to Miko and Xavier Carver. You see this weighted sap on which we found the blood of those victims, as well as traces of Anthony Strazza's.

"How did all these items come to be in your possession, Mr. Knightly?"

"Please refer your questions to me," Drummond told her.

"Why? He hasn't told you dick. You know it, I know it. When did you get the idea for it, Kyle? The costumes, the drama of it? It had to take you a while to set it all up. We found the mini cams, and the recordings from them on your comp. Easy to see how you'd plant them in your cousin's place—and you were smart enough to take them out on the night you beat the crap out of him and raped his wife. I figure you did some legwork, slipped into the other places—and the ones you've yet to hit."

Keeping her gaze on Kyle's she leaned back. "Jacie and Roderick Carbo, Gregor and Camilla Jane Lester, Toya L'Page and Gray Burroughs—and more. We've got a team going to the residences on your target list, taking the cams you planted into evidence. You watched them in their own homes, you perverted little fuck—"

"Lieutenant!" Drummond objected, but she just rolled over him.

"You listened to the their private conversations. It gave you your windows—when they'd be out and gone, their schedules, their routines. And you watched those recordings in that room, imagining what you'd do to them, especially her."

"Fix this." Kyle turned on his lawyer. "Now. I'm not going to sit here and listen to this bullshit."

"Lieutenant, I'd like another moment to consult with—"

"I don't want to *consult*," Kyle exploded. "I said fix this, and fix it now."

"Lieutenant, I require time to speak to my client off this record."

Eve shrugged, rose. "Dallas and Peabody exiting Interview. Record off."

Peabody blew out a breath. "He really thinks the lawyer can just wave a magic lawyer wand and make it all go away."

"Because it happened that way before. He gets in a little jam, somebody takes care of it. A bigger jam, somebody fixes it. I expect we'll uncover a lot of that."

"The thing is, the lawyer looks shocked, but not really surprised."

"Good eye, Detective. He is shocked, but as it comes out, bit by bit, he's starting to think of things, remember comments or gestures or behavior. Maybe he remembers funneling money to a woman who cried rape or abuse, a woman he probably didn't believe at the time. Or he believed her, but tidied it all up for his client."

Eve stepped aside when Drummond came out.

"Ready?"

"I . . . I am no longer Mr. Knightly's attorney of record."

"Probably a smart move on your part."

"His choice, not mine. Still, I've never handled a capital case. Kyle . . . he needs an attorney experienced in capital crimes. He needs a psychiatric evaluation. He—"

"You're not his lawyer," Eve reminded him. "He's entitled to one, as experienced as he can get. He will be evaluated. Excuse me." She stepped back to the door, glanced back at him. "How many women? How many did you pay off after he raped them?"

Drummond merely shook his head. He looked sick, Eve thought, physically ill. But he shook his head and walked away.

She went into Interview.

"Record on. Dallas and Peabody reentering Interview. Mr. Knightly, have you dismissed your attorney?"

"Dismissed? I fired his useless ass."

"Do you wish to contact and engage other legal representation at this time?"

"Oh, I'll get legal representation." Contempt rolled through his voice, glittered in his sneer. "I'll get the best lawyers out there, believe it."

"Do you wish to contact a lawyer at this time?"

"I need to do some research, conduct interviews."

"Very well. Peabody, arrange for Mr. Knightly to be taken back to his cell."

"Bullshit. Bullshit. Bullshit! I want a hearing." He jabbed a finger on the table. "I want a goddamn hearing, I want bail, and I want out. Now."

"None of those things are going to happen. You can bring Mr. Drummond back in to represent you, contact another lawyer or representative, waive your right to legal representation at this time and talk to us, or go back to your cell. That's the full menu."

"I know my rights."

"You should, we've read them to you twice. And I don't believe we're the first. Where in there does it say Kyle gets to go home because he wants to?"

"You think you're smart." He let out a crack of a laugh. "You think swaggering around with a weapon and an attitude makes you sexy? Dunne *played* you sexy. It's called *acting*."

"Choose. Lawyer, another lawyer, waive the lawyer and continue the interview, or go back to your cell."

"I'm not going back to any cell. Sit down. And you." He pointed at Peabody. "Go find somebody who knows what they're doing around here and get me a hearing."

"No."

His nostrils actually flared. "What did you say?"

"No. Anyhow, are you waiving your right to legal representation at this time? Because otherwise, you're heading back, and I can go grab a snack. I missed lunch."

"Ha ha. You're the funny one, right? Nothing funny about you. And you need to lose ten pounds."

"Ouch." Peabody looked at Eve made exaggerating sniffing noises.

"Waive legal counsel at this time," Eve snapped. "Yes or no. Any word other than yes, I take as a no and you're in a cell."

"Yes." A note of panic escaped before he sat back, shrugged. "Why the hell not? It's not like you two worry me. Get me a drink," he told Peabody.

"Gee, I'd be happy to. Would you like me to make you a martini?"

"Could you?" Knightly said with a fresh sneer. "Make it a ginger ale, on ice, twist of lime."

With a snort, and a nod from Eve, Peabody left the room.

"Peabody exiting Interview. Where do you want to start, Kyle, at the beginning or at the end?"

"You've barely got tits and a teenage boy's ass. Still . . . How many of the brass did you have to fuck to make it to lieutenant?"

"But we're not here to talk about my sexual habits, Kyle. This is all about you. You're the star of the show. This whole place is buzzing about you. I've never seen anything like it, not even during the Icove mess."

She paused a moment, gave him a thoughtful study. "Jesus, Nadine's going to be all over this, probably get another book, another vid out of it, especially with the whole Oscar deal right now. I mean, look at you."

She sighed, shook her head, could actually see him preen at the attention. "Brains, looks, money, style, and power, too. Add in a whole bunch of sex and it's pretty heady. I hear people around here saying how Neville's looking like a pussy, a limp-dicked pussy. I can't argue it."

"Because he is."

"You sure as hell proved that. Screwing his wife right in front of his face. That shows who has the balls in the family."

"I see what you're doing." Still smirking, Kyle circled a finger in the air. "You're trying to butter me up."

"Just saying what is. Why do you think she brushed you back the night you met, the night at that party when the three of you met?"

"She didn't."

"Really?" Eve frowned, consulted a file. "But she said—"

"She's a liar. She said she was with that asshole when I gave her a tap, but she wanted me. Clear as day."

"But . . . didn't she leave with the asshole?"

"Only because I decided not to waste my time. And what does she do, she comes back."

"To you? Do you mean later or that same night."

"The same damn night. She used Neville, gave him the eye to get me stirred up, then she leaves with the asshole."

"But she married Neville, even after you gave her a few more taps along the way. Did she do that to get you stirred up?"

"What do you think? You said it yourself, he's a pussy."

"Peabody, reentering Interview." Peabody slapped a tube of ginger ale (she'd deliberately ordered diet) on the table. "Take it or leave it."

Kyle picked it up, cracked the tube, sipped while sending her a look of cold loathing.

"Okay, so Rosa married Neville to get you stirred up—because you're the one she really wanted, at least sexually. And maybe—just a guess—she married him *because* he's a pussy."

Kyle shot out a finger. "Bing-fucking-o. You're smarter than you look."

"Smart enough to know a lot of women say one thing and mean another. Some women, probably most women, they marry a pussy because they figure they can control him, get everything they want. When a real man, a man with real balls, he controls *them,* and they do what *he* wants. Like you. People do what you want. Actors, directors, lawyers. Women."

"I built my own studio."

"Well, you and Neville."

"Hell, I could've done it without him. I took him along for the ride."

"It sounds like you did him a favor."

"He's my cousin," Kyle pointed out. "We go back, and he's got good ideas. He needs me to jump-start them, implement. He puts in his share, the time, the money. But I'm the one with vision."

"So you brought him along for the ride, Rosa married him because he's a pussy. He sure sounds like a weak sister. Does he take after his mother or his father?"

"His father's worse than Nev, trust me. No balls, no spine. Second-rate director."

"Interesting. Did your aunt stay married to him to stir you up, Kyle?"

Eve slid a photo of Astra Patrick out of the file.

22

EVE SAW HIS REACTION, THE DESIRE AND DELIGHT FLICKING FAST INTO RAGE.

"You know her problem?" he demanded.

"I don't."

"Playing it safe, locking herself into society's rules. Look at her. I mean, just look at her. She's got it all. The face, the body. Beauty and style and sexuality that doesn't quit. She's got it all," he repeated, trailing his finger over the face in the picture. "Except for one thing."

"Let me guess. I bet I know. Vision."

Obviously pleased, he lifted the finger, shot it at Eve. "Right in one. No vision. She's stuck in this rut with a loser, just coasting along."

"And you could offer her so much more."

"I *did* offer her more."

"And she chose the rut." Eve shook her head, studied the photo. "I bet she gave you the kiss off, but in a way that left that door open, just enough to keep you dangling."

"Neville makes her some bullshit necklace out of beads for her birthday, and she makes like it's the crown jewels. I gave her a ring, something real, told her what I felt, how it should be. She wouldn't even *take* it. She tells me I'm confused. How I'm *sweet,* and she's flattered, and more bullshit about how I'm going to find the perfect girl one day."

"How old were you?"

"I was fifteen, and already more of a man than that Brit pussy she married. She *humiliated* me."

"You don't strike me as the kind of man who takes no for an answer so easy. You don't take the pussy way."

"I waited. Figured I needed some experience under my belt." He smiled, patted himself. "Get me?"

"Oh, yeah. Some of that experience was with . . ." Eve pulled another photo out of the file.

Kyle studied it, shrugged. "Doesn't ring a bell."

"You were eighteen when she accused you of sexual assault, recanted after your father gave her a cool million. Does that ring the bell?"

"That one?" He leaned forward, jabbed a finger in the eye of the photo. "She wanted it, then got all whiny when I gave her what she wanted. She cost me three months in some fucking rehab center. I lost my whole goddamn summer break."

"That's tough. But you gave Astra another chance, didn't you?"

"Right after my twenty-first birthday, I went to London on my own, booked the best suite in the best hotel. I asked her to come."

"How'd you get her there? You had to be subtle about it, right?"

"Wanted to take her to dinner. The asshole's off on location, and Neville's still at university. I'm in town, let me take you to dinner. Drinks and dinner, fancy and elegant."

"And she bought it."

"She knew what I was saying. I was just giving her cover. I had champagne and flowers, her favorite foods, everything all set up. She wore a blue dress." He closed her eyes, lips curved. And when he opened them, the rage came back. "And she pretended to be shocked when I kissed her. Shocked and angry. She *slapped* me. Slapped me and stormed away before I could . . ."

"She humiliated you again."

"I should've shown her, that was my mistake. I should have shown her. I apologized. I shed tears." He tapped his cheeks, grinning. "You have to think of the long view."

Eve nodded. "You have to have vision."

"Exactamundo. I could wait. Plenty of substitutes. She'd see how successful I was, how important I was. How I could have any woman I wanted, and she'd come to me."

"But you couldn't have any woman you wanted. You couldn't have Rosa."

"I saw her first!" His voice rang with sheer and sincere outrage. "You think I could let them get away with that, doing the same thing to me? You think I could let that bitch brush me off, give me the same line as Astra—I'm *confused*, she's with Neville?"

"Playing the same game." Eve expelled a long breath that signaled perfect agreement. "Teasing you, daring you. Holding out on you to stir you up. But you know how to wear the mask, right? The loving cousin, the solid business partner, the loyal friend."

"There's nothing I can't do."

"Because you learn, you don't make the same mistakes. With Rosa, you didn't make the same mistakes you'd made with Astra. You needed to show her, and you did." Eve tipped back in the chair. "If she wanted to stay in that rut—with Neville—that was her loss, but she'd have a taste of a real man first. The Dracula bit, that was genius. Symbolic. The vampire—the king of vamps—he takes the woman he wants, takes her over, body, mind, soul, right?"

He smiled, shrugged, looked away.

"Come on, Kyle, take the credit. You earned it. The planning, down to the last detail. Using the robbery as cover—it worked. And beating the crap out of both of them. Especially Neville."

"He deserved it. I saw her first."

"But you thought of Astra when you raped Rosa." Eve took Rosa's photo out of a file, laid it beside Astra's. "Look at them. Rosa could be Astra's daughter."

"You see that, too."

"Sure. Just like I see she was meant to be yours. Both of them are. First Neville's father's in your way, and now Neville, after all you've done for him. I'm surprised you let him live."

"Thought about killing him, but we're family. And it was about making them *live* with it. About watching them try to live with it."

"Oh, I get that. You were in a little bit of a hurry with Rosa and Neville. I get that, too. It had all built up, and you needed to *have* her, show her, make her admit she wanted it. You ripped her clothes. With the others, you had them strip. So much more seductive. And more humiliating for the man."

When he said nothing, she shook her head. "We've got the evidence, Kyle. You're not stupid, you know what we found in your loft. So we've got what we need. I'm just . . . well, I've got to admit, I'm pretty fascinated by how you played all this."

"His lawyer's going to fix it," Peabody added. "He can afford a damn platoon of high-priced lawyers."

Now Eve shrugged. "That's not our problem. We did our job. I just like hearing how anybody could plan all this out, time after time. The precision, the planning, the smallest details. Well, it's exquisite actually. Did you really decide on the woman at that gala? The ah, yeah, here it is. The Celebrate Art Gala? What pulled that trigger."

"They couldn't stop talking about wedding plans. Rosa and Neville going on and on and fucking on about them. Everybody we know who comes by the table starts up on the wedding. Can't wait, how perfect they are together, what a beautiful bride she's going to be. Made me sick to my stomach. Made me want to puke."

"So you looked around, milled around, and began to see all the women you could have. All the married women. Women you'd show, men you'd punish. Did you already have the cameras in Neville's place?"

"I did him a favor. He's got the nerve to ask me if I can hang out at his place, wait for a delivery while they're moving in together? The asshole doesn't even notice."

"You watched them whenever you wanted. Watched them in bed together."

"So what? All it did was prove to me how much better I was at it."

"Your timing was—bears repeating—exquisite. Right after their honeymoon. Just as they're really starting the whole married gig together."

"Now she'll know, for the rest of her life, she settled. He'll know she had the best sex of her life with another man."

"And Lori, Lori Brinkman." She pulled out the photo. "How did you pick her?"

"Ah, Lori. That face, that body, the laugh. It was her laugh that got me. The laugh said sex. Pulled one of her scripts out of the vault— not bad."

"Astra's a screenwriter, too, isn't she?"

"It's more a hobby, just like with Lori. And they wouldn't need a hobby, would they, if they weren't married to losers. If a man keeps a woman satisfied, she doesn't need anything but him."

"You could see Lori wasn't satisfied, sexually."

"Stuck with that boring fuck? Give me a break. Lori was really the one who inspired it all. Why stop at Rosa, that's what I thought.

I thought, right here, in this room there are a dozen women like that. Stuck in that rut, trapped in the rules. I picked them out, and saw how it could be. And after Rosa, I knew how it could *feel*."

"You planted the cameras."

"You're a cop, right? I don't have to tell you people think they're secure in their own homes, and they're not. You just have to be observant, take the time, be smart. I could've made a living with e-work. Everyone said so."

He shook back his hair, obviously comfortable now, completely in the groove of his own arrogance.

"But, Jesus, how many electronics experts get covered by the media, have stars coming to them? Do on-screen interviews? E's just a hobby. And watching all those lives, those small lives on screen? Hell, I almost ran out of popcorn."

He laughed, finished off the tube of ginger ale.

"Watching, you got to know their routines, and their secrets." Eve's hand flowed over Lori's photo. "It made it easy for you to time when to break into Lori's house, set everything up, wait for them to get home from vacation. Hell of a welcome back, right?"

"She was excited. You were right, I wasn't in such a hurry this time, so I had her strip. She was so ready for it, trying to pretend, pulling out the tears when I went for that loser she married, but so ready. I gave her a break, told her to beg for more. And I gave her more. That asshole she married—what's his name?"

"Ira."

"Right, old Ira won't be able to satisfy her now."

"Why did you wait so long between Rosa and Lori, then for Daphne?"

"I believe in rehearsals. If you want a performance to shine, and I do, you rehearse."

"You had the droid for that?"

"The droid, LCs. And Daphne? She was going to be special."

"Why is that?"

"She likes it rough. That rich doctor she hooked knocked her around plenty, and she'd come back for more. He'd tie her up, blindfold her, and bang the shit out of her. Choked her, too, just enough. Then he'd get out his med bag, fix her up. She'd cry and cry, but she did what the hell she was told. He knew how to run that house. I had to respect that."

"He was stronger than the others."

"He wasn't a pussy, I'll say that. A man who knows what a woman's for, and how to make her show respect. She said what he told her to say, wore what he told her to wear, fucked the way he told her to fuck."

"Like a droid?" Peabody put in.

"Hey, he paid for her, didn't he? He put the roof over her head, the food in her mouth, the clothes on her back. If she needed reminding, he reminded her."

"I bet you got off watching him *remind* her."

He answered Peabody with a cocky grin.

Homeland had watched her father beat her, Eve thought. Had watched him rape her, a child of eight. Had done nothing. The thought of it made her insides want to shake, so she pushed that new echo away, blocked it out, focused on the moment.

"You respected him," Eve repeated. "It even sounds like you admired him. But you killed him."

"Hey, he brought it on himself. Absolutely self-defense. He came at me."

"You know, I did read the scene like that." She looked at Peabody who gave a grudging nod. "Walk us through that, Kyle. To me, it looked like he broke out of the chair you had him restrained in while you were out of the room."

"That's just what happened." Kyle shoved the empty tube aside so he could lean in closer. "Let me set it up for you. I've got Daphne in bed. She's half out of it—that's what some serious sex will do to a woman, right? I choked her a few times to give her a better orgasm. Might've held it a little long on the last because we were both into it, but she was breathing, and going in and out. He's out, all the way, so I leave them to pick up a few things I'd earmarked, get a drink. He kept some exceptional unblended scotch in his room upstairs. When I come back, holy hell."

"He'd busted out, and charged at you."

"He'd busted out and was screaming at Daphne, smacking her, choking her. Said how he'd kill her. I'll kill you, you whore—he's screaming that. She's still tied up, not much she can do about it. I've gotta say, made me hard. Then he spots me, *then* he charges. He was crazy, out of his fucking mind. Moved damn fast, too, knocked me back some, and that's when I grabbed that big vase. I had to defend myself, so I smashed it over his head, put him down. Lots of blood," he said, reminiscing. "He's flat out, she's barely conscious, all glassy-eyed. I figured she was dead at first, but she was breathing. I did her again, real quick because the whole thing stirred me up. Then I let her go, like I do. She just lay there, out of it. She ought to thank me for bashing that vase over his head. If I hadn't, she'd be as dead as he is. Anyway, I broke down the set, got my things, and left. Yeah, she ought to thank me. She'll be a rich widow now instead of a dead whore."

He flicked his fingers on the empty tube. "I could use another."

"Go ahead, Peabody. Kyle's doing thirsty work."

As Peabody exited, Eve took him back over the Strazza assault to refine details. When Peabody came back in, she shifted to the last murders.

"Why did you kill Miko and Xavier Carver?"

"I was getting into a rut. Before I bashed the crazy doctor, I was already getting into a rut. If you don't change and grow, that's what happens. I wanted the experience. I wanted to know how it felt. The whole thing with—what's his name?"

"Anthony Strazza."

"Yeah, Strazza, it was fast, so in the moment. Whack and done. I like to plan and anticipate. It's why I'm good at what I do. And I wanted to experience it while I was still revved from before."

"You went in planning on killing them?"

"It was time to change things up. Take it to a new level."

"You knew she was pregnant. You had the cameras."

"Didn't apply." He waved that off. "Anyway, they pissed me off with their perfect little lives, they're perfect little plans. I gave them a big, important death."

"They should thank you."

He laughed, sucked on the tube. "None of this is going to matter."

"Why is that, Kyle?"

"Because your scowling friend there is right. I can hire a platoon of lawyers. Hell, an army of them. The kind who'll keep this in the courts for years while I'm out on bail. The kind who'll piss all over your evidence and make this go away. The kind who'll have every woman I banged admitting they wanted just what I gave them. We can put together a deal now, save us all time and trouble. Putting together deals is one of my specialties."

"What sort of deal do you have in mind?"

"I'll cop to going into the houses, setting the stage. Hell, let's face it, I can eat out on that story for years. I did it for research, for first-hand experience for upcoming projects. I pay a fine, even do some community service, no problem."

"You killed people, Kyle."

"Strappo—"

"Strazza," Eve corrected.

"Whatever, that was self-defense. You said so yourself. I gave him a whack in self-defense. The others, I got caught up in the moment. I lost it. Temporary insanity as a result of taking a life, right? I'll agree to therapy, even make some financial restitution. Which would include a generous donation to the NYPSD. Say a million."

"You're offering to give a million dollars to the NYPSD."

"I can afford it. With say, another ten percent of that to each of you. Petty cash considering who you married, but this one?" He jerked a head toward Peabody. "I bet she can use it. A nice little bonus for clearing this all up without wasting my time."

"He's offering you a hundred thousand to smooth this all over, Peabody."

"I heard. That's a lot of money against a detective's salary."

"There you go. You ditch this recording, or I'll help you edit it so we can all cover our asses. I pay some fines, do some good works, talk to a shrink and donate a nice chunk to the police. Win-win."

"That sounds really interesting, Kyle, except for the fact three people are dead, four women were raped, beaten, and terrorized, four men were brutalized."

He actually rolled his eyes as she spoke.

"Lives were violated, lives were taken, and everything you've said here, on record, in this room, demonstrates unequivocally that you knew exactly what you were doing, planned what you would do, and feel no remorse whatsoever."

He turned to Peabody. "Better talk to the rich bitch, sweetie, or you're going to be out a hundred k."

"You can take your hundred k and stick it up your ass." Peabody pushed up, slapped her hands on the table as she leaned into his face. "You'd better hire those lawyers, you fuck, because no matter how many, no matter how much they cost, you're going down. All the way down. You'll be whining in a concrete box for the rest of your life. You can live another hundred years, and I hope to Christ you do, and every morning you'll wake up to the same view. A box and bars. And I hope to *God* there are some big sweaty guys with dicks the size of jumbo kielbasas serving with you who'll be able to say, 'Hey, he wanted it,' after they're done with you."

"Get out of my face, you stupid cunt, or I'll make you sorry."

"Try."

Eve rose, nudged Peabody back, put herself in Kyle's face. "In case my partner hasn't explained it clearly enough, you're now further charged with attempting to bribe police officers. It's just a nice little cherry on top. No deals, you son of a bitch. Peabody, arrange for this revolting piece of garbage to be taken back to his cell."

"I'm not going into a cell. I want to talk to your superior, right now!"

"That's not included in your rights." Eve gathered her files. "Got you cold, Kyle. My only regret? As bad as Omega is, we don't have worse. You deserve worse."

"I'll be out on bail in an hour!" he shouted.

Knowing it ranked as the biggest insult, Eve just laughed as she all but shoved Peabody out of the room.

"I want to punch something."

Eve eyed her. "If you punch me, I'll punch you back, which would be a shame as I've never wanted you more than at this moment."

Peabody choked out a laugh, scrubbed her face.

" 'Dicks the size of jumbo kielbasas'?"

"I couldn't think of a better metaphor in the heat of the moment."

"Gave me an image. Shake it off. Go hit the gym later if you need to, take it out on a sparring droid, but shake it off, get a couple of big, sweaty uniforms—no measurement on dick size—to haul that miserable bastard back to a cell."

"You were good cop." Peabody took a breath, then another. "You reeled him in acting interested, even fascinated. It worked. I got to be pissed off cop. Sort of bad cop."

"You were badass cop. Badass cop," Eve said more sharply as Peabody's eyes filled. "Don't fuck it up now."

"It made me sick. You'd think after all this time, seeing what we see, dealing with the excuses for humans we deal with, it wouldn't. But he made me sick."

"We got him, Peabody. We did the job, did it right, and we got him. See that he's put back in a cage. Then write it up, okay? Write it up, and go home. Beat up a droid, bang McNab, make some soup, whatever it takes to shake it off."

"You said 'bang McNab.'"

"Don't make me regret it."

She walked toward Observation as Reo came out.

"You make my job easy."

Eve glanced back toward the Interview room. "I figure it'll take a full year on Omega before he starts to actually consider he may be fucked."

"I really hope to make him realize that sooner, but I'd take it. Do you want me to contact the victims, tell them we have him?"

"Anyone we spoke to on the potential target list. That would help. Olsen and Tredway should tell the Patricks in person, and the Brinkmans. I'll take Daphne Strazza."

"I'll take care of it." Reo squeezed Eve's arm, then walked away to do her part of the job.

Eve waited while Mira came out with Roarke, held up a finger and moved to speak to Olsen and Tredway.

"Fried him up like a kielbasa," Tredway said.

"I'm never going to be able to eat one of those again, but, yeah, he's fried. His ego and entitlement made it pretty damn easy. It's not going to be easy on the Patricks."

"No." Olsen shook her head. "It's going to gut them."

"It should come from you. They have a closer connection with you. The Brinkmans, too."

"We'll take them," Tredway agreed. "We'll handle it. Damn good working with you again, Dallas. Feeney's got a hell of an eye."

"Let's get this done before it leaks. Then you and me, partner?" Olsen tapped a fist to Tredway's arm. "We're going for a couple of brews."

"I hear you."

Eve stepped away, up to Mira and Roarke.

"I guess you caught some of the interview," she said to Roarke.

"Most, I think. You played him perfectly."

"He wanted validation, wanted his dick stroked—so to speak. It was easy to see that, and to give it to him. We had him without it, but it's tied in a bow. He's not insane," she added, turning to Mira.

"Sick, delusional, sociopathic, psychopathic, but no, he's legally sane. It wasn't easy to give it to him, but by doing so, you tied that bow."

"That part's done. I could use you—or Daphne could use you. I need to tell her face-to-face."

"I cleared time. When can you leave?" Mira asked.

"Pretty much now if that works. We found her," she said to Roarke. "I think—unless Mira says otherwise, it would be good for you to be there, too."

"I'll take you both."

"I'm going to let her know we're coming. She might want her family there. The Patricks and Brinkmans have each other. Give me five minutes. I'll meet you in the garage."

When Eve strode away, Mira laid a hand on Roarke's arm. "She has you. This has been brutally hard for her in many ways, but she has you."

"And you."

"Yes. And the next victim."

E ve thought of the next victim as she rang the buzzer on the door of Daphne's suite.

Tish answered, eyed all three. "Daphne's in her room. Has there been another? You said there hadn't, but—"

"No, there's not going to be another."

"You caught him." Tears sprang to Tish's eyes. "Why didn't you say so when you tagged us? God, God, what a relief. Our parents are out. We talked them into going out, taking a walk in the park, but—"

"I really need to speak to Daphne."

"Sure, sorry. God, thank God. Are you Dr. Mira?" She asked as she gestured them into the parlor area. "Daphne described you."

"Yes."

"I'm glad you came. She feels—says she feels—calmer with you. You're Roarke. I recognize you. I know you found her, helped get her to the hospital. I'm her sister. Please, everybody sit down. I'll get her. This is going to help her so much."

She started toward a bedroom, stopped. "Shit, sorry. I should offer you something. We've got a nice little kitchen area."

"Why don't I make some tea?" Mira took off her coat as she spoke. "Daphne may like some."

"I'm for popping some champagne, but, yeah, tea. Thanks. We'll be right back."

Eve went to the window, looked out. "I love New York. Despite the fact that people like Knightly inhabit it, I love it. It's helped make me what I am. It gave me my place."

"You're still sad."

"In Dallas, those last days in that awful room, I could see out the window. But there was nothing real, nothing I knew or understood. My world was that room, and my world was a nightmare. Even after I got out, after I killed him and got out, it wasn't my world. It was like something on screen. Sometimes he let me watch screen. It was like that, and sometimes there were monsters on screen, just like in my world. We've got monsters here, but I know them. I'm not afraid of them."

She closed her eyes a moment. "When this is done, can we—I know it's cold—but can we go home and take a walk? Just walk in the cold and snow for a little while?"

"I'd love to take a walk with you."

"If it's dark—"

"We'll turn on all the lights." He walked to her, laid his hands on her shoulders, kissed the top of her head. "It'll be our world."

She reached back, laid a hand over his. Let it drop when she heard the bedroom door open.

She turned her back on the city she loved.

Epilogue

D aphne's lips trembled, tears gleamed in her eyes, but she moved straight to Eve, gripped her hands.

"Tish said you caught the devil—the man. You caught him. Did you?"

"Yes."

"Oh, God." Now she threw her arms around Eve, clung tight. "Thank God. Thank you. He can't come back? He can't ever come back?"

"No, he won't come back. Let's sit down."

Mira came out with a tray.

"Oh, Dr. Mira." Daphne rushed over to take the tray. "I'm so glad you're here. I feel . . ." Daphne carried the tray back, set it on the table in front of the sofa. "I don't know, exactly. I feel like something's ready to break inside me, and I don't know what'll be left when it does. Is it all right if I tell Dr. Nobel?"

"He said to call him Del," Tish reminded her, and began pouring tea.

"It's just he's been so kind and concerned. My parents! Tish, we should tag them."

"They'll be back soon anyway. Have some tea, Daph. Take a breath."

"Daphne." Eve waited until Daphne took the cup, shifted toward her. "The man who attacked you is named Kyle Knightly. Do you know him?"

"I . . . No, I don't think so. Do you think my husband knew him?"

"I doubt it. This person put cameras in your house, hid them. He watched you and your husband for several weeks."

"He . . ." The cup rattled before she set it down. "He watched. He . . . recorded us?"

"Christ, sick bastard," Tish exploded, passing Mira tea.

"Daphne, I'd already concluded that Anthony Strazza abused you, battered you, raped you."

"He was my husband. He gave me everything. I owed him—"

"That's bullshit, Daphne." Tish snapped out the words. "You know it's bullshit."

Daphne shook her head. "Please, Tish. He's dead. He was my husband. I can't say bad things about him. You shouldn't expect me to."

"I can expect you to tell me the truth." Eve said it sharply enough to have Daphne's head snapping up, to put just a hint of fear in her eyes. "He abused you. He struck you, and then treated your wounds so no one would see. He threatened to do worse if you told anyone, if you tried to leave. He raped you if you objected. He threatened your family in order to make you sever ties with them."

"It doesn't matter now," Daphne began.

"It does. Record on. I'm going to read you your rights."

"What!" Tish leaped to her feet. "What the fuck?"

"Quiet. Daphne Strazza, you have the right to remain silent."

Eve read out the Revised Miranda, took a breath.

"I'm putting this on record, I've read you your rights because this is going to protect you. Do you understand your rights and obligations?"

"Yes, but—"

"Don't lie. This will be harder for you, and for your family if you lie. Remember, too, we have Knightly's recordings. Did Anthony Strazza ever strike you?"

"Please don't—"

"Did Anthony Strazza ever strike you?"

"Yes, yes, yes." When she lowered her head, her long dark hair fell around her face like a curtain. "I would do stupid things or say the wrong things or—"

"Don't be stupid now. Did he threaten you with physical harm?"

"Yes." Daphne covered her face with a hand. "But—"

"Did he threaten to harm your sister, your parents?"

She dropped her hand as tears fell. "Not at first. Not at first, don't you understand? He was so kind, so attentive, so romantic. He made me feel so special, he told me I was . . . I was perfection. Then I'd do something to upset him. He was sorry he struck out at me, he'd be so sorry."

"Until he did it again."

"Yes. He said my family wasn't my family. He was all I needed. And they weren't mine in any case. Just substitutes, just obligated to house and clothe me. I knew that was wrong, but he'd get so angry. Once, just once, I was so angry, too. Not shocked and afraid, but very angry. I slapped him and I tried to run. I shouted I was going to my family. And he . . . hurt me. More than he ever had before. He kept hitting me, and he broke my wrist, and he said if I ever tried to leave him he'd kill them. That he knew how so no one would know, and he'd kill them, and it would be my fault."

"So you didn't leave him."

Daphne shook her head. "If I did what he wanted, he hardly ever got angry. If I wore the right dress, said the right thing, he could be very pleased with me. He could be kind, even gentle when he was pleased with me. I tried to make him pleased with me."

"But sometimes he hurt you anyway."

"It would be my fault if a man looked at me too long or said something my husband didn't like. It was an insult to him, and I'd instigated it. I had to be punished, be reminded how to behave properly. If I begged him to stop or tried to crawl away, he'd hit me harder, longer. He would choke me until I passed out, and later I'd wake up."

"There was a white silk cord and a white silk blindfold in his beside drawer."

Daphne's face flushed; her breath released on choppy hitches. "He'd use the cord to tie me, and the blindfold. He'd rape me, and hurt me. But it wasn't rape because I belonged to him. He said it wasn't rape, but I knew it was. I knew, but I stayed. I didn't know what to do. He was important, and everyone would believe him. He had the droids watch me. He knew everything I did. If I left the house, he knew. I couldn't leave unless he said I could."

"How long did this go on?"

"He hit me the first time on our honeymoon. He was very sorry, but I'd insulted him, upset him by flaunting myself on the beach. And men had been ogling me."

"So the abuse began at the beginning of your marriage and continued. Escalated."

"Yes. It doesn't matter now. It's over now, isn't it? I just want to forget."

"You're not going to." Eve said it flatly. "On the night you were attacked. You came upstairs with Strazza. Was he pleased with you?"

"No." She brushed away a tear. "No, he wasn't. People had stayed too long, and I had failed to be a good hostess. A good hostess knows how to end an evening. He gripped my arm so hard, and I knew he would hurt me, but the devil was in the room.

"Please don't make me say all that again."

"Kyle Knightly, disguised as a devil, struck Strazza, assaulted you. Is this correct?"

"I don't know who it was. But if you say that's who it was . . . Yes. Please. I don't want to think about it."

"You remember more than you did. You lied to me when I asked you yesterday. If you lie it's going to eat at you and eat at you. You won't forget, and you won't have a prayer of moving on. Knightly restrained you, then your husband. Is this correct?"

"Yes, but he let me go again when my husband was tied up, after he struck him in the face. He let me go, he held a knife—no, it's not a knife, it's smaller and silver and sharp—to my husband's throat and told me he'd slit it unless I took off my clothes. Slow, he said. Take them off slow. I didn't want to. I wanted to run, but Anthony said: 'You stupid bitch.' And I did. I took off my clothes, and I laid back in bed because the devil said to. He tied me again, and he slapped me, hard, hard, and he raped me. The lights were red, and there was smoke. I think.

"He said it was hell. Fire and brimstone, sulfur and smoke. He cut me and he hit me, and he raped me, and he laughed. He left us after he hurt my husband again, after Anthony told him the combinations to the safes."

"What happened when he was gone? When it was just you and Strazza."

"My husband raged at me. I was a whore, a weak, filthy whore. I'd let the devil have sex with me. I'd said it was the best I'd ever had. I tried to tell my husband the devil forced me, had said he'd kill me if I didn't say it, but my husband was so angry. There was blood on his face, his face was red and black, like the devil. Then he came back, the devil came back and he hurt Anthony again, and he raped me again. He took a pill, and raped me again, and choked me. He'd choke me, like my husband would, and I'd go away, and I'd come back and he'd rape me again. My husband, the devil. Again. Why doesn't he kill me, why isn't it over? And he went away again. I think. I think. It's mixed up."

Her eyes brimmed over. "It's mixed up."

"What do you remember? He went away again. Then?"

"He went away, and my husband was like a madman. He broke the chair, he beat and beat and the chair broke. His face, red and black, and he was standing in that red light, and I thought, Help me. Help me. It hurt, my throat, when I tried to talk, but I said: Help me, Anthony. Hurry. He'll come back."

"Did he help you?"

"He was on top of me. My husband. The devil. His face. My husband."

Pale as ice, Daphne pressed her hands to her temples. "Now my husband's the devil, and he's choking me, hitting me. He said he'd kill me for this. Kill the whore. Worthless whore. I was going away, finally going away. This time I wouldn't come back. He'd end it this time. But he jumped away. And the devils, they fought. I saw in the light, through the smoke, the one struck the other with the vase, and the lilies scattered."

Her eyes, glassy now, stared through Eve.

"I hate the smell of them. I had to have lilies because my husband said, and I hated the smell. They were scattered on the floor and the devil—no, no, my husband was on the floor. Blood, so much blood. Then the other, he laughed, and he came back. He raped me again. It didn't matter. It just didn't matter. I couldn't feel it. I couldn't feel anymore.

"Then it was quiet. So quiet. Dark and quiet, and I got up. It must have been a terrible dream. I didn't feel anything. But I could smell the lilies and the blood, and he was on the floor. I had to help him because he's my husband. Anthony? He got up. Blood on his face. He hit me."

Absently, she lifted a hand to her cheek. "He hit me, I fell back. I fell, I think, and went away again. But I came back. The room, it's spinning, it won't stand still. The devil—who is it—the devil was shouting and storming around the room. I tried to get up. I got up, but I think I fell. Did he hit me again? I don't know, I swear I don't. 'I'll kill you, and they'll think it was him, they'll think it was the one you fucked. Whore. You let him have you. No one will ever touch you again. I'll kill you.'"

Trembling now, her hands rubbing hard over her heart, she said it again and again. "'I'll kill you, I'll kill you, I'll kill you. I couldn't run. Did we fall? I think we fell, and the vase was in my hands. He grabbed my ankle, tried to, grabbed it, I don't know. It's so mixed up. I hit him. I hit him with the vase, hit him as hard as I could. Stop, please stop. And hit him. and he stopped, and it was quiet. and I couldn't feel anything. I just wanted to go away. I just wanted to be somewhere else. Away from the devils and the smell of blood and lilies.

"Then there were angels—you," she corrected. "You were there. And then I was in the hospital."

She let out a broken sob. "I killed him. I killed my husband." Weeping, she curled herself into a ball. "I'm so sorry. Tish, I'm so sorry. I didn't remember at first. I swear, I didn't remember. I killed him."

"Be quiet." Tish leaped to wrap arms around her sister. "Daph, you be quiet. I'm calling a lawyer."

"Yes, I'd recommend that," Eve said. "Just hold on a minute."

"I'm not giving you the chance to—"

"Shut up," Eve ordered. "You want to help, hold on to her. Daphne, you killed Anthony Strazza."

"Yes, yes. I'm sorry."

"You killed Anthony Strazza in self-defense. Everything you've told me corresponds with the evidence gathered through this investigation. Your statement here, your recounting also corroborates the confession given by Kyle Knightly. You should contact Randall Wythe. He may advise you to hire another lawyer, one with criminal expertise, but I'm telling you, on the record, no charges will be brought against you."

"But . . . I—"

"You were attacked and brutalized by Kyle Knightly. You were further attacked and brutalized, and your life was threatened by Anthony Strazza. I believe Dr. Mira will agree your state of mind was one of panic, confusion, and survival."

"I will," Mira confirmed.

"What you've told me here corresponds to what I evaluated on scene, through interviews, what the chief medical examiner concluded. I'm going to need you to come in tomorrow, with your attorney, and go through this again. The APA will be present at that time. And at that time, I'm telling you, this will be determined self-defense."

Still clinging to Tish, Daphne stared at Eve. "You're not going to arrest me?"

"For what? For defending yourself against a brutal attack and the threat of death? No. Record off."

Eve picked up a cup of tea that had gone cold, downed it to soothe her own throat. "You have people to support you. Remember it. Remember this, too. Even without the circumstances of the attack Saturday night, Anthony Strazza would have made good on his threats, sooner or later. He'd have kept at you until he'd gone too far. You stopped that from happening, and that's no crime. It's no sin. It's not wrong."

"I remember hitting him. I dreamed about it, and I was afraid to tell you. I wanted to believe it was just a dream. I was afraid to tell anyone."

"Now you have. It's going to take a while before you're not afraid. This is the start."

Eve got to her feet. Tish rose with her.

"You needed her to say it all, on the record. For her own sake."

"I needed her to say it all, on the record."

Tish stepped forward, held out a hand. "Thank you."

"Just doing my job."

"That doesn't mean we don't owe you. We'll all come in tomorrow. We'll come with her. Can Dr. Mira be there?"

"I can and will," Mira assured her. "I'm going to stay for a bit now. Is that all right, Daphne?"

"Yes, yes, please. I feel—it broke, and I feel. I'm still not sure. Lieutenant Dallas, I can agree to truth testing. I'll do that if it helps."

"I'm pretty good at being a truth tester, and Mira's the same. This guy, too. Set up the time tomorrow to work with Dr. Mira's schedule."

"Will you be there?"

"I'll be there. You'll get through it, Daphne. We've got to go," she said to Roarke.

He put an arm around her in the elevator, felt the light tremors. He said nothing, just kept an arm around her until they stepped outside.

"You knew. You knew before you had Knightly in the box."

"Yeah."

"When did you know?"

"Had to wonder when I saw the crime scene. Had to wonder more when I talked to Morris. It's the only thing that made sense. Her finishing him off, I mean. Then getting a sense of Strazza, getting a sense of her, it got pretty clear she'd done it, and I leaned toward either self-defense or just snapping."

"It's what made you so sad."

"I couldn't tell you. It felt like it would be . . ."

"A betrayal," he finished, turning her to him, ignoring the helpful doorman who held open the door of the car.

"When I put it together it was too much like looking in a mirror, or hearing too many echoes. I needed her to get it out, one way or the other."

He kissed her, turned her to the car, rounded it, and got behind the wheel. "She's no more a murderer than the child you were."

"No. If she'd just snapped, I'd have thrown what weight I could toward diminished capacity, and I wouldn't have been wrong. But I kept asking myself if it was because of her, because of the circumstances, or if it was because of me."

"It's all. Because of you, you were able to see her and the circumstances more clearly, understand them more clearly. I'm unspeakably proud of you. Don't say it's your job," he told her before she could. "This was more. Strazza was your victim, but so was she, in every sense. You uncovered the truth for and about him, but you stood for her. The one who most needed it."

"She'll get through it."

"I believe she will."

"So will the Patricks, even though this is going to shake their foundations and leave a hell of a crack in them."

"They have each other, as you said. So do we." He lifted her hand, kissed it. "I want that walk with you."

"Until we're half frozen, then we can thaw out by the bedroom fire."

"What do you say we get a little drunk by that fire, see what happens next?"

"I say: I know what happens next, and I'm all for it."

Steadier, much steadier, she looked out the window. Snow blackened against the curbs, people rushing to get somewhere else, traffic thoroughly pissed off. Horns blasting and ad blimps blaring.

The city she loved, Eve thought. Her place. It looked absolutely perfect to her.